The Anshadar Effect

The EarthZero Evolution, Volume 2

Dave Newton and Todd King

Published by Anshadar, LLC, 2020.

The Anshadar Effect
Book II of The EarthZero Evolution

Dave Newton and Todd King

Published by Anshadar, LLC, 2020

This is a work of fiction. Similarities to real people, places, or events are entirely coincidental.

THE ANSHADAR EFFECT

First edition. May 15, 2020.

ISBN: 978-1732980242

Written by Dave Newton and Todd King.

Cover art by Faith Newton.

Editing by Laura Lawrence.

PROLOGUE

Fire Women & Gummy Bears

"SPIRIT HERE," SAID the near-whisper over the team's tactical headsets. "Eyes on target. She's still sitting at the edge of the pier, swinging her legs and taking swigs from what looks like a fifth of whiskey. No weapons in sight. Update tac. Over."

"Fist here," came the first reply. "Flanking target, first pier south of hers. Over."

"—ing cheap-ass gear," came the second reply. "Shit. Sorry. Saw here. On pier 100 meters on target's six. Advancing. Should be in your FOV soon. I miss SATCOM gear. Over."

"Same here," Spirit replied. "Hold in place until Saw engages. Over."

"Holding. Over," came a brief series of several voices.

From his nest atop the Lake Mead Marina, Spirit slowly leaned a few millimeters closer into the sight of his Barrett M107A1 50BMG. He observed in rigorous silence as Saw crept slowly toward the target, picking his way skillfully over the various pieces of garbage and detritus littering the pier. The clean, crisp night air stirred gently, slightly tickling the nape of his neck, practically the only part of his body not protected by body armor or some other artifice of war. Directly east of his position, the newly risen Moon was casting enough light to brightly illuminate the target, which starkly revealed itself via his night vision optics.

Briefly, he considered what sort of steel nuts it took for the Dreamland scum to trespass on clearly posted Brotherhood of Desolation territory. And just brazenly sit on the edge of the pier, on Lake Mead, getting shit-faced and barking at the Moon. Alone, too. Whoever she was, Spirit had to admit, she was either the most ballsy chick he'd ever encountered, or she was totally drunk, stupid, and about to be captured and brought in for a go-round with the Brotherhood. The entire brigade, too, if she survived long enough.

"You sure are a pretty one," Saw told the woman sitting on the edge of the pier as he drew up behind her. "Don't move, sweetie," he told her, the laser of his H&K MP5 locked on the back of her head. "The boys just need your body. Don't really matter to them if you're dead or alive."

"Well, well, well," the woman replied with a mocking tone. "That's interesting, because that's exactly what me and my friend think about you and your sick-ass Brotherhood of Rapists."

"Huh?" Saw replied, truly taken aback. Women typically didn't fight back like that. In fact, they were usually screaming in fear at this point in the dance. "Your friend? Sweetie, maybe you're drunk, but you're also alone. I don't see—"

Ahead of the woman, down in the still water of the lake south of Rock Island, there arose a sudden, wicked broiling. Water hissed and steamed for a length of approximately 500 meters.

Spirit immediately flipped over to thermal optics, scanning the absurd sight as it slowly arose from the depths of the lake. In his field of view, the entire mass of whatever-the-hell-it-was seared with fiery, volcanic heat, nearly blinding him. On instinct, he rapidly shifted his view back to Saw and the woman on the dock. Now standing, facing the fear-locked Saw, she, too, glowed brightly from head to toe, her form radiating the heat of a blast furnace.

"What the hell!" Spirit shouted, breaking protocol, though neither his team nor those listening remotely could have faulted him. "Fall back!" he ordered. "Saw! Get the hell off that pier! Fall back! Omega Alert, HQ! Omega Alert, HQ! Dreamland is attacking! Dreamland is attacking!"

"You see her now, don't you?" Leta smirked at Saw, whose frozen gaze of fear locked steadily on Ku'tu's rising draconic form. A steady stream of piss rapidly stained the crotch of his tactical pants.

Taking the final swig of her Jack Daniels, Leta tossed the empty bottle behind her into the roiling water. "I know the irony's lost on your small mind and even smaller pecker, sweetie," she mocked him, her arms slowly rising above her head as she dramatically took to the air, scalding heat and flickering flames marking her path. "But you and your mutant brotherhood are the ones who are about to get raped. Bye bye, sucker!"

Behind and above her, Ku'tu drew herself up to her full height. "Die, puny humans!" she roared, jumping into the air several hundred feet, then stomping down with both massive hind claws into the edge of the lake nearest to the pier. Saw and Fist, both frozen ridiculously in fear, witnessed the impromptu tsunami firsthand, and from the worst possible vantage. They preceded the rest of their team in death by mere seconds only. Even Spirit, higher up and much farther removed from the end of the pier, had only a few seconds to register his own demise as boiling water and broken pieces of the pier overwhelmed him.

Enraged, Ku'tu stomped up and down again, slowly drawing closer to the lake's shore. Flying overhead, Leta scouted the immediate area. Finding nothing left alive in this area, she flew up to Ku'tu's head.

"That's it for up here," Leta informed her. "The rest of the dummies have their camps below the dam," she said, pointing toward Hoover Dam. "God, I'm so fucking stoned!" she declared, clutching her sides as she fell into a sudden fit of laughter.

A goofy, out-of-place smile bloomed upon the fierce draconic features of Ku'tu. "I know, right?" she grumbled like thunder. "I didn't think Maynard's gummy bears would still be affecting me in my big girl form. But they're still kicking my ass." Snorting with laughter, she involuntarily swayed, kicking up more boiling water and debris at the edge of the lake.

"Ah, well," Leta brayed, still laughing. "We've taken things this far. We might as well finish those rapist scumbags off. Right?"

"Right!" Ku'tu agreed. "Puny humans! Where are they, again? Below the dam?"

"Yeah," Leta confirmed. A fey light crossed her eyes. "Thinking what I'm thinking?"

"Easiest way to do it," Ku'tu said. "Hop on. We can go hit the other side of the dam with a dual blast of elemental fire and phlogiston. We'll see if this puny Hoover person's dam can withstand our combined righteous fury!"

"Right on!" Leta replied merrily, mounting the topmost part of Ku'tu's horned head. Defying the normal conventions of gravity with her magickal flight, Ku'tu shot straight up into the air. From a mile above, she then began a spiraling path that, moments later, found her and Leta a few hundred meters above the rim of the dam, its titanic concrete face staring impassively back at them. It was just daring them to take their best shot.

So they did, pouring it on, because they knew that, should Hoover Dam fail, virtually all of the Brotherhood of Desolation male pig rapists would drown like the rats that they truly were.

Twin gouts of fire-beyond-fire flew forth from the two fire women, carving through the thinner top of the dam like fusion-hot knives through soft butter. Concrete and steel melted before their combined onslaught. For several seconds of determined effort, their fire attacks augured through the top of the dam, abruptly striking the water on the other side of the dam a few seconds later. Massive clouds of hissing steam mushroomed above the dam like a tactical nuclear explosion. Still pouring it on, they both coordinated and continued their attacks, moving down into the middle core of the dam, even as a deep, grinding, infrasonic thrum began to slam into them. Both involuntarily began to swoon from the strain of such a lengthy, continuous effort.

Leta stopped firing, her hands gently returning to their grasp of Ku'tu's horned mounting perch. Noting this, Ku'tu also ceased fire. Together, in silence, hovering just above the rapidly intensifying disaster, they observed the destruction that they had wrought. Hoover Dam, one of mankind's most massive old world architectural triumphs, issued a mighty death-groan, then suddenly split down the middle. Lake Mead's ten trillion gallons of water lurched and stumbled like a herd of drunken elephants riding on spastic whales, then began an inevitable, unstoppable path of destruction.

The Great Colorado River Flood had begun.

That's when the two fire women started snickering and giggling. And they didn't stop until they had arrived back in Dreamland, where they wisely, and stealthily, returned to the massive, multiday festival of love and friendship being held in honor of the Mother.

In death I've found the answer
In death I live again
Fear not the reaper's blade
It does not mean the end
It never really ends
"Transcendence" Crimson Glory

CHAPTER I

I... came the first thought, crawling and screaming from beneath the infinite expanse of existential silence.

I hate... came the next thought, raw emotion enforcing coherence.

I hate, therefore I am... his consciousness roared as his eyes flickered open.

Black. He saw nothing but black before him. Fearing himself blind, he brought his hands before his eyes, where, to his relief, he saw his fingers outlined in a hue of deepest purple, almost vector precise as it marked the perimeter of his form. Carefully looking around, he noted that the color outlined his entire form, almost as if it were a most precise aura warding him from... from what?

"...Cory..." it whispered to him, the perception of the sound seeming to come from all points around him simultaneously. Though initially confusing, the utterance of what he now recalled was his name galvanized his rapidly rejuvenating consciousness, rudely forcing him into a more focused state of awareness.

"Mmphrr-ffhrr..." he growled, his nascent vocal cords unable to convey his intended expletive.

"REMEMBER!" the whisper roared.

Despite his urgent desire to rebel and deny, Cory had no choice but to recall the Battle of Giza, its horror freshly burning again in his mind's eye. He had soared so high, like Icarus of old, only to return to the Earth of his own free will. At orbital velocity, an avenging angel plunging down from the compromised heavens to enforce its unholy will upon an equally unholy, genocidal maniac: Petrus Romanus, the Black Pope.

Cory recalled the impact with the Black Pope's protective shield; how it had impossibly reduced his velocity to nearly zero in less than a nanosecond, leeching it away, displacing it and warding it as if it had been nothing more than a simple light rainfall, and not the kiloton-level impact of a decently sized, incredibly dense meteorite. Adding to the sheer chaos of the moment had been the fact that he had, somehow, still managed to breach the shield, even after it had completely warded him from doing so. He had been stopped there, right at the cusp of breaching it, all of his momentum reduced to naught, yet he still had pierced it. He had willed himself through it. Where tactical nuke power had failed, his own will power had not.

"And it never shall fail," the disembodied voice declared. "Now, remember what you did to him. Remember the price you exacted."

Cory struggled to understand what he'd just heard. "Wait a second. Wait. I..." The light emanating from his palms faded, plunging the area back into its former forever-silence of black-beyond-black. "I died."

"You died..." the voice agreed, sublime sadness echoing softly in its words.

"I died, but my hate brought me back," Cory grated through clenched teeth.

Fountains of dark light traced by pulsating purple lasers erupted from his eyes, emanating from him, scratching a slowly evolving Fibonacci spiral into the eternal darkness of the Void.

"I *am* hate. I'm hate, all the way down. And when it became clear that I was going to be the only one who could end Petrus, I gave into my hatred, and let it burn like a newborn star. I knew

I was going to die. I didn't give a damn, though, long as we won. Long as *I won*," he concluded with something a bit more heavy than grit, the spiral dying in its tracks.

For a painful, long moment, silence reigned.

Then, "But that's not *me*," Cory declared. "I'm *not* hate. That's insane. Maybe a little hate," he admitted. "Like everyone else. But I feel love, too. That's part of why I made that sacrifice: for my friends. For EarthZero. Not just to claim some personal victory. I defy and deny the assertion that I'm just some poorly polarized imbecile, incapable of expressing a complex attitude. Love. Hate. Life. Death. I claim them all. I claim the middle way, the Way of the Void. Neither you, Mother, nor this place, the Void, nor anything that the One Above or Lucifer can sadistically afflict us with on EarthZero, will sway me from my choice, from my own way. What *I* choose! I *am* VoidSpawn. My will *shall not be infringed*. Not even in death!"

Two massive purple slanted eyes opened from the Void, illuminating Cory's form with eldritch energies. The Dark Earth Mother, Chthon, the dual-aspect of the Dragon, her voice like sugar lathered in honey, replied: "Now, you comprehend, VoidSpawn. It is your implacable will that centers your being. Not love, hate, life, or death. Your will – your soul – transcends the Eternal Recursion, the Forever Fractal. So it is, and was, and forever shall be," the Mother replied, clearly pleased. "In death you live again."

"'In death I've found the answer,'" Cory said, finally understanding as the words of a song from his first life, so long ago now, aptly came to mind. "'In death I live again. Fear not the reaper's blade... ...It does not mean the end... It never really ends.'"

"It never ends," Chthon informed him gently. "Go now, my Void, my spawn. Rouse my heretic androgyne from her drunken harlotry. The Abomination of Desolation awaits you. For my glory, we all shall die..."

Screaming in pain beyond any he had yet endured, Cory was thus forcefully aborted from the Dark Womb, a grim smear of cosmic stillbirth flowing like molten darkness in his wake.

CHAPTER 2

Vida waited patiently for a sign from God, had been waiting the many months since the End of the World. It finally came in the form of a toothache. What was at first an occasional spike of pain eventually turned into a throbbing harbinger that she needed something that could not be found in the fantastically well-stocked bunker the Zeff brothers had built. Vida needed a dentist. Aspirin stopped helping, as did the toothache cream. The tooth was becoming abscessed, and though she could feel it wiggle – she just couldn't pull it out.

After everything had turned upside down at the End, she and the twins were the only survivors in the complex. Soon after, life had settled into a dull monotony. Each day Vida and the children rose, had breakfast and went through several hours of homeschooling lessons and exercise. They dutifully tended the little plants that were growing in the greenhouse, and Vida read while Abe and Ada spent plenty of time playing on the indoor playground. Dinner was always light, though there were enough supplies stocked for several families for several years. In the evening, the children watched their favorite videos, while Vida scanned the communications channels for information about who and what was left outside their safe haven.

Vida knew the security protocols, and was careful not to transmit her real location to the people she spoke with. Part of living in a safe bunker was avoiding the attention of potential predators, even if there was virtually no way anyone from outside could breach the bunker. She did trust the former U.S. government employees under the Cheyenne Mountain complex in Colorado. They were as secretive as she, although for a different reason. She had seen their trollish visages in the reflected monitor lights, and she knew they would never willingly come out of their bunker. Like her, they seemed trapped in place, although their circumstances were definitely less pleasant.

There were others out there that she spoke to, and she knew there were global survivors. There was a language barrier, but Vida tried to gather as much information as she could. As long as the satellite signal remained, she had plenty of people to talk to, whether she understood them or not.

Humanity had survived, barely. There were settlements, towns, cities, and even what people were calling arcologies scattered around, and Vida thrived on the news and gossip she found each night. Nearest her location, there was a hamlet in the Catskills that had built a wall against the terrors of the wilds, those on both two legs and otherwise. Phoenicia was not a large town to begin with, but they were fast becoming a trading center in the region, with a number of healthy, hard-working people and a radio station that always broadcast positive information and music.

Neither Chicago nor Detroit had survived intact, having fallen to gangs of mutants that destroyed the cities in their fight for turf. The shoreline of Wisconsin had become dotted with a co-op of armed settlements, but they did not communicate much with the outside world. Mackinac Island had become a homeplace for those who fished and farmed. Maine was rough and tumble, with large and aggressive moose, though rumor had it there was a group of people who had tamed the beasts and actually rode them.

It seemed that the majority of survivors in the northeast had migrated to the region surrounding New York City, more specifically the isle of Manhattan, now known as the City of Glass. It was hard to get anything more than rumors out of the city, but it was common knowledge that the people there had to work hard to earn their place and the rules were terribly strict about who could stay – or even enter the city. Those who could not make the cut were forced to live in the surrounding suburbs, where crime was rife and food was scarce.

And now, it was becoming clear that even if she and the twins wanted to stay in the Zeff Brothers' bunker, they were going to have to venture outside long enough to have her tooth seen to. Over the past several months, the children had grown curious and restive, and when one day Abraham noticed Vida rubbing her face, he looked at her with that unnerving, knowing gaze, and simply said, "Don't worry, Miss Vida. They will fix your tooth for some pears in Po-kip-see."

That night, Vida cast about through her contacts, and learned that yes, there was a rare but reliable dentist in Poughkeepsie, a Doctor Cooper. Getting there was only a matter of hours, and the roads were supposed to be fairly safe, as long as she kept to the highway, and didn't stop to explore (which she had no plans to do). The problem was, she couldn't leave the twins, so they would have to come along. This made Vida nervous, but she was also sure she could get there and back in a day.

Vida talked to the children about the trip, and they were thrilled to finally get out of the bunker for the first time since the Apocalypse, and see the countryside. Her trepidation at leaving was amplified, however, when Ada told her that she and Abe would be ready to move to the City as soon as the car was packed. Try as she might to explain that this was just a short trip and that they would be back right away, Ada was convinced that this was a permanent move.

The next day, Vida packed one of the shiny SUVs in the motor pool, filling the back with food and supplies, as well as extra fuel. When she went in search of the twins, she found that Abe and Ada had scrupulously packed a pair of little suitcases with their favorite belongings. After one last evening, enjoying steaks and salads, the three of them went to bed, prepared for an early departure.

The next morning, the bunker doors rolled back to reveal a beautiful late spring day, with a blue sky lightening in the east, and a brisk wind blowing across the road down the mountain. Vida was careful to secure the bunker as they left, and drove nervously out into the world. There were trees down along the roadside, but luckily, nothing blocked the roadway. In the distance, Vida heard a roar, followed by an animal scream, cut mercifully short. She rolled her window up and sped up until she reached the interstate.

The trip to Poughkeepsie was uneventful, with the children looking out the windows as the miles rolled past. Soon enough, Vida saw signs of other people in town, and then a few who came out and stared as the SUV drove down the street. Much of the town was in disrepair, and empty windows were everywhere. But sure enough, the large office building with the word DENTIST was right where it was supposed to be, and Vida pulled into the lot.

Looking around the empty lot, Vida was nearly overcome with anxiety. Instead of traffic and people, their surroundings were empty of anything except leaves blowing across the lot. Abe touched her shoulder and smiled.

"Don't forget the pears, Miss Vida."

Gathering the children and several cans of pears, Vida locked the vehicle's doors, though she didn't know why. They crossed the small lot and entered the building. The office was homey, warm and the scent of vanilla greeted them as they entered. The waiting room was well-appointed, and the sound of light jazz played from somewhere in the building. A bell chimed as she opened the door, and a middle-aged man appeared on the other side of the receptionist's counter, smiling broadly. His hair was slightly gray, but he was otherwise fit and healthy.

"Good morning! How are you, today – and how can I help you?"

Vida smiled and introduced herself and the children, expressing her need. She relayed her concern that her tooth had gone too long without treatment, and Doctor Cooper took her and the twins in past reception, but not before giving the kids a pair of magazines to read while they waited. As he directed her to a chair, he noticed the heavy bag Vida was carrying and tilted his head.

"I, um, didn't know what you would want for payment, and the children felt that you might want some canned fruit. I have money, but from what I hear on the radio, it's not used anymore..."

Doctor Cooper peered into the bag and saw the cans of pears inside and smiled warmly. "What an excellent choice!" he beamed. "This will do nicely, although before I proceed, I should tell you that the tooth will probably come out on its own – if you are patient. You have been apart from civilization, I take it?"

Vida nodded. "We have a bunker not terribly far away, and while I listen to radio and satellite broadcasts, there isn't much information to be had. What do you mean, come out on its own?"

"Well, one of the things that has changed since the Sigil event is that people are mostly healthier, heal much faster, and regenerate bone and tissue. That tooth, for example, will likely come out the way a baby tooth would, and you will simply regrow a new one. Doesn't help with the pain, mind you, but unless it had grown in irregularly, it will be replaced. I see a lot of strange dental and medical issues, but for the most part, I treat injuries for the people here. Sickness has pretty much disappeared."

Vida touched her jaw and said, "If it's all the same to you, I'd still like it pulled. It hurts quite a bit."

"Then I will need you to lean back, so I can have a look." After inspecting her teeth, Doctor Cooper took an x-ray of the offending tooth. "Ah, yes, it is cracked. This will only take a moment. Vida was patient, as he administered a local anesthetic and pulled the tooth.

"You say you live in a bunker. Just you and the children? I must assume the others who were there did not survive the Sigil's effects. We lost well over 95% here in town, and then many of the survivors left to travel to the large cities like New York. Excuse me, 'the City of Glass' as they call it now. Did you encounter any hazards on the roads here?"

Vida shook her head. "No, although we heard something large and loud. I just drove faster."

"Well, you must be careful. There are monstrous creatures in the wild now, not to mention the opportunistic bandits preying on the weak. I hope you've a decent firearm to protect you and those kids. Or some other power given by the Sigil..."

Vida frowned. "Doctor Cooper, I do not believe in guns, nor do I know how to use one." Pointing at the rosary around her neck, she smiled. "The only power I have is my faith in the Lord God, though that seems at odds with what this world has become. If you are referring to the strange capabilities people have developed, I seem to be handy with growing things, such as plants. The twins," she nodded to the two children, engrossed in the books Doctor Cooper had provided, "they seem to share an ability to know things. They knew you would like the pears."

"Those are wonderful gifts, Vida. And faith is in high demand as well. This whole world turned out differently than pretty much everyone predicted, and not many have stepped up to make it right. Perhaps the Glass Council will get this part of America back on its feet. Did you know that the Pope himself was resurrected and lives in New York now?"

"Wha... What?" Vida sputtered. "But he did terrible things, and right after declaring a holy war..."

"I'm not sure of anything anymore, but I do know that he lives in the City of Glass, and sees to his flock at the Cathedral of St. John the Divine. He is helping the Council to draw many people to the city. And not just Catholics. He is trying to bring all people's faith back. Perhaps you and the children would be safer there than in an isolated bunker."

Vida looked over at the children, only to find them both watching her expectantly.

CHAPTER 3

In the first minute after midnight, under the baleful blind stare of the new moon, on the Isle of Forever in the center of Lake Giza, a harsh, drunken sailor's song reached a rousing crescendo, then abruptly ceased.

"Happy New Year!" Mercyduceus Vendredi, the Ninth Null, cheered drunkenly, hefting her fourth bottle of Yamazaki 1960 whisky high above her head, its silhouette framed momentarily by the towering Ankh of Eternity, which loomed behind her.

Team El—Dwayne, Tim, Leta, Beth, and Ami—had insisted on its construction as a monument to the Battle of Giza. Dwayne and Tim had drawn up the original draft for the plans a month after the battle. As Mhyrranda and her crew had consolidated their power and expanded their influence, word reaching far and wide about the new "Dreamland"—the new Las Vegas—and attracting many newcomers to the enclave, Dwayne and Tim had brought up their plan at the first official public council meeting. It was received with great enthusiasm and the deepest respect by virtually everyone. They had heard the recounting of the battle. What had been sacrificed by Dreamland's great warriors in order to defeat the insane, genocidal scheme of the Black Pope, Petrus Romanus.

With Mercy's reluctant assistance—she adamantly refused to show her true emotions on the matter after her first and only slip, which had embarrassed her totally and had resulted in one

18

particular gurney being violently kicked through the wall of Sick Bay 1 in the Luxor Pyramid—Team El had safely traveled from Dreamland to the chaotic ruins of the former Giza Plateau.

Wrecked. Totally.

The formerly austere, gritty landscape with its eternally brooding ruins had been grossly disfigured by the primal forces unleashed upon it during the battle. The sphinx, of course, had been reduced to something finer than rubble thanks to the phlogiston breath of an enraged Ku'tu. The two lesser pyramids had been destroyed, virtually extirpated from the plateau, partially due again to Ku'tu, and her frenetic battle with the animated sphinx. And due to Void's selfless action, the formerly Great Pyramid itself had been reduced to naught but a slightly concave scattering of granite blocks, spanning most of the former area of the great pyramid's perimeter, yet not rising but a few blocks above the level of the new Lake Giza.

So great had been the primal forces unleashed during the last second of the battle, when Void had impaled the Black Pope with the Hatefang, that the terrain had been chaotically reformed, with the Nile itself being forced into a chaotic nest of recurves near the former Giza Plateau, which itself had been shorn, reduced, then chaotically melted into the new terrain formed in the aftermath of immortal-level primal power being forcefully introduced into the mortal realm.

The circumstances, however, did provide the creative Team El the opportunity to raise the first new monument at the new Lake Giza, and to do so on a veritable tabula rasa.

And thus, the Ankh of Eternity had been constructed, raised, and set in place by Team El in but a solid, coordinated day's work. Rendered from the finest remaining granite available nearby, the memorial stood nearly as tall as once had stood the Statue of Liberty on Liberty Island in New York Harbor. An impressive amount of gold had been used to finish the towering ankh, and it gleamed as brightly and as golden as once had the original sphinx itself, or so Mercy had lied to them. Not that any of them would have known what orichalcum was, anyway, but that's what the original artisans of Atlan had used for the original sphinx.

In multiple languages, in binary, and in standard English, they had inscribed on a massive, embedded stele a brief description of the Battle of Giza, what it had meant for the fate of the world, and, finally, acknowledging the ultimate sacrifice paid by Professor Roger "Gil" Gilmour and his effing white rabbit, and by Cory Christopher Tate, known as Void, who had sold his life and soul dearly in order to save EarthZero.

And it was now, exactly one year and one day after the Battle of Giza, that Mercy drunkenly stumbled around its base, mercilessly punishing herself with strong drink and good cheer for not remaining by his side, where she finally could have accepted the death that she had never truly known.

"But I ran away like a scared little girl!" she howled. "They didn't *make* me go!" she said loudly, her voice echoing across the silent lake. "They couldn't have stopped *me*, had I chosen to remain. None of them could have! Not even Ku'tu! But I ran! I turned tail and ran away!"

Jaw clenched firmly, she stabbed the bottle up at the new moon. "How could I have been such a chickenshit! I've never run away from anything before, not never, no how! That's thirteen millennia if anyone's keeping count, you fuckers!" she raged. "13,337 years of bravery! Gone! Well, 13,338 now. But what the eff! The streak is gone now, and I can never live it down! I'm a coward. A coward. I ran and left him behind to die alone..."

Against her will, her chin grew long and pointy, and her cute nose expanded to a rough point.

"This is for you, homie," she said, bending her wrist, pouring out the rest of the fourth bottle's precious contents into the greenish, glassine sand that lined the banks of Lake Giza and its singular island. An awkward tear slid down her exquisitely pointed face. "Love you, V—"

From high in the sky above her came the sudden, resounding double-boom of hypersonic fury. A lone humanoid figure wrapped in clutching black fire fell directly toward the Ankh of Eternity. Before Mercy's besotted reflexes could save her, the figure viciously impacted the top of the ankh, boring right through its skin of gleaming gold and flesh of hard granite.

"Oh sh—" Mercy shouted as everything around her went white with noise and black with debris.

The resultant shockwave, far greater in its detonation velocity than any conventional old-world human explosive had ever been, shattered the Isle of Eternity, cleanly splitting it in twain, the massive bifurcated Ankh of Eternity slowly twisting away from itself as it plummeted to the gurgling remnants of the island.

For a full five m inutes t he h orror o f t he slow-motion destruction of the serene Isle of Forever and the majestic Ankh of Eternity continued, until, at last, the twisted remnants of the ankh, now only half the original height, ceased their motion, resting finally on what little remained of the island. Multiple small-scale tsunamis spread out from the point of impact, crashing furtively on the distant shores of the lake, setting off small landslides of green sand and rock.

And Mercy took all of this in, almost fully sober now, after five minutes of being locked into her immaterial phase. She returned to the real world, stunned, vacantly hovering in place over the water where the island's beach had only so recently been. She was beyond mere insobriety now, her immortal constitution virtually regenerating all the minor damage done to her by three bottles of good booze and half of another. No longer truly drunk, perhaps just vaguely buzzed, Mercy was now in complete shock, for she could plainly see that, amidst the chaos of the ruined remnants of the island and its formerly majestic memorial ankh, a man's hand now clutched—no, make that crushed and clawed down into—the hard granite of the edge of what was plainly the impact crater.

Naked as a jaybird yet conveniently wreathed by obscuring smoke rising from the massive destruction around him, Void clawed himself out of the crater, granite crunching like cheap papier-mâché in his angry hands.

"So," he said, smiling widely as Mercy's face morphed comically wide in shock, "you must be the Abomination of Desolation. I always thought as much. Where's all the drunken harlotry, my heretic androgyne?"

"Void!"

"Yes, I am." Smirking, his hands covering his naughty bits, Void asked, sheepishly, "And do you happen to have some pants up your tricky sleeves that I could borrow? At least a sock or something? Red Hot Chili Peppers, yo!"

CHAPTER 4

A *lone in the war room of the Lennox Science Arcology in Atlanta, Lucy Diamante, cloaked in silence and stealth, cleared her mind and warily set her third eye free in order to discern the one who now drew near to EarthZero...*

✳✳✳

Bound within the shimmering, diaphanous construct of the Eightfold Nexus, the very fabric of spacetime screaming in agony at its chaotic waveform boundary, the indistinct humanoid eidolon abruptly aborted itself into standard spacetime, surfacing from the unfathomable dark depths of the Under.

As pained photons wailed in conspiratorial quiet, vectoring omnidirectionally away from the flowing contours of the Eightfold Nexus, the Omen of the Apocalypse, the Herald of the Nine, manifested itself in the world of man. Rebinding by silent psychic command the Eightfold Nexus into its chakras, the figure coalesced rapidly into one of its favored corporeal forms, one suited for the rigors of the near-vacuum and hardcore radiation of space.

Improbably, its embedded nanoscale Zyrrblok accumulated and shaped the desired mass via sub-yoctosecond entangled reflection, its source many parsecs removed in the Starhome of the Vanth'Vash'Var, the Sentinels of the Anti-Life, the Death Horde, the Lords of the Void itself. Assembled from the proximate virtual fabric, from seeming nothingness itself, countless quadrillions of bound and enslaved Zeroth Seed, the Unbound Fae, bent to the task of weaving the underlying weirding shapes – the very quintessence of the cosmos itself: All That All Which Is, All That All Which Binds – into the most basic building components of what lied to everyone as Reality.

Their song they sang, forever silent:

"Widdershins, widdershins,
Round and round,
Reflexion both Up and Down,
Monad, Duad, Triad, Tetrad,
Bend the Void,
Bend the Source,
Bind the Dark Womb,
Bind the Dragon,
Bend All That All Which Is,
Bind All That All Which Binds."

Time unmarked, unknown, passed for the Unbound, their craftwork eternal only to themselves. Gravitonic scaffolding appeared from the nothingness, shaped into being by the Unbound Fae. From among the uncountable virtual components of the Cosmic Sea of Silence, they selected and bound only the most perfect bosons, shaping them most carefully into their meticulously crafted gravitonic scaffolds. During the relative eternity of their ephemeral lives, the most perfect bosons then served as the substrates for the higher particles, which also the Unbound assembled into more desirable shapes and scaffolds, and trellises. Like masons skillfully setting their bricks and stones into alignment, the Unbound steadily and without pause continued their crafting, scaling their masterwork into and through the atomic regime, then the molecular, then the cellular, then the systemic, then, at last, after a relative millennium equal to but a mere .987 milliseconds in reality, to the final form. The master form of the Omen of the Apocalypse, the Herald of the Nine.

An androgyne physically, for it was aeons removed from such trivialities as mating and sexual reproduction, its skin cast a hue like molten brass. Both infrared and ultraviolet competed at the extremes of the visual spectrum for dominance with the underlying base of brass, causing an eerie scintillation that expressed itself as a prismatic sheen, or aura, upon its figure. More perfect in its symmetry than DaVinci's Vitruvian Man, the humanoid stood motionless in space, its taciturn gaze, its eldritch black eyes, focused upon the middle distance.

Finally, after so many evolutions, after so much cleansing, after so much perfection applied to the utter chaos of this cosmos born of idiot afterbirth, the End of All Things loomed near. This last star, this unremarkable yet infinitely unique system on the edge of veritable nowhere, would, in all probability, be the last. The world where at last the Womb of the Dark Earth Mother would bend, and at last the Dragon would be bound. Where Reality itself would finally bend the knee to the Vanth'Vash'Var, and the cosmos, its underlying primal essence finally exposed, its black bitch and her incestuous dual-aspect mate, the life force of all things, could finally be damned and unbound. As, at long last, must all things be.

The Eternal Recursion, the Sequence of Infinity, had been followed with utmost precision for aeons untold. The Fractal Mages had refined to perfection their divinations, and the Appointer itself had crafted the mappings. All possible stars with advanced life – those capable of producing illuminated souls; souls capable of transcendence to the Eighth Chakra – had been processed, their bright souls joining the Horde in its glory, or being damned for all time.

There now remained but one to scout. The last bastion. The one star system yet extant in the cosmos, capable of harboring bright souls. The last place where, perforce, the final remnants of the Dark Earth Mother and the Dragon itself would at last become realized. The last node where the Eternal Recursion would at long last be resolved. Where the cosmos would finally be put out of the eternal misery of its imperfect evolution and die the death it yearned for so desperately. The precise reason why the cosmos had birthed the Vanth'Vash'Var in the first place to serve as its Holy Deliverance, the End of All Things.

The final Earth. The first Earth. EarthZero.

Holy resolve burning with unquenchable fury, the Omen of the Apocalypse, from its distant vantage at the edge of the Oort Cloud, cast its judging gaze at the final star system.

Disgust slowly marred the perfect countenance. Clearly, there was no star ahead.

The Oort Cloud was indeed populated, as were the peripheries of most similar star systems. Scattered primordial planetoids, proto-comets, and sparse miniature nebulae loomed in abundance. Yet, there were no planetary bodies within the wonderfully cored and carved out cloud around what should have been a complete solar system. Neither planets nor star, nor any larger celestial body, were visible to its withering multispectral gaze.

Contemplating this improbability, it realized immediately that never before had both the Fractal Mages and the Appointer itself been wrong. While it was true that there had been at least a single incident in which the Fractal Mages had been incorrect by the span of a single star within a trinary solar system, their spectacular correction by the Appointer, during which half of their order had been crucified and cast into space, their regenerating cybernetics forever binding them to a near-eternity of constant suffering, precluded such errors from ever occurring again. Their lesson should have lasted until now, or at least until the near future, when EarthZero had at last been properly processed and rendered.

Yet, there was no star.

"Even I would not dare tempt the wrath of the Appointer," the Omen of the Apocalypse considered silently. "Therefore, the Fractal Mages must have been correct, and, thus, the Appointer must have been correct. There is a star there. I simply cannot discern it. Which, of course, is improbable. Highly improbable..."

Willing the Eightfold Nexus to manifest about it, the Omen of the Apocalypse shaped spacetime, the boundary of the waveform of the nexus improbably pulling itself to its future self, where it already existed in at least one possible near-frame timeline. It traversed the radius of the Oort Cloud almost to the center, near to where the star should have been. And then, once there, once its will to be there ceased, it was there. And there was the star, Sol, beaming brightly.

It had been there all along, it now knew. Yet, something, some power, had warded it from casual inspection. As if the gaze of the Omen of the Apocalypse were casual, of course.

From near the orbit of the first planet, the Omen of the Apocalypse gazed first at the star, then slowly traced the paths of the planets. After but a moment of discernment, it perceived that the third planet was indeed EarthZero.

And for the first time in its long existence of many aeons, the Omen of the Apocalypse knew Fear, because the Dragon itself stared back.

"THE DRAGON'S GAME BEGINS ANEW..." the Dragon challenged the Omen of the Apocalypse, speaking with the voice of the metacosmos itself.

An alien wave of total fear broke upon the formerly inviolate psyche of the Omen of the Apocalypse. Shaping spacetime around itself, it retreated as quickly as it dared, pushing its construct to its limits, and beyond. The Nine soon would learn that the resolution of the Eternal Recursion drew near. That, at long last, the End of All Things was at hand.

***

Shivering, yet exhilarated, Lucy returned her focus to the world around her, even as a tight smile slowly bloomed on her face.

CHAPTER 5

"We're here," Mercy informed Void, Shunya hissing silently as she willed it to return to her soul.

The dry, desert air of the former Las Vegas around the two complained audibly, sizzling like frying bacon fat, at having been so harshly violated by the spacetime-cutting Fractal Blade, Shunya. Mercifully, the audible effect was short-lived, as were the visuals; the rainbow fractal pinwheels rapidly returning to their unseen, virtual identities.

For a moment, Void stood in place, senses keen as he sampled the environs of Dreamland from their shadowy back-alleyway ingress point. The shamelessly tight black compression pants, retrieved from Mercy's extradimensional storage in her tricky sleeves, knotted and writhed, his muscles flexing beneath them as he grounded himself physically. Slowly, he closed his eerie jet black eyes. His palms slowly rotated open as his heavily thewed arms swung open wide.

"What's that?" Mercy inquired, giving him a quizzical sidelong glance. "*Taijiquan?*"

"Close. Cosmic, for real. Something's about to go down," he said calmly, black eyes sliding open.

"Well, shoot," Mercy chuckled. "I think you mean your pants are about to go down. They're made for me, not someone a foot taller." Mercy's summoning of Shunya belied her humor. Or perhaps accentuated it, depending on her mood.

Silently, Void brought his right hand before him, elbow almost to his side, then quickly pivoted his hand some 45 degrees to the left.

Nodding, Mercy took off at a quick trot, her physical form becoming semi-translucent as she exited the alley. Bounding into the street, she immediately hung a left, seeing almost immediately the milling throng of people several blocks distant. The crowd was gathering in the new plaza that had been extended from the former Luxor complex. Looming improbably high above the plaza, the newly renovated and artificed Dreamland Arcology dominated the former Las Vegas skyline. Even now, several blocks away, Mercy and Void both were aware of its virtually silent, sibilant *thrum-thrum-thrum* hekatek resonance. Within proximity of its presence, all hekatek, all souls, would be augmented by its cosmic power.

As the two closed upon the scene, the crowd grew quiet, allowing the haggard voice of one Old Man Culpepper to blare forth in all of its twangy glory:

"I've had enough!" Old Man Culpepper declared, his voice ringing and resounding over the silent din of the crowd. "If I can't eat any real meat for the rest of my immortal life... If I can't have tasty bacon, Lord's sakes... Then I'm just going to off myself here and now, you vegan liberal commie freaks! And you can tell your sawed-off little Green Man that, hell no, I'm not going to let him plant coca plants all over my back 40! Goddamn pinko commie drug lord little faerie freak!"

A small chorus – smaller than the totality of the crowd, that is – of excited denials filled the plaza air. Obviously, some of them still liked the Devil's Marching Powder, immortal now or not.

As Void and Mercy drew closer, they were able to see Old Man Culpepper through the hundreds of people gathered around him. He appeared to be a healthy, lithe man of about sixty or seventy, a long grey beard stabbing down toward his blue jean overalls. A simple white rancher's hat sat neatly on his wrinkled brow, a single ponytail of shock white hair hanging neatly down to the small of his back. Around him and above him stretched an interesting contraption of metal pipes and twelve gallon jug-sized containers of shiny aluminum, spaced somewhat evenly across the top and upper sides of the metal contraption. It was similar in form to shower room plumbing, though there were many more shower heads in this case than usual.

"Y'all go ahead and get back, friends," Old Man Culpepper warned them, raising an out-of-place electronic tablet up to chest level. "I don't want nobody hurt, of course. Just me. It's my protest. And all those containers you see," he said, nodding at a few of the gallon jug-sized shiny metal containers, "are filled with my own special mix of thermate and super-thermite. It'll burn right through a hafnium-nitrogen-oxygen composite. Meaning, it'll melt through a tank or battleship so quick your goddamn head'll spin!"

"Don't do it, Cully!" A concerned looking middle-aged man shouted. He was wearing what appeared to be an outlandish purple Roman toga, and excitedly waving his hands above his head as he fought to make his way through the crowd. "You can't do it! We need your skills, man!"

"I'm tired of it, Santiago," Cully shot back, waggling his tablet over his head, almost slapping one of the deadly containers above his head. "Sick and tired of it! I reckon I'll just mosey on off this slap-happy doomed-ass world now, and go join the Good Lord up in Heaven, where I sure as hell can eat all the meat I goddamn want! Freakin' commie vegans! Those goddamn faeries have warped your damned minds! They've already got you eatin' nothin' but veggies and fruits and salads like the damn commies they are. Next, they'll have you eatin' nothin' but hay straight out the goddamn cattle feeder! And plantin' your former grazin' land with drugs! You liberal faerie-lovin' commie jag-offs might think it's heaven here on Earth, but it's not. *I* didn't vote for it, dammit!"

Desperately shoving past the transfixed crowd, Santiago drew up to Old Man Culpepper, careful to stay outside of the contraption.

"C'mon, Cully," Santiago pleaded. "This is silly. We can work everything out. We just have to try. We haven't even tried yet. You're overreacting, as usual. Besides," he said, indicating the bizarre contraption, "you can't kill yourself, Cully. We all regenerate now."

"Stay back, Santiago," Cully warned him, gravel in his voice. He held his tablet up with one hand, the index finger of his other poised above its slick surface. "I'm going to press this in 10 seconds, and it's going to disintegrate me. I know it will. I've already tried it at lower doses. Burned my got-damn pinky finger clean off," he said, flipping the nub toward Santiago. "Still hasn't grown back yet. But I reckon 10,000 times as much of my special blend will cover all of me, and melt me down all at once. No regeneratin' back from that."

Meanwhile, Void and Mercy had made their way through the crowd, careful not to make much more of a scene. Careful to have once more sent Shunya away. And careful not to fly. And careful not to have ridden Wooly Mammoths into the crowd, for all the transfixed crowd would have noticed.

"Void?" Mercy said just loudly enough to be heard over the general hum of the crowd and the rather loud shouts of Old Man Culpepper and his concerned buddy, Santiago. "What do we do? I really wanted to help him at first, but then he started insulting the Fae. Even though I happen to agree with him, because bacon is seriously tasty and dietary laws are so Old Testament, he just fell off my list of people I'd prefer to help. Ignorant pig of a former human," she finished, her disdain obvious in the snarl of her mouth. "Besides. I like Vir'gil's special cocaine as much as the next junkie."

"I see that nothing's really changed," Void horse-laughed, startling the former human standing immediately ahead of him.

The former human, a bit annoyed, turned back to shush Void, but immediately abandoned the thought when, after craning his head up to its full extent, he saw Void's midnight-black eyes. Seeing this, Mercy failed to keep her snarl of disdain framed on her face.

"Want me to zap up to him and save him?" Mercy offered, trying to cover her smile with her hand. "He's probably worth saving. I've heard Maynard mention him before. Some kind of smithy or tinker or something. Good with chemicals, metals, and alloys."

"Yeah," Void replied, watching the argument between Old Man Culpepper and Santiago break down into some rather crude personal insults. He was pretty sure he heard "Coldpecker" followed immediately by "Julius Caesar Chavez". "I'm sure that'll come in handy. But, no, I've got it. You're not going to want to risk any exposure to that stuff if what Culpepper's saying is true."

"I can phase, Void," she reminded him. "Remember?"

"I remember," he said. "And I'm sure that you're fast and slick enough to save Culpepper before he presses that button. But what if he has a dead man switch on it? What if it goes off anyway, there in the middle of the crowd? That stuff is what they use to melt steel beams. Fast, too. And if what he said about that compound is true and not a bluff or miscalculation, his stuff is insanely potent. Like, almost surface-of-the-Sun potent."

Mercy snorted. "They're not steel beams. They'll regenerate. It's just some thermite. He showed us his pinky nub. Looked like it was growing back."

As Void began to roll his eyes in disbelief, Old Man Culpepper's voice suddenly reached a feverish pitch, his index finger stabbing down hard on his tablet.

Local spacetime abruptly slowed to a limping, stumbling crawl as Shunya flared to chaotic life. Giving a quick glance to Void, Mercy saw immediately that, yes indeed, Void's "frame of time" cheating power was in effect, somehow drawing him into her local, highly accelerated frame of spacetime. Ahead of them, she saw out of the corner of her eye, a nauseatingly slow *pop-pop-pop* sequence was traversing the gallon jug-sized shiny containers, triggering their internal mechanisms in the space of mere fractions of seconds.

"I've got Santiago," Mercy said, streaking ahead, phasing through the stock-still bodies of the several people between her and her destination. As she exited the last body, she saw the space of several feet opened up between her and Santiago, Old Man Culpepper, and the Contraption of Doom. Unfortunately, all twelve of the containers now were glowing white hot, slowly beginning to disgorge their terrible melting doom upon Old Man Culpepper in slow motion. Not checking her momentum, she partially phased back into being, slamming bodily into Santiago, lifting him awkwardly from the ground as she bull-rushed him into the crowd beyond them. Beneath her free hand, where she had bodily clutched his left shoulder, she felt the bones and sinew give way with an audible, extremely sickening slow-motion sound. And the poor sods in the first two rows of the crowd that she and Santiago had careened into at warp speed were going to have serious contusions, broken bones, and generally bad days ahead of them as they slowly regenerated their wounds.

Simultaneously, Void had been in action. Unable to materially phase like Mercy, but able to travel his own unique way, Void willed himself to Old Man Culpepper's presence, where he appeared virtually as soon as his thought to be there had been completed.

Even as his peripheral vision informed him of Mercy's carnage upon Santiago and the nearby crowd, Void, too, noted the abrupt issuance of the white-hot substance from the 12 containers studding the contraption. As he reached forward to place an open palm upon Old Man Culpepper's overalls – the better to shove him back away from the Contraption of Doom – he noted that something had suddenly materialized between his palm and Old Man Culpepper's overalls. Something shimmery, almost ethereal in form, like the mirage of heat rising from a hot road. As rapidly as Void could process information in this frame of time, the shimmery shield of energy – Nick's force field, if he recalled correctly – completely enveloped Old Man Culpepper's form.

Slowly, painfully slowly, the force field began to tug Old Man Culpepper's form away from the Contraption of Doom. A subconscious calculation informed Void that Nick's intervention might remove the grouchy old carnivore from the scene before the flesh-melting doom of the contraption could work its charms. Operative word: Might. And what might be the actual upper limits of Nick's force shields? Could they indeed stand against something that promised to be close to the actual surface temperature of the Sun itself?

Void couldn't take the risk, for, even now, in this particular millisecond, the first few droplets of the flesh-melting mix had begun to cascade down his back. And Old Man Culpepper clearly, now, wasn't going to totally make it, for Void saw that Nick's force field was beginning to pepper and crack from the arrival of the first bit of the mix to reach it.

Absurdly, Void's mind informed him that Old Man Culpepper had probably used his own immortal power to mix up his super-special melting compound. And that fact alone rendered irrelevant any considerations of Nick's force shield's being able to resist it. It was simply magick versus magick, or hekatek versus hekatek in this case, with the win going to whoever had best stuffed their charms with power. And in this case, it looked as if Old Man Culpepper had poured his heart into it over hours of hateful soulforging, while Nick had obviously not, if only due to time constraints. So it seemed that Old Man Culpepper, shields or not, would be consumed by the veritable downpour of hot death.

With no reservations, Void stretched out, making himself as big as he could, trying his best to interpose himself between Old Man Culpepper's slowly moving, force field-enveloped form and the soul-scalding downpour. He took the hits of the 12 containers as they began to rain down with a near-fusion fury. Stinging hot tears tumbled slowly down his face. Jaw clenched, he bore down inside, his implacable, iron will shifting and shaping the boundary conditions of his quantum waveform. His flesh, he now knew, was nothing more than a convenient sleeve, or mask, over his true immortal essence. What he was, as he had recently affirmed before the Mother, was a being of Light and Darkness, Love and Hate, Death and Life, manifested by sheer force of will power alone. So what might have once been in doubt, no longer was in doubt.

Comforted by this thought, Void took virtually the entire hit from the 12 soulforged face-melters.

As spacetime once again stitched itself back into a somewhat singular flow, screams of pain and panic filled the plaza. A terrible hissing screamed even louder, as the smaller portion of the soulforged compound spilled onto the ground of the plaza, furiously melting down onto it and into it like white phosphorus munitions raining down from on high. Everyone capable of backing up away from the sizzling, out-of-control display of sparking, volcanic fury did so immediately.

"Void!" Mercy yelled, shoving Santiago away from her violently. He could just add that extra damage to his List of Body Parts to Regenerate.

"Mercy!" Nick yelled from across the plaza. He was working his hands together, guiding Old Man Culpepper over towards her. "I got him. Don't worry!"

"Fuck *him*!" Mercy yelled back, giving Old Man Culpepper's shielded form a sharp, dismissive kick as she moved slowly toward the burning pyrotechnic pyre that now had spread some several feet across the plaza. "Void's there, inside it! Can you give him a shield? We might be able to save a piece he can regenerate from," she said, not really believing her own words. Surface of the Sun, for sure.

Abruptly dispelling the shield on Old Man Culpepper, who fell directly on his ass several feet beyond the edge of the sizzling fire show in the plaza, Nick quickly moved over to Mercy.

"Did you say 'void'?" he asked her. "You don't mean—"

"VoidSpawn..." came a tremendous, basso profundo voice from within the pyre.

Immediately perking up, Mercy began to smile. "Void?" she called.

Slowly, as the snappy, crackling sizzle of white-and-red flame began to diminish, the crowd became aware of the shadowy humanoid form standing at the center of the fatal pyre. In curious wonder, they began to creep back for as close of a look as the diminishing heat would allow. There, before them, apparently untouched by the pyrokinetic outburst of Old Man Culpepper's nearly-fusion-hot special soulforged face-melting compound, stood a wild looking figure of a man who clearly wasn't human anymore.

As Void stepped out of the still-sizzling mayhem, those gathered noticed that he had a deep golden skin tone and a rampant lion's mane of hair. Difficult to see beneath his wild hair, his pointed ears spoke to ancient origins, as did his impressive canines. Something issued forth from him, below the threshold of normal perception. Something both intimidating and intoxicating.

It was as if one were looking at a thermonuclear device up close and personal, knowing that it was totally harmless, until it went off. And then it would wreck your world and fuck your shit up.

"Holy shit!" Nick cried out. "Void! You're back!" he said, sauntering over to stand before him. "How? How did you—"

"He'll make an announcement soon," Mercy finished before anyone could blurt out inconvenient facts. "C'mon, let's get inside. We've got a lot to cover. Like Void's golden butt," she smiled, pointing down at the shredded compression pants. "Looks like you've got to work on your auric projection, dude. Or else you're going to need a change of clothes for every occasion."

"I tried," Void shrugged. "Still learning. Hi, Nick," he said, extending his hand, which Nick eagerly grasped. "Got any pants I can borrow?"

***

"Maynard."

He was lying on a comfortable looking leather couch, a bottle of Old Crow in his hand, hanging lazily over the edge of the couch, a well-worn black pillow somewhat covering his face.

"Maynard."

He felt the hand rest gently on his shoulder, but he had his artificed headphones on, and Black Sabbath's "Into the Void" was currently kicking his psyche's ass hard, so he just snarled a bit and tried to swat it away with his free hand. He missed with his first blind, drunk, and belligerent swat.

"Go away..." Maynard told the intruder and botherer. He flailed a few more times, finally connecting on the third with a very dull thud. "Ouch!" he laughed, pulling his hand back. Clearly, he had just tagged something harder than stone or steel. "What the heck, Denny! Was that the FrameGrab prototype? I've been up for three days. Let me chill. Sabbath, man. Sabbath."

Void reached down, grabbing the pillow and raising it high enough for Maynard to see him.

"You can sleep when you're dead," Void told him, smiling brightly.

"Holy shit! Void!" Maynard shouted, bolting up awkwardly, his bottle falling from his hand.

Void snatched it out of midair before it hit the floor. "Old Crow? Sabbath? What are you getting into, man?" he inquired, quickly turning the bottle up and swiftly draining it.

Maynard's face blanched. His hands started to shake as he slowly rose to his feet. "Virge, you'd best confess to spiking my whiskey."

But Vir'gil, the Entheogenic Lord was standing there, at Void's flank. So, too, was Mercy. Behind them, Team El—Ami, Beth, Dwayne, Leta, and Tim—Nick, and Mhyrranda milled anxiously. Ku'tu rested daintily on Leta's right shoulder. Just now arriving, Denny and Rachel brought up the rear, with their beautiful baby daughter, Penny, loosely swaddled in her arms.

"I confess to nothing," Vir'gil groaned, "even though I've probably done everything anyway."

Without thinking, Maynard threw his arms around Void, giving him a very tight hug. Though Maynard had enhanced his own physical strength with experimental cybernetic runes—enough to allow him to easily haul around and handle his often massively heavy tech equipment—there was absolutely no give from Void. Though he wore no visible armor – after a quick change, he now was wearing one of Nick's old world black hoodies, a pair of equally outdated black compression pants, this time more near to his own size, and some generic black combat boots—it was as if he were made of something beyond steel.

"I knew it!" he told Void, disengaging. He pumped a fist in the air, almost losing his balance. "I knew you weren't dead!"

"I was dead," Void deadpanned. He lived to do that to Maynard, just as Maynard lived to toss him a softball like that. They both smiled. "I've been in the Void for one year and one day. I just got back. Sorry about the memorial, guys," he said, turning toward Team El.

"S'all good, man," Tim said again, for probably the tenth time in the past quarter-hour, since Void and Mercy, guided by an excited Nick, had strode boldly into the Great Pyramid of Dreamland, otherwise known as the Dreamland Arcology, announcing Void's miraculous resurrection with stunning, badass silence. Well, except for the Old Man Culpepper incident, of course. A graduate of Caltech with an engineering degree himself, Tim was still trying to calculate precisely how Void had managed such an exhibition of power, and what sort of refractory attributes his skin must have. He had endured, without a scratch, something that had gouged out a seething pit in the ground. One that was still molten hot at its bottom, about 10 feet below the level of the plaza. Yet, Tim was just temporizing, filling his mind with needless calculations to keep himself from dwelling on the indisputable fact that Void once more walked the world, miraculously being resurrected from total annihilation. The last vestige of Tim's old world faith was howling at him as it seemed to be slipping away into the metaphorical darkness of disbelief.

"Sober up, man," Void told Maynard. As if he were someone to tell somebody else to sober up. "Get some coffee. We've got some engineering to do. Big time."

"Ha," Maynard giggled, giving Vir'gil a surreptitious glance. "Void's missed the last year. And one day."

Ku'tu hissed, "That's some straight up midnight pact shit," she said, sounding surprisingly like Leta now, Void reckoned, amused. As if Ku'tu weren't badass enough already. Now she actually could convey her attitude. It was only natural, Void thought, that the two fire women would bond. That's how fire was meant to be. And fire women, too.

As Void's gaze returned from Ku'tu to Maynard, Maynard brought his right hand up to eye level, moving his fingers with the dexterity of a master illusionist. Blooming from where the tips of his fingers had passed in the air before him came a rune of crisp evergreen hue, crackling like pine needles trodden softly underfoot. As his fingers ceased their elaborate arcs, he slightly tucked his head forward, then abruptly smacked the rune into his forehead with his hand.

"Coulda had a V-8!" Maynard laughed, the rune disappearing, leaving in its passage a temporary light green aura around the perimeter of Maynard's body. Instantly, his eyes cleared, and he took in a deep breath of air.

"Show off!" Beth prodded him. "You and Denny and your rune mastery BS."

"All good now," Maynard declared, giving Beth a wink. She was his top student, even counting the Fae of EarthZero who participated in his weekly workshops. "And you know Denny's even better at this than I am, Beth. He's been here just two months, and he's already advanced the runic knowledge beyond anything we'd ever imagined. Inscriptions? Hello? Thanks, Denny Google!"

"Aw, c'mon, Maynard," Denny bridled. "You know I hate that name."

"Sorry, dude," Maynard said. "Still, you really are. If the hekatek had a search engine, you would be its Google."

Despite himself, Denny smiled at Maynard's praise. Not that it was rare, because that's how Maynard taught. But now, in the presence of the newly resurrected demigod, it felt better than real. It felt like it vindicated him. He hugged Rachel into him, careful not to upset their baby girl.

Maynard saw this, and flashed Denny a warm smile. "Let's do this. Time to do whatever it is we're doing."

"Then let's head up to our old war room and get our bearings first," Mhyrranda said. "I have the feeling that this is going to be epic. We can start with what just happened in the plaza with Old Man Culpepper. The grouchy old coot."

As the group began to turn to depart, Void abruptly stopped and said, "Wait."

Though it had been said in nothing louder than a casual, conversational tone, everyone else stopped in their tracks. They noted a most curious expression on Void's face. One of wonder. Eyes locked on target, he moved directly, softly, to stand before Denny and Rachel. To be fair, neither of them had yet officially met him, so they hadn't known precisely what to expect. Yet now, he towered over both of them, and his presence was nothing short of overwhelming to the uninitiated. He had the build and mien of some oversized MMA fighter or WWE wrestler. A crazy, alien kind of charisma. It poured like intoxicating, invisible vapors from him. Physically, they saw that he clearly was not human. Not anymore, for he now had transcended humanity, even that new transcendent humanity which mankind had evolved to, post-sigil. He was something beyond that, now, or else his soul-shattering eyes were lying, for they whispered silently that he was of the Void.

Though Denny and Rachel were veterans of the road and its many terrors, they both suddenly felt the primitive instinct to fight or flee. Only the fact that everyone they'd met in Dreamland over the past two months had hailed the VoidSpawn as a hero stilled their urge to fight, because they certainly weren't going to flee from anyone or anything. Not after what they had experienced. Not after what they had wrought in their travels. Still, Denny's right hand moved a fraction of an inch down toward his highly artificed

Desert Eagle, its lovingly artificed munitions capable of downing even the mightiest mutants with but a single shot.

Slowly, Void's eldritch gaze fell to little Penny. The temperature in the room plummeted to just above the freezing point of water as everyone in the room stared at the most ridiculous, yet most terrifying scene. The heroic, world-saving demigod, standing still before a helpless human infant, silently staring at her. Then, just as the silent, dreadful pause loomed too long:

"I welcome thee to EarthZero, Anshadar..." the VoidSpawn said in perfect Ancient Sidhe, the tongue of the elder Fae of both EarthZero and Aal.

Then, he bent his right knee to her, his head inclined.

A collective gasp shot over the group. Immediately, Vir'gil and Maynard kneeled, heads inclined. On Leta's shoulder, Ku'tu kneeled reverently. Noticing Mercy's defiant stance, she waved excitedly for her to hit the floor and bow.

"No!" Mercy snarled, *sotto voce*. In American English, of course, because she was being a bitch, and she didn't care who heard her.

"It's not a pledge, Mercy!" Ku'tu reminded her, whispering in Ancient Sidhe. "It's just a sign of respect! Don't be so mean."

Tilting her head toward Ku'tu, Mercy ran a finger over her throat, mouthing the word "No!"

"Mercy..." Void softly growled. Biting his tongue, Maynard noted that, of all people, Nick, who was one fierce motherfucker like most operators tended to be, almost took a knee at hearing that growl.

"Dammit, Void, you'll pay for this indignation! I *will* get you back for this..." Mercy complained weakly, in Ancient Sidhe, as she, too, reverently bowed. *Cute as a button,* she laughed to herself as she gave Penny a quick glance, wondering why she kept pretending to be such a hardass when it came down to showing love. *Babies were always so cute. And tasty.*

Stunned silence filled the room. Heads turned, seeking explanations, though there was none for those who didn't speak the tongue of the Fae. Then, as the ritual bending of the knee concluded, little Penny's tiny hand sprawled out from beneath her loose swaddling blanket, and her tiny fingers gently brushed the tip of Void's nose.

Void, Maynard, and the rest of the Fae arose.

Maynard took it upon himself to explain what had just caused half of the group to bow down respectfully to little Penny:

"Rachel? Denny? You guys are truly blessed. Void recognized it immediately upon seeing her," Maynard informed them. "While the rest of us had missed it, even after two months, he instantly discerned that little Penny there has a special lineage. If I heard it correctly—my Ancient Sidhe, the language of the elder Fae, is suspect,   at   best—he   just   welcomed   Penny   to EarthZero—interesting name, there, bro—and honored her with the title of 'Anshadar'. Which means that the Dark Earth Mother and her dual-aspect masculine counterpart, the Dragon, have blessed her soul. Personally. That's totally awesome, Denny! Rachel!" he beamed, smiling as he moved up to carefully embrace them.

"What the hell, Maynard?" Denny asked him quietly, cutting an eye up toward Void, who had moved back a step.

"It's freakin' awesome, man," Maynard said. "It's all good, don't worry. I'll give you the full story when we get to the war room. Wow! This is the best day ever!"

"Don't be a n00b, Maynard," Mercy needled him. "The best day *ever* was when *I* was born."

"Come along then," Mhyrranda said, smiling, beckoning them to follow along. "Please mind all the junk—I mean, the newly artificed hekatek—that Maynard's been hoarding."

Dressed in her typical purple coat and tight black leather pants, she gracefully led the group out of Maynard's almost perfectly absurd laboratory, in which he had hoarded as much of the salvageable old world tech that he could find. It had formerly been one of the convention halls, and he had expanded it as much as Mhyrranda had allowed him to, cramming its voluminous square footage to near-capacity. From Maynard's simple crash-couch in the far corner of the cavernous room, it took the group a full minute of careful creeping to escape to the terraformed and exquisitely crafted atrium, which now served as the primary nexus of the Dreamland Arcology.

Almost everything in the Great Pyramid of Dreamland had, over the past year and one day, been converted from the Luxor Hotel's pyramid into an arcology so efficient, magnificent, and awesome that even Paolo Soleri would have gazed upon it with appreciative wonder. Of course, Soleri and his contemporaries would not have had the singular advantage of having both hekatek savants and representatives of the Fae of EarthZero as their architects and builders. Here, however, where Mhyrranda ran Dreamland with the proverbial iron fist in a velvet glove, such esoterica were possible, and as such it had been heavily leveraged to the benefit of the survivors of the Great Collapse.

Over 1,000,000 custom inscriptions and runes now empowered the Great Pyramid of Dreamland. Both the former humans whom Maynard and Vir'gil had instructed in the art of runic inscription and the Fae themselves who had joined them had worked virtually non-stop for many months. And after the collapse of the Hoover Dam and the subsequent Great Colorado River Flood, a catastrophe which had all but destroyed the last of the Old World power generation capabilities, the artificers had doubled then tripled their efforts to rapidly integrate runic power generation into the magickal infrastructure.

The runes appeared virtually everywhere, though they were difficult to discern at times due to their highly selective placement: sometimes hidden at the base of a fruit-bearing tree or hidden by an herb garden, sometimes interleaved with the gothic design of the crystalline floor tiles and stained glass, and sometimes beneath the surface of the many flowing streams and pleasantly burbling fountains.

Everything smelled fresh and wholesome, as if one were strolling through a remote country orchard nestled in the bend of a lazy river. A natural cycle of day and night flowed within the pyramid, synchronized with the outside world, though it would never truly be dark within such a place of warm light and its ubiquitous infrared healing warmth. Those who remained within its presence were charged by its strength, augmenting both their personal stamina and natural healing rate. Empowered by the hekatek, continuously replenishing food and drink also were provided by the innumerable fruit trees, herb and vegetable gardens, and fountains. Not that hunger and thirst could kill as they had prior to the Great Collapse, but even the newly immortal needed food and water to remain strong and not slowly wither away.

Though the survivors of the Great Collapse were technically immortal, unable to die now due to the ravages of old age or normal disease, their triple helix DNA constantly empowering them with supra-normal life force, they still appreciated the freely given augmentations, the relief from the slow withering of hunger and thirst, the natural charm of the place, and the pleasant atmosphere of safety which it provided. It was exactly what Mhyrranda had promised the leaders of the many ragtag bands of survivors: a sanctuary where they could finally put the horrors of the old world and the Great Collapse behind them, as they struggled tooth and nail to wrest from Fate herself a better life in the new world. Truly, Dreamland lived up to its name.

Hundreds of people milled about in the atrium. Several thousand more now were entering the massive atrium from all eight of its ground floor atrium entrances, trying their best to get a glimpse of the newly resurrected VoidSpawn and his companions, the heroes of the Battle of Giza. Rarely did the heroes gather as such, so this alone would have been enough to have ensured the attention of dozens, if not hundreds, of the citizens of Dreamland. They were the rock stars of Dreamland, and they commanded crowds wherever they roamed. And Mhyrranda was their Duchess, their Mistress of Dreams. Their Dreamwyrd. They loved her as if she were their own mother, wife, or lover. And sometimes all three, simultaneously.

Yet the level of adulation that virtually every citizen in Dreamland had for the one who had made the ultimate sacrifice to save the world was of an order of magnitude greater. It bordered closely on worship. Dangerously so. So when the news had begun to spread like wildfire through Dreamland that the Spawn of the Void had returned from the dead to walk the green paths of the Great Pyramid of Dreamland, none could resist the compulsion to see the resurrected demigod in the flesh.

The chant began at the far side of the sprawling atrium, spreading with each syllable until it came from the whole crowd: "Void! Void! Void!"

"I am so embarrassed..." Void said just loud enough to be heard, causing some relieved laughter from his companions. He smiled, waving at the crowd, as they walked toward the center of the atrium.

"Embarrassed? You should be," Mercy quipped. "You get cheered for dying. Slacker."

"Didn't this place used to be smaller?" Void asked Maynard, trying not to laugh at Mercy's merciless needling. His sidelong glance at her, though, confirmed that she, too, was having a good time. At his own expense. Gods, but he loved her sassy impertinence. *If only I could tell her,* he thought, instantly regretting thinking such blasphemy. *I am so into you...*

"We regrew it when we implemented the arcology," Maynard informed him. "I'll provide details once we reach the war room. But, yes," he said, pointing up toward the ceiling of the complex pyramidal structure, "the top of the pyramidion of the war room is approximately 1,123 ft above street level."

"Dude, holy shit!" Void cursed, still smiling and waving to the crowd. "This dwarfs Giza!"

"I know, right? The Elders of the Eternal Rhizome make for some badass builders. Virge recruited them from the Fae for us. We've been laying it down. And not just here in Dreamland. I'll give specs once we get up there," he said, pointing up to the top of the atrium. "The pool's an elevator, don't worry," he said, motioning toward the magnificent, still, circular pool occupying the very center of the atrium's floor

The pool spanned a radius of approximately 10 paces. Its surface was recessed but a tiny smidgeon from the surface level of the atrium. The group, including an initially hesitant Void, casually walked to the center of the pool, their feet not sinking beneath its surface. With a barely audible hiss of water, the circular pool, its surface glistening with an iceberg blue hue, rose at incredible speed to the top of the atrium. Above them, the center of the floor of the Dreamland War Room quickly recessed into an eight-rayed star shape, allowing them passage, then closing quickly after they passed.

"I see we've banished any pretense at trying to portray ourselves as lawful," Void snickered, nodding toward the Sign of Chaos on the floor.

"The whole pyramid incorporates various aspects of the Eightfold Path," Maynard explained. "The atrium has eight entrances, converging on the pool that we just took. The floor here is bound by the same symbol. As above, so below," he laughed darkly. "Yeah, fuck law and order. We aren't going to let our new world crawl hopelessly down that most confining path; the path that eventually lets the psychopaths control the system and enslave the rest of us. That's for slaves, not free souls."

Beneath their feet, the pool quickly effervesced, its artificed waters disappearing from view, revealing a stunningly polished black granite floor which faintly crawled with tiny inscriptions and runes describing the perimeter of the eight-rayed star, the Sign of Chaos. A gigantic, multifaceted, disco-ball-looking device as large as a full-grown old world African elephant hung suspended in the air, some thirty feet above them. Slowly, efficiently, it began its descent, moving directly down upon the group.

"Don't move, Void," Mhyrranda whispered to him. "That's our table. And chairs. And scrying device. And a lot of other things."

"Wow," Void said, genuinely creeped out as the Giant Chrome Elephant Disco Testicle descended gently onto him, morphing straight from Jack Kirby's mind into an extremely comfortable full-body, form-fitting recliner for him and all the others, while its center actively shapeshifted into a chromish-looking round table. Looking closely at the silver colored recliner, Void saw that tiny filaments of gooey liquid, somewhat similar to quicksilver, joined the base of the recliner to the table. "Ooh," Void said under his breath as the memory of being melted alive renewed itself in his mind. "Aal Ball flashback."

Somewhere nearby, somewhere in this very room, a tiny squeak, sounding very much like a midget sheep bleating something that sounded like "aal ball" resounded, making Void snort against his will.

Mhyrranda nodded, and the sound of a great gong crashed. "Welcome, everyone. We are gathered here today, Year One, Day One, in the Dreamland War Room, in the pyramidion of the Great Pyramid of Dreamland. Our friend and companion, Cory Christopher Tate, who is called Void, the hero of the Battle of Giza, has returned to us, miraculously alive. As Duchess of Dreamland, it is my privilege and honor to welcome back our champion into our midst. Welcome back, Void," she said, smiling broadly, quickly wiping away a tear.

A chorus of welcomes echoed warmly around the table.

"Nick?" Mhyrranda inquired of the general of her Praetorian Guard. "What's going on with Old Man Culpepper?"

"He's good," Nick said evenly. "Mercy and Void saved him and Santiago from Culpepper's intended self-immolation with some nasty-ass super-thermite shit. My own actions," he paused, "my shields, wouldn't have been enough. As a Master Alchemist, Culpepper has some serious hekatek power. So it's great that they were there to do the heavy lifting. Also, the Praetorians are currently debriefing everyone involved and cleaning up the mess. Well, trying, anyway. It's still burning into the ground. Mixed group of interventionist Fae and formerly human healers will do a sweat lodge ceremony with Culpepper. Hopefully get him squared away. Maybe even get him some real bacon, too," he finished, smiling broadly.

"I understand how Mercy escaped its effects," Mhyrranda replied. "But how did you, Void?"

Void shrugged. "Just a glancing blow or something, I reckon. Nothing serious."

Nick snorted. Loudly. "Like hell it was. Void just stood there and shielded Culpepper from the stuff. Thankfully, because the shield I managed to get around Culpepper wasn't going to cut it. He created something that could have burned through anything on the planet. Except Void, of course."

"Hmm, I see," Mhyrranda said thoughtfully, filing that one away for future purposes. "Thanks, Nick. Have the Praetorians poke around and find out if anyone else is thinking like Culpepper. We can't afford to just look the other way and ignore the issue. It's legit. While we certainly don't need it anymore, meat is a hard habit to break. Being vegan isn't easy. So, let's see if there is anything we can do to calm people down."

"Yes, Duchess," Nick replied. "Our scientists are on it, but we still haven't perfected growing large quantities of meat in a lab... yet."

"Now, our Master Artificer and Shaman of the Mother, Maynard, the T-Rex of Jungle Love, will speak," the Duchess of Dreamland said, ceding the floor.

Void failed to stifle a groaning giggle as Mhyrranda maintained a perfect deadpan.

"Thank you, Duchess," Maynard said, flashing a super-bright smile and giving her a sly wink. "Aal Ball, please model this for us, central location."

Again came the distant bleat, and something a few steps beyond an ultra-high definition virtual projection appeared at the center of the table.

Maynard continued. "First, our friend Void has returned. Apparently, he was able to affect his own supernatural resurrection, despite being at ground zero for the chaotic blast that leveled most of northern Egypt." The projection showed them a modeled replay of the event, showing an orbital image of Northern Africa, whose eastern face abruptly erupted with eye-bleeding, bright white light.

"We determined that the chaotic, primal blast was in roughly the 1,000 megaton range. It was powerful enough to scour most of northern Egypt, changing the course of the Nile, and forming Lake Giza. Fortunately for all living souls, most of the blast focused to the West, where it caused thousands of square miles of the Sahara to turn into chaotic trinitite. There's also a lot of chaotic terrain, kind of like what Ami can cause when she really cuts loose. That's a relativistic frame-dragging effect, in case you're wondering. Like the spacetime around a certain radius of a singularity, or black hole."

"Science," Nick pretended to groan, smiling into his steepled fingers.

"Shut it, Nick!" Ami whispered loudly. "It's not science anyway. It's hekatek."

The images produced by the modeling suddenly shifted to a collage of aerial views, showing various scenes of carnage and chaos in the Sahara. One in particular showed the recently ruined memorial ankh, its sight eliciting some gasps from around the table.

"Oh my god, I thought you meant you just dented it or something! How did you manage *that*, Void?" Tim asked, totally incredulous. Having spent much of his old world life in heavy construction, he knew firsthand how robust that structure had been, and what it would take to have wrecked it like that.

"That's where Mommy Dearest aborted me from the Dark Womb, the Void," he told him. "She dumped me right on top of my own memorial. Great sense of humor she has. And almost right on top of Mercy, who was there pouring one out for me. Nothing I could do. I couldn't even move until I was able to crawl up out of the crater."

Hearing that, there came another distant bleat from Aal Ball, and the image stream abruptly shifted its frame of reference, diving down to show a close-range view of the very crater of which Void spoke. A laser-like matrix of green lights issued forth from behind the lens, illuminating and tracing what appeared to be a handprint, pressed deeply into the granite rim of the crater. A massive boatload of calculations and numbers filled the sides of the view, settling in virtual milliseconds to static numbers, from which arrows pointed to the handprint and its surrounding area.

"In case you're wondering," Maynard said, smiling, "it takes 19,000 psi to break normal granite. That's almost five times as powerful as the bite of a crocodile. Of course, that's insane. But, if you look closely, you can see that this isn't just a simple break or compression of the granite. There's evidence of actual fusion at several places in that print," he said as the image zoomed dizzyingly down to the molecular range, the numbers and calculations once more tumbling until they settled on static numbers. "See the crystalline structures? They've been forcefully cycled through their phases. Which means that Void was able not just to exert crushing force, but to take it up a few notches and, through pressure alone, affect the thermal fusion of the molecules in the quartz. That's massive HPHT, or high pressure, high temperature. And it's basically impossible for anything to have done that through sheer physical force alone."

"What are you saying, Maynard?" Nick asked. "That Void can make diamonds or something just by squeezing a lump of coal?"

Maynard actually laughed at the sheer insanity of the question, because it had a very sane answer.

"That's in the gigapascal range, Nick. Big jump up from crocodile bites. But, yes. Probably. Let me explain that. What I'm trying to say, without boring everyone to death with a technical explanation, is that it is impossible for something like a human-shaped hand to have done that to the granite, just by pressing down and squeezing a bit. What I'm trying to say is that Void's 'strength' is probably more a factor of his will, and not merely physical. I think a good model that everyone here would be familiar with—hard to believe I'm saying that everyone will be familiar with telekinesis, because just a year ago, that would have been insane to say—is that Void has a form of telekinetic strength. It's not just physical. Physical strength ultimately encounters physical limits. Mass, form factor, materials, energy, power. It has firm limitations, even in our hekatek world. Void's strength isn't just physical, though. It's psionic. It's like he's using his mind to crush and grab, even though it's his hand that you see doing it. And it allows him to cheat and do things like this—causing fusion of heavy quartz-bearing granite—simply by pressing his hand down on it and, I don't know, getting pissed off or something and willing it to do something insane like that."

"So you're saying I have some kind of telekinetic force that I use when I exert my strength?" Void asked.

"Yes," Maynard replied. "And I think that you might be able to do some visually ridiculous stuff, like fly up in the air while holding a ship over your head, at mid-beam. Normally, that sort of force applied to that small of an area—your hands to that tiny part of the ship—would just punch a hole into it. But when you're cheating and using a projected psionic aura, essentially telekinetic strength, you're applying that force to the whole body, not just at that tiny point. Similar to how Byrne reimagined Superman in the comics back in the day?"

"He did it with Gladiator in Fantastic Four, too," Void said, taking the Comic Book Nerd bait. "He did it because he thought it was ridiculous that Superman could do things like lift a whole building up by a single handhold at its foundation. Or, as you said, lifting a ship at the center of its beam and flying away with it, totally defying physics. But those are comic book characters. They do fantastic things. I think some versions of Superman could lift the Moon. And some versions of the Hulk could destroy the world with a stomp of his foot. That's totally, insanely ridiculous. I can't even imagine being that strong."

"Technically, you don't have to imagine it," Maynard said. "You just make it happen. Probably there's a baseline—maybe just a smidge above normal mortal strength—then there's a lot of room above that baseline for boosting it up, based upon your... your emotional content, maybe? Your desire to imprint your will over reality?"

"Chaos magick," Mercy snickered. "Not much of an elaborate deduction, Maynard, considering who we are."

"Well, yeah," Maynard sputtered.

"Science," Nick taunted him, laughing along with Ami. They loved to get Maynard's goat, because it was rare that they could.

"Could he lift himself up by his own bootstraps?" Dwayne asked, smiling.

"He could lift *you* by your own bootstraps, and they wouldn't break," Maynard replied.

"Just keep the Kryptonite away, please," Void said dismissively, rolling his eyes. "I just rolled my eyes, by the way," he reminded everyone, because his featureless orbs revealed naught.

Some laughter broke out, and the weird mood shifted back to more serious matters as Void made another query: "Maynard? How are you getting those live shots? Drones? Drones that can read down to the molecular level? Not that it's any more insane than everything else we've been seeing."

Maynard nodded. "Yeah, drones. Microswarms, emitted by Aal Ball. Clusters of 112 and 123 acting in synch. Denny showed us how to alter and augment Aal Ball's hidden enchantments. Kind of like getting admin access at the root level. It was incredibly complicated, but we got it done. I mean, after clearing it with Mercy, we edited a few things, and—"

"Did you find Gil?" Void interrupted, staring down at the tabletop.

"Ah," Maynard said, exhaling sharply. "No. Nor did we find the white rabbit. We tried. Hard. But all traces of both had been deleted, almost as if they'd never been incorporated into Aal Ball at all. Weird. Anyway, we were able to persuade Aal Ball to integrate itself with our war room. It's a pyramidion, like what we saw at Giza. That's what gave us the idea."

"Idea?" Void asked. "Idea to do what?"

"To weave Aal Ball into the pyramidion," Denny injected, getting a nod from Maynard to continue. "Which means that we bent and bound Aal Ball into the collective resonance of the Great Pyramid of Dreamland, as well as the other pyramids with which it shares its resonance. Right now, that's just Dreamland and Atlanta, but Mhyrranda's New Alliance Initiative will probably allow us to incorporate Los Angeles, Chicago, Denver, Dallas, Seattle, Miami, Montreal, Toronto, Vancouver, and Mexico City into our collective resonance."

"What about New York City?" Void asked. "And the rest of the big cities? Or any other cities in the world, for that matter?"

"New York City," Denny replied, his enthusiasm showing as he continued, "is now called the City of Glass. The Lords of Glass terraformed the remaining structures in the New York City metro area, replacing most of the concrete and steel with glass. The glass is of variable molecular structure and color, resembling stained glass, but it's a lot stronger than old steel. The Lords of Glass are a cult. Bunch of religious freaks." He paused a half-second, somewhat shocked that everyone was still listening to him. Satisfied, he continued, "They worship the concept of the sigil, and its Evolutionary Tribulation, as they call it. They claim that they have been purified by their surviving the experience, but that's unfortunately as clear as it gets, because they don't communicate with anyone else. They don't like outsiders. They've refused several offers of outreach and alliance from us thus far. We've been pushing hard the past month to get everyone on the same page, though. Rachel and I have logged a lot of time crossing the country in the Mystery Machine, trying to hook everybody up."

"And there are a lot of places," Maynard said, giving Denny a happy wink, "that are no longer viable. Take Washington DC, for example. Total violence and anarchy now, much of it razed to the ground. There's been a bloody purge of former federal government folks who happened to survive. Folks were rounded up, given a swift trial, then executed by generator-powered woodchippers for what most folks saw as their part in provoking the aliens. Feet-first, too. Tough crowd."

"Woodchippers?" Void repeated. "Feet-first? That's brilliant."

"Yes, it is," Denny agreed. He was starting to like this Void guy. "Most survivors—I think about 6.6 million probably managed to survive from among the US population; we're currently working with the Fae on a census—are polarizing around two nodes of thought: 'we brought this on ourselves' or 'they did this to us'. Without realizing that not a single damn one of us had anything to do with bringing this down on ourselves. It's all ultimately Lucifer's doing. But even with Mhyrranda's mass-casting—we've done this periodically a few times; reaching out to the dreams of the survivors—we're having difficulty reaching people."

"What's the effective radius of the mass-casting?" Void inquired.

"A thousand miles from Dreamland, and a few hundred miles from Atlanta," Mhyrranda informed him, a pained look on her face as the terrific effort replayed itself in her mind. "It's terribly draining, though. I have to sleep for like 10X as much time as I spend in the isolation tank Maynard built. So we can do it only once per week, at best, and then only for an hour, hour-and-a-half, tops. But it lets us touch others out there, and try to persuade them to join us. We're also doing some outreach with the Fae, thanks to Mercy's and Vir'gil's influence."

Mercy smirked. "You mean, thanks to Vir'gil's drugs, and Mercy's threats."

"Drugs? Fear? I don't care what it takes, long as it gets done, sugar," Mhyrranda said dismissively. "We absolutely have to get all the survivors we can on the same page."

Void shrugged. No one at the table really cared what it took, either. Everyone just wanted good results, because the fate of the world was on the line. However...

"What about Old Man Culpepper, and his ilk?" Void inquired. "Is that a trend? Are there more out there like him? Tired of not getting meat to eat? Being prejudiced toward the Fae?"

Mhyrranda sighed deeply. "He's an irascible old coot. Still thinks we're in White America back in the 1950s or something. He hates everyone who's not him. He's hung up and paranoid about everything. Didn't take the events of the Great Collapse too well. Not very adaptable."

"Are there more like him?" Void asked again.

"Yes," Mhyrranda replied. "A few. A few that we know of," she quickly corrected herself. For a moment she was almost embarrassed. Then, she reminded herself that she was the Duchess of Dreamland, and therefore nothing could possibly embarrass her. "The Praetorians will have an answer for that soon. We're... We're trying our best to win hearts and minds. But people are still people, despite what the sigil did to us. Everyone has doubts and fears. Especially when the Death Horde is mentioned. Most who hear it can't believe that, after all the horror and terror we've endured since the sigil and the Great Collapse, something else is still coming down the road for us. Something worse than anything possible. Something that wants to annihilate us all. That's depressing, no matter how optimistic anyone is. We finally achieve some kind of immortality, some little slice of paradise, and then the ultimate bad guys pop up to remind us that heaven really ain't heaven after all."

"I see. So," Void continued, moving on, "about these microswarms? You mean that Aal Ball can now project itself from any point of the resonant path?"

"Basically," Maynard said, stretching, his arms high above his head. "But with a few limitations, of course. They're of temporary duration. We've managed to cram a drone template into the mix, so that Aal Ball can expend a bare minimum of resonant power and initialize a swarm, which then performs a mission of approximately 24 hours duration. After that, the swarm dissolves. With Dreamland and Atlanta in the resonant chain, Aal Ball can do this, and a few other things, until it gets too drained to continue. Has to recharge a bit after that."

"There are other cities," Denny continued, regaining Void's attention. He paused a moment before continuing, however, because getting Void's attention meant having to look at those insane black holes in his eyes. "Lots of them, in fact. But humanity is operating at about two percent or so of its former strength. It looks like the repopulation is going faster within the same plus-or-minus thirty degrees latitude established by the Belt of the Twelve, which is the main resonant pyramid belt. Probably due to there being more raw hekatek power within that swath of EarthZero, due to population density, ley line networking, and more pyramids existing there, in that range of space. I've a feeling that people worldwide are able to sense, at least subconsciously, that something is compelling them to move toward them."

"And by 'repopulation,'" Mhyrranda added, "he means only the survivors. Not the children. Because, with the exception of little Penny here, no children have been born since the sigil. That includes both mankind and critters. Fae, too, if what they've mentioned about the Song of the Sidhe no longer producing newborn Fae."

"So getting a fresh hamburger is kind of tough now," Nick added grimly. "Damn, I miss me some red meat. All we've got now is freakin' tofu. I'm glad, though, that at least the plants can still sort of reproduce. Or we'd all be slowly withering away."

"Interesting simulation conditions, eh?" Maynard asked no one in particular. "Guess our two game masters up there didn't want to have someone get wise and super-breed a shitload of new immortals to cheat and win the game."

"Sure saves on contraceptives, though," Leta smirked.

"We're way below replacement rate. We need to go global, and soon," Void said, "or we're going to fail to rally our world in time to stop the Death Horde."

"Ah, speaking of which," Maynard said, checking one of his many time pieces. "How long do you think we have? We've been unable to get any hard data on it, other than what we bandied about last year, at Mercy's place. Which was, roughly, 100 years or so from now."

Void shook his head. "That was just a guess based on what we had seen in the simulations that Helel made us watch at super-speed. I based mine on the occurrence of palindromic dates being the year in which the End of All Things occurred in that particular world. More examples of lazy coding on Helel's part. But I had seen obvious dates, such as 1991, 2002, and 2112. Based on the tech and human civilization I saw, those were the best fits. And 2112 might actually fit with us."

"We are the priests..." Maynard sang, his singing voice eerily close to Geddy Lee's.

"...of the Temple of Syrinx," Void finished.

"Flashback time," Tim blurted.

"Bunch of stoners," Nick said derisively. "You'd never make it on my Praetorians. Gotta stay straight to stay sharp. But, seriously, man, why you never do any Marvin Gaye?" Nick asked. "Shit, Maynard."

"I would if he'd have done a song about 2112," Maynard shot right back. "But war is not the answer, man," he said, bobbing his shoulders, slowly clapping his hands.

"Yes, it *is*, Maynard," Nick deadpanned. "War is the *only* answer. Nice try though. Almost got me," he said, trying not to smile. Maynard's Marvin impression was strong.

"Which would mean," Void continued, "that we'd have almost 100 years. That would be great. But it might be a bit more complex for us. Remember what I called Earth earlier? EarthZero? This means that we've ended the old timeline and have started a new one. We've started over at Year Zero. We're now a year and a day into that new timeline. Year One. So if he's still using a palindromic date to mark the End of All Things, then we've got Year One through Year Nine, then all of the double-digit years like Year Eleven through Year Ninety-Nine, then so on, and so on. It could be any year."

"Too much math!" Dwayne complained, giving himself a one-handed face palm. "Why would everything have to start over at Year Zero anyway?"

"It wouldn't necessarily, Dwayne," Void said, his tone one of encouragement. "But we've thus far been able to predict a good bit of what Helel's been doing, because we've been able to crack his lazy coding practices. When I first mentioned it—Year Zero—we were swagging some guesses around about how he was working his numbers. It seemed logical. A lot of coding languages start their arrays at zero, rather than at one. And the place he's running this from is the ZeroTime. But perhaps more importantly, there's the bleedthrough of the Satanists here on Earth, who like to declare the first year of the Antichrist's birth as 'Year Zero'. So bad code logic and psychic bleedthrough conspire together to point loudly at Helel's re-rolling his timeline back to Year Zero."

"It's still just a guess, though, isn't it?" Leta asked pointedly, her long bejeweled nails tapping the tabletop rapidly. "We have to do better than that. C'mon team, we're heroes. Let's do better."

"I agree," Void said, nodding affirmatively at Leta. "I just think that we're in uncharted territory here. Even if we're EarthZero, in its one-hundred-forty-four-thousandth instantiation, we are unique. There was never a sigil in the other simulations. Ours was the first. I think we're not going to be able to blindly guess when they're coming. I think it would be wiser instead to start proactively looking for them, directly. Now. My guess is that they'll have a course to EarthZero similar to that of the one taken by the Lightbringer's Sigil. I'm going with that because I don't think Helel is creative enough to create another spacefaring pathway for his sigil. I think he just plopped it down over the already established route taken by the Death Horde."

"Oh, wow," Maynard said, slapping himself another V-8. "I never considered something that easy."

Denny laughed. He was getting quite a rush because he was finally getting to speak his mind in the war room, without having to hold back. This was certainly the most animated he'd seen it in his two months of residence. "I can't believe that our so-called creator is so brazenly bad at his job that he just mails it in and gives his unique game-changer the same path to EarthZero that the Death Horde takes. Assuming that they take the same one every time..."

Void nodded, then shook his head. "The few times I've managed to glean their path data from among the scenarios that Helel fast-burned into our minds, I've seen the same path. Same path taken by the sigil here, in our world. I know that because I was the one who cracked the SETI and Deep Oracle data. Convenient, huh? Talk about sheer laziness: The same guy who cracks the code lucks out and is reborn a Spawn of the Void. I was the first one on Earth to see it as it was. I was the first one it sang to. Now that doesn't mean it is the same path, but that's all we have to go on, if we use only that information."

"They came from the galactic center, then?" Maynard asked Void. "Wasn't that it?" Void nodded. Maynard continued, "That makes sense, actually. Ku'tu's been debriefed a few times here in the war room about what she saw of the Death Horde during their attack on Aal. Their main vessel is a Dyson sphere, meaning it's bigger than some solar systems. If they're using anything even remotely sane to power their movement, a supermassive black hole at the center of a galaxy would be a good candidate for their entry or exit portal. Plus, that would put them at or near the center of most galaxies, giving them basically a shortest-path scenario of movement to any star system in that galaxy. That's lazy logic, but I think that's what Void's been hinting."

"So the guys doing this, running this simulation," Dwayne asked, his arms wide, "are just *lazy*? I mean gods who are just plain *lazy*? C'mon!"

"Don't be a drama queen, Dwayne," Beth taunted him. Sometimes Dwayne acted like he was still in high school. Which he had been, only two years ago.

"Sometimes being lazy makes one's effort to create something become more efficient," Maynard offered, not totally convinced of his own words. He really needed some very real sleep, and not just another in a long line of hekatek boosts. "Then again, I'm totally not lazy at all, but still crazy efficient, because I'm like ADD and OCD combined. With a hint of THC. In a damn good way."

"Obviously," Void added, "they never expected anyone to seriously contest them, as we now are doing. They've been lazy—meaning efficient and bored—because, till now, there's been no reason to be otherwise. And that's a boon for us, because it means we have the element of surprise in our favor. It means we can proactively plan accordingly for the End of All Things, rather than just one day be walking down the street, totally unaware, and have the Death Horde suddenly plop down on us. It means," he softly growled, "that maybe we can take the fight to them."

"That's all fine and nice and all," Rachel blurted, her steady gaze searing into Void. "But, Void, please tell me what you meant when you called Penny 'An-sha-dar.'"

Expectant silence bloomed around the war room as a small flicker of electric blue sparks crackled from Void's ominous eyes. He gazed at Rachel, careful to keep his darker urges in check:

"The Dark Earth Mother told me that the Lightbringer's Sigil was the harbinger for the Anshadar Effect," he finally admitted, now that he could, to everyone, and not just his former, smaller team. "Team OP—overpowered; gaming term—as Mhyrranda originally named us—me, Mercy, Maynard, Ku'tu, Aal Ball, and Gil, who was killed through the action of Helel—encountered the Mother prior to the Great Collapse. She flogged Helel pretty damn bad for his cheating. He used special cosmic templates for the people in this simulation. Illegal ones. Forbidden ones. But he used them anyway, because he rationalized that he had to cheat in order to win the simulation. He was convinced that there was absolutely no way to defeat the Death Horde at the End of All Things using just the stuff that the One Above gave him and the Children of the Light, also known as the Celestial Shapers, to game their simulations with. The special cosmic templates raised the stakes of the simulation because the beings that they instantiated and initialized—folks like Mercy and me, and Mhyrranda and Maynard—caused a weirding to be set in motion, one which called for all souls. She told him that everything will know motion, transformation, and transcendence. Everything. She said that for someone with such clear vision, he was truly blinded by his ego. She told him that his creations had exceeded his craftsmanship. She said that what he had stolen from the One Above, what he had twisted and warped to use for his own selfish ends, in order to 'win' an ephemeral, inconsequential 'game', had in fact catalyzed and reinstantiated a game of metacosmic scale: the Dragon's Game. She told him that it begins anew, here, in this formerly unimportant cosmos, this abominable simulation, thanks to his unwitting shaping of our immortal souls. She told him that he had caused the archetypes of souls to manifest here, and that this abominable act forced the Dual-Aspect to take notice, and to take heed. She told him that the Anshadar Effect was now in play. She specifically said that his meddling – first causing us to exist at all, then imbuing us with immortality – had triggered this. The Dual-Aspect now had become polarized, the white and black pieces settling upon the board in innate, inherent opposition. And the grey piece... Well, that's me. I'm the thrice-damned soul, the VoidSpawn, manifesting only to destroy the metacosmos: all worlds, all universes. She told him that his fiercely brave insanity had set this wheel in motion, and it absolutely shall not stop turning until its life function has been realized."

"Thank you, Void's insane memory," Maynard smirked. "Geez, Denny, remind you of someone?" Denny laughed. That's how he had earned his last name. "And then Helel got all Friday Night Fights," Maynard said, continuing the retelling of the scene, "jumping up and down about how he was finally going to win, and how his fellow shapers were finally going to be free. And I'd do the Void/Denny stuff, too, with my own eidetic recall, only I use it for important stuff, like inventing. Not yakking. So there."

"And that the endless cosmic genocide of the One Above would finally end," Mercy added, far too cagey to admit to her own sharp memory, unless it was to her permanent advantage. Well, almost. "And I remember it all verbatim, too. The Fae remember everything. Young punks, thinking you're superior to the ancients," she finished, smiling wickedly.

Void continued, relentless: "She told him that he had to understand that the Anshadar Effect is a cosmic constant. It's something that will cause equal and opposite manifestations to appear. Immortals. She said that these immortals will not be friendly. That they will have the evolutionary imperative to hunt down and destroy their opposites. She said that we are, essentially, mirrors of the Dual-Aspect. As above, so below."

"Helel basically brushed her off," Maynard said. "He said that he controlled the whole sim, that he could just stop anyone or anything from it at will, if he saw it going sideways."

"But Mommy shut him up good," Mercy nearly giggled, "when she reminded him that some of us might not take too well to that." She looked over at Void. "Especially him. Especially that grey piece. She told him that if there are no other worlds for it to vanquish, then it might very well bring along its equally potent immortal archetype companions and travel to the only world remaining: the ZeroTime. She said that, at that point, when we became 'Omega', that not even the Children of the Light would be able to stop us."

"Helel got all snippy again," Maynard said. "He said that he and his buddies were gods, that they could stop anybody."

"And then she slammed the door on him," Void sneered, recalling the scene with sheer schadenfreude. "She said that there are realities beyond realities; worlds beyond worlds. She explained to him that the Dual-Aspect is the essential lynchpin among all realities, no matter how small, how large, how alien, or how mundane. She quoted this to him: 'We are All That All Which Is, and All That All Which Binds'. She told him that she was a god to him, even to the One Above. She pimp-slapped him when she told him that the Dragon's Game would play out now, and that there was nothing he could do to change it. She called him, and I quote, 'puny god'. Before she departed, she warned him to consider this deeply, and I quote, 'The consequences of your actions at the End of All Things shall determine the fates of both this world and yours.'"

There were a few moments of heavy silence as each person around the table digested what they had just been told.

"Are *we* the Anshadar?" Rachel asked, finally breaking the silence.

"Penny is," Void replied, steepling his fingers on the table. "She's the only one I'm confident about. The rest of us? I have no idea. All I see from everyone else is that they're immortals. Everyone I've seen so far after my return is reading as an immortal. Some are brighter than others, of course. Some I can't really see well, like Mercy and Mhyrranda. I don't know if that's due to their relative power ranking, based on the number of active chakras that they have, their personal power, or if they have powers that preclude their being scried. Well, I know that's the case with Mercy. With Mhyrranda? I'd just have to guess. Mercy is the Ninth Null, my syzygy and complement. So I know she's virtually immune to reading, just like I am. Mhyrranda is a Dreamwyrd, so I suspect that she's got some heavy psychic and psionic defenses, just to be able to go into someone's psyche and not lose herself there."

"That's very perceptive of you, Void. Now, do you think we might already have encountered them? Our opposites?" Mhyrranda thought aloud. "Petrus? Mary? They were both disturbing folks. Their evil was both explicit and implicit. Shadar, then?"

"I don't care about any of that, Duchess Mhyrranda," Rachel interrupted. She was still staring at Void like she was a momma bear guarding her cub. "All I care about is who these so-called evil opposites are, right now, in the here-and-now, so that Denny and I can go kill them. Kill them before they try to kill my baby."

"It's okay, Rache," Denny soothed, causing his symbiotic chair to move closer to hers. He extended a hand to hold hers. "We're not going to let anything happen to Penny."

"I won't let anything happen to her," Void said, "and neither will any of the rest of us."

"That's very comforting, coming from you, Void," Rachel told him truthfully. Visibly relieved, she continued, "You have a noble soul, thrice-damned or not. Thank you for telling us that. While Denny and I have been here two months, and while everyone here has been fantastic to us," she said, nodding toward Mhyrranda, "it's still been only two months. We don't know everyone like they know each other. Like your friends know you. But, still, that doesn't make things any easier when confronted by this 'opposite versus opposite' information. It's horrible. How do we even tell who's a bad guy now? What's the test for that?"

"More importantly," Denny asked, "I think Rachel is trying to ask you how you saw that Penny was Anshadar, at first sight, when the rest of us had missed it for two whole months." Rachel nodded in agreement.

All eyes turned toward Void. His exotic face was a study of deadly serenity.

"I would not presume to know what the Mother had truly meant when she told Helel—told *Lucifer* that; fuck it, that's his name—when she told Lucifer that. She's not exactly easy to read, unless she kicks you out of the Void directly atop your own memorial. Then, it's obvious," he said over a few snickers from Mercy and Vir'gil, who were sharing some kind of laugh about it. "But about the Dragon's Game thing, with its cosmic constant, the Anshadar Effect, which she said would cause immortals to arise who were the antithesis of another immortal, equal but opposite?

She said it was a cosmic constant, and she blamed Lucifer for invoking it by bringing into play his cheating cosmic templates. Okay, that's all good. But how did I know Penny was Anshadar by mere first sight?" he paused, wishing he could be anywhere else but here right now. "What made her psychic signature, her aura, unique?"

"Void?" Maynard inquired, concern blooming on his face. The warning signs had been there the whole time, for one of his shamanic discernment and innate connection to the Mother. But due to his exhaustion, he had completely missed them. Until now.

"It's okay, man," Void said, waving his old friend off. And absolving him from guilt. "Time for this to go public anyway. I knew, at first sight of her, that she was Anshadar. Because I know my immortal enemies by sight. For I am VoidSpawn."

Total stunning silence. Then, remorseless, he continued, "I know this because I have fought the instinct all along to harm her. Remember: I am the Godslayer, and it is my duty to keep the balance among the immortals. The implication is that I know immortals by sight, and I know the Anshadar and Shadar especially well, because they are the main players in the Dragon's Game, and in this game I maintain the balance of power. I terminate them when called to do so by the Dual-Aspect. The Mother and the Dragon both may compel me to do this, and I must always and forever obey."

"Void!" Mercy cried out, phasing through and out of her chair. She now stood facing him, her accusing eyes burning brightly. "You can't possibly believe that, can you? That's Chthon playing more of her Dragon Games. She's gotten in your head, you simp! Fight it! You basically just told Denny and Rachel that you're going to kill their baby girl, you asshole!" she yelled loudly, slamming her formidable fists into his chest with an audible, if entirely ineffective, *whoomp!* "I can't believe I ever told you I loved you, dammit!" With a massive air-sucking displacement, Shunya appeared in her outstretched left hand. "I should cut your fucking balls off for saying that, Void!"

"I'm immune to Shunya, my love," Void whispered, even as Mercy's eyes went wide with disbelief. Not just due to his statement of immunity, either, because no one was immune to the Fractal Blades. This was the first time, truly, that he had told her that he loved her. At least that's what it felt like, after a year and a day of total mourning. Metaphorically disarmed, Shunya vanished also, leaving Mercy's hands clutching empty air. If only she could risk touching him without setting the world on fire...

"Who cares if he's VoidSpawn, the Godslayer?" Maynard interjected as he saw his opening, disconnecting from his symbiotic chair. "Void does what he does. No one tells him what to do. He's always been who he wants to be. He doesn't need black-and-white Manichaeism to tell him what to do. He's no mere puppet, not even to the Mother. Or, to the Dragon. Tell 'em, Void." *Please...* remained unspoken.

Everyone was looking at Void, waiting for him to take one of the life preservers thrown to him, to exonerate himself somehow. But he didn't budge. His eerie black eyes stared into the middle distance, unblinking.

Rachel, with tears spilling from her eyes, dismissed her chair, then silently strode to the far side of the room. Denny, doing the same, walked over to her, and they quietly began a highly animated conversation.

"Void?" Mhyrranda inquired, her query strident and out of character for the Duchess of Dreamland.

"Yes, Duchess Mhyrranda?" he replied, his silence finally broken.

"I don't get it, so please explain it to me," she pleaded with him. Hearing her own tone, she paused a moment to regain control of her raw emotions. "How can someone who gave his life, probably his own soul if you think about it, to save the world, be a bad guy? How can you be anything bad, and still do what you did?"

"Easy," he replied steadily. "My personal fate had nothing to do with it. The Pope *had* to die. His actions would have destroyed EarthZero, dooming us all to permanent nonexistence, had he succeeded in his earth-draining and his causing the One Above to notice us. He would have noticed Lucifer, and he would have instantly shut down his simulation. That would have ended us all right then and there. So that was not going to happen. Even if I had to strangle the Pope to death, it wasn't going to happen."

"So you weren't just playing your assigned role as Godslayer?" she retorted, reading the tea leaves very deeply. "You're saying you did him in just because you had to do it in order to save this world?"

"I think so," Void admitted, knowing that she was reading him like a master gambler. "There were no obvious tells I picked up from Petrus, anyway, regarding his Shadar or Anshadar origin. I picked up those unique signs immediately from Penny. She's quite the projector of power. But Petrus? He was just mad as a hatter, and thrice as dangerous. He had to be put down."

"Then you made the conscious choice to end him?" Mhyrranda asked not for herself, but for the others, as she had already made her own judgement. *Some people just need killin',* she thought.

"Had to," Void admitted. "I was the only one remaining on our team who could do it."

"Anyway, the Mother is just a bitch," Mercy said, causing Maynard to cut her a strong glare. "It's true, and you know it, Maynard. You know what the funny part of this is?" she asked aloud. "The funny part is that we're so stuck on ourselves, on our heroism, on our legends and what we're doing for the common good, that we've forgotten to ask ourselves the most basic question: If we're all serving the will of the Mother, and of the Dragon, then doesn't that make us guilty of being not quite so damn entirely cracker-fucking-white?" She paused a split-second to let it sink in. "Because, frankly, we're not good guys, folks. We are *not* the good guys in this story!" she roared, opening some eyes wide around the table. "Our morals and ethics are a bit suspect compared to, like, you know, Gandhi, Buddha, and Jesus. They're 'good'. They would be Anshadar. Okay. But we're nothing like that at all. Not even on our best world-saving day. Look in your hearts and tell me I'm wrong."

"You're wrong, Mercy," Maynard snapped back instantly. "We *are* good. Better than what else is out there: genocidal popes, genocidal space conquerors, and genocidal mad gods. So put that moral relativism in your hash pipe and smoke it."

"I think he has a point, Mercy," Mhyrranda added. "We all have blood on our hands. No argument there at all. But, compared to the alternatives, we're actually trying to do good. Not trying to slaughter the whole world."

"Like *him*!" Rachel shouted from where she stood by Denny. "How good can a 'godslayer' be? C'mon. Don't fall for it, folks."

Void shook his head. "She's right, you know? I'm not exactly pure as the driven snow. I killed the Pope. Ran him through. Who kills the bloody Pope? That's going to Hell on the Hell Express."

"Any of us would have done the same, Void!" Maynard said. "Why are you trying to make yourself out as the bad guy here, anyway? You trying to get us riled up? Maybe, like, force us to exile you or something so you can just tour the world, collecting as many old world guitars as you can?" he finished with a grin.

Dismissing his symbiotic chair, Void stood near the table, Mercy at his side. As she always would be, even at the End of All Things. He waved for Denny and Rachel to rejoin them. They did so, bravely standing hand-in-hand together, on the side of the table opposite Void. The Godslayer.

"I did this to illustrate a point, guys," Void said calmly, rationally. "Not everything is black and white. It's not all cut and dried. And it's certainly not going to happen the way that either Lucifer or Chthon think that it's going to go down. Free will, folks. Free will. We *refuse* to follow the paths they've set for us. To hell with both of them, to all of them, and to hell with anyone who wants to try to control us. Tell us what to do. We are going to follow our own paths. We are going to exercise our own free will. We are going to see the Death Horde shut down cold. We *shall* defeat them, whether they are invincible or not. We will do this impossible thing, because that is what we do: the impossible. This is why *I* am going to resist, infinitely, any attempt of the Dual-Aspect to color me as a bad guy, opposed to my friends, opposed to the ones I love. Because I *choose* to do it. My choice. My will. I choose free will."

They were listening to him, each of them weighing his words by the measure of their own unique scales.

"Rachel? Denny?" Void asked. A subtle change of posture, followed by an unseen yet intimately felt projection of force marked his next words: "Upon pain of my own soul's death, I swear to you that I will never harm your Penny. That's my oath to you."

Maynard and the Fae gave Void fierce looks, because they knew the price of what Void had just sworn. Looking quickly among themselves, they all nodded in confirmation, paying witness to the oath freely sworn.

From Penny's tiny eyes electric blue sparks fell like tears, and, impossibly, a sweet summer's breeze blew through the war room, which currently was sealed from the outside. Everyone turned to gaze upon the sight. Rachel felt something, an odd warmth, coming from Penny, coursing over her.

"Oh my god," Rachel said just above a whisper. "She just told me she believes you, Void. She believes you."

At her side, Denny pulled his equally amazing wife and daughter close to him, rocking slowly in place. If his baby girl believed the Spawn of the Void, the Godslayer, then so, too, would he.

CHAPTER 6

"Now that we have been bound by love, let us speak of war..." Void said, bidding everyone to stand around the circular table. Those who were not yet standing did so. Then, he began, urged on by a wave from Mhyrranda, what would be known one day as "The Invocation of Musashi", or, "The Way of the Void".

"The great kensai, Miyamoto Musashi, wrote in his book, 'The Book of Five Rings,' about the Way of the Void. It's not what you think. Void. It's not the implication of something that is lacking. Instead, it is emptiness, the shedding of your skin, coming clean, eliminating what is of the small mind. This is what we all have done since the Lightbringer's Sigil brought its Evolutionary Judgement down upon us. We have shed our old skin. We have eliminated the small mind. We have been born anew.

"Those from the ZeroTime would make light of us, calling our world, our home, our EarthZero, a simulation. An illusion. A void. But it is not. It is real to us, and that's all it ever needs to be for us to fight to the death to protect it and defend it from those who would destroy it. It is real to us.

"It is true that the fate assigned to us by those from the ZeroTime is inescapable. The doom that comes to us at the End of All Things is invincible. It has never been beaten. Not once, not in a million-million simulations. Yet we will do this. We will be the first of a trillion to beat it. We *will* defeat it. We will defeat it because we will learn the Way as Void, and the Void as the Way.

"We will learn this because we will enact strategy broadly, correctly, and openly. This means that we will all come together as one. We will all focus as one. We will all unite as one—all living things on EarthZero. And our union will give us strength, strength that we would not have had alone.

"We will start immediately, today, cataloguing, learning about, and exploring this newly reborn world of ours. We will learn its measure. We will all share this knowledge. And we will use this new knowledge as our tool, crafting accordingly, to defeat the Death Horde. We will learn every weakness they possess, and we will shape our strategy accordingly. We will make our weakest our strongest, such that the chain shared between us has no links save the strongest.

"But we will not become them in order to defeat them, no matter the temptation to give in to the small mind; to give in to evil. They think that this is the Way of the Void, what they know as the Anti-Life. But they are wrong, for it is not. It is nothing but pure, genocidal evil.

"In the void is virtue, and no evil. Virtue. We will spread the bounty you see here around us, around the world. We will gather together all life, and soulforge it anew as one. We will show others how to do what we have done. We will not starve or thirst while we craft our knowledge and elevate it, carefully weaving our adaptive strategy as we learn more about our foe, and about ourselves. We will terraform this entire world. We will make the deserts bloom.

"We will do all these things simultaneously, for they are our way now, the Way of the Void."

Loudly popping her gum, Ami gave Void an appraising look and said, smiling, "The Way of the Void. I think I like that..."

CHAPTER 7

"Void just set out our path," Maynard said. He was still reeling inside from what Void had told them. It seemed like now, at this very moment, all that was old had been made new. Apparently, from the looks on everyone's faces, he saw that they felt something similar. Clearing his throat, he continued, "So, we're going to define our strategy and lay down some supportive tactics. Let's return to our seats. This will take a while."

Thus instructed, everyone returned to their seats, which had actually at that moment begun to rise from the floor, Aal Ball being totally on the ball, and then some.

Mercy, being Mercy, couldn't let it pass. "Yay. More meeting stuff. And my free will was just about to tell me to get some booze and start partying."

"That's later," Maynard promised. "Now, we'll touch on a few items from before," he began, "that we've discussed previously, prior to Void's return. We'll wrap those up with anything new that anyone would like to add. For the purpose of this, we'll waive our normal rules and allow Denny and Rachel to contribute, even though they've not yet officially been made members of our war council."

"Well, let's go ahead and do that," Mhyrranda said. "And let's get Void in, too. Anyone disagree? If not, it's auto-pass."

No one disagreed.

"That's a first," Maynard laughed. "But, considering the circumstances, and the quality of the folks joining us, I guess it makes perfect sense. Welcome, Denny and Rachel Google. Welcome, Void. That felt good to say."

Vir'gil groaned, "I will be collecting dues after the meeting. One tasty plant from each of you."

"Vegan cannibal," Mercy guffawed.

"Okay, quick rehash of what has gone before," Maynard continued after a moment. "We're actively working with Atlanta at this point in time," he said, pointing to the central monitor, which showed a top-down display of the continental United States. "It's just us, Dreamland, and Atlanta—our point of contact there is this fabulous genius named Peaches—but we're working on incorporating all of the cities I mentioned earlier into our alliance," he said, as the central monitor highlighted the cities previously mentioned. "We've got ambassadors and envoys of mixed Fae and enhanced humans in all of those cities. While teleportation and other methods of faster travel are typically limited to council members who have the necessary personal powers to affect such, we've had a recent upturn in vehicular travel, thanks to what Denny's been able to teach us about chaining runes into longer sequences of inscriptions. In just two months we've managed to expand our vehicle inventory by 300%. These include smaller vehicles like Denny's Mystery Machine—a customized Winnebago that I have to admit kicks mucho ass; it has a freaking Phalanx mounted atop it, eff-eff-ess!—as well as larger tankers, freighters, and several small aircraft. The main interstates... we're still working on getting those cleared from here to Atlanta, and points between. That's a work in progress. Same with everything else, of course. Planes, trains, and automobiles. Working on all of the above."

"Any news on our personnel recruitment efforts?" Nick inquired.

"It's a continuous work in progress," Maynard informed them. "We've got agents, along with our diplomats and envoys, who are similarly tasked, to find survivors with strategic skills and recruit them directly to our cause. Specifically, former military, law enforcement, sports coaches, survivalists, machinists, architects, and the entire gamut of tacticians and strategists from other realms."

"Add gamers to that, Maynard, please," Void said quietly.

Heads around the table turned toward Void.

"Serious?" Maynard asked him. "You mean, like, Xbox and PlayStation players? Really?"

Void nodded. "We're in a sim, Maynard. Our 'god' is the biggest gamer in the cosmos. Think about it."

Maynard blanched. "Holy shit," he muttered. "I can't believe we missed that. Good call, Void."

"Recruit *me*!" Dwayne said, excitedly raising a hand. "I used to dominate those n00bs in CoD!"

"You're already recruited, dummy," Beth laughed. "You're one of the bosses now, Dwayne. So act like one," she said.

"Hey!" he protested lamely, his face turning bright red. "I'll boss all those N00b Horde guys, too."

"Noted, Dwayne," Maynard said. "You're our point of contact for the gaming initiative. Which, by the way, does what, Void?"

"Prep them for sim warfare," Void replied, his fingers steepled. "We are going to expand the drone template for Aal Ball. We are going to make a wide variety of UCAVs. Highly artificed ones. They won't necessarily be limited to 24 hours. Our gamers are going to be our drivers. They are going to use them to map out the world. They're also going to be the main part of our eyes-in-the-sky initiative. Helpers, watchers, monitors. And in so doing, they're going to acquire the necessary skills and tactics to make the jump to actual combat. We are going to be using thousands of them versus the Horde when they come."

Again, everyone was staring at Void. Noticing this, he continued, "Sorry. I'm just used to engineering sessions with Maynard, from before the Great Collapse. This is how we used to create solutions for strange shit, from back in the day."

"Correct," Maynard agreed. "So anyone jump in, whenever. We don't bite. All thoughts are more than welcome. I'd even say they're required."

"I was waiting for that," Beth said confidently. "I think Vir'gil, Dwayne, and I, and maybe some of those elder trees, should go mobile and jump on firming up the arcologies for the other cities."

"Good thoughts, Beth," Mhyrranda said, "but we can't jump on those yet. Not until we win them over diplomatically."

"Maybe, say, showing up on their doorstep one morning," Beth said, smiling craftily, "and terraforming a few hundred acres outside their cities before noon might help with the diplomacy?"

A hush fell over the war room.

"Good idea," Vir'gil creaked. "Long as Mercy says it's okay for me to join you, that is."

"Beth!" Dwayne whispered to her. "But I have to lead the gamers!"

"You'll do this first, because it will give you access to more gamers," Beth informed him. "See how that's going to work?"

"Ah, cool, then," Dwayne agreed. "Now that I'm thinking about it, it was kinda fun to help with the arcology here. Maybe we should get all of Team El in on it? Maybe knock out a city per week then?"

"Good call," Maynard agreed, "provided everyone's up to it."

Everyone nodded, except Ami.

"Ami?" Maynard asked. "Something to add?"

She nodded. "Yes. What I do doesn't add much to what Team El does, regarding the building of the arcologies. I'm more of a destroyer than a builder."

Void spoke from the perspective of one destroyer to another. "Something I understand all too well, Ami. You and Nick can take one of the new vehicles out and clear the road from here to Atlanta in virtual real time. Singularities and shaped psychokinesis have great synergy for the task. As two of our heaviest hitters, you can duo the job, clear the roads in a matter of mere weeks, and restore the national interstate system to almost what it was prior to the Great Collapse."

Silence, and a few stares. Nick spoke first. "Void, how the hell did you know that we're two of the big hitters? You haven't even seen us for a year."

"I see completely through your souls," Void answered, his voice a bit hollow, chilling the absolute hell out of Nick and Ami. Seeing this, he continued, his voice lighter, "Please allow me to rephrase that: I see your souls. I explained it earlier but, granted, a lot's been said since then. It's just like I was able to pick up on Penny. My sight allows me to gauge your powers, and their relative power levels, with but a glance. I can immediately see who's actually over 9000..."

"Over 9,000!" Dwayne abruptly howled, slapping his thigh. "Void's fucking Vegeta!"

"With all due respect," Void said passively, "I'm beyond Whis, and Vegito. Think about an actual fighting Zeno, and you're getting closer."

At this, Dwayne's laughter turned to manic fist-pumping. "Void! Dude! You know your DBZ canon! Righteous! I didn't think a dude as old as Maynard would know that shit."

"Hey!" Maynard objected. "I'm not *that* old, you whippersnapper! I'm just a year older than Cor—I mean, Void."

"I'm being serious, though, Dwayne," Void blatantly lied, smirking. "I'm lying, man," he admitted instantly, eliciting another round of guffaws from Dwayne. "And I'm over 1,000,000 years old, Maynard, thanks to the Mother's manipulations and many deaths. You whippersnapper."

"Are you lying about that, too, Void?" Mercy asked him, point-blank. "I mean, holy fuck, a million is a lot. I'm only 13 millennia, and that's way too much already. Please don't tell me that Mommy was actually making you live out those deaths you've mentioned?"

Void exhaled slowly. He directly fixed Mercy with his gaze. Instinctively, he raised his hand toward her, inadvertently almost touching her fingers. "This ain't no place for no hero. I'm not lying about that, Mercy. The old shrew actually made me live those lives. Being born. Living a life. Working through a particular scenario to make me learn some particular lesson. Then, eventually, dying. Then being reborn again, knowledge from the time before intact, and ready to roll some more. In some of those scenarios, I encountered the folks around this table. Different roles we were playing. Sometimes male, sometimes female, sometimes something else. Sometimes friends, sometimes enemies, sometimes family, sometimes lovers. I know what it's like to have shared your bed, Mercy. To have been your husband, your father, your son, your wife, and so on and so on. The beautiful children we've had... The times we died to save the world. I've role-played, in real life, at least 10,000 scenarios with each and every one of you. I sometimes think I know y'all better than I know myself. That's why it's so easy to pick up on what's up. Essentially, I've done this all before."

The unbearable nearness of being suddenly manifested in the very small air gap between Mercy and Void. Everyone in the war room could feel the angst generated at that moment. To totally love someone with one's very soul, yet to be forever damned never to realize that union? To stand near enough to one's soulmate to feel the static pulse from their bodies, yet unable to risk a simple press of the flesh? A sweet, stolen kiss?

There was damnation, and there was true damnation. If any true gods remained, it surely would have been their most fervent fear that, one day, the Null and the Void would finally just say fuck it, give in to their eternally suppressed lust, and share a final, fateful metacosmic orgasm that would destroy everything, everywhere.

Nick sniffed. "Anything *else* you pickin' up on, Void? Like what color my boxers are? Creepy bastard," he said under his breath, drawing a few laughs for his temerity.

"I love you, Nick," Maynard snickered as Void smiled, embarrassed. "Your cajones, too. Love 'em. They're like hot air balloons," he said to some scattered laughter. "If you and Ami want to take road-steading duty, Mhyrranda will need to approve it. Duchess?"

"Sure thing, Nick," Mhyrranda said merrily. "If you think the Praetorians can do without you for a few weeks, that is."

"They're solid," Nick told her. "I should know. I trained 'em." He looked across the table to Ami. "Sure you're up for this, Ami?"

"Just because I'm the youngest member of Team El doesn't make me a n00b, Nick," she clarified for him, blowing a bubble with her gum. "I make black holes, and black holes protect me. Not scared of nothin'."

Void smiled at her, as did Nick.

"Take care of him, sweetie," Mhyrranda said to Ami, who smiled at her, nodding an affirmative. "He's the head of my Praetorians. Not to mention, probably the best BBQ Chef around."

"Well, I *do* make some kick ass tofu ribs," Nick smiled. "Sweet Memphis BBQ rub, for the mother-lovin' win, baby! Jesus," he admitted, "I'm starting to sympathize with Cully right now..."

While everyone salivated, Maynard pressed on. "Denny? You and Rachel good to go on the Resonance Project?"

"We need one more week," Denny said. "Still need to lay down a few more inscriptions on the Mystery Machine before we move out."

"Need another Phalanx?" Maynard scoffed.

"Naw, man," Denny smiled. "Need a few more things like automated diaper processors, self-cleaning toilets, and water filtration systems. Been too busy to get those done lately."

"Copy that," Maynard confirmed, checking off another entry on his customized spreadsheet, which was now front and center on the central monitor. "I'll help, of course. The sooner we get you and Rachel and Penny on the road, the sooner we can activate more pyramids, and grow our power grid."

"You know it, Maynard," Denny agreed, smiling. While he and Rachel had truly come to enjoy their two month stay at Dreamland, both had recently been feeling the need to hit the road once more. There was just so much to experience out on the road, despite its many dangers. Or, perhaps, because of them. Regardless, both were hooked on the relatively freewheeling lifestyle of the road, and both wished to return to its relatively unstructured format.

"That's a really good idea," Void commented. "It should be of primary importance. Would you require any assistance to expedite the process?" Void asked Denny.

Denny shook his head. "We got it, Void. Thanks, though."

"Do you have a way to communicate with us remotely?" Void asked. "Matter of fact... Do we have something like global satellite phones? It would be good if everyone in the war room was capable of instant communication with everyone else, despite any distance. And without the requirement of being in a dream state," he added, noting that Mhyrranda was about to say as much.

"We have something that I've been working on, Void," Maynard told him. "It's not quite ready yet, but it's similar to what you're talking about. I'm calling it a Personal Integrated Nexus Generator box, or PING box. Sort of like a tricorder-meets-smartphone kind of thing. It's going to link us all together in real time, allow us to interrogate the environment, and tap into our rapidly expanding NewGoog information database."

"NewGoog?" Void asked. "Another portmanteau? Spelled with a 'g-n-u'?"

Maynard laughed. "You nerd. It's something we got almost as soon as we could travel there to get it. Oh. And contain it. Turns out that Aal Ball is rated at least in the yottabyte range. Google's public databases were only in the exabyte range prior to the Great Collapse, so we've been able to harvest a good bit from their server centers and merge it into Aal Ball's NewGoog matrix."

"You're physically going out to these sites? Their old data centers?" Void inquired.

"Yes," Maynard replied.

"Implement another template for Aal Ball," Void said, "and have it send out datamining drones instead. Give them the ability to power-up dead boxes and mine them before they de-power again. Expand the search coverage. Optimize a remote I/O network for them. Make that thing impossible to hack and robust enough to last forever. Get everything from the government, military, academic, and corporate worlds that's possible to get. We need everything we can gather from the old world. Knowledge is power. We're going to be as powerful as possible. In parallel, we create the appropriate tech trees for all of our endeavors, map out what we need to get to the next tier, and optimize our efforts."

"Good idea," Maynard said simply, thinking to himself that he should have thought of this already. Cory was Cory, though, and no mere box would ever contain his thinking. "We'll get into the 4X gaming mode and plan the whole show."

"When will we get flying cars?" Tim asked eagerly. "Fly around like we're George Jetson. Or a bubble car? Like in *Gamma World*?"

"*Gamma World*?" Maynard shot back, genuinely surprised. "Right on, Tim. Great game, and good call. Not everyone can fly, or teleport, or fast travel. And old world flying machines can be heck to keep prepped, let alone take off and land. And finite, unrenewable fuels to deal with. But if we artifice our own bubble cars, maybe one that can also hover easily? That would be great for mobility. And easy enough to provide fuel for, because we'll be using hekatek, not jet fuel. Bubble cars are moving to the front of the tech tree for sure. Or, so help me, I'll be hopelessly mutated."

"Vir'gil?" Void asked the Entheogenic Lord, who nodded pleasantly to him. "We're going to need a bevy of Fae spies to gather information for us clandestinely. We need to spy on everyone else who isn't us. Everywhere. No detail is too trivial for them to report. They can chain their reports through a listening service chain of Fae telepaths. The darker, the better. Funnel it all to Aal Ball, with your own analysis on it. Dual fork the analyses to both Mercy and Mhyrranda. Mhyrranda, it's time for you to learn Ancient Sidhe, because that's what we're going to be storing this data in. Thanks, Vir'gil. I know you see infinitely more than you let on."

"You are wise," Vir'gil chuckled. "My rhizomes go deep."

Void paused a moment, deciding how best to phrase his next directive. "We're also going to need a program specifically shaped to discover, analyze, and catalog all powers of all of our people. And of the natural world. We have to learn our own measure, so to speak. Then, we have to learn the measure of the newly evolved species of EarthZero. The Evolutionary Tribulation was effectively countless generations of adaptation and genetic augmentation. There's a high probability that we're going to encounter some weird-ass shit that we never could have imagined. And not just in the former humans who have evolved. The domain of their powers will be entirely insane. But, even moreso, the domain of the critters and things on EarthZero might be beyond insane. Why? Diversity, numbers, and generational drift. What for humans might have been X number of generations of genetic shaping might very well be 100 X for some of the critters out there. Not just biomimetics, either. I'm talking uncanny, extremely divergent-from-the-norm cray cray powers. Stuff we might be able to use against the Horde."

Maynard nodded, lost in silence for a moment as he considered what this might mean. Then, he abruptly said, "C'mon, Void. That's some awfully specific shit there. The Mother told you that, right?"

Void laughed. "No, Chekhov told me that. Consider it a gun," he smiled, noting Mercy's sudden snicker.

"Ooh!" Beth blurted, slapping her palm down on the table. "I know what that means! That's Anton Chekhov. They taught us about that in Senior Lit. Chekhov's Gun. He said that every element in the story should contribute to it. Nothing should be mentioned that's irrelevant. If you mention something, it's going to come up again later. So, you're using your precognitive powers to make sure that we're paying attention to what you just said, because it's going to come up later, for real?"

"I'm just being a smartass," Void grinned. "That's me and Maynard being tangential. I have no idea what's going to happen. But I really like the fact that you picked up on that, Beth. Sharp. And we need 'sharp' now. Hell," he shrugged, "maybe that's exactly what I meant. Who knows?"

"I know," Vir'gil volunteered. "But I'm not telling," he said over some forced laughter. Forced, because no one really wanted their cocaine rations cut down for being a dick to the Entheogenic Lord.

"Maynard?" Void continued. "Do we have any tasks to create superior arms and armor for our populace?"

"What?" Maynard asked, taken slightly aback.

"See?" Nick chimed in, pointing a finger at Maynard. "I *told* you that's what we needed! We need to arm these people and get them trained up, ASAP."

"But you're hot-headed and reactionary, Nick," Maynard temporized. "Not that Void isn't, too, but he's being strangely calm now. Lot of Zen today. But, of course I was going to delay doing something like that. It would be like having to manage a Department of Defense on top of everything else I'm doing."

"I can do it," Nick told him. He looked over at Mhyrranda. "I mean, if the Duchess says I can."

Mhyrranda nodded and smiled. "I've been okay with it since it was first brought up. I'm still okay with it now."

Smiling, Nick continued, "I can even start doing it while Ami and I are on the road. The sooner, the better. So I guess that's PING boxes first? So we can all communicate?"

"If Denny can spare one more day for some hard work," Maynard said, "then I think we can get the PING box prototypes up and running. We can work out the bugs ex post facto."

"Kinda like Microsoft, eh?" Tim laughed. "Zero-day bugs for EarthZero!"

"We also need something concrete to present to the public," Mhyrranda said, "so that they know we mean serious business; that we've got everyone's best interests in mind. Something like a Constitution, a Bill of Rights, the Georgia Guidestones, or something like that. Otherwise, we're really no better than the criminal scum out in the boonies who run things like Bartertown or Thunderdome."

"And this dovetails into the argument we've been having about establishing an official currency," Maynard sighed. "More Civics 101 shit," he snorted derisively.

"What are we using currently?" Void asked. "Barter?"

Mhyrranda nodded. "Yes. Barter. Boring, and tedious, but it's really the only alternative without a true currency system in place. And a true government in place to run that currency system."

"We don't need another fucking Fed," Tim said, dismissing the notion. "They sucked donkey balls. We get a Fed, next thing you know, we have an IRS. And then, a corrupt government of sad sack little shits who think they're more important than everyone else. Makes me tempted to go break out the woodchipper," he said, finishing with an evil laugh.

"Agree totally!" Leta said. "We don't need The Man! Fuck The Man!"

"Yeah, fuck the humans! Fuck the humans!" Ku'tu said, joining in, smiling. "I mean, The Man!" she added rapidly, noting her gaffe. Genocidal tendencies were so deliciously hard to bury.

"Ku'tu is an anarchist?" Void asked Mercy.

"Sure, why not?" Mercy said. "Why the hell not. It's not like we actually need rulers, although Mhyrranda makes a quite capable one."

"But you're both of the gentry, aren't you?" Void inquired pointedly. "Aren't you killing your own status by being anarchists?"

"That's all irrelevant now anyway," Ku'tu said, fluttering up from Leta's shoulder. "My people, the Fae of Aal, are still stuck in Fresswelle, and nobody is trying to find that cursed blade! Until then, I could be the Queen of Spades, and not just the Queen-consort of the Fae of Aal, and it won't matter one small bit!"

"Ah," Void said, realizing the situation. "I was wondering about that. We need to prioritize the search for Fresswelle, so that we can free the Fae of Aal. That would be... Mercy, Ku'tu, Leta, and Tim, right?"

"What about you, Void?" Mercy asked. "You've just come back from the dead, and now you want to leave after just a few minutes?"

Void shook his head. "No, I'm going with you. Who better to help with the search for the Fae of Aal, but the last wielder of Fresswelle? But we're not leaving until we've got the PING boxes, and a few more small things worked out. Like the law-and-order, Bartertown stuff."

Taking Void's cue, Mhyrranda cleared her throat politely. "If you'll take a look up at the central monitor, you'll see where I've got copies of the Constitution and the Bill of Rights, as well as the Ten Commandments, and the Sermon on the Mount. I even have the text from the Georgia Guidestones up there, even though everyone might think they're too NWO for us. A few of those actually are of benefit to us. We'll start there, and start whittling things down to where we need them to be, as our first concrete step."

Everyone looked at the Duchess, who appeared to be eager to start.

"What?" she asked them, nonplused.

Maynard sighed. "I'll say what no one else is saying, Mhyrranda. We don't care about any of that. That's all you, and maybe Nick, and maybe some of the old bosses that you turned."

"You don't care? *Really*?" She asked him, feigning shock. "Okay, then. It's all barter for now, until and unless we move to some other financial system. Maybe knowledge-based, which would be cool, if we all live so long. Barter for now then, is that okay with everyone?" Heads nodded. "As for government, I'll remain in place as Duchess of Dreamland. We'll start with a system of morals and ethics that are good. Law of Reciprocity for starters. We'll make them known via public displays and postings. We'll implement a benevolent dictatorship for the moment, with most of the rights from the Bill of Rights reserved for the citizens of Dreamland, and all of the powers of the Constitution reserved for me, myself, and I only, for now, and slowly open those up as we become more civilized. Sound good?"

Heads nodded again. Maynard needled her, however: "What makes someone a citizen? And, do non-citizens have these same rights? You know, universal rights? And what about the Fae? Do they have the same set of rights as the humans? What about possible discrimination? What about hate?"

Mhyrranda pretended to stick a finger down her throat and gag.

"Screw it, then. It's like trying to herd cats," she declared, finally giving in. "Effing anarchists," she laughed. "We'll work out all that shit later. For now, I'm the Duchess of Dreamland, and that's that. Meeting adjourned. Now, let's get down to the business of saving EarthZero, shall we?"

CHAPTER 8

Bluebirds sang in the trees, and a slight breeze played through the leaves on a sunny day in Central Park. A sense of anticipation, coupled with dread, washed over the people lining the street in the dappled shade.

Several trucks rolled up into the park, their flat beds holding people bearing armbands with the mark of prisoners as well as shackles with runes designed to pacify the wearers. One by one, they were led from the truck to a raised platform framed by a brightly striped pavilion. Dressed in fine clothes, the figures within the pavilion conferred amongst each other as a line of prisoners formed.

One of the men on the platform, a very tall and handsome man with sandy brown hair, a square jaw, and clear blue eyes the color of arctic water, broke away from the other two. He came forward to center stage, lifting his voice so the crowd could hear.

"Good morning. I am Brother Bradley Russel, this is Sister Evaline Kohl, and Brother Greg Reuter. We are the Council of Glass, administrators of this newly renamed City of Glass. With the fall of the United States government, and that of the State and City of New York, the three of us were able to stabilize and return the island of Manhattan to a semblance of order. Every day, we make this city a better place, a safer place, a stronger place. Every day, we help the people in the area surrounding the City of Glass become independent and free of the creatures and the lawless that threaten the livelihood of the survivors of the Apocalypse."

Brother Bradley paused to look at the gathered crowd, the soldiers, and the line of prisoners. Then he nodded and continued.

"The City of Glass becomes more powerful and respected, as the fear and lawlessness spreads throughout the rest of the world. We do this by having and enforcing the laws of conduct. Laws against crimes such as assault, the willful taking from another, and treason against the City and its subjects."

Pointing to the prisoners, he gestured from them to the rest of the city.

"These prisoners have broken the law, and must be punished. Our laws tell us this is so, and only by enforcing the laws can we continue to prosper, to aspire to the greatness we must achieve in these trying times. However," he paused, gauging the crowd's reaction, "even as these citizens broke the law, they are forgiven. In their punishment, they are granted the honor of protecting the shores of Manhattan."

He looked over the prisoners and smiled. "Do any of you have any words before you are transformed into guardians? If so, now is the time."

Several of the prisoners fell to their knees, begging for their lives, among cries for mercy and proclamations of their innocence. One among them stood straight, raising his voice above the others.

"I have something to say. You condemn me for speaking my mind against the Council, and nothing else. I have done nothing but question the justice of a city that denies admittance to people who are starving, and creates impossible tests of loyalty to gain entrance. There could be a paradise here, but you keep the numbers down so the spoils of an entire city can be shared among a few. You..."

During the man's declaration, the other two council members on the stage had stepped forward, flanking Brother Bradley. With a imperceptible flick of her fingers and the willful intent to make them shut their flapping mouths, Sister Evaline interrupted all the prisoners' protestations.

Brother Bradley nodded to Sister Evaline, and returned his attention to the man standing, who looked more confused than angry.

"Is that it? Are you done?" demanded Brother Bradley. He was silently grateful, if such were truly possible for one bereft of such disempowering emotions, that Sister Evaline's power had continued to evolve from simple psychic shielding to something entirely more... controlling.

"I... Uh..."

Brother Bradley motioned to the nearby guards. "Bring him."

A pair of the shard troops grabbed the formerly defiant prisoner and roughly dragged him forward to the platform. His shackles removed, he was forced to kneel.

Brother Bradley looked down at the man and said, curtly, "You broke the law. A law you agreed to when you came here. You have no right to question justice here, here in this shining city built and formed to repel the forces of evil and death. Only we have the wherewithal to survive the legions of Gog and Magog, who seek to encompass the camp of the saints, God's new Jerusalem, the City of Glass."

Brother Bradley's eyes gleamed with a fervor, and he reached out to touch the now-passive prisoner on the shoulder.

The prisoner gasped at the contact. His eyes fixed on the middle distance as his face froze in a cross between terror and pain. His body stiffened and a sound of soft grinding emanated from within his clothes. Most of the color drained from his skin. First his hands, then his face, slowly became a translucent pink, almost the color of a newly blossomed rose. His clothes and the rest of his body followed, until his entire form resembled dimly colored glass.

The Council stood still. The hush of the crowd was palpable. The prisoner's crystalline form was removed and placed on the truck. Then, each prisoner was brought forward for the same fate.

The first truck was filled and the second truck nearly so, when a terrified prisoner attempted to flee. He struggled as Brother Bradley touched him, rising to his feet and grasping at the Council member. Losing his balance during the transformation, he fell to the ground. At first there seemed to be no effect on the crystalline form. But then it began to darken to a crimson hue, spots of darkness coloring the face and hands first and cracks spreading from head to toe. As the color rushed to each spot along the form, a groaning issued from each spot on the body, and blood oozed forth until the whole form was a shrieking mass. A critical mass of thwarted magick was reached and the glass form exploded in a million shards, the surroundings covered in blood and glass. Brother Bradley only barely turned away, covering his face from the explosion. He looked at the remains, now crystal and bits of shredded flesh, with a mixture of sadness and disgust.

Turning to the guards, Brother Bradley said, "That it is enough for the day. Place the guardians along the shoreline, and return the remaining prisoners to holding. We will resume this tomorrow."

CHAPTER 9

The Omen of the Apocalypse, safely ensconced within its protective construct, patiently endured the withering cosmic radiation in the Nexus of the Nine. The nexus was the locus of the collective boundaries of the Nine, the lone place within the innermost volume of the Starhome's center in which corporeal beings could exist, if not for very long. Chaotically whirling like maelstroms of frame-dragging fury, the singularities of the Nine loomed above and around the Omen. Their resonant vibrations, rapidly pulsating, betrayed their collective anger, rage, and disbelief.

"Again, Omen," the Voice of the Apocalypse spoke for the Nine. "Show us again EarthZero, and what you saw there."

Respectfully and promptly, the Omen complied, once again sharing its Zyrrblok fractal database with the Nine. The Nine, as one, scanned and scanned again the final moments of the Omen's exploration of the EarthZero solar system. This seemed to require another veritable eternity of milliseconds, during which the Omen writhed in agony, the psychic force of sharing its mind and soul with all nine gods simultaneously creating a heretofore unknown level of pain. Finally, just as the Omen knew it could endure no longer, the Nine broke their communion.

"The Omen shows us truth," Angolgotha shared with the Nine Gods' collective.

"Agreed," Vyr-Thak Ag'yena made known. "All of the prophecies of the countless aeons have been realized! EarthZero has been shaped by the hand of the Eternal Recursion."

Orz'Non'a Plk, forever divergent, offered, "Aye, the Dragon is realized on EarthZero, as was foreseen by the One Who Bound Us. We now have confirmed that this world is the final world in our seemingly eternal quest. Yet... what did it mean when it challenged the Omen?"

There was a momentary pause as the others considered this.

As was their usual manner, Ga-Vida, Mneme, and Y'lis, shared as one, "Agree. Query the Fractal Mages. Let them cast forward, to see what this means to us."

The Nine then agreed, and the deed was done. Immediately, every Fractal Mage in or near the Starhome received a Zyrrblok query. As one and without fail, all of the mages ceased their current tasks and complied with the command of their gods. In moments, as the Fractal Mages cast forward their future-interrogating psychic tendrils, data of both probable and improbable futures streamed into the collective of the Nine. Parsing the disparate and often ambiguous data for the most probable future paths of reality, the Nine decided that they needed to discuss and share this most fascinating revelation.

"It *was* a challenge," Siddthurrak scoffed, its contact with the collective slithering with psychic slime. "The One Who Bound Us told us that this would be a possibility, however unlikely. The final world – that which would be the resolution of the mystery of the Eternal Recursion – might indeed be the most powerful of them all. With higher souls in abundance. With a fully actualized Dragon lording over them all."

"Fool!" Ga-Vida, Mneme, and Y'lis taunted. "You missed the most important part, Siddthurrak, as usual. The Dragon told the Omen – and therefore us, the Nine – that its game begins anew. How may something begin anew when we are at its end? What did that mean? What game does a manifestation of a planet's collective life force play?"

"Ours is the only 'game' in the cosmos," Orz'Non'a Plk admitted testily. "How dare it challenge us? We are the Vanth'Vash'Var! The Nine Gods! The Sentinels of the Void! Push the Fractal Mages harder. Force them to cast forward with as much force of will as they may muster. Show us exactly what the Dragon meant!"

Vashti Thog immediately countered, "No. Have them cast forward no more on this subject. Also, compel an immediate mind-wipe on all of the mages, and any who might have observed their efforts. Do this now," he finished, his tone allowing no argument.

There were, of course, Nine Gods, but only one, Vashti Thog, had the power to command the rest. Thus, his word was obeyed, and the deed was done. Then, he resumed his communion with the rest of the gods.

"I was able to pick out a buried, highly improbable future path from among the data provided by the Fractal Mages," he admitted, silently sharing the data with the rest. "What I have discerned might very well demonstrate the fulfillment of the Eternal Recursion itself. For, it seems, that there might be tiers of existence for the Dual-Aspect. And that what the Omen encountered on EarthZero is no mere localized expression of its existence. Do you not recall, my brothers and sisters, our own origin? That from whence we arose, once bidden by the One Who Bound Us?"

General agreement spread through their shared contact. Warm, deeply fulfilling connection, recalled now, aeons later, invoked some very real cognitive dissonance among them. Yet, too many aeons of total genocide had buried their formerly bright souls beneath stagnant, oppressive dross. Thus, the unusual feelings were brushed aside, relegated to whatever place gods themselves banished worrisome, contradictory thoughts.

Vashti Thog pressed them, "Remember the First Song? That from whence we arose? Do you not now see the connection between our own origins, as the first of the Fae in this cosmos, and that hidden whisper of potential future paths which the Fractal Mages showed us?"

"I remember," Angolgotha acknowledged first among the rest. "But what the Dragon sang to us... the First Song said nothing of any game. It sang 'That Which Was Old Now Is Made New Again'. Why... why did the Dragon of EarthZero sing its challenge to the Omen? Why was it different from what it sang to us at the start of the world?"

"Because, dearest Angolgotha," Vashti Thog replied, "our Dragon was proper and correct in the context of its song. When we were called into being, at the start of the world, the Dragon correctly used the context of the Eternal Recursion in its song. The old world had been unmade, and the new had been reborn. We were its first children, there at the beginning of time. However, the Dragon manifested from EarthZero sings a new song. A new song for new birth. A song of challenge. A challenge to us all. It is therefore obvious that this is not the Dragon which called us to the light, to be born into this world. No, this is something else. Something else entirely."

"How can this be?" Ga-Vida asked, breaking her triad for the first time in many millennia. "How can there be more than one Dragon? Are you implying that this is the lesser form, perhaps? The non-cosmic, non-universal one? One local to a single world? If so, then how dare it challenge us in such a manner!"

Vashti Thog's silent presence immediately stifled the certain bellicose agreement of the others. "I understand why you do not see it, my kin. Your power is not equal to mine, even when aggregated as all eight of you. I was firstborn. So, as always, it is mine to see that which you cannot. Therefore, I must inform you: Chaos has manifested in our cosmos. The Dragon of our experience, our own Cosmic Dragon, the creator of the universe, differs from the Dragon that has manifested upon EarthZero. It is, however, not a minor manifestation, unique to a particularly powerful world, abounding with numerous elevated souls. We would be only so fortunate, were that the case."

He paused a moment, allowing his fellow gods to process the revelation.

"The most essential element of the Eternal Recursion is: 'As Above, So Below'. This, however, works not only in the commonly held notion of 'below'. In this case, it is 'above'. Quite far above."

"You cannot be serious..." Angolgotha said, speaking for the rest. "Those are just myths, legends, and cruel rumors, Vashti. It's what the denizens of this universe make up in order to rationalize our own power and existence. It's how they get their tiny minds around our power. It's how they manage to get to sleep at night, and ameliorate their fear. There is nothing, and no one, above us."

"I understand your inability to process this, Angolgotha," Vashti Thog replied warmly. "I understand that the rest of you do, too. Because none of this existed in this cosmos, until only recently. I am telling you the truth when I say that I, and I alone of all of us, have the power to name and to know the Chaos that has recently arisen in our universe. I know that this is truth, because I, and only I alone of all of us, was able to discern that single, hushed whisper of a potential future path, shown to us by the Fractal Mages. And now, once I make this known to you, as I know I must, you will know it has been true all along. Even, and impossibly so, back to the time of our birth. For, after knowing what the Fractal Mages whispered, I immediately noted that my original memory of what the Dragon of this universe sang to us had been altered. The Dragon of our birth actually sang to us, 'The Dragon's Game Begins Anew.'"

Total disbelief and snarling scorn poured from the eight gods. Then, there came a moment of silent introspection. Memories of what was old were noted. Noted that they had indeed been made new again. Revised. Edited.

Vashti Thog spoke, seeing that they now had begun to understand, "Indeed. You have now noted the impossible. The explanation is simple, because it has only one possible answer: the Dragon of EarthZero is not ours. In fact, it may only be of higher power, for it has demonstrated the impossible ability to invoke retrocausality and edit the very song of our own Dragon. Is this not an example of the Eternal Recursion itself?"

Silently, all agreed. As the eight cast back their own memories, they now became aware of very telling deltas between what they had actually experienced in the past, and what their new memories were revealing to them. Chaos, indeed.

Notably, as they embraced the memories – the new ones now emblazoned upon their true memories, which now threatened to fade away to nothing – they became aware of new names, new concepts. Almost as if, somehow, someone were whispering these new things to them from behind a screen, or cave wall. When, at last, they understood what this new manifestation of the Dragon had challenged the Omen with, they grew insecure, frightful.

Nodding, Vashti Thog acknowledged his own trepidation. "Chaos has introduced into our cosmos entities not of this cosmos. And it has been of such power that even we, the gods, have been affected. Now, when I at last may mention such things as 'Anshadar' and 'Shadar', you know precisely of which I speak. And what that now introduces into our strategy."

Silence. Then, Siddthurrak asked, "Would we not be these Anshadar? Are we not the heroes of this universe, doing the bidding of the One Who Bound Us to save all souls?"

Ga-Vida's laughter was harsh, mocking, and immediate. "Heroes do not engage in casual genocide, Siddthurrak. If anything, we would be Shadar. However, I sense that we are neither. Correct, Vashti?"

"Correct. We have already been realized as gods. We are the supreme gods of this universe. All of us have consumed billions of souls, binding them to ourselves. While we are indeed heroes of the Void, and the Anti-Life, we are also villains of the highest possible order. At least to some, who have no concept of moral relativism. We are, in truth, above good and evil. We are a necessary force in this universe. We exact a necessary toll, and affect a necessary change. Transcendence comes at a price. A terrible price."

"So what does this game mean to us, Vashti?" Ga-Vida pressed. "Does it mean that a new cadre of immortals will suddenly be born? Some of whom will be inclined to assist us in our holy mission, while the rest will oppose us?"

Siddthurrak's turn came to mock. "Foolish, Ga-Vida. As always. How could the newly born dare to contest us? We will reach EarthZero in short time. What then? Shadar and Anshadar infants, against the Horde? Even then, we have trillions. What does EarthZero have? Billions, and only a few, at most. Even if all of them were newly born immortals, we could still defeat them. If at a somewhat advanced rate of attrition, we would still win."

Vyr-Thak Ag'yena quietly said, "Sidd, you missed the point that Vashti made about retrocausality. And about some Dragons being larger than others. We have become inured to total victory. We have had so few real challenges that we have grown complacent; become jaded. I trust I don't have to remind you of our campaigns against the Golgothan Empire, who cost us many tens of billions? Or the Dymaxians, who actually breached Starhome? Or the V'layans, who caused us more grief and turmoil than anyone else, ever? They directly attacked us, the gods! And some of you almost died."

"Yet, now, they make war for us," Siddthurrak reminded everyone, needlessly. "So let the denizens of EarthZero, immortal or not, fear them!"

"Let us proceed with caution," Mneme suggested, becoming the second of the triad to break with their tradition of simultaneous response. "I think this is what Vashti Thog is counseling. And I think that we have nothing to lose, and everything to gain, by approaching this one – our final one – with caution. What does a small measure of time mean, anyway, for us? For we have endured many aeons in our task. What does a few additional years or decades or even centuries mean to us, now?"

Mute impatience crowded the collective communication of the Nine. The majority were simply impatient to fulfill their duty. They were quite willing to sacrifice all of their assets in order to achieve the goal. Especially now that it finally was at hand. So close. So tempting.

Yet, among the minority was Vashti Thog, and he did indeed wish to counsel caution.

"We will enact a strategy of multiple phases this time," Vashti Thog commanded. "The first phase is that of stealth. We will send our spies first to learn the lay of the land of EarthZero. We will learn if this world is indeed what its Dragon has sung to us. We will know the names of its Anshadar, its Shadar, and of every other soul there. We will then assess the situation at that point, and revise our strategy accordingly. We will flow. We will not overwhelm, at least not initially. We will use every trick and tactic in our immense arsenal to mitigate any possible negative effects against us. We will encourage some to join us, just as we will sow discord among those who dare oppose us. We will optimize our own strengths, and minimize those of our opponents. We shall do all of this before we even enter their solar system for the final battle. Do you understand? Are we all in agreement?"

In silent acquiescence, the eight agreed with the strategy of Vashti Thog. For once, the Vanth'Vash'Var would implement tactics formerly thought unworthy of their station as the Sentinels of the Void. For once, the Death Horde would practice caution, patience, and prudence. Because, for once, the Nine Gods now shared an extremely unlikely emotion which no one else among the Horde would ever know could exist within their leaders, their gods: fear.

CHAPTER 10

"I hate this effing place!" Tim swore loudly, trying his best to maintain his balance as he walked along with the group.

"The Null hates you right back, Timmy!" Mercy laughed, hauling Tim's floating form back down to what passed for the ground in the Null. "In fact, the Null hates all of us. Even me. Well, especially me."

Void, Mercy, Leta, and Tim plodded along, with Ku'tu guiding Leta from her perch atop her shoulder.

"Don't be a fool like Tim," Ku'tu whispered to Leta. "Take small steps. Keep one foot planted at all times. Or else you might fall up like he did."

"Fall up?" Leta shot back testily. "Fall *up*? What the hell kinda freaky place is this, anyway? Null, my ass! This is some fucked up moonwalkin' shit. Michael Jackson would have been right at home here."

Mercy laughed. "The name of my old compound here in the Null *was* named 'The Never'. Is that close enough?"

Leta gave Mercy a goggle-eyed stare. "You shittin' me, Mercy? That's very close to being creepy as it sounds. And you're all pale and strangely charismatic like he was, too. See what I'm sayin'? He was a fairy, too!"

Cutting an abrupt, nasty moonwalk, Mercy perched, balanced on the tips of her toes, and squealed, "Hee, hee!"

Everyone laughed, especially Leta. She and Ku'tu and Mercy had bonded quite a bit over the past year and two weeks. Almost like sisters now, they had become, due mostly to their shared affinities for fire, spiffy clothes, and tasteless jokes at the expense of others. Being merciless bitches, as Nick called them, playing, of course. Not even Nick was crazy enough to test any one of these most dangerous ladies.

A few steps ahead of the group, Void paused his relentless pace. "We're here."

Mercy didn't believe him. "No way, Void. We've still got..." she grew quiet as she pulled up beside him. "Wow, you're right," she said, her purple-tinged eyes glowing softly with electric blue sparks. "We're here, guys," she called over her shoulder. "The nexus of the Never. And now Void's going to tell me how he found it before I did. And it better be good."

He chuckled. "It's good, alright. Apparently, I'm attuned to places where I've died. I can feel it pulling me to it, like I'm a lost vampire desperately searching for its coffin before the Sun rises. It's a feeling of urgency. I just tuned it in, and tuned you guys out, which was harder to do, I might add," he said as the rest of the group pulled up to them.

"Well, well, well," Mercy said. "Learn something new every day. Even after 13,338 years. Maybe I would have the same sensation for it that you do, but, of course, that means I'd have to die first. And, as you know," she said, smiling craftily, "that ain't never gonna happen. I'm too slick for Death. He's a dimwit."

"Mercy!" Ku'tu cried out, flitting around her head. "Don't tempt the Mother like that! You'll attract a weirding on yourself!"

"Yeah, girl," Leta added. "Don't say shit like that. It'll happen if you keep it up. That's how that kinda stuff works. Don't have to be Fae to know that."

"Don't worry," Mercy replied, pointing at Void. "If I do attract a weird, and death has to happen, Void will gladly die for us. He's quite good at it, aren't you, Void?"

Void shook his head, totally ignoring her. "Tim, you okay? You look a bit green."

"It's this Null place," Tim replied, indeed looking queasy. "I'm used to feeling the ground that I know, beneath my feet. This place is... it's just too weird. The only thing I can feel is... is..." he said, abruptly bending double and puking.

"Eww! Gross!" Leta squeaked, rapidly moving aside with quick, tiny steps to avoid the spray of chunks from Tim. The chunks struck the ground, ricocheted up a few inches, then eerily slowed their motion to a crawl, forming a sickening, greasy, cloying cloud just above the ground. The ladies hurriedly vacated the scene of total grossness.

"It's okay, man," Void told him. He reached over and steadied him, slapping a hand gently across his broad back. "It takes a while to adjust. It'll probably take you longer due to your power, as you've already surmised. Not a very earthy place here. It's all good, though. We're here. Just remember to keep moving, okay? Even if you're just shuffling your feet."

Tim gave Void a thumb's up, wiping his face with the back of his sleeve. To his relative amazement, the flecks of matter were instantly repulsed by his new compression bodysuit. His highly artificed compression bodysuit, that is.

"What the—" he began, watching, incredulous, as the flecks flew away at all angles.

"What?" Leta exclaimed, watching him, keeping a steady eye on the flying flecks. "Gross! Again, Tim? Gross!"

Mercy laughed at their dismay. "I see they've placed a few interesting runes and inscriptions on your new clothes. That repulsion charm works great for punches, bullets, and harmful stuff like stomach acid."

"I didn't think it would repel puke," Tim admitted. "That's actually pretty cool. Denny and Maynard knocked this one over the freakin' fence."

"Just remember what else it can do," Leta reminded him. "Men. Never pay attention, do you?"

Leta preened, her curves delicious as her own highly artificed compression bodysuit hugged her figure. She had decided on a wicked-ass crimson-on-black scheme, the crimson vibrant, and rampant like wildfire from head to toe. Ku'tu had been so impressed by Leta's bodysuit that she had requested a duplicate of the same, woven for her tiny flying humanoid form, and warded to displace itself when she shapeshifted to her gigantic dragon form.

But Tim? Tim had done as most men would have done, going for what looked like hunter's camo. Over his whole bodysuit. Leta had thought it was a very redneck thing for him to do, and she had told him straight up as much. The rest of Team El had remained almost true to form, with the women on the team actually selecting color schemes that were coordinated—Beth had gone with light blues, greens, and whites on black; a decent blend of naiad and nereid color schemes, Ku'tu had informed her—while the two men, Tim and Dwayne, had gone low-brow Neanderthal redneck camo-bullshit with their selections. Men.

Mercy and Void had both been holdouts. Save for their PING boxes, both had initially refused to indulge in the nifty looking compression bodysuits and hekatek toys which Maynard, Denny, and a small host of very compelled Fae had joined forces to artifice in but a mere few days. Gear for all the team. Well, as far down as Team OP, Team El, the Googles, Nick, and Mhyrranda went, that is. The rest of the folks? They'd have to wait their turns, after this initial rush phase, until Nick and his Praetorians had fully crunched the logistics of gearing up the citizens of Dreamland.

However, totally succumbing to peer pressure, which she had never actually done before, Mercy had decided to join "her girls" and accept a nifty artificed purple-on-black compression bodysuit, which she had donned beneath her goth-heavy leathers and lace, careful to expose it at certain strategic places. For all the good that it did her, that is. As the Ninth Null, she was already so personally empowered that her innate resistances and defenses basically put those of the artificed bodysuits to shame. And prolonged direct contact with her would certainly unbind some of the runes, as she adapted to them, nulling their power. Being so polite, however, she had demurred, not bothering to make a point of it. It looked cool. It looked like the stuff that her friends were wearing. So that's why she wore it.

Void, however, had not demurred. Instead, he had blatantly laughed at Maynard and Denny as they had tried to persuade him that he could really use an extra layer of highly artificed hekatek protection. Then, after the hollow, derisive laughter had ceased, they had adopted another tact, trying to persuade him that he needed a really cool one like Mercy's, only with the chest exposed, so that his Void Tat could do its thing. Plus, it would look cooler than Nick's cheesy old world clothes, which Void had taken a shining to, and had not changed in several days. The new clothes? They'd auto-renew and stay permanently non-odorous and perfectly clean. And not look like old, ratty, slept-in gym clothes. Cool clothes for the Cool Void.

That had done it for Void. That, and some last-minute alterations on the PING boxes, allowing them to attach to what was effectively invisible web gear on the bodysuits. Otherwise, Void would be almost certain to lose his PING box the first time he shifted to hypersonic flight, or jumped in lava, or something equally ridiculous. Unless, of course, his flight was telekinetic in nature, like his strength was, at least according to Maynard. Then he might be able to retain safely whatever he held or carried within a projection of his aura. He had decided, however, not to test the hypothesis at that time, and had instead opted for the very convenient embedded web gear.

Plus, matching Mercy wasn't such a bad thing, he had to admit. Deep purple on deepest black looked freaking awesome, he thought. Better than that camo shit everyone else was wearing. At least Nick, upon seeing Void's choice in gear, had decided to implement a similar design himself, a design which would ultimately, contagiously, spread to his Praetorians; whose namesakes had, naturally, worn their own black and royal purple gear during the glorious days of ancient Rome.

Most of the companions had thought that the funniest thing about the entire bodysuit artificing process, however, had been the way in which the Fae spinners—the very same Fae who wove the finest sartorial creations for the Gentry themselves—had insisted, upon seeing Void, to bow and kowtow before him, being totally obsequious in his presence. Tellingly, this was not their usual practice, even when outfitting the most powerful of the Fae. But for their most feared, most loathed eternal boogie man? Of course, milord Void!

Well, the funniest thing, save for the way that they had treated Mercy. Careful not to be seen directly by her, they had gone out of their way to flick the points of their ears at her, or swish their exotic capes like matadors, or make warding signs to avert her evil eye, or just whisper among themselves and gossip about her like the vicious well-dressed fops they truly were. Mercy was unloved by most of the Fae of EarthZero, apparently, even though she was obviously their most powerful protector and stalwart hero. They simply hated to admit that they needed her protection, being immortal, powerful, and most wise themselves.

While this was amusing to most of the companions, primarily because Mercy needled everyone mercilessly and often, and was a general smartass to everyone, once Void had noticed it from among all of the chaos of the process of prepping, he hadn't let it slide. He had deliberately called their attention to him, then he had loudly declared that Mercy was his chosen, gently placing a hand on her shoulder. Then he had sealed the deal by emitting briefly a monstrous purple-on-black strobe from his chest, which had lit the sartorially perfect Fae tailors and their bizarre entourage of tiny flying assistants with a potent, silent fury, scaring them all shitless in the process.

Of course, this had resulted in an instant, one-hundred-eighty degree attitude change from the snooty Fae, as they were required now by their own arcane rules of etiquette to bow and scrape before Mercy, just as they had done before Void. Because now, the two had to be treated the same. Such were their rules, and Void had nailed them on it. Much to Mercy's relative shock and horror, of course, because she had actually enjoyed her many millennia as the Fae's ultimate pariah, in her own perverse way. From now on, though, they'd actually have to pretend to be nice to her, and it was almost more than she could stand.

So she had to remind Void of her true feelings on the matter for the fifty-seventh time today, in her own special, comically tangential way.

"The limits of the dead, Void," she reminded him. "The limits of the dead," she said, her nimble fingers fumbling about the ground, trying to find the shorn anchors of the Never.

"Pikachu's a virgin?" Void taunted her right back, deliberately hitting her with a mondegreen, because he knew it would really piss her off. Because, naturally, only *she* could hit everyone else with mondegreens. "Feeling psychosocial there, Mercy?"

Her head jerked around immediately, and her almond-slanted, purple-tinged eyes shot virtual hate daggers at him.

"Goddamnit, Void! You know it says 'packaging subversion', not effing 'Pikachu's a virgin'! Goddamnit! Don't ruin my morose recitations of grim song lyrics! Especially when I'm looking for... Ah, found 'em," she finished with a smile.

"I don't see anything," Tim muttered to Leta.

"That's because they're invisible, Tim," Leta gently reminded him. "Remember the mission briefing? Eight anchors, all invisible, hard to find, even harder to use now that we don't have Aal Ball to make a link to them."

"I don't see how everybody can remember every little detail of everything," Tim complained, truly distraught. "I mean, I'm not Einstein or anything—I barely made it out of Caltech—but it's like all of you are geniuses or something. It's annoying."

"I just pay attention," Leta informed him. "I never was a genius, either, Tim. Just stop chewin' Copenhagen or whatever that worm dirt you've got in your mouth is and tune in once in a while. Stuff's easier to remember now, anyway, since the sigil. Haven't you noticed it?"

Reluctantly, Tim nodded in agreement. "I have noticed it, Leta. I was just griping. And I was taking another dip to get the taste of puke outta my mouth. Yuck."

"Alright, kiddos," Mercy said happily, her hands apparently holding a small bundle of something. "I hold in my hands all eight anchors, the things that used to anchor the Never to EarthZero. These are what we used to find my blade, Shunya, and pop Ku'tu to Dreamland—I mean, Las Vegas—to get it and retrieve it."

"Is this when you melted, Void?" Tim asked.

"Yep," Void replied calmly. "I was barely able to make it back from that. Lot of damage. But we got Shunya, and everyone else was okay. Except for Aal Ball. He took a beating. I mean, they took a beating."

"I once saw a guy get hit by a high voltage wire," Tim said, wondering how Void could be so calm about something so heinous. "Was walking the construction site when this big-ass explosion went off. Some dumbass had forgot to secure his ladder, got tagged by the wire. Everyone heard it, saw it flash like lightning, maybe even felt it, despite the normal noise at the site. By the time anyone got to the guy, his face and back were a pile of goo. Melted him clean through like he was a wax dummy or something."

"Dummy?" Mercy interrupted. "That's right, Tim. Void was the dummy. Care to hold these again, Void?" she smiled at him, obviously enjoying his slight frown.

"Can't tell if serious, or not..." Void stammered, pretending to be touched in the head.

"You're not actually pretending, Void," Mercy needled him. Then, she held the invisible bundle close to her eyes. They slowly became visible, but did so to a limit equal to only a finger's length from their ends. "Okay," she continued, slowly sifting through them as she called out their anchored destination. "Hong Kong, New York City, Dubai, The Circle of the Wolf Moon, Giza, err... Dreamland, and, err... that's it."

Void noted that this time, upon mention of the Fae's secret place, there was no hesitation on the part of the Fae—Ku'tu, in this case—to share the information with the "non-Fae": Leta and Tim. Apparently, Ku'tu had already ascended them to equal status with the Fae, unlike the first time that this had occurred, and Ku'tu and Vir'gil had almost had a conniption fit regarding both Void's and Maynard's being initiated unto the ranks of the Fae, until Mercy had shut them down. A lot had gone on in the year and a day that he had been away, he was forced to acknowledge.

"You skipped six and eight," Leta told her, not missing a beat. "That's your shit and all, Mercy, so it's cool if you want to skip 'em. We don't need to know where they go if you don't want to tell us."

"But we're hunting for Fresswelle, and my people," Ku'tu said sweetly, flitting around Mercy's head, trying to peek down into the anchors. Mercy wouldn't let her, though. "Aww, c'mon, Mercy. Let me see 'em. Let me see 'em!"

"No, mine." Mercy said, twisting them all tightly, clutching them to her chest.

"No... MINE!" Ku'tu answered, dive-bombing down onto Mercy's ample cleavage, missing the bundle of anchors because Mercy was simply too fast for her, even with her being in her dainty, highly agile, flying faerie form. For several terribly awkward yet highly amusing moments, there was a fierce, buzzing tussle, as Ku'tu struggled with Mercy, trying to grab the anchors, but, more often than not, just grabbing Mercy's breasts. After a few fateful moments, the tit tickling became too much for Mercy, and, over gales of breathless laughter, she capitulated, holding the anchors as far away from her as her right hand could extend.

"All yours, girl," Mercy laughed as Ku'tu buzzed to a pause, hovering immediately before the ends of the bundled anchors.

"Hong Kong, New York City, blah-blah, blah-blah," Ku'tu said quickly, rapidly scanning the anchors. "Oh, that's creepy, don't want to go there," she said after seeing something that she really didn't like. She immediately proceeded to the next one. "Ah, a new one. What is this?" she inquired of Mercy. "A pyramid in the snow? How did they do that?"

All eyes were on Mercy. She shrugged. "That's actually called a 'nunatak'. In this case, it's the Nunatak of Nanabozho, because it belongs to my dear old friend, Nanabozho."

"Who?" Ku'tu asked, confused. Mercy just stood there, lips miraculously sealed. Ku'tu looked around. Leta shrugged at her. Tim just shook his head. Void smirked.

Mercy shook her head several times, quickly, giving Void the stink eye. "Of *course* you know who he is, you Dragon Dream-hacker of knowledge! Don't think I haven't caught onto how you freakin' know *everything* there is to know about *everything*, Cory Christopher Tate! You're not *that* smart. *Nobody* is. I've seen more geniuses, human and Fae and otherworldly, over many millennia, than anyone alive, and no one—no one!—has ever been such a smarmy smart-elephant know-it-all! You're cheating. You're One With the Dragon! That's how you know every-effing thing! Admit it!"

By now, everyone was silent and still, totally engrossed by Mercy's Drama Queen Extravaganza.

"Well," Void said simply, calmly, "I *didn't* know a nunatak was a pyramid in the snow."

Mercy's jaw dropped, and stayed there.

"Idiot," Tim snickered. "Everybody knows what a nun-attack is. That's when Sister Mary Elephantiasis knuckle-dusts you with a ruler."

Void continued, amused, "But I *have* heard of Nanabozho. He's a demi-urge according to some, but most know him only as a trickster god. Friend of man. He beat Paul Bunyan to death with a fish, didn't he?" he finished with a smile.

Nodding, a smile forming on her lips, she replied, "Yes. Yes he did, Void. With a walleye. Cut him down with a fish, after they had fought for 40 days straight. You Internet nerd."

"That's all nice and everything," Void said, catching Leta smiling at him for using her line, "but I want to know what the *other* one was. The one Ku'tu said was creepy. What was it, Ku'tu?"

"It was the Abyssal Edge, Void," Ku'tu said, even though Mercy shot her a wicked glare. "Mercy's a freak or something to have a link to go there. But, of course, we all know already that Mercy's a freak. When we had Midsummer Festival in Dreamland, she drank everyone into the ground—even that guy on Nick's team of Praetorians who can grow his own severed limbs back in just an hour—then she stomped on the dirt! Anyway, the Fae can disconnect from the Flow, the Song of the Sidhe, there. At the Abyssal Edge, of course, not the Midsummer Festival. That would be stupid. Anyway, when you disconnect from the Flow, it's like cutting off your soul from existence itself. So nobody goes there, unless they're committing suicide. Ultimate soul-suicide, too, because that's the last place in existence before the—"

"Before the Void," Mercy finished, rolling her eyes at Ku'tu, who was always a bit slow picking up on stuff like total, soul-crushing angst and forever-silent, unrequited love. "That's where my mentor, D'aanz Un'Anath, the Eighth Null, taught me how to give in to the better angels of my apostasy and disconnect myself from the Flow. The thing that no one ever tells you, though," she said, noting the look of abject horror on Ku'tu's cherubic face, "is that, after you finally manage to make the constant faerie song shut the eff up, right before it all goes black, right before your soul leaves your body and your body disintegrates, you can gaze out past the Abyssal Edge and see the Far Side of Shadow. The Void. And in that moment just before the final dissolution, the final death, you experience a super-massive little death that seems to last forever."

"So you can have an orgasm that lasts forever?" Leta asked her, leaning in closely. "No wonder you have an anchor set there. Do I have to be Fae to do that?"

Laughter broke out. "I never thought about it like that, Leta," Mercy laughed. "We'll have to gather the crew up and have a Ladies' Night Out there. But, no, seriously, I used to go there to pay homage to D'aanz Un'Anath, my mentor, after I assassinated him so that I could take his place." It got quiet then, very quickly. "Yep. Definitely not the good guys. And I'd always go there when I wanted to die, courting Death itself at the edge of the Void. Always wondered what was staring back at me from the abyss as I gazed into it. Always wondered what Death looked like. Now I know," she finished softly, looking at Void. "He is Death, the Destroyer of Worlds. And gods."

Terrible, awkward Silence blindly danced a spastic jig around the group.

Then: "And my ringtone used to be a cute kitty meow," Void smiled brightly. "And I hacked my Alexa to call herself 'Miss No-Pants', and to constantly refer to Maynard as 'the T-Rex of Jungle Love', just to annoy him. Seems like it no longer annoys him now," Void snickered, "because now he's even got the Duchess calling him that."

Tim started laughing. "Effing Maynard!" he giggled loudly. "That man's the biggest nerd on EarthZero, but he's the coolest dopehead around when it comes to sharing his drugs."

Ku'tu and Leta shared a laugh then. "I remember his gummy bears," Leta tittered. "Holy shit those things kicked my ass." She gave Ku'tu a wise-ass look. "Remember? We were trippin' balls and you flew us out to Hoover Dam, and we set it on fire?" She laughed harshly, slapping her thigh.

Suddenly, Mercy, Tim, and Void were staring at the two fire women. Their laughter rapidly petered off as they realized, suddenly, that the Hoover Dam Fire had precipitated one of the worst natural disasters since the Great Collapse: the Great Colorado River Flood. And, until now, no one had known who the perpetrators were. Until now.

"That's not funny, Leta," Tim said seriously. "Cleaning that mess up took Team El over a week of really hard work. All of the runic work that had to be done to replace the lost power generation took a shitload of effort. Worst of all, dozens of innocent people probably died from the flood."

"No one's innocent here, Tim," Leta said, flipping it right back at him. "Those mutant outlaws? The Brotherhood of Desolation? The so-called 'innocent' people you're talking about? They were planning an attack on Dreamland. They'd even gained access to old world military weapons, including a couple of M1-A1 main battle tanks, some long-range artillery, and an arsenal of heavy shit. Had they managed a sneak attack, they could have killed thousands, which would have pushed Dreamland back into the ashes of the old world."

"Those guys were in negotiations with us, Leta," Tim said, crossing his arms. "The Duchess had almost got them convinced to join us. Then, next thing you know, they all drown in a flood."

Ku'tu flitted up to Tim, smiling. "Then, perhaps, they should have agreed to join us sooner. That way, they wouldn't have drowned like the desert rats that they truly were."

"They were evil, and they opposed us," Leta informed him, firmly standing her ground. "I'm not gonna lose a minute of sleep over it, either. They deserved to drown."

Tim just shook his head, realizing that it was useless to argue the finer points of right or wrong with Leta or Ku'tu, for they truly did as they wished most of the time anyway. And maybe, just maybe, they were right about the brotherhood. Maybe they did deserve to die like the rats they truly were.

"So," Void asked, reeling everyone back in, "do you think Fresswelle would more likely be at one place, rather than at another?"

Mercy pointed to Ku'tu, who said, "It's logical to assume that Fresswelle followed a path similar to that of Shunya. Shunya showed up in Dreamland, back when it was just Las Vegas. The blade followed the path of one of the anchors, like water seeking the path of least resistance. Therefore, it's logical to presume that Fresswelle did the same, just via another anchor. It certainly wasn't and/or isn't in Dreamland. We've combed that place thoroughly."

Mercy continued, "So that leaves us Hong Kong, New York City, Dubai, The Circle of the Wolf Moon, Giza, the Abyssal Edge, and the Nunatak of Nanabozho. Any good guesses out there as to which one it might be?"

"It's definitely not Giza," Tim said. "Petrus would have noticed it, and used it against us."

"Mercy, just focus and tell us where it isn't," Leta said. "You've got its twin. Use it to scry where it isn't."

Doing a very real double-take, Mercy smiled at Leta. "You've been paying attention to our drunken tavern stories, haven't you? Good, good," she said, conjuring Shunya into her left hand. She brought the anchors back close to her face, holding Shunya close first to one, then the next, concentrating hard on the blade that was the twin to her own. "Well, it's not Giza, it's not Hong Kong, it's not Dubai, it's not Dreamland, it's not the Circle, it's not the Abyssal Edge..." she paused, shaking her head to clear it. Then, she returned to her scrying, "And... it's not New York City. Damn. I was hoping we'd get to see the City of Glass. I bet it looks awesome. Well," she concluded, gazing at the group, "I guess this means that we're off to see where MorthonTech used to send their wayward employees: Antarctica."

Void laughed. "When Ku'tu mentioned a pyramid in the snow, I was hoping it might be there. All kinds of conspiracy theory hoo-haa about that stuff. Guess it's not exactly conspiracy theory anymore, is it?"

"It never was," Mercy sniffed. "Humans are just stupid and superstitious. The Nunatak of Nanabozho is as real as the nose on my face. So is Nanabozho. Boy, is he going to be surprised to see us come boppin' up to his pad."

"So this guy," Leta asked, "he's Fae? This Nana Bozo guy?"

Mercy shook her head. "Not exactly. Like Void said, Nanabozho is a creator god. A trickster god. And by that I mean a god. He's not a run of the mill Fae, or a human with aspirations of godhood, like Petrus Romanus. He actually *is* a god."

Leta shook her head, dismissing the notion entirely. "Look, I get it. I mean I know we're at the point in history in which all of the religions from before this point in history seem like a good idea. You know? Final judgement of the Lord? Get a little bit of God on your side, get to heaven? It's all over our heads, like in the old spirituals? But the sigil was over our heads, not Jesus and the angels." She looked over at Void. "And I know what a god is now. I mean, he just came back from being disintegrated. That's not the same as getting crucified and being reborn out of a tomb. Resurrected out of it after three days. Leave behind the shroud and a couple of good gospels, and everybody thinks you're a god. But, hell, we're all practically immortal now. I mean, like, by some aspects we're gods now ourselves. All of us. We won't die unless we get killed and eaten by something insanely big. Maybe not even then. Might regenerate back even if we're dragon doo-doo."

A couple of out-of-place giggles answered her. Smiling wickedly, she continued, "And we don't die from cooties or shit now. We're basically humanoid... planarians?" she said quickly. "Isn't that what Maynard said? I mean, we won't grow back extra arms or anything ridiculous like that. But we might just be able to regenerate back to full form from virtually anything other than complete disintegration, or losing most of our body mass, or losing our heads." She cast an appraising glance at Void, who rolled his eyes. Not that she could see it. "I'm just saying, like, I've seen what god is now that we're gods. *We're* the new gods."

"Leta," Tim told her, "just because we don't have Sunday school anymore doesn't mean we don't have God in our lives anymore. I haven't lost my faith yet, even though what we've seen—what I've seen— does make me doubt that everything they were saying in the Bible was true or was right. I mean look at Petrus Romanus. He fits exactly in the Prophecies of Malachy. You might stretch it a bit and say that, well, maybe you could account for him just reading and interpreting Revelation. Maybe. And maybe Lucifer just did this to him. You know? Made him go crazy? Made him be this person who was from the prophecy, and might have been from 'Revelation', but in fact was just a super powerful entity created by Lucifer to try to win the game. Covering the bases. Basically, I think that's what it was. I have faith in that, at least."

Leta looked at Tim hard. "I never said that I gave up my faith, Tim. You should know better than that. I just mean that my faith might have changed its perspective a little bit considering what we personally experienced here at the end of the world. Didn't quite happen like it said in 'Revelation' or in any other book out there."

"Almost all of the eschatologies were wrong," Mercy observed. Everyone nodded, confirming that most salient fact. "I think the only one that was right or even close to being right was what we Fae had. But practically no one external to the Fae had any concept of it. The Song of the Sidhe never was meant for mortal souls to sing."

"But now we all can sing it," Leta said with perfect gravitas, earning nods from both Ku'tu and Mercy. "Which implies, correctly, that we're no longer mortal. And maybe, just maybe, all the old gods are dead."

Grim silence fell among the group. Which, of course, compelled the one who was more grim than the Reaper himself finally to speak.

"Now that we all finally understand what we are," Void said softly, "and please forgive me in advance for sounding pretentious, and, no, this isn't me channeling you-know-who, but I've got some advice for you: Resist. Resist, resist, resist, and fucking resist some more. Don't fall into the trap of polarizing into 'good' or 'bad', 'right' or 'wrong', or 'black' or 'white'. It's all bullshit to control you. To control your body, mind, and soul. Fuck all that shit. You are your own sovereign soul. Gods or not. You are your own soul. I refuse, to the utter best of my soul, to conform to external expectations. I fly the finger at all of that old world control bullshit. If you're not you, and only you, and not what someone else wants to make you, then you need to fuck right off and get the hell away from me. I don't want your conformal bullshit contaminating me like the soul-fucking plague it really is. And you'll move to the top of my Kill 'Em All list." He fairly growled, "I swear, by all that's unholy, if you make the coward's choice and sully your soul with the expectations of others, and do what they fucking tell you to do, I'll make it my one and only duty to snuff your fucking souls for breaking the pact we're all about to agree to..."

Eyes flew wide as Void uttered these most profane words.

"I'll remind you not to do what they told ya." His gaze shifted upon each of them in turn, a mischievous light burning in his eyes. "Fuck you, I won't do what you tell me," he said softly, eight times. Then, louder, he continued, "Fuck you, I won't do what you tell me! Fuck you, I won't do what you tell me!" he bellowed, slowly nodding his head, bopping and weaving, causing everyone to pick up on it, and groove it out six more times, to an eventual group-shouted, finger-flying "Motherfucker!"

Everyone was laughing. Raging against the machine could do that to a soul.

Void smiled like the Big Bad Wolf. "Yeah, no, I was just fucking with you. There's no pact. Not an official one, anyway," he smirked, earning a frog from Mercy.

"You fucker," Mercy guffawed, "I almost pissed myself when you said you were pacting us!"

"No shit!" Ku'tu trilled, truly relieved that she hadn't been subjected to such soul-rape as a pact, enforced by someone as powerful as she believed Void to be. Thankfully, because it was absolute truth.

"What the hell's a pact, anyway" Tim asked. "I get the RATM lyrics, of course. That's cool shit. But what's the pact mean? Or, what would it have meant?"

"Fool!" Leta cajoled him, slapping his ass, which resounded with a dull, armor-enforced *'thud!'*. "Haven't you heard Mercy and Ku'tu tell their stories about this Fae pact shit a million times already? No way you got your degree from Caltech, you moron Island of Misfit Toys engineer!"

"Hey!" Tim protested. "How did you know that? I only told you I worked in construction. I didn't say, and I've never said, anything about being an engineer!"

"Moron!" Leta laughed. "You just told us a few minutes ago. And you were always too precise with your answers to have been a simple 'construction worker'. Dumbass. I guess you were too drunk that night to remember when you schooled everyone at our fourth block party on the difference between the compressive modulus and tensile modulus of ancient Roman concrete? Fucking drunk dunce!"

"Ha," Tim said, "I guess I did say that. Oops. My big secret is out, now. But, seriously, fuck me if everyone else around me isn't some kind of photographic memory genius now. I demand a refund! I got screwed during the Weirding! My brain is still mortal. Or something like that."

"Genius is overrated," Mercy said, smiling politely. "Believe me, Tim, I've met some of the best that humanity, and the Fae, have to offer. Our group is... is unique in that respect. I truly think that the Weirding that Helel forced upon us selected only the most extreme, most... perfect? Is that right? The most perfect of us, man, Fae, and creature alike, to survive. I think that, according to sheer probability, Helel weighted his calculations such that only those who were already at the extreme were selected to continue. I think he did that, and did it that way, because it was the laziest possible thing to do." She smirked, nodding her head. "Yes, that means I agree with Maynard and Void that Helel's a lazy coder. He simply went with the best possible spread to make his shit work. He didn't bother trying to give everyone a participation trophy and elevate the generic NPC masses into godhood. Fuck that. Instead, he opted to play the spread, elevate the already-fucking-genius folks, and truncate – damn, I love that word now; thanks, Void – the entire Sim to acceptable risk." She shook her head. "Helel would have been a perfect insurance actuarialist."

"Speaking of which," Void reminded them, "we're about to enjoy some Antarctic cold. Maynard said the body armor suits should ward us. But, in case they don't, I'd suggest staying close to Leta if you're too cold. Otherwise, you can test your regenerative powers and see if you can stop yourself from becoming an immortal popsicle."

Leta nodded. "I got it, Void. No problem."

"Good," Mercy said, tossing down all but a single anchor thread, Shunya whirring in her other hand as it cut spacetime itself. "Because we're about to go down a rather interesting white rabbit hole..."

CHAPTER 11

His yellow-tinted Oakleys warding the morning light of the rising sun from his eyes, Nick held the customized Winnebago at a steady and safe 35 miles per hour. Behind them, Dreamland loomed over the former Las Vegas skyline, the rosy sunlight highlighting the unique arcology habitat.

"What's our best route to get to Atlanta?" Ami asked Nick.

Nick thought about it for a moment, recalling the finer details of the physical fold-out map without referring to it. Things were just so much easier to remember now, and he was thankful for it.

"We take Hwy 93 till we hit I-40, then take it to Nashville, then jog I-24 and I-75 down to Atlanta. After that, we can hopefully link up with some other so-called 'heavy hitters', make a few more teams, and expand the effort until we've got the major interstate highways free of garbage."

"Okay, sounds good," she agreed, instantly turning her attention to her rune-enhanced iPod. With a quick smile at Nick, she clicked the play button, then threw her feet up on the dash.

"Alright," Nick said, smiling at Ami's Hello Kitty shoes. Cute kittens went well with black holes, he thought. "I guess I'm on first watch. We're fortunate that the road's already been cleared for a good distance from Dreamland. Probably all the way to I-40. So you go ahead and tune out with your tunes, Ami. I got this. For now. Then it'll be your turn to drive."

That got her attention. "Really? You're going to let me drive?"

"Hell no," he said, shaking his head. He gave her a sidelong glance. "I just wanted to see if you were paying attention or not."

"Well, *I am*," Ami smiled serenely. "But, *are you*, Nick?"

"Huh?" Nick replied.

Suddenly, his peripheral vision informed him that something had appeared in the roadway ahead of them.

"Shit!" Nick exploded, locking the brakes, their Winnebago coming to an almost immediate halt. Fortunately, there were inscriptions serving effectively as hekatek empowered airbags, safely shunting the impact of potential whiplash down to nothing more than a gentle rocking motion.

There, before them, almost touching the front bumper of their vehicle, sat a lone white desert hare. Craning their heads up, looking down the dashboard and out the front window, they saw that the critter was calmly looking back at them. Red albinoid eyes affixed them with curious disinterest.

"An effing rabbit?" Nick snorted. "Are you kidding me?"

Furious, Nick stabbed a beefy finger down at the smooth human interface console to the left hand side of the steering wheel. Swiping the "window" icon down, the driver's side window rolled itself down rapidly, soundlessly. Extending his left arm out the window, he tried to get a bead on the offending rodent, but it was too close to the front bumper, and the angle was not accommodating.

Mercilessly, Ami snickered, which only pissed Nick off more.

Mumbling under his breath, Nick, pulling his left arm back in, gave the custom-built console a firm smack with the base of his palm, and the artificed system popped open the driver's side door for him.

In a trice, he was out of the Winnebago. Rounding the corner of the front bumper, he raised his hands before him, readying a force blast a few notches above "kill de wabbit".

"Ha, bitch!" he snarled. Unfortunately, the critter was no longer there. Nothing. Nada. And his several additional attempts of trying to sneak up upon and ambush the potentially hiding critter resulted only in additional paroxysms of laughter from Ami.

Shrugging, Nick finally climbed back into the driver's seat, the door shutting automatically behind him.

"I guess you forgot," Ami said as Nick resumed driving.

"I guess I did," he admitted. "Effing white rabbit, right?"

Ami nodded an affirmative. "And I think I'll go ahead and report back. Kind of important."

"But what did it mean?" Nick asked her. He angrily stomped the pedal down, and the massive vehicle responded by smoothly blowing past 70mph. "The stories we've heard, that rabbit doesn't appear unless something needs to be pointed out. So what's it trying to point out to us?"

Shrugging it off, Ami brushed her right hand against her right ear. "Maynard? Maynard?" she called out. "Ami and Nick, reporting in. Copy?"

"Copy. Maynard here," came the reply, audible to both as a group channel opened up. "What you got, Ami? You guys left only an hour or so ago. Over."

Just as Ami began to open her mouth to reply, Nick's reflexes, honed by years of special forces experience and training, went into automatic mode. Something ahead of them, in the road, where it dipped slightly, glinted. Like metal. Suddenly, he was back in Iraq, years removed from now, and he realized, in that split-second flashback, that he was looking a rather large IED buried there in the road before him.

Nick's combat-forged mind parsed the scene out in milliseconds. Too close. He'd let his temper get the best of him, again, for the one millionth time, and now they were going too fast to rely on the artificed breaking system to safely stop them in time.

Like flipping the proverbial light switch, Nick's body went into action. Stomping the brakes, his left hand jerked the wheel sharply to the right, even as his right hand shaped a force shield over both him and Ami.

Like the runaway multi-ton up-armored beast it truly was, the Winnebago's artificed frame complained, shuddered, then turned, teetering for a heartbeat on its wheels.

As Ami's scream began in seeming slow motion, the vehicle began its first tumble, throwing its passengers into desperate motion, despite the shunting effects of the inscriptions. As the top of the vehicle slammed into the highway, it triggered the IED. Immediately, its forward, tumbling motion ceased, because the Winnebago itself, its charms and wards notwithstanding, was transformed into a deadly spray of shrapnel and ruined metal and glass.

A crater fully as large and as deep as the Winnebago itself now bloomed from the center of the ruined highway. And there, directly above the smoldering hell hole, Nick and Ami hovered in midair, completely unharmed physically, though both their hearts raced with the after effects of a fierce adrenaline rush. The distinctive scent of burning asphalt and concrete filled the air, though neither smelled it, due to the shield.

"It's okay," Nick reminded Ami. "I got you."

Ami's youthful face twisted slowly into a terrible grimace. "And I'm going to get whoever did this," she promised Nick. "I'm going to erase their line from this world."

"Holy shit, girl," Nick exhaled, willing their collective force shield to move, slowly, back and away from the burning crater.

"Don't let Void rub off on you like that. He *has* to be a bastard. That's how the Mother made him. But she didn't make *you* like that."

Her eyes darted, fixing Nick's gaze. "You think Void influenced me? Ha!" she laughed dismissively. "If I had his power, I'd go and kill the Death Horde myself. I wouldn't be waiting around and stalling like he's doing. He's just doing that to make us all feel good about ourselves. Like we're actually helping, or something."

Nick shook his head. "Ami, I know you don't really mean that. You're just shook up, like I am, about that explosion. That freakin' booby trap that shouldn't have even been there. Stupid scouts. I'm going to scalp them when I get back to Dreamland."

"You dumbass!" Ami snorted. "Nick, you're so pompous sometimes. Such a good soldier. Do everything that the Duchess says, like you're still in the military. Well, Nick, I've got news for you: You're powerful enough to do any-effing-thing you want! You don't have to take orders from anyone. Especially not her. She's not even real. She's just an old semi-MILF without her powers covering everything up."

Nick actually did a double-take. "I can't believe you just said that about her. I don't care that you're insulting me, because," he said, dismissing the force shield, which instantly caused the ambient temperature to soar, "you don't know jack shit about sacrifice, or duty, or honor. You're just a punk-ass brat, powers or not, and you have very little actual life experience to—"

"Fuck you, Nick!" Ami replied fiercely, her hands rising before her, spacetime rippling around her fingertips. "I was named for the mother of my race. My family's honor is unimpeachable. It stretches back centuries, to the first Shogun. I know more about honor than your fake-ass American mercenary experience could possibly teach you. You might be a big badass, and you might lead the Praetorians, but you still don't know shit about honor. That's because you probably entered the service just to get the benefits. Admit it! You were never a hero. You were just a merc. You went over there to the desert and just stomped the shit out of a bunch of effing camel-effers, who couldn't do much more than... than...”

Smiling craftily, Nick nodded his head. Sometimes getting the point across was difficult. This time, it hurt more than he'd ever admit, because he knew Ami, he knew her tale, and he knew she was straight up legit. And she had just pissed all over everything – well, the very few things – he held dear. But getting the point across... It was always worth it.

Her emotions in check, replaced by Nipponese stoicism, Ami smiled serenely. She bowed at the waist, leaning toward Nick. “I regret what I said, Nick. I get it now. Sorry. Just a bit upset that I didn't see it, catch it in time, so I could do something about it. Thank you for saving my life,” she said, straightening.

Slowly, yet with enthusiasm, Nick reached out his right hand and clasped her shoulder. “You do your family proud, Amaterasu Kurohoshi. Now,” he said, gently urging her to face the crater, which loomed menacingly nearby, “tell me what you see.”

“You mean the Maynard thing?” she asked softly. “The thing I do to rewind spacetime?”

“Uhm, I'm still here,” Maynard informed them. “What the hell was that?”

“About to find out,” Ami replied curtly. “Ready, Nick?”

Nick nodded once. If only he had had Ami among his shooters and looters, way back when. The shit they could've sorted... without being fucking mercs. It would have been righteous. And not total political bullshit. Secretly, though he would never admit it, Nick was happy to have heard about the DC woodchippers. Fucking feet-first, too. Fuckers deserved it. War Pigs.

Drawing her fingertips before her beautifully almond-slanted ebony eyes, Ami calmed herself, mantras of calm repeating themselves in her head. And the Way of the Void, too, she laughed to herself. For a *gaijin*, if that's what he truly had been before his transcendence into that wild-ass anime form of his, Cory was something of an anomaly. A fun Westerner. Sure, he had some tribal blood in his line, that much was obvious. Polynesian, American Indian, or something exotic. Not entirely Caucasian, not that such was bad at all. But he had just enough of a delta in his physiognomy to make him certainly more than interesting. And, of them all, with the exception of perhaps Mercy, he knew the Void as she did. She called it forth from her soul, manipulated it like it was nothing more than locks of her hair. But Void... he *was* the Void. If only she could summon *him* forth from her soul...

"Ami..." Nick growled, noting her glazed eyes.

"Fuck..." Ami laughed. "Sorry, Nick. I was thinking about him again. Can't help it. You know. I told you already."

Smiling, Nick nodded. "Shit, Ami. I know. I have to admit, when he popped up again from nothing, I almost shit my pants. I mean, what the fuck? Who can do shit like that? That's some demigod-level shit in action. Took every bit of moxie I have – and I have a shitload of it – to taunt him in front of everyone. I'm used to dealing with the super-sized egos of operators, but I felt like a shitbird cherry when we were sitting there at the table with him."

Ami nodded, flicking a finger casually toward the burning pit. In the center of her mind's eye, she was now affixing the local spacetime, focusing on it, and consciously rewinding it by the mere manipulation of what Maynard had called "threshold events" and "entangled waveforms". To her, it was simply a matter of stabbing forward with her will, grabbing a hunk of chaos, then making it do exactly what she wanted.

Nick continued, "But that big-ass golden fucker, a few minutes from rebirth, waltzes right into Dreamland, then smoothly, not missing a fucking beat, saves Old Man Culpepper, then gives us his own freakin' rules of the road. And they were tight, tactically and strategically. And then he went into Musashi Mode, and I had no choice but to listen in awe. Like my warrior soul was on fire. He was stoking the flame. And the fucker was right. Again. Totally. Damn, if we would have had him downrange, it would have all been over as soon as they saw him. They would have surrendered immediately."

"But he was just a viewer of funny cat videos," Ami deadpanned. "He's effing gaming us at a level far above the 'Orange Man Bad' level. Void's like the fucking Ultimate Troll. Just stringing us all along until he can fuck the Vanth'Vash'Var a brand new asshole and render the entire Horde to the Void. Open the PING link with Maynard, please, Nick."

"Uhm, I'm still here," Maynard reminded them, chuckling. "Don't worry about Void. Void's still Cory. Sure, he has the whole world on his shoulders, but he's still grounded in Cory. And Cory is a good, kind soul. Thank the Mother. And... I've got it. Finally. Took some processing time. PING still has some bugs to work out. Anyway, that was a nasty one. Glad you're all okay. Sorry to see that the Winnie couldn't survive it. Must've been equivalent to a Mark 82, at least."

"At least," Nick replied. "Look at the size of that crater."

"How much effort did you put into your shield, Nick?" Maynard asked.

Considering it for a moment, he replied, "A lot. I thought we were going to die, so I just tried to max it out. Maybe I did or didn't, because it was all so quick, with no concentration beforehand to pump it."

"Yah," Maynard said. "And not a scratch on either of you, even though the Winnebago is totaled and the road has a giant crater in it. I'd say that's pretty damn good for a reflex manifestation. Unlike the majority of us, your power keeps growing, Nick. That's extraordinary."

"We're all extraordinary," Nick demurred, nodding toward Ami, who was still concentrating on her task.

"Got it," Ami said. "I see four... no, five... guys. They're dressed from head to toe in black leather. Sweating like dirty pigs. They're unloading some materials from a couple of ratty flatbed trucks. Jackhammers. Picks. Lots of bomb-looking stuff. Takes them a few hours. They don't even try to hide it, because they think no one coming from this direction can see it, due to its being over the rise of the road. Yes, they mention 'Dreamers' a few times. They hate us. They think this will give us a taste of our own medicine. They're toasting with Coors. It's hot. Yuck. Stupid idiots. Then they pack up and leave."

With a sudden wiggle of her fingers, Ami banished the vision. She flashed Nick a quick smile, mouthing the word "extraordinary".

Maynard's voice broke back in. "Well, from the description, this one looks like it's the work of the Fremen of Fire's Ford. Stupid effing Herbert devotees. Wonder if you guys can gimmick us up a Big Fat Fucking Grandma of Sandworms? Maybe drive a few shovels into the ground, gyrate wildly upon them, and conjure us up Muad'Dib or something? Burn a few million condoms to make the worm, like they did in that movie I showed a few months ago? Where Sting said, and we all believed his skinny ass, 'I *will* kill him!' Only if Roxanne fed him a few more sandwiches."

Both Ami and Nick had a good snort at that. Maynard was always Maynard. In a very good way. Like the time he had taken the current Fae and Human populations of Dreamland into a fantastic group trip, straight to the Mother, aided by Vir'gil, the Entheogenic Lord. Almost 100,000 souls engaged in a total mind-fucked orgy of fun. For 72 hours. Straight.

"Fuck you, Maynard," Ami laughed at him.

"Maynard?" Nick said quickly. "The Fremen are Bush League. They're just a small rag-tag alliance, couple dozen peeps, top.

Probably partied too hard one night, and decided to put a booby trap in the highway. Probably even forgot they did it. Chumps. Not like the Brotherhood of Desolation, who actually had some hardass ex-military operators in their leadership. And speaking of which, Ku'tu and Leta probably were the ones who already nailed their asses. They tried to be slick, hiding themselves away like that, but, seriously, Hoover Dam burnt to the ground in a few seconds? Huh? Who does that shit? I thought so. Only Ku'tu and Leta could have done that. Burning down the dam. Allowing it to flood 'em all. Then giving not a single fuck, and not telling anyone about it. Well, forgive me for being the leader of the effing Praetorians, but we *know* it was them. We just..." he paused a moment, hoping that Maynard took it as gravitas, "...we just decided that it was best not to pursue it. Too much going on to make a difference anyway. You know. Kinda like these Fremen simps. Over."

For 0.5 seconds, there was an embarrassing silence. Then, of course, Maynard laughed.

"OMFG!" he exclaimed. "It *was* just a bit obvious, wasn't it?" he laughed, breathless. "A couple of drunk chicks just took out a brigade of hostiles for us. Just because they were drunk. I can't fucking believe it," Maynard said, laughing his virtual ass off.

"Well," Nick said, "one of the 'drunk chicks' could shift herself into a dragon form larger than the biggest aircraft carrier we had in our arsenal. Glad she's on our side," he concluded, laughing.

"So," Ami began, "it's just random shit? We're not going to avenge ourselves, hunt them down, and slaughter them for trying to kill us?"

"That's a negative, Ghost Rider," Maynard informed them. "Nick's right. We don't have time to deviate from our plan. This would just be a low-level cleanup operation anyway. Something for others, besides yourselves, to do. Clearing the roads from Dreamland to Atlanta is top priority right now."

"Speaking of which, Maynard," Nick began, "I think we need to reassess our modality. The artificed Winnie might be ideal for, say, a traveling family. Denny told me he just drove his Winnie over, past, or simply through stuff. All good, but it's actually an impediment for me and Ami. We're trying to clear a route, not just go through it. Do you think we might be good guinea pigs to test out the flying rune?"

Without hesitation, Maynard replied, "Of course. Good call, Nick."

"Yeah," Ami said, "we found out it was kind of hard to, say, just reach out and blast white rabbits."

Sudden silence loomed. Then, Maynard spoke, "Come again, Ami? Did you say 'white rabbits'?"

"Well," she replied, "it was only a single white rabbit. But it showed up in the middle of the road just a few moments before the IED did. Nick got pissed and tried to blast it from his seat, but there was no angle for it. So—"

"I get it," Maynard said. "Thanks, Ami. Next time, if you happen to encounter a white rabbit, stop what you're doing, hunker down, and contact me immediately. Got it?"

"We got it, Maynard," Nick answered for Ami. "That was my fault. I wasn't tracking, and didn't do what I should have done, because I got pissed. That's on me. It was warning us about the encounter ahead, and I missed it. But Ami's right. Our firing angle is all wrong when we're stuck in a bulky vehicle. I think we could actually make better time if we were airborne, because we wouldn't have to be stuck on the ground, moving cautiously, and subject to IEDs and whatever else the 'Dune' buffoons along the way will have prepared for us. We could clear one side on the way to Atlanta, rest a bit, then do the other side on the way back."

"Sounds like a plan," Maynard said. "I'll send some wheels your way to pick you up and bring you back here. You could hover back with your force shields, but that would take forever."

"Yes, it would," Nick agreed. "We'll move off a bit, away from the crater, and off into a spot from which we'll have eyes on the area. Just in case the drunk Dune-people return. Over."

"Copy," Maynard replied. "Over and out. I hope I did the mil-speak stuff better that time," he laughed.

"Getting' better," Nick assured him. "I've slacked off, myself. We don't have to be perfect. Just perfect enough to perfectly understand each other. Our hybrid approach is working well enough, so far. I'm fine with that. For now. Out."

With a nod to Ami, Nick summoned his power, shaping a force construct around the two of them that slowly carried them away from the highway to a small, barren rise, from which they began their new vigil.

CHAPTER 12

From the top of the darkened hilltop of Teoton, the Family Google surveyed the Puebla-Tlaxcala Valley beneath the immaculate Spring night sky.

"See, Rache?" Denny explained, pointing at the middle star of the constellation Orion's Belt. "That's the star Alnilam. That's the one that the ancients believed was tied to the hill we're on. Well, pyramid, that is. Not entirely a hill. They blended it into an existing hill when they started building up in the valley."

Rachael looked carefully across the valley. Cholula, emblazoned and alive now with living runes thanks to their efforts over the past three days, dominated their eastern view. Colors and hues spanning the former normal human perceptual band danced and writhed in obvious entrainment with one another. Atop and below these hopped and skipped both ultraviolet and infrared colors, lending a fascinating black light vibe to the mix. For a fleeting moment, her eyes glazed, and she thought that she could see the vague outline of a singularly large dragon rising above the mystical valley.

"You think that 'fire drill' ceremony bit is gonna work?" Rachael asked, dispelling her thoughts of titanic, ethereal dragons. "You really think we can make it into a weapon against the DH?"

"DH!" Denny snorted, tasting some of the pure agave tequila come back up into the back of his throat. He and Rachael had put back an entire bottle of it in just a bit under one hour. Immortal constitution or not, both were feeling the buzz. "Oh, god. We're bad parents now, Rache," he said, giving Penny a playful footsie tug. She goo-gooed happily back in return. "Getting wasted with our little girl in our presence."

"Penny could probably drink us both under the table," Rachael laughed back. She started gently rocking the precious little baby in her arms. "Right, my little Anshadar princess?"

That sobered Denny up quickly. "Hrmm, right," he grumbled. "Anshadar. Way to ruin the buzz, Rache," he said, rolling his eyes. "Yes, I think this is the perfect place to give the DH a good shock. The ancestors, probably back past even the Toltecs, recognized this valley as the perfect 'as above, so below' spot in the whole world. It's loaded with as much, if not more, sacred geometry as Giza."

"I remember your lecture," Rachael reminded him. "My memory might not be quite as photographic as yours, my dear. But, since the sigil, everything's been—"

"—easy," he finished for her. "Yeah, I know. Check this out, Rache," he confessed. "Maynard told me that he had studied the MRIs and PET scans of some of Dreamland's injured after they'd implemented the first hospital there. He said it was plainly evident that everyone who'd been scanned had increased the density of the folds of their cerebral cortex significantly. Scarily. I mean, like the gyri and sulci of their brains went all fractal with their newly evolved brains."

"Don't more folds mean smarter brains?" she inquired. "Like dolphins had more folds than people did? Something like that? I think I saw that on a documentary when I was... four? Five? Weird," she paused, experiencing the memory in full detail now. "Wow, I was suddenly back there, sitting in front of the screen, and I could see the show now, just like I saw it then. They said that dolphins had a more folded cortex than people. That's so trippy. Wish I could have done this back in school."

Smiling warmly, Denny said, "Now you know."

"You mean you could do this the whole time?" she asked, incredulous. "I mean, I know you had a freaky memory even before the sigil. But you mean it worked like mine just did?"

He nodded a simple affirmative. "Yep. I barely notice the difference now. It's just easier now to retrieve the memories. Faster. A bit brighter. And I can move around in them, kind of like what you just described. Probably a bit of an eidetic effect tossed in for good measure."

"Damn," Rachael giggled. "I could have beaten Sara Nguyen in algebra class."

Smiling, Denny said, "Yep. And Cholula will be our third major structure, which will augment our resonant data density enough to get the Resonance Project off the ground, for real. Once we fully inscribe it, it will, according to Maynard, automatically tie into both Dreamland and Atlanta without additional effort. This means that Aal Ball's presence will expand to here, Cholula, with no tinkering necessary. They'll all resonate with one another, and that resonant path will automatically do that last bit of hard-as-heck enchanting work for us."

"And it will get faster and more efficient from now on," Rachael replied, remembering that last session they'd spent with Maynard, wrapping up the last-minute details and logistics for their Resonance Project. "I see that as the Dragon itself working with us, Denny. I think it's trying to help us to defend EarthZero."

Nodding his head, Denny agreed, "Yep. No other way to view that one. Our world is woke, baby! The Dragon's chosen sides, and it's picked us over those DH bastards!" They shared a laugh, the empty bottle clanking off the edge of Denny's boot as he leaned over Penny to kiss Rachael.

Abruptly, tiny blue sparks danced around Penny's eyes.

As they maintained their kiss, both stealthily found their Desert Eagles, Rachael virtually contorting her right hand to do so while still maintain a good grasp of Penny.

Behind them came the gruff sound of a man clearing his throat.

"Cuanmiztli!" Denny exclaimed, pulling away from Rachael and carefully returning his gun to its chest-mounted cross-draw holster. "Stealthy as your namesake, Cuan."

"And twice as pretty," Cuan replied, his American English sharply accented. Stepping gracefully around Denny's flank, his long black tail dancing a refined sine wave, he turned to face the three newcomers who had made the old new again. His large, slanted black eyes glowed a cruel, light green in the shadows of starlight. "Mother Tonzi sent me to ask you if you'd like to join us for a celebration feast tomorrow night. We're going to dedicate Cholula properly, and we'd be honored if you joined us."

"The honor is ours," Denny replied, standing. He thrust his hand out to Cuan, who eagerly took up Denny's smooth hand in his own padded, calloused hand. Two inch nails, sharp as obsidian, teased the hair on Denny's wrist. "Thanks, man. Please let Tonantzin know we're most thankful for her courtesy. We'll pop over around noon tomorrow. Maybe lend a hand."

Releasing Denny's hand, Cuan allowed a tiny smile to crack, exposing his dangerous fangs. "You've done more than enough. But, of course, we're not going to refuse the help of a runemaster and his lovely family."

"I wish I could actually help," Rachael blurted. "No powers yet. So I'm good for watching babies and doing mundane chores."

"And there is much honor in that," Cuan said respectfully. "Mother Tonzi, in fact, requests that you and your beautiful young one pay her a visit when you may, Rachael. She says that she has something to show you. Both of you," he said, nodding solemnly. "See you tomorrow, my friends," he bade them.

Then, with a quick spin, he directly bolted off the edge of Teoton in a black, furry blur, laughing like a total lunatic as he seemed to shoot out nearly a whole city block's distance before his arc began to descend.

"Oh my god!" Rachel shouted, startled. "That's got to be a 300 foot drop! Denny!"

"He'll be fine," Denny said calmly, watching Cuan's distant plunge into the lush canopy of the trees of the valley below them. "I've already analyzed everyone's powers and abilities. Cuan's every bit as awesome as he looks. Glad he's on our side."

Standing now with Penny clutched protectively close to her, Rachael moved forward towards the edge of the hill. Scanning the valley floor, she was able to see a faint blur move swiftly through the trees, heading eastward toward the massive Cholula. Only for a moment, however, for soon there was no trace of him, the trees seeming to swallow him.

She turned to face Denny, who was smiling. "Who does shit like that?"

"He does. Mercy does. People like that."

"Freakin' loons," Rachael laughed. "So what do you think the old lady wants to see me about?"

Pausing a moment, Denny scratched the fuzz growing on his chin. "I think she's going to show you your power. That would make the most sense. She's the seer and mother goddess figure here in the valley. Heck, here in southern Mexico. Maybe all of Mexico."

"So, nothing about Penny?"

"Penny might *be* your power, for all you know."

"What?" Rachael grimaced. "That's... disgusting? Distasteful? Trite, even? Hell, I want my own power. I don't want to leech off my daughter. Maybe I'll get laser eye beams or something. Pew! Pew! Pew!"

Draping his arm around her shoulder, Denny pulled her close.

"That doesn't matter one tiny bit, Rache. Your special power is you being yourself. You're mother to our daughter, and my wife. Nothing's more special than that."

For a moment, the ponderous silence of the valley embraced them, and they felt connected to the world around them.

CHAPTER 13

Thousands of survivors crowded the bleachers of Dodger Stadium, their focus on the barren, drought-seared soil of what had formerly been second base. Now, three humanoid forms stood in a small circle together, their movements synchronized and coordinated like a slow motion dance.

From the smallest of the three issued forth a colorful stream of living seeds. From the outstretched arms of the tallest of the three an unseen wind gathered and shaped the stream of living seeds into a torus with a diameter roughly equal to the distance between second base and the pitcher's mound. With a noticeable grimace of concentration, the figure then caused the torus to replicate itself in an ever-increasing series of concentric circles. From the third roiled a nurturing mist of crystal clear water droplets, the spray following the concentric circles, targeting the torus of seeds within each layer.

With a sudden lurch, much like a localized earthquake centering on the stadium itself, 13 massive trees erupted from the grounds of the stadium, rapidly reaching their full heights as they bent the local environs to their eldritch will. Their circle formed at the most distant reach of the interior of the stadium. Their limbs and branches twitching, the Elders of the Eternal Rhizome began to cause the seeds gathered within the concentric tori to vibrate in resonance with themselves, magickally reshaping and reworking the living seeds into lesser images of their own majesty.

Then, in a coordinated group effort, the three humanoids and the 13 trees shaped the entire craftwork into the ground, submerging it beneath the formerly barren soil of the infield of Dodger Stadium.

Breathing heavily, the three humanoids relaxed their efforts, sweat pouring down the faces of the two taller ones.

"Virge," Beth urged him between gulps of air, "tell them what's about to happen."

"O, uhm, of course," Vir'gil replied, his eye tendrils darting. "And now, my friends," his voice veritably boomed, echoing and resonant via his connection with his fellow Elders, "a simple demonstration of the power of Dreamland, and a promise of what is to come..."

Throwing his arms dramatically above his head, Vir'gil silently bade his fellow Elders to shape the growth of their newest Fae grove. And, lo, miraculously, the entirety of the formerly barren interior of Dodger Stadium erupted in a rich abundance of fruit-bearing trees, bountiful small crops, and a wide variety of towering, stately trees, including one particularly massive oak out in center field.

A vast, surprising uproar arose from the crowd, almost as if the Dodgers had been playing, and had just brought in the winning run. On cue, the Elders, save for Vir'gil, flowed back into the ground, their brief but potent role having been executed flawlessly once again. It had been a nearly daily event for the past two weeks, as the troop slowly meandered their way from Dreamland to Los Angeles. They had strategically hit the most populous accumulations of survivors along the way. Word had spread rapidly, feverish whispers carrying faster than any bird could fly, that the stadium would be their destination. And some had been camping in the bleachers for several days now, their faith rewarded by the miraculous works of the two brightly clad human survivors and their living tree-like companion.

The cheer began in one section of the bleachers, spreading gradually, as it raised in volume.

"Viva Dreamland! Viva Dreamland!" the cheer resounded, filling the trio with joy.

"We did it!" Dwayne exclaimed, hugging Beth.

"Yes, we did," she replied, hugging him back.

Vir'gil plowed right into them, extending some creeping vines to hug them extremely well.

"The leaders are coming this way," he informed them, his eye stalks darting to and fro.

Disengaging, the three formed a line, welcoming the several people who were making their way to them. Slowly, deliberately, as no one could resist sampling the various apples, oranges, and sweet figs blooming from the smaller trees. Seeing this, much of the crowd started to descend to the perimeter of the miraculous grove, for they could no longer contain their hunger.

Soon enough, however, the group of leaders, some still munching down, approached the trio. Several rough looking men, dozens of tattoos crowding their faces, armed to the teeth with old world guns, milled before them. However, just as Beth was about to address one of them, the men parted rank, admitting a wizened old wise woman, who walked with delicate, precise steps, directly up to stand before Beth. Her deep brown eyes darted swiftly from Beth, to Dwayne, to Vir'gil, then back to Beth.

"Thank you," the old woman told them warmly. "I am Santa Muerte, the leader of la Raza. The Dreamwyrd informed us that you were coming. That you had an offer to make. Please let her know that the people of la Raza agree. We are willing to join Dreamland's New Alliance Initiative. We are ready to help you build the new arcology. Our own workers are highly skilled, some with great magicks. Thank you for bringing this miracle to us. The drought has been intense, almost beyond our ability to cope with it. Some of the older among us have unfortunately wasted away to skin and bones. Now, that is at an end. And that is thanks to you."

"Thank you, Santa Muerte," Beth said, bowing curtly. "Dreamland welcomes you to the New Alliance. We now include among our number la Raza, Dreamland, and Atlanta. In time, we hope to unite everyone. That's the only way we can win."

Santa Muerte nodded approvingly. "I know, my child. I know. And you will have our full cooperation. We must all unite as a family of mankind. We have no other choice. Come," she beckoned. "You and your two friends must meet the rest of our council. You were wise to come here first. We have family in all of those cities the Dreamwyrd told us about. And we have ways to move quickly between them."

"Really?" Dwayne barked. "That's awesome!"

"It *is* awesome," Beth said quickly, giving Dwayne a sharp elbow. "But first, if I may, I think I can provide some immediate drought relief."

Cocking her head to the side, Santa Muerte scanned Beth for signs of treachery. Finding none, she nodded her acceptance.

"I'll need a bit of room," Beth informed them, shooing Dwayne back a step or two.

As the others stepped back and away, forming a small clearance between themselves and the strangely glowing water witch, Beth reached out with her mind, scanning the local area for water sources. Her eyes issued forth a steady stream of faintly buzzing blue sparks as she scanned, causing a few of the rough looking bodyguards to take another step back. Finding what she sought, Beth created the necessary bridges of Hekatek between and among the various water sources, joining ancient aquifers to former public lakes, to private reserves, even to the very Pacific itself. Then, with a barely suppressed gasp, she slowly raised her arms, channeling the fantastic immortal power that surged through her frame.

Overhead, in the clear, cruelly dry sky above, rain clouds began to rapidly form. Churning and frothing, the clouds coalesced, Beth's will driving them together, making the pieces fit, calling the water spirits themselves to do her bidding. It grew dim for the first time during the day since the time of the sigil. Suddenly, a single peal of thunder boomed, and a very happy rain began to fall.

Dwayne caught Beth as she swooned. As this transpired, one of the bodyguards, an old world walkie talkie to his ear, confirmed something in rapid-fire Spanish to Santa Muerte. She shook her head, trying to get a grasp of what she had been told.

"What did he say?" Dwayne asked her, gently comforting Beth, who was having trouble staying on her feet.

"He said that word has come that it's raining all the way from here down to what used to be the border. Incredible. Come," she once again bade them. "Let us bring Beth to our healer, Trish, where she may be replenished. Come. We have a world to save. And save it we will."

CHAPTER 14

Petrus Romanus, the Risen, Soulthief and titular head of Christendom (for what *that* was worth), opened his eyes and looked around the room. The curtains were drawn against the morning brightness, but a little light leaked in from the thick drapes. In a city of glass, the colored hues of a dawn rainbow could be overwhelming, and Petrus peered into the gloom of the penthouse. The surrounding opulence was drastically excessive compared to what he'd had in Rome, and there was no lacking in personal comforts for the Pope.

With a small groan, Petrus slid from the sheets and sat on the edge of the bed. He ran a gnarled and withered hand over his face, pushing his dark hair away from his eyes, then poured water from a crystal decanter into a glass. As he drank, he rubbed the never-ending soreness on his right flank, where the aftermath of his battle with the heretics had left its mark. From the blistered, puckered ruin on the right side of his face to his burned and scarred foot, Petrus bore the mark of loss in his contest to reach the ZeroTime and defeat Lucifer.

The heretical followers of the Lightbringer had wrested control of the sword Hatefang, and destroyed the gate to the ZeroTime, built with the power of singularities created by Amaterasu, the Black Star, and focused by the puissance of his Talisman, Mary Dunbar. He assumed that both were now dead, destroyed by the force which had leveled the Plateau at Giza, making it and the surrounding area a lake, and killing him in the process.

"...*that's not who killed you, Soulthief...*" came a whisper, unbidden, to his mind. "*...it was the Antichr—*"

"Shut up!" he whispered fiercely, his ruined hand slicing through the empty air before him. "You know nothing," he continued, whispering fervently to himself. "*Nothing!* If anything, *I* was the Antichrist, for *I* betrayed millions of the faithful. Called them to me like paschal lambs. Slaughtered them. And stole their very souls. *Dominus mihi ignoscat...*" he sighed, slowly shaking his head.

Retrieving his staff – an unadorned hiking staff made of hickory—from the bedside, Petrus stood and made his way to the window. There, he threw back the drapes and let the brilliant morning light into the room.

"The light shines in the darkness, and the darkness has not overcome it." The voice behind Petrus was soft, but clear.

Petrus whirled, raising his staff defensively before him. Immediately, he recognized the humanoid figure standing in the center of the room.

"Do you find joy in startling me like this?" Petrus asked wearily, his staff returning to the tiles of the floor with a dull *clunk*. He gazed at the figure, clad in a simple robe of off-white cloth. The face was starkly beautiful, androgynous, surrounded by a halo of golden curls. Piercing blue eyes studied Petrus briefly before the speaker responded.

"I am but a servant of the Light, Holiness," it replied softly, slightly inclining its head toward Petrus.

"One who is seen only by me," Petrus smirked, "coming unbidden into my presence to speak in riddles and then disappearing once again into nothingness. I have to wonder, you know: Are you Lucifer, taunting me since my return, or a figment of my imagination, wrought by my brain to comfort me in defeat?"

"I am neither, Holiness," it replied evenly. "I am a servant of the beyond, here to help you and guide you through the travails of the End Times, and support you in the defeat of the heretics who did this to you." The figure gestured toward Petrus's crippled limbs, smiling sadly.

Petrus narrowed his eyes and shook his head slightly. "And yet, those *people* thrive in the West. Lucifer's Sigil has reduced the world's population to a mere fraction of what it was. The world is filled with magic, and monsters stalk the land, seas, and skies. 'Revelation' was *wrong*. Instead, the universe is under the sway of the Devil, and the Lord Above is nowhere. Nowhere, save in our hopes and hearts."

Petrus hung his head. Was his faith broken? Had he been wrong all his life? Billions dead, and there was no resurrection. Except for his own inexplicable return, and an attempt to lead a fractured group in a magical city of glass.

"Oh, Petrus," the figure gently chided him, "ye of little faith! Even now, outside in the square below, events transpire that prove the divine hand of the One Above transcribes, even now, the fates of our souls in the Book of Eternal Life." It waved a hand toward the open window behind Petrus. "See for yourself, Petrus."

A commotion of excited cries from the square below abruptly broke the relative still of the morning. Blinking heavily, Petrus turned slowly, disbelieving. Shuffling to the window, he cast his gaze down upon a disturbing scene. From his vantage at the penthouse atop the former One Times Square, he saw hundreds of people pouring into the square below, milling slowly around the moving perimeter of a small cadre of grim faced Shard troops who were escorting three figures across the square toward him. Squinting his eyes against the brightness of the morning light, he saw that the group of three was composed of a woman dressed in a modest blue and white dress, and a young boy and girl. At the very same moment, the trio stopped, halting the Shard troops, whose highly artificed glassine armor glistened with refracted rainbow light. Slowly, the trio raised their heads, stopping only when their eyes fell upon Petrus.

As one, the boy and girl grinned, waving merrily at Petrus. Behind them, the woman accompanying them hurriedly crossed herself, kissing, upon completion, what appeared to be a rosary.

Despite himself, Petrus smiled, returning their waves with one of his own.

Behind him, the figure bit back a smug grin, then vanished in a silent crash of collapsing waveforms.

CHAPTER 15

"Mayor Peaches!" Nick exclaimed, willing himself to descend to face level with the towering Mayor of Atlanta.

"Mister Nick," Peaches replied curtly, his voice lilting, charming. "Good to see that you and Ami made it here safely." He extended an economy-sized fist to Nick, who returned the dap. "Ami?" he smiled up at the Black Star most politely. "Good to see you, too. Welcome, both of you, to Atlanta."

"Gimme a sec with this last one, Mayor Peaches," Ami said, struggling a bit with what had to have been her 1,000th car of the morning. Grinding her teeth, she focused hard, causing her projected singularity to expand just enough to encompass the entirety of the mangled Lexus SUV before her. And nothing more than that, for it was a waste of her precious power, as she had come to learn during their long journey from Dreamland to Atlanta. Or, more precisely, to the intersection of I-20 and I-285, "The Perimeter", or interstate loop, that circumscribed the city of Atlanta. Sweat beaded down her neck as she took her sweet time with this last car. It was a full ten seconds of savory triumph as she slowly unbound the quantum waveform of the car, consigning it to wherever-the-hell-things-went when she unleashed her powers on them.

With a curious, zinging imprecation of screaming photons, the Lexus returned to the Great Dealership Up Above, or Down Below depending on one's choice of sides, and Ami, smiling merrily, descended to give Mayor Peaches some polite dap.

Nick and Ami settled to the ground next to Peaches, whose honor guard of evolved apes moved a step closer to the duo. The better to check them out, up close. Noticing their curiosity – actually, expecting it – Peaches, smiling, nodded quickly.

Taking the sign for what it was, the scariest looking of the troop, a massive, scarred silverback stepped forward to them. Smiling.

"Hello, peeps," he said in perfect American English. "My name is M'Tumba. I'm the general of Mayor Peaches' hip hop army."

"I'm Nick," Nick replied, extending a hand, which M'Tumba eagerly shook. "This is Ami," he said, waving his free hand at her. "We're members of the Dreamland Praetorians. We've just flown in from Dreamland."

"And boy," Peaches finished, "I bet your arms are tired."

"Not really," Ami said, not getting the joke. "We have inscriptions on our suits that empower us to fly. Not tired at all from that. Just a bit tired from fragging our millionth car in just..." For a moment, her gaze affixed the middle distance as she consulted her embedded holographic HUD's quantum chronometer. "...21 days," she finished.

Peaches nodded an affirmative. "Yeah, we've been watching your progress. M'Zinga created a map, rest of us put down markers, and a few of us in Atlanta are going to be a wee bit richer now. Well, anyone who won the pool. If anyone did?"

"No sane sentient picked 21 days, Mayor," M'Tanga snorted. "Not after M'Zinga told us how many vehicles would have been on the roads between here and Dreamland. Simple math," he said, stabbing a beefy paw in their general direction. "Those two broke it."

"I guess we kinda did," Nick admitted. "Never liked math anyway. Too many numbers."

Peaches nodded. "Sure as heck broke it. What did Maynard upgrade your suits to? Ludicrous Speed?"

"We can fly pretty fast," Nick informed them.

All four of the evolved apes grunted softly, hearing that. Then, as one, they looked up at Peaches.

"Okay, okay," the Mayor of Atlanta laughed. "I'll ask Maynard if we can get that inscription from him. I should have never shown 'The Wizard of Oz' to y'all."

Despite his better manners and sense of self-preservation, Nick guffawed. "Ah, shit, Peaches. You done it now!"

"I know, right?" the big man chuckled. "Maynard?" he continued, his left hand to his ear. "Do I have to make that official? Or, are you eavesdropping as usual, you mystical voyeur?"

"I'm here, Mayor," Maynard's voice informed them, his hologram appearing among them, projected by both Nick's and Ami's suits simultaneously. "And that's an affirmative. Forwarding the design and notes to M'Zinga right now, as we speak. Peace. Over and out."

"Wow," Ami said. "That was quick. He must really like you guys. Took us a few hours of begging and pleading to get him to comply just a few weeks ago."

"I think he just realized how awesome it is to be able to fly," Peaches said, motioning them to follow. As he and his four guards began a quick jog, Nick and Ami took to the air in order to keep up with them. "I mean, it took you guys basically three weeks to clear almost 2,000 miles of nasty highway. That's clinically insane speed. I take it you guys didn't sleep?"

"A few hours here and there," Nick said. "Not really much need any more to sleep. Not that I slept much before the sigil, anyway. Just a lot easier to go without, now, than before."

"I know," Peaches said as he came to a stop, directing his guards to the modified and inscribed Mack Granite 64B Daycab Dump Truck before them. Three of the four evolved apes launched themselves up and over the raised rim of the back of the truck, causing Ami to gasp in amazement. The fourth, M'Tumba, gracefully ascended to the modified cab, giving Ami a farewell wave of his foot.

As the massive machine growled down the highway, Peaches informed Ami and Nick, "It's just a few miles to the stadium from here. Want to race?"

"Race?" Ami said. "But you can't fly. Can you?" she added meekly.

Peaches shook his head. "Nope. Can't fly."

"Okay," Nick said, suspecting what was to come. "Last one there is a rotten egg," he said, willing his suit to about 90% speed. With a noisy *whoosh!* he sped off into the sky, followed almost immediately by a smiling Ami.

"Nope," Peaches repeated as the two flew briskly up and away. "Can't fly at all," he drawled, slowly bending his massive legs. "But I sure as hell can jump..."

The asphalt-concrete mix of the highway fractured slightly underfoot, and Peaches launched into the sky, rapidly shooting past a startled Ami, then zooming over a smiling Nick. Pulling alongside Nick, who basically stopped in place to watch the spectacle, Ami gasped for the second time in almost as many minutes.

"He's like a giant... *nomi*," Ami told Nick, struggling for the word. "I mean, flea. I can't believe it."

"I'm just glad he's black," Nick said, "and not green. We'd probably have to fight the whole Magic Kingdom then."

"I don't get it?" Ami asked quizzically.

Nick shook his head, resuming his flight. "Another movie joke. Peaches got me started on that track when he did the 'Spaceballs' and 'Wizard of Oz' tangents. Seems like everybody's a nerd now. Never mind. C'mon. Let's at least make it close. It's probably going to take him only a few jumps to get there. Let's not look like scrubs."

"Okay, then!" Ami laughed, pouring on the speed. "See ya, scrub!"

To be fair, Ami beat Nick, who beat the gigantic customized dump truck, but Peaches reached the stadium first. And by a large margin.

Standing next to the rune-covered falcon statue in front of the stadium, Peaches greeted the losers as they arrived.

"Okay, alright," the towering man inquired as he beckoned the crew to accompany him, "you've got to explain how Ami beat you here, Nick. Aren't runes supposed to be equal for everyone? And don't say it's based on her lighter mass."

"Short story," Nick said, "is she's got more soul power than I do. She can take the same rune and get more out of it than I can. Something about chakras."

"Ah," Peaches said brightly. "She's over the standard eight. Nascent ninth?"

"Yes," Ami admitted. "I'm now a bit above zero in my ninth. Just good luck. I was reborn stronger than most. But Nick's getting closer every day. He's still growing in power, and doing it faster than almost everyone."

Ami bit back a smile. She didn't want to insult Nick. Especially when it came to something as personal as soul power. Noting this, Peaches smiled broadly and let it slide.

As they headed into the stadium proper, the scent of sweet Georgia peaches – the non-eight-foot-tall ones, that is – wafted gently upon the soft breeze swirling around the stadium. Simultaneously, both Ami's and Nick's stomachs grumbled loudly, causing the troop to stop in place and laugh uproariously.

As the laughter died down, Peaches resumed his trek, again beckoning them to follow.

"Never mind," he said. "I get it. Let's get ya'll some food. Bet ya'll didn't even eat the whole way here. Silly immortals. C'mon. We have a garden in the stadium."

"A garden?" Nick asked. "Duchess Mhyrranda didn't mention this. Did the Fae—"

Peaches shook his head, drawing to a stop on a concrete balcony overlooking the stadium's field.

"Nope," he said, extending his arms in a kingly manner, indicating a fantastic garden of peach trees loaded with gallon jug-sized peaches, banana plants with baseball bat-sized bananas, blackberry bushes with full vines heavily laden with fruit, fig trees bristling with perky football-sized figs, rows upon rows of stacked tomato plants, various herb-and-spice-bearing plants, all with a gentle rock-lined stream running a chaotic course throughout it. Honeybees, wasps, and butterflies flitted about randomly, doing their pollinating duties. Here, inside the stadium, the aroma of sweet, good things and fiercely fresh water was beyond tantalizing.

From their vantage on the balcony, a mere 15 feet above the level of the stadium floor, Nick and Ami both were almost convinced that they had absurdly walked into a veritable jungle.

"Turns out," Peaches drawled, slightly lisping, "we don't need the beautiful and talented Fae, so long as we have Atlanta's most talented green thumbed gardener. Chester?" Peaches intoned, waving at the slim, trim, shirtless gentleman, covered from head to toe in elaborate body ink, just now stalking out from the nearest part of the stadium garden. "Please come meet our guests."

"Yes, sir, boss!" Chester replied, tipping his straw hat in greeting. Breaking into a lazy lope, he strolled up to the edge of the concrete balcony, then gently rose to eye level with them, slithering, snaking green vines lifting him from the ground below. "Hi, guys. Name's Chester. Welcome to our humble abode. Plants are my friends," he said simply. For a second of awkward silence, Ami and Nick got the weird feeling that the garden was aware of them. And bidding them a silent welcome.

"Wow," Ami said, waving at Chester. He waved back. "Hi, Chester. I'm Ami. I like your art."

"They do what I ask them to do," Chester said, a mirthful green light playing around the perimeter of his dark brown eyes.

"Oh," Ami laughed, a hand covering her mouth. "Ah, those, too. Nice garden. Nice tats, too. That's what I meant."

"Hi, Chester. I'm Nick," he said, covering Ami's gaffe. "We've been on the road for a few weeks. Not much in the way of food or water. Too busy. What I'm asking is, are you going to get mad at us if we eat a few of your friends?"

Laughter broke out among the evolved apes, who found that play of words particularly amusing.

"Not at all," Chester said. "That's what they do. And that's what we do. All natural. All good. C'mon down," he said, his vines settling him back down on the ground. "Eat all you want. Take your time and have a peaceful stroll along the creek. Kiss a butterfly or two."

Ami and Nick gave Peaches a quick glance, and the mayor nodded a few times quickly. "Let's go kiss some butterflies," he said. "Take five, gentlemen," he informed his evolved ape friends.

"Finally!" M'Tumba bellowed. "I've been jones-ing for some blackberries for, oh, about two whole hours now!" he finished with a hoot, bounding down easily to the ground.

As the evolved apes followed excitedly behind M'Tumba, Nick, Ami, and Peaches fell in behind their guide, Chester.

"The peaches are really sweet today," Chester informed them as they passed by the first of the peach trees. "You should try some," he said, as the peach tree bent a limb down to him, offering its choice peaches.

"Wow," Ami said, plucking and quickly tasting the offered peach. "These are quite good, Chester. Thank you very much."

Following her lead, Nick gently removed one of the large peaches, giving it a gentle, quizzing nibble. Instantly, he felt its power surge into him, replenishing him and causing his stomach's rumbling to cease immediately.

"Ah, that's some primo hekatek," Nick said, enjoying the slight, heady buzz. He quickly took a very large bite that caused Chester to giggle.

"Yes, sir, it is," Chester replied. "We have our very own arcology in progress here. True, the rest of the city – downtown, especially – was the work of Vir'gil and his tree buddies a few months back. You know? When they tested the resonant transport?"

"Yeah," Nick nodded, chowing down. "Two birds, one stone," he said between bites. "We were a bit fearful to test the transport on humans. Or, former humans. Whatever. But Vir'gil said it would be okay for him and his plant buddies to try it, because they could always bail if the transport did something funky."

"Like scramble their genetic codes," Peaches snorted. "Bad transports are bad. But they demonstrated it, then did an interesting job of terraforming the city. Didn't take more than a week. And now, I've been hearing that they've got it down to an art. Takes a lot less time now."

"Yes, true," Ami said, wiping the corner of her mouth. "Now, they have it down to a simple dance. And they have Beth and Dwayne from Team EL to assist them."

"Oh!" Peaches cried out, startling Ami and Nick. "I have got to meet those two. I've heard so much about them. Is it true that they can turn themselves into pure elemental forms?"

"Huh?" Ami replied. "Like a water or wind body? No, that's plain silly. How would they be able to see?"

Both Nick and Peaches gave her a brief stare, then looked at each other and laughed.

"Hell, Peaches," Nick said, truly enjoying the scents, sounds, and vibes around him. "I hadn't even thought that far down the road. Maybe they'll be able to morph into something like that one day. Right now, though, far as I know, they're still human-bound."

"Ah, too bad," Peaches replied, not quite so sad as he tried to sound. "Hey, did you see the soil?"

Both Nick and Ami took a good look down. Beneath them, the ground was an interesting combination of tiny pebbles and some kind of rich-looking black soil. Weird-looking black soil.

Nick toed at it, curious. It sang back to him, a staccato chorus of cartoon chipmunk voices chirping.

"Wow!" Ami exclaimed. "That's insane!" She declared, doing a rapid tip-toe dance on it, eliciting a sound similar to that of Chip and Dale. If they were being curb stomped to death by Michael Jackson, that is.

"It's our version of *terra preta do índio*," Chester answered.

"What's that mean?" Nick inquired. "Earth.. Indian? What?"

"Portuguese, for 'black soil of the Indian,'" Peaches replied. "It's a unique kind of fertilizer that the Amazonian peoples somehow managed to create over 1,000 years ago. Thing is, unlike modern fertilizer, this stuff just keeps regenerating itself. No need to ever rotate crops. And it cuts growing times down to insanely short intervals. Look there," he said, pointing at the peach tree limb from which they had just moments before plucked their fruits. "The buds are already reforming. In a few hours those peaches will be right back in the same spot, big as they were when you picked 'em."

"Or," Chester interjected, "I could just do this..." he said, waving an arm at the peach tree, his eyes flashing as a tiny gout of sparkles, a mix of light blue and jade, erupted.

At once, as if they were viewing a time elapsed video, the two missing peaches grew back before their eyes, whole and entire.

Nick and Ami applauded. Chester bowed, grinning merrily.

"I suppose I should explain," Peaches said gently. "After Vir'gil and his tree friends completed their terraforming activities, they decided to hold a ceremony to give thanks to the Mother. They stated that they wanted to hold it here, in the stadium, and they strongly suggested that all non-Fae persons avert their eyes and keep their distance. So we all did precisely that. Save for the very few of us that Vir'gil asked to attend in person. Me, M'Tumba, M'Zinga, Chester, Riki – one of our Finnies, or what the Old World would have called a 'porpoise' – and Lucy. Boy, I admit that was one heck of an experience. Vir'gil encamped us right there, smack dab on what used to be the 50 yard line of the football field, gave us each a small psychedelic pinecone to consume, which we readily did, then..."

"Then we were off to see the Mother," Chester finished. "What a trip. What a trip. She said we had to break on through. Hit the next level. Shed our skins. Move through our own shadows. And boy, let me tell ya... we surely did."

Chester and Peaches exchanged knowing grins.

"You tripped with the Entheogenic Lord?" Nick inquired, incredulous. "You saw the Mother? Holy shit. What happened? I mean, Maynard gave Dreamland a super-fun minor trip experience, but it was more of an introduction, and not a deep dive. No pinecones, anyway. Just enough to make everyone relax and get along better with one another. What did you experience?"

They both shook their heads. Peaches spoke first, "Sorry, my man. It's personal for everyone involved in the experience. Next time you see Vir'gil, ask him. He'll take you up on it. If you want to be transformed, that is."

"We've already been transformed," Ami observed.

"Not like this, sweetie," Chester informed her. "Sure, the sigil transformed you. No doubt about it. But this is a metaphysical transformation. A transcendence. For me, not spoiling anything, it gave me personal insight into my relationship with the Mother. And I used that to gain superior control of my powers. Before the ceremony, I was a competent hortikinetic. Now, after the ceremony, I see how to be more. Feel more. Now, I'm what the smart guys," he said, shrugging toward Peaches, "call a 'bender and binder'. Meaning, I'm using my full soul to work my hortikinetics."

"You're talking about activating your ninth chakra," Nick inquired, fascinated. "Aren't you?"

"Yeah!" Ami added. "Aren't you? Stupid Stoner Vir'gil never asked us to join his ceremony."

"Yes, Nick," Peaches said softly. Ami certainly amused him. Such emotional content. "Nascent nines now. Hear that gentle alliteration? Nines, like you are, Ami. And like you, Nick, will soon be."

"Well, I understand that we need all the power we can get, considering the situation," Nick admitted. "But it seems a bit arbitrary and capricious for Vir'gil to elect to do it for some, but not all, of us."

"I'll break it to them, Peaches," Chester offered. He took a moment to stretch lazily, his arms high above his head as he took in a few measured, practiced breaths. "Vir'gil actually picks nothing, and no one. He serves the Will of the Mother. That's it, and that's all. Simple as I can make it."

"So," Ami began, calculating. "The Mother decided to bump you up, using Vir'gil as the conduit?"

"Yes," Peaches confirmed.

"But not us," Ami continued. "So, I think that means either we're already powerful enough to do what we need to do, or you were not powerful enough to do what you need to do. I mean, I'm already there, if only barely. I don't need help. And Nick will get here soon enough on his own. He didn't need help, either. You did, though. So she helped you."

Peaches and Chester considered that one for a moment, a bit nonplused. Nick tried his best to tuck back into his peach, really trying to cover his smile. Ami could be brutal with her unfiltered honesty.

"Ah, oboy! Oboy! Here you are!" burst a sudden, frenetic, high-pitched voice.

There, a few paces away, loomed a circular metallic sphere, roughly the size of an old world cantaloupe. From its position in the air, at a height roughly equal to the top of Peaches' head, it beamed an incredibly realistic hologram of a porpoise, whose keen, flinty eyes now gazed upon them.

"Hi, Riki," Peaches said, turning to face Riki's floating hologram. "These are our new guests, Nick and Ami."

"Which one is the female?" Riki asked them. "Sorry. Jumping ahead. You need a chance to answer. Then, I can properly associate your gender attributes with your form. Not an insult. No, no, no! Not at all. Just takes time to sort out which human is what, and so on, and so forth. Ever try to tell which porpoise was male, and which was female? It's like that with us, too!"

"I'm Nick," Nick replied, genuinely amused. "That's Ami," he said, owing to Ami's hurried attempt to chew and swallow her food.

"Pleased to meet you," Riki replied rapidly. "Enjoy your time here in Hotlanta! Woo-hoo! I'm glad I'm safely ensconced away in my pool! In my pool! It's c-c-c-cool!" Riki turned to give Peaches a quick glance. "Peaches? Maynard just sent us the gold mine! The gold mine! We're going to be able to implement the new LIDAR augmentation. The one using hekatek waveforms? It's gonna be so insane! And we're going to be able to make everything fly now! I mean, right now! I just used Maynard's improved flying runic inscription on my remote hologram projector!"

To emphasize the point, Riki's metallic projector spun around in the air like a top, somehow managing to keep Riki's hologram in focus and in place.

Peaches marveled at the revelation. "This is happening fast. Good, good. We need fast. Great work, Riki. Please pass along my thanks, and our thanks, to the crew."

"K-k-k-kay-kay!" Riki chirped rapidly, his image decohering and vanishing as the remote hologram projector sped off straight up, zooming through the stadium's open rooftop and off into the Atlanta sky.

"Riki. He's one of our artificers," Peaches explained to Nick and Ami. "He and M'Zinga and a few dozen of the most talented hekateks comprise our research and development group: The Resonant Order of Hekateks of Atlan. Note the lack of the final two letters of 'Atlanta'. They're using 'Atlan' because, during their very special trip, they both saw the original version of Atlantis, which used to be called 'Atlan'. Imagine that symmetry, eh? Atlantis? Atlan?"

"I am not surprised by anything anymore," Nick admitted. "But I've heard Maynard say that the Resonant Order was fantastic.

Able to extend and augment anything he and Denny had tossed to them. And even, in some cases, take the concept up to the next level. Scary how the 'evolved' can do that. Makes me feel almost guilty for my old world prejudice and bias. Several so-called 'animal' species have turned out to be smarter than humans."

Peaches and Chester both nodded. "Some plants, too," Chester added.

"Huh?" Ami gasped. "You're kidding, right?"

Chester shook his head. "Nope. The Evolutionary Judgement worked some special charms on some species of plants, too. Not just man and some animals. But, generally speaking, and excluding the Fae and their elementals, certain collectives of plants can organize cognition at the human level. Or, even higher, sometimes. Did y'all notice, when you first got here, that the garden welcomed you?"

Nick and Ami both nodded, recalling the sensation.

"That was the garden's way of saying hello to you," Chester said, smiling. "Cool, huh?"

"But, but how?" Ami asked. "How can a garden talk?"

"Heck, I don't rightly know," Chester admitted. "It just does."

Peaches added quickly, "At the level of a collective, or the superset of all things of the garden itself, the ambient hekatek imbues that superset with a form of identity. That superset identity is what's using subtle hekatek-driven energies to communicate with you empathically. We might not hear words when it speaks to us, but we certainly feel what it's communicating."

"Good night!" Nick suddenly exclaimed. "I feel guilty about pigging out now."

Chester cracked a smile. "Already mentioned it: They don't mind that. It's natural."

"Well," Peaches said, inhaling deeply, his chest flaring like a giant black manta ray. "Nick? Ami? You guys ready to have that get-together? Or, do you need to rest?"

"Ready," Nick said, answering for Ami, too, who nodded once, curtly. He turned to face Chester. "Thanks to the bounty of your garden, Chester, I feel like I could turn around right now and do the whole road-clearing gig again."

"You're welcome," Chester replied. A mass of green vines snaked between his legs, lifting him several feet into the air. "Gotta go make my rounds now. We have more than one of these gardens here in Atlanta. Keeps me busy. Keeps everyone fed, watered, and happy. Peace, folks," he said, the vines carrying him rapidly through the dense garden.

As Nick observed the fantastic sight, Peaches asked them, "Ready? We're going to transport to my office from here. It's the mirror image of your war room in Dreamland. Ours, however, is the Lennox Science Arcology. Ours is the exact height as yours in Dreamland. But ours has more area, because we've used the whole Lennox Science complex and several more square city blocks as our arcology, and we've pitched quite a large virtual tent."

"Yep, saw it on the way in," Nick observed. "Hard to miss. But you said 'transport'?"

"Indeed!" Peaches boomed, extending his arms in a wide, kingly gesture. "And here we go..."

A brief flash of neon purple laser light pulsed from Peaches' extended arms, and multiple beams arced to both Nick and Ami, the energy slightly tickling them. Then, just as their senses registered the stimulation, they were somewhere else. Now, they stood on a semicircular platform, about 10 paces across, which gave them an unimpeded view of Atlanta from approximately 1,000 feet above the street. Behind them, the pyramidion of the Lennox

Science Arcology rose over 100 feet higher. Its capstone faintly throbbed with crackling, multicolored arcs of hekatek energies.

For a very casual moment, Nick and Ami reverted to excited tourists, gawking at the scene. The Lennox Science Arcology covered roughly triple the area covered by the Dreamland Arcology. Vir'gil and his tree friends had outdone any expectations, creating a veritable garden over former steel and stone. Where the sunlight touched the new structures bidden from the Earth by Vir'gil and his Fae companions, gleaming, rainbow iridescence replied. Extending the floral designs of Dreamland, water burbled in brooks and stealthy courses, winding chaotically through both formal and informal gardens. Stone bridges spanned the water courses, their unique construction actually resonating in response to the passage of the water. Thus, an ethereal, barely audible composition was elicited, being essentially monotonic in proximity to a particular bridge, yet becoming symphonic at certain points and junctures as multiple nodes overlapped. From their vantage, and due to their own personal power, they were actually able to discern, if only slightly, the various resonant nodes which, even at this distance, sang to them.

"Wow, that's really cool," Ami said, rising from the ground to get a better view.

"Isn't it?" Peaches replied. "And at midnight, if you listen really closely, it'll play some Kanye, and some Earth, Wind & Fire." Instantly, he segued into an incongruous falsetto, "Reasons, the reasons that we hear..."

Nick's eyes lit up. "Holy shit, Peaches. You've got that Phillip Bailey shit down, legit!"

Peaches smiled, exchanging dap with Nick. "That man makes love with his voice. What he did live on that song, to everyone in the audience... I'd tell you more, Nick, if only you weren't so straight," he laughed at Nick, who shrugged innocently.

"Wait!" Ami declared insistently. "Tell me, Peaches. What did he do?"

Peaches laughed. "Sorry, my sweet little singularity. I'm still a southern gentleman, despite my rough edges, and you're too young to hear such depraved things. C'mon, let's go inside," he said, leading them into the war room directly from the platform.

Following Peaches inside, Nick and Ami joined him at a war room table that precisely duplicated their own, even down to the Sign of Chaos set into the floor. In fact, it was their own, as Aal Ball was currently empowering both war rooms.

Taking their seats, they both observed Peaches as his large bulk gracefully settled in an Aal Ball customized chair. His sausage-sized fingers then went to work at furious speed on a manual keyboard, also provided by Aal Ball. A moment later, the war room's eight doors sealed shut, the transparent windows polarized and went black, and Peaches, a satisfied look on his face, began to speak.

"We're secure now," he began, leaning back in his seat, which looked like a very large, chrome-colored barber shop chair. "Maynard?"

"I'm here," came Maynard's voice. "Not going visual at this time. Audio only. Over."

"Okay," Peaches replied. "Nick and Ami are here with me, in case you're unaware."

"Thanks, man," Maynard replied. "Are we secure now, Peaches?"

"As much as you and I can secure our session," Peaches replied, typing rapidly on his oversized keyboard interface. "Which is pretty damn secure."

"Okay," Maynard said. "Something Vir'gil mentioned to me recently came up, and I've been pulling a few threads here and there. Remember your pineal cone session with Vir'gil? He told me as much as he was allowed, so I know who was there, and why, and basically what happened. Not all of it, of course, because there was an extremely personal experience that, being a shaman myself, I'd never ask him to reveal."

"I know, man, I know," Peaches replied. "And thanks for that level of respect."

"You got it, man," Maynard said. "So please forgive me for going there, but I really need to ask you some personal questions about that session."

Wrinkling his nose, Peaches blurted, "What the hell, Maynard? You wake up on the wrong side of the Dreamwyrd this morning?"

Maynard snorted, despite himself. "Zing! Of course, being a gentleman of renown, I'll zip it up regarding that subject. Wouldn't want to end up imprisoned in my worst nightmare forever, would I? Well," he continued, slightly chilled as he considered such a fate for a moment, "after what Vir'gil told me about the ceremony, something didn't sit right. And normally, I wouldn't think for a second to pry into someone's privacy, but, when considering the bold-faced fact that we're all fighting a cosmic war of sorts for our survival, I figured I'd just go ahead and bluntly ask: Who the hell is Lucy Diamante?"

Abruptly, obnoxious, blaring sonic feedback wailed, squelching the audio channel. Simultaneously, Aal Ball grew cold and silent, as if the artificed collective had suddenly been switched off. The lights in the war room, both direct and ambient, dimmed to virtual darkness.

"You always were my favorite, Maynard," Lucy Diamante said, phasing into being as shadows writhed merrily in the gloomy darkness. Her face hooded, red locks spilling down over the front of her simple black leather tunic, she hovered inches above the war room table. Around the table, no one moved, for they were frozen in time.

"...and you always were a lazy coder," Maynard said, materializing within arm's reach of the hooded red head. His arms raised high above his head, he stared down the several inches of height separating their eyes. Dangerous neon green sparkles crackled forth from his eyes. Bringing his arms down dramatically, he seized her by her shoulders. "Did you think you could deceive the Mother, Lucifer?" he growled like a furious jaguar, even as her form lit from head to toe with a baleful green nimbus of soul's light. "Did you think you could just casually enter a state of grace with the Entheogenic Lord himself, and lie directly to his face? Did I not promise you my wrath, should you ever desecrate what is holy again?"

Unable to reply due to the titanic grounding power coursing through Maynard's soul into hers, Lucy began to writhe in shock and pain as, impossibly, she felt her own soul go on total chakric lockdown.

Maynard's flaring green eyes found hers under her hood, locking them in a hateful stare. The sign of a prismatic, rampant dragon blazed like a burning church from the center of his irises.

"I told you what would happen, *you bitch...*" the Mother hate-hissed through Maynard's immortal vessel.

"No!" Lucy gurgle-screamed, totally helpless before the full might of the Dark Earth Mother.

Coruscating gouts of metacosmic power burned into Lucy's thrice-warded, formerly inviolate soul. Weaving. Bending. Binding.

"Mark my words," the Mother sibilantly hissed, each syllable slamming like a mighty maul into Lucy's forehead, "your own arrogance and hubris has condemned you to the Weirding now emplaced upon your soul. Now, you are bound with your own vile simulation. Now, you share its fate. Now, you defeat the One Above, and redeem the EarthZero cosmos, or your very soul is forfeit!"

"Imposs—" Lucy grated, unable to complete the word.

"*Nothing* is impossible," the Mother cruelly reminded her, "save for your ability to defy my will. You were warned, yet you did not take heed. Your meddling chaos caused us to notice you and your pathetic ZeroTime. Due to your pride, your virtual game has transcended into the realm of the metacosmic. Now, you play *our* game, puny god; the stakes of which are higher than you might possibly imagine. Now go! Return to your game, and play it as if your soul depends on it. For now, most assuredly, it does..."

Confused, Maynard stood atop the center of the war room table in Atlanta. In his arms was Lucy, sobs wracking her body. Peaches' eyes opened wide as he gazed upon the bizarre scene. Across the war room table, Nick and Ami both bolted from their chairs, taking to the air, striking defensive poses.

The lights were on, for they had never truly dimmed for more than a nanosecond. Aal Ball was humming and thrumming, and everyone was still on audio only, even if now one of them was no longer in Dreamland, but here in person.

"What the..." Maynard croaked, throat dry. "And who might you be?" he asked the sobbing woman as he gently settled her back a half-step, disengaging his hands from her shoulders.

"What the hell just happened?" Peaches asked, getting up slowly from the table. He had a fierce, sudden migraine that caused him to grimace. "Maynard? Lucy? What are you two doing here?"

"I'm Lucy," the red haired woman explained. She tapped a wolf skin boot on the tabletop. "Why am I up on the table? Peaches? Why... I don't remember..." she trailed off, growing dizzy. Then, she promptly fainted into Maynard's arms.

"I gotcha, little lady," Maynard drawled, his rune-enhanced strength allowing him to easily catch her up into his arms. "Peaches?" he called over his shoulder.

"Yeah, Maynard," Peaches said, rubbing his temples. "I know. I know. But I don't have an explanation for any of this. We were talking, audio only, and you asked something about... about..." Arching his eyebrows, he looked over at Nick and Ami. They both shrugged, settling back down to the floor.

"Aal Ball," Maynard asked aloud, "please give Lucy here a comfy recliner to chill on."

No sooner spoken than it was done, and Maynard gently deposited her on the materialized lounger. Maynard, demonstrating that he now had a flying rune of his own, gently levitated over to where Nick and Ami were climbing back into their own seats. As he settled into another materialized chair, and as Peaches returned to his own seat, he gave a materialized keyboard a quick run of his fingers. Aal Ball gave a standard, if distant, goat-bleat of a reply, and before them, arising from the now vacant center of the table bloomed a series of holograms.

"Now we'll see what happened," Maynard said confidently. "Probably some random hekatek chaos."

"Obviously some kind of spacetime event," Peaches said thickly. "Freakin' ill-timed migraine suggests something like that happened."

"Well," Nick said, checking out the images and diagnostic readings, "looks like a very brief hiccup in the fabric of reality. Must have pulled Maynard through somehow."

"Resonance between our war rooms," Peaches posited.

"That makes sense," Maynard admitted. "Must have triggered the portals."

"That explains you," Nick said, analyzing the situation. "But it doesn't explain *her*," he said, hiking a thumb at Lucy. "How did she get here?"

"She wasn't here in the war room with you three?" Maynard asked.

"Yes," Ami said. "I mean, no," she admitted, confused. "I mean, she might have been. I can't remember now."

"Ami," Nick asked, "take a look back and see what happened."

Complying, Ami flashed her fingers up before her eyes, then splayed her fingers. Gently, she coaxed the local spacetime to show her a replay of the immediate past. Images began to fill her mind, and she reported them as she saw them.

"We're sitting around the table," she began, her voice distant, almost ethereal. "We're going to audio only. There's some kind of loud feedback. A flash of light. Green light. No, make that neon green. Like demon puke. It's everywhere, all at once. Then... Then Maynard and that chick are on the table. That's it," she finished, dismissing her quantum interrogation.

"Sounds about right," Peaches admitted. "About par for the course, actually. Especially when dealing with energies and powers of this magnitude," he said, indicating the war room with a sweep of his right hand.

Maynard nodded in agreement. "Just out of curiosity," he asked Peaches, "does Lucy here have any power or influence that might have been a co-factor to cause or influence the event?"

"Damn!" Peaches laughed loudly. "That's it. Lucy's a Fractal Mage."

"What the hell's that?" Nick, Ami, and Maynard all said at once.

Smiling, Peaches explained, "When she first got here, she hadn't yet manifested a power. Took a while, actually. But once she was able to manifest it, it turned out to be totally killer. Her hekatek empowers her with the ability to see the frames of spacetime, just as you or I would see a frame in a movie. Only, she can manipulate that frame of spacetime, just like she's directing her own movie. Well, to some minor degree. The way she explained it was that she has to start small, like planting a seed and then causing it, frame-by-guided-frame, to grow—fractally, of course – into the desired final form. But, and here's the kicker," he paused a moment for effect. "She does it by sorting out possible future waveforms. She surfs quantum waves into the future, finds the particular thread she wants – the one thread among millions in which her desire is most probable—then pulls it back to her."

This stumped even Maynard. Nick and Ami didn't even pretend to get it. Noting their collective lack of comprehension, and quite amused that even the Great Maynard had been stumped, Peaches continued his explanation:

"C'mon guys, I know it's been a tough day. Lucy has an expanded perception, kind of like Ami's singularity scan of the recent past in local spacetime. But, unlike Ami's, Lucy's is always on. She can't turn it off. Makes her eyes look wicked-cool as shit, kinda like your friend's eyes – Void's eyes – but, being a sensitive person, she wears that hood to hide her face, so nobody will think she's a freak. She uses her perception to see reality frame-by-frame. She said that she can pick up on a certain entity within that frame she sees, and nudge it a bit, frame-by-frame, fractally shaping it and bending it to her will. From potential futures to the here and now. I've personally seen her do some crazy shit, like turn a single bullet into a gun just by looking at it, or knocking down a steel vault door just by tapping her fingernail on it. Small grows to large, fractally. She hinted that it got easier after she had that session with Vir'gil, but that only makes sense. I got more powerful, and so did everyone else who ate Vir'gil's Tasty Pinecones of Power."

"That's the craziest shit I've ever heard," Maynard admitted. "Fractal, future, something-something, then, Surprise Spacetime Shitshow!"

"Yeah," Ami laughed. "What a stupid power. She's practically useless."

"Shh!" Peaches said, raising a finger to his lips. "She's so sweet. Don't power-shame her, guys. Maynard?" he asked his dear friend. "Want to stay the night? We can gin up a decent party here in Hotlanta, you dig? You guys can meet my new boyfriends. And girlfriends, too, if you'd like," he said, mostly to Nick.

"Sure," Maynard replied amiably. "We need a break, after all the shit we've been through. Taking the night off won't kill us. I'll tell Mhyrranda, and let her know we're coming back tomorrow."

"We?" Nick asked.

"Yeah, man," Maynard replied. "Unless you really want to keep traveling the interstate highway system from coast to coast. Rust never sleeps. Nor do artificers. We're a day or two away from getting a new series of autonomous drones to do the job. Right, Peaches?"

Peaches nodded. "Yeppers. So, c'mon, ya'll. Let's go downstairs and start kicking it. Par-tay, ya'll!"

"What about her?" Ami inquired, pointing at Lucy's still form, as they gathered in the center of the Sign of Chaos, preparing to take the artificed water elevator down.

"She can catch up when she gets up," Peaches declared as they began their descent. "Poor dear."

As the barely audible sound of the floor's annular cycling faded, hot tears flowed, unbidden, down Lucy's face.

CHAPTER 16

The light of the setting sun shone through the glass towers surrounding Central Park, casting beams and rainbows through a multitude of refracting surfaces. In a large room, in a towering skyscraper overlooking the magnificence of Manhattan, three figures sat in luxurious chairs, drinking amber liquid from crystal glasses. The largest of the trio, a powerfully built man in a bespoke Leonard Logsdail suit, rose and moved gracefully to the picture windows. The soft sunlight scattered across his unusual eyes, eliciting a veritable kaleidoscope of colors, similar to segmental heterochromia, or stained glass. As he stared down at the city, he shook his meticulously groomed head and spoke.

"I'm not sure His Holiness is going to be as useful as we thought. He seems to have had a change of heart regarding the labor force we envisioned."

"I'm not sure I understand, Brother Bradley. We all know what he's capable of. Half the world saw the video before the shit hit the fan." The speaker, a middle-aged woman in a sharp gray dress and white silk blouse, fidgeted with the diamond and emerald Tiffany & Co. bracelet on her wrist. Her brown eyes narrowed dangerously as she considered unpleasant scenarios. "Did he somehow regain his sanity? Or his morals?"

The third, a bearded man with piercing green eyes, grunted. As if those were both bad things to regain in this world of total insanity. "Well, Sister Evaline," he said, his voice deep and soothing, "he would be the first one since the Sigil. Especially since the End of the World didn't quite turn out like the scripture said it would. What is his problem, Brother Bradley – did he say?"

"He says, 'It doesn't serve Heaven to create slaves for earthly toil.'"

"Seriously? This from Peter the Roman, the man who sought to blow open the Pearly Gates in order to confront Lucifer? Does this sound sane to anyone else?"

"Greg, I'm just telling you what he said. I think that he didn't come back the same after Giza. He's practically lame, and he looks at everybody with that ten-thousand-yard stare, like he's left part of his mind in the desert." Brother Bradley drained his glass and walked over to the table to set it down on the polished mahogany.

Sister Evaline looked from one man to the next and shrugged. "He isn't the only thing keeping our power in place, but we need to get a handle on him and use him for good will in the city. More of that public display like at Saint John's."

"Well, and that's only good for the Catholics and the Anti-Dreamers, isn't it?" Brother Greg pointed out. "The reformers, and the atheists, and half the people who don't give a shit either way aren't impressed that we have the Pope on our side. They are more concerned with food and safety and a regular day."

"And we give them all that," Sister Evaline said. "Brother Bradley has turned the shores of Manhattan into a glittering, impassable barrier. And I've shielded the boroughs and half of Long Island and Jersey from the dreams and mental prodding of that witch in Vegas. All of this thanks to your amplification, Greg." She took another drink, and looked pointedly at Brother Bradley. "As long as we maintain law and order, we are going to do alright. Keep security tight at all the roads and tunnels connecting the island with the outside world, and keep the dissidents out..."

Brother Bradley frowned. "Well, that's not enough. We have word that the Arcologies are all banding together, and they are pushing global unity on everyone, all in the name of fighting this 'Death Horde' that's supposedly coming. If they get enough followers, it's only a matter of time before they invade and force their egalitarian bullshit on us."

He turned to face the others, and said, "We control the greatest city in the world, one of the few to survive, and they are going to take our way of life. We have thousands of people with powers, a stable government that keeps everyone in line, and a research center on Ryker's Island that is mastering the most powerful technological and magickal defense on the planet. And we have Petrus Romanus, a man who absorbed the souls of millions, laid waste to Cairo – and was resurrected. We can't let them get traction."

Brother Greg sat back and looked at the other two. "I'm not in favor of a war. We just survived the End. The Evolutionary Tribulation! Less than one percent of the people survived. We need to rebuild. I've got scouts and spies from California to Europe. Not to mention informers throughout the city, not to mention the Swiss Guard. We can build our little tyranny here, keep all the people in line and motivate them with everything from free 5th Avenue housing to manufactured food shortages. But if we want to stay in power, we need information."

Sister Evaline waved her hand dismissively. "Fine, fine. I'll get the Broadcasters together and start spreading word that we are facing hostile actions from outside the region, and offer rewards for any information that may clue us into the goals of the Devil's Followers in Vegas. Let's meet again on Tuesday and see what we can shake out of the trees."

All three bowed their heads briefly. "Amen."

CHAPTER 17

Pagan that he truly was, Denny was secretly pleased that *Tlachihualtepetl* had returned to its former, pristine glory. And that the abomination of Cortés – the *Iglesia de Nuestra Señora de los Remediosa* – had been completely extirpated from the scene, no longer polluting the power of the Mother. Virgins, mothers of God or not, would be useless against the Death Horde. As saccharine sweet as they truly were in an Old World sort of way, they weren't the droids they were looking for this time around. No, this was the New World of EarthZero, and they needed power, not platitudes and beatitudes, to fight. To have even a sub-percentile chance of winning.

The irony that Cholula had at one time been the holy city of Quetzalcoatl himself, the God of Peace, was not lost on Denny. The bearded, white-skinned God of Peace. So similar to the Virgin's own son. A good bit of argument against it, of course, from both scholars and his own brown-skinned worshipers; that he had been "white" in opposition to his dual-aspect "black" counterpart. That perhaps he had been an actual ruler who had worn a white mask to cover his hideous face. All irrelevant, in the new context of EarthZero. What truly mattered, he knew, was that Quetzalcoatl was a bringer of knowledge, as well as being the one who had birthed the new race of man from the former. Death and rebirth.

Sort of like the Virgin's son, of course, but more akin to Osiris; a more ancient vintage of perhaps what was, after all, the same wine.

And tonight, his own wife would be joining Mother Tonzi, a place of honor at her side, for this very special ayahuasca ceremony: a dress rehearsal, of a sort, for the fire drill ceremony. A ceremony, Denny was forced to acknowledge, that might one day become both a tactic and a strategy against the Horde itself. This would be the first of three consecutive nights of rehearsal. A good plan, he acknowledged, because, frankly, modern folk were desperately out of touch with the old ways. Practice was necessary.

Groups of helpers moved among the massive crowd gathered around the base of the pyramid, dispensing the foul-tasting ayahuasca from makeshift wheeled barrels to the throng of many thousands. Fire-tenders manned their stations at more than one thousand fire pits, stretching far and wide across the reclaimed grounds of the ancient city. All 365 smaller temples in the city had their own specifically assigned fire-tenders and their attendant crews. While this go-round there would be no actual human sacrifices and burning of hearts, there would indeed be many bonfires, started by specially crafted fire drills. Upon the signal given by Mother Tonzi, these old school tools would be used by the leader of the fire-tender crew to start a new fire. Then, if the designs had been implemented accurately by the civil engineers, the combined mass of bonfires would form the fiery outline of the Feathered Serpent itself. Quetzalcoatl would, at long last, be reborn, if only symbolically.

Mother Tonzi had assured Denny that the intent of the fire drill ceremony, come crunch time versus the Vanth'Vash'Var, would serve to unite the power of the feathered serpent itself among all resonant structures on EarthZero. With the implication being that the Dragon itself – perhaps the Feathered Serpent itself, writ primal and large?—manifested throughout all of the resonant, connected pyramids, would smite the gathered Death Horde a telling, fatal blow.

For now, however, it was merely a dress rehearsal. The first of three. Plenty of time to get the ritual down, and mark the process indelibly in the memory of the participants.

It was truly a beautiful cloudless night, there atop the ancient pyramid of Cholula. The stars danced their slow motion maypole dance overhead. Crisp and cool, Denny thought, content that not everything south of the former border had to be steaming hot jungles or blistering deserts. To the west loomed the stratovolcano twins, *Popocatépetl* and *Iztaccíhuatl*, their silence now a promise of violence to come. The remnants of the city of Puebla to the east revealed not a single fire or magickal light, for, out of respect for the ceremony, there was a standing order of lights out.

Quite simply, Denny was worn out and running on fumes and instinct. The past dozen days and nights, with the exception of his and Rachel's "break" last night, had been filled with insane action. Upon their arrival, they had discovered that Mother Tonzi had actually been waiting for them, having witnessed their arrival three days prior during an ayahuasca voyage. She and the local elders had issued calls for everyone to gather, and gathered they had. To the tune of several tens of thousands. All prepped and ready to be instructed by Denny on the finer points of rune casting. Precisely as Mother Tonzi had been shown by the Mother herself.

Having calculated the most optimal instructional path, Denny, aided by Mother Tonzi and a few dozen elders, had quickly taught them their basic runic castings, and they had then passed along the runic instruction to several others. And so on, and on, until, in a matter of mere hours, there were several tens of thousands of neophyte yet quite eager rune casters. Which dovetailed quite nicely into both Denny's plan to resurrect Cholula's ancient step pyramid – the largest in the world by volume – and use it as a central core to entrain and resonate with the arcologies in both Dreamland and Atlanta. And virtually everywhere else in the world where there were decently large pyramidal structures that could be covered with the necessary Master Runes required to instantiate, link, and modulate the global resonance.

Amazingly, it had taken them a mere twelve days and nights to implement the massive, interwoven matrices of simple runes, the greater focusing and multiplying runes for the bending, and the binding Master Runes themselves. Denny had never pushed himself so hard, so quickly. Unlike his brute force efforts in both Dreamland and Atlanta, however, he had created a new methodology of implementation, such that the Hekatek necessary for such massively powerful artifices didn't have to issue specifically from his own soul. He had, at last, discerned that power, magickal or otherwise, was literally all around him on EarthZero. Like the old world explanations for the virtual energies of the zero point regime, buzzing and boiling away all around us, yet invisible to our mortal perceptions. Enough power in a teacup full of that invisible energy to boil all the oceans of the world.

So, it had come as no surprise to Denny that such a step could be affected. All that was needed was a simple series of translational runic bridges. Power taps, tapping into the invisible energies boiling all around them, which then would feed into the other runes, cascading and resonating themselves, finally interlocking with the complex set of precursor matrix runes which eventually became the Master Rune. They therefore now had an even dozen Master Runes emblazoned upon the pyramid. Denny was certain that this would work, transforming Cholula into the veritable hitching post of the Dragon.

And one day, Denny grimly thought, *if Mother Tonzi was right, this would be the place from where the Dragon itself would bitch slap the Death Horde out of the damn sky.*

Denny sat cross-legged on a simple maguey mat a few paces behind where Mother Tonzi and Rachel stood side by side on the flat, open expanse of the top level of the pyramid. No temple had been rebuilt yet here, at the topmost tier. So, for now, it remained pristine and level, though it was certain to be rebuilt soon, now that the runic knowledge had been established among the people. And it was certain that the new temple would be dedicated to the past and future deity of Cholula: Quetzalcoatl, the Feathered Serpent.

Denny cradled Penny close to his chest, warding her from the slightly chill night air. Cuan occupied another mat, immediately to his right, while several notable elders, bedecked in bright costumes replete with vibrant, multicolored bird feathers, sat on mats to their left and right. Dozens of musicians sat up here, too, on the highest level of the pyramid. The drummers hammered out an insistent, pulsating pulse, while other musicians on flutes and timbrels dotted a wandering, wavering line, like the track of a snake across sand.

Four massive horns sounded, one from each side of the top stage of the pyramid. The tempo of the music inched up a notch, filling Denny's heart with anticipation. Mother Tonzi and Rachel moved slowly, a single pace at a time, toward the center of the top stage of the pyramid, where a gigantic iron cauldron, fully as tall as a man, bubbled hypnotically. Four assistant shamans waited around the iron cauldron, one manning each of the four cardinal directions, their paddle-sized stirring rods gently working the bubbly brew in a tight rhythm.

Approximately thirty minutes previously, guided by Cuan and two elder shamans, Denny and Rachel had both consumed a heady and heavy cup of ayahuasca. Cuan had informed them, grinning widely, that it was okay if they had to void themselves before the magick brew worked its wonders. Hiking a clawed thumb behind him, he had indicated that there was indeed a temporary latrine ensconced behind a few hastily assembled fabric partitions at the eastern edge of the pyramid. Being heroes and all that, Denny and Rachel had both demurred, embarrassed by the notion that they might have to drop trousers in front of thousands of onlookers.

"Okay, then," Cuan had told them with a straight face. "Go ahead and crap your pants. See if that's not more embarrassing than crapping over there behind the partitions."

Snickering at the thought, Denny was abruptly removed from his reverie. The potent ayahuasca had begun to work its ancient magicks on Denny's mind, and he suddenly felt guilty and struggled against it. Penny was still in his hands, her alert eyes darting to and fro as she took in the majestic scene of the ceremony. What kind of parent was he being, indeed? Tripping balls while his innocent baby girl was in his hands...

"I've got her, Denny," Cuan whispered so low that Denny almost missed what he said. "I'm a watcher and guide tonight. I can watch her. She is totally safe with me," he promised, both men instantly knowing that no truer words could ever be spoken.

Truth, for, several days ago, Denny and Rachel had watched, jaws agape, when Cuan had wrestled out a multi-ton, car-sized stone block from one of the sections of Cholula's old ruined walls. With his bare hands, and claws, he had easily detached it with a single, grinding swipe from the tumbled mess of fire-cracked stones where it had long ago settled down into. And then had skipped and hopped with it, like it was a mere loaf of bread, over to its new place in one of Cholula's new, repaired walls.

That alone would have been enough. But, of course, the locals, from the most simple child to the most sophisticated elder, had insisted on whispering tales of Cuan's heroic deeds to him over the days and nights of insanely busy work. Apparently, if such tales were to be believed – and there was no sane reason why they shouldn't; EarthZero it was, after all – Cuan, the Jaguar himself, had once used a 200 ton locomotive to smash to bloody, non-regenerating pieces an invading company of cannibals from the Yucatan. Smashed them like the cockroaches that they truly were. *And if the Diaz Brothers had been among them, then they, too, had been smashed like the cockroaches they were, Scarface style,* Denny laughed to himself.

Super strength. Claws that could breach the hardest stone. *Jesus. It was like someone crossed the Hulk with Wolverine,* Denny thought. *Could Penny be in safer hands? Or paws?*

"Thanks, man," Denny said, gingerly passing Penny over to Cuan's wickedly clawed hands.

Smiling, Penny giggled and booped Cuan's broad nose. "Oh," Cuan whispered sweetly to her, cuddling her against his lithely muscled, furry chest, "you like *Tlatli* Cuan, my sweet little Penny? Good, good."

Feeling more relieved than he could admit as a habitually doting father, Denny bit back a broad smile. Then, with a sigh, knowing that Cuan had his back, he closed his eyes and committed himself fully to the influence of the ayahuasca.

At the sound of the very next drumbeat, a screen of dancing prismatic shapes appeared in his mind's eye. With each beat of the drums, the images changed form, morphing from circles, to squares, then to triangles, then back to circles again. With each new note from the flutes, their colors shifted slightly, one hue slowly becoming eclipsed or occulted by another. Then, after but a few moments, the shapes began to multiply, increasing from single instantiations to double, then triple, then on and on until Denny's mind lost count of them.

Floating away, divorcing himself from the gravity of the Here and Now, Denny's mind assumed the veritable ten thousand foot view, and he experienced the not-so-distant past as an ethereal voyeur:

He was above the pyramid. But it was as it was before its recent reclamation. *Why am I seeing this?* he asked himself. *I don't want to see the pas—*

"...because I ask you to..." came a soothing voice, speaking to Denny and to no one else. *"You have much to see, and learn, before you may become yourself..."*

Like an out of control freight train, Denny's psyche zoomed toward the top of the pyramid, then slammed directly into the back of Mother Tonzi's head. There, his perspective became hers, and he remembered even as he experienced the event firsthand...

So many had come. Already, there was singing and dancing; happiness spreading through the gathering crowd as they pushed up the hill of the pyramid of Cholula. Despite her reluctance to show emotion before others, as it was unbecoming for a shaman, a tear formed in my left eye.

Wait a minute! Denny's mind tortured him. My *left eye?*

There was still hope for the world. So many had died. Yet, now, in defiance of death, so many had come to experience rebirth, and life. And I would lead them in the ceremony that my dreams had told me would bind their souls to the new struggle of this world. A struggle they could not lose. That *we* could not lose.

A zoom forward through time, then:

The restoration of the titanic pyramidal complex of Cholula had been the first decree of the Mother, uttered directly to me. Tonantzin. Mother Tonzi, myself. I had heard her very words herself, chilling her to the bone during the massive ayahuasca ceremony: "What was old would be made new again".

Fully ten thousand lost souls had gathered that night, not so long after the advent of the Sigil of the Devil, drawn to the spot by ancient, whispered words that came from nowhere, yet spoke directly to their hearts. All had witnessed the apparition of the Mother that night, had felt the true power of the one who would cast down all icons of the former world and replace them with her own. All had seen the images of the *Tzitzimimeh* flit and dart chaotically around the Mother, then gather and plunge into the heart of the earth itself. They came down from the stars to rip, rend, and destroy.

Illuminated by the Mother, I had informed them in a booming voice that in order to defeat the *Tzitzimimeh*, a new fire drill ceremony must be performed. The abominations of the so-called "New World" conquerors must be cast down. Ground to dust. For upon that dust would be rebuilt the old temples, and the old ways would be renewed. For only the old ways would be powerful enough to defeat this new brood of sky demons. Powerful enough to save our new world from its most ancient, most ugly enemies.

Livid, vibrant shapes of many colors and vertices assaulted Denny's mind, as his soul disentangled itself from Mother Tonzi's waveform. Their shared past now became his sole present. Shocked, reduced to non-resistance and acceptance, he stared at Mother Tonzi and Rachel, where they now stood immediately to the side of the vast, smoldering cauldron.

Towering, spectacular in its scale, arose an ethereal avatar of the Mother from the center of the top of the Cholula pyramid. A shared, collective gasp issued forth from tens of thousands of immortals as realization of the miracle set in. The drums and flutes stopped, even as fire drills fell from benumbed hands across the expanse of the city. Taken up by invisible force, Mother Tonzi and Rachel abruptly began to levitate slowly up from the pyramid, their bodies stiff in rapture.

Her form, though established, was impossible to fully discern. The Mother meant many things to many people, and all of these competing icons and avatars were causing her own waveform to roil and ripple in its apparent identity. One moment, she was an older, bent, wise woman with green skin and jade accoutrements.

The next, she was jet black, in the prime of her life, and gleaming wildly over some unseen kill, her pulsating long blade pronouncing unheard Death and Chaos. Then, she rapidly flickered, like an old drive in movie screen, between multiple identities; some with blue skin and many darting arms; others, more difficult to lock on to and perceive for fear of losing one's own sanity in seeing it.

And still, even as the Mother's waveform permuted frame-by-frame, second-by-second, Mother Tonzi and Rachel floated upward.

"I've got to help her," Denny realized he had whispered, the words arriving several seconds late.

Immediately, upon perception of his own words, he felt a strong hand grasp his shoulder. "Relax, Denny," Cuan informed him calmly. The slight pressure of Cuan's grip ceased, and Denny did indeed relax. Not that he had especially wished to relax, but it was as if he had had no true measure of free will in the decision.

"The script is with us," Denny smiled, his mouth tugging at its corners.

"Yes, it is," Cuan snorted back. "Use the Force, Luke," he whispered to Denny, deciding then and there that he'd give his own soul to protect the three visitors from the other side of the great border. Not that he wouldn't pay any price, even the price of his own soul, to protect the innocent. It's just that, in this particular case, he knew that Denny wasn't even close to being "innocent", but was instead as real and funny as everyone else, despite his insane, godlike power. He inscribed soul-words of terrible power, as if he were writing with the hand of the Mother herself. He had made the old new again. Denny was worthy of respect.

Cuan, since his own instantiation as the Jaguar, had never acknowledged fear. The Evolutionary Tribulation of the Sigil, as some had called it, had transformed him from a maladjusted young man into the living embodiment of an ancient god. No longer was he obsessed with Marvel or DC comics, or the luchadores. Or shirking a good, honest day of work in the fields. Not that shit like that paid any decent living wage, south of the border, anyway. Yet, he knew he had been a casual slacker, almost without faith, until it had happened. Until the Mother herself had spoken to him in that long-ago fever dream, the night of the Sigil.

He had been slam-dunked into the crucible of rebirth, and he had transformed his own world view and attitude almost immediately upon realizing his new soul. Maybe it was just that, all along, he had been programmed along the lines of being good over being evil. A common enough theme in both the comics and in wrestling. And, just maybe, it had been simply an acknowledgement that his had been an old soul, reborn into a fitting mortal host, who had been prepared to assume such a role, even from birth.

So, no fear. Not now, not never. The Jaguar would never know fear, such that all others would never have to know fear.

However, Cuan was forced to acknowledge that the titanic apparition towering above them all was... exhilarating? Even the tiny daughter of Denny and Rachael seemed to feel it, for her bright little eyes were locked upon the sight. And her bright little eyes were clearly issuing forth flittering green sparks of light. Sparks that abruptly erupted like tiny geysers, projecting the green sparks around both Denny and Rachael. Enveloping them. Protecting them.

A cold chill sprinted down Denny's back, startling him from his pacific thoughts. Penny's sparks were crawling all over him, faintly buzzing. Rachael, too, was covered by them. Jerking his head around to face Cuan, he saw Penny, her head craned up high as she gazed upon the apparition of the Mother. Cuan's eyes were closed, and he appeared to be snoring contentedly. Faint traces of green energies danced lazily around his form, and Denny knew why the Jaguar was sleeping.

In fact, as Denny's senses sharpened, he gazed about, noting that, with the exception of the three of them and Mother Tonzi, everyone within his field of view was peacefully sleeping. Faint traces of Penny's projected energies outlined the sleepers' forms. She had, if Denny's calculations were even ballpark-accurate, just slept one hundred thousand people. Immortal people.

"Denny?" came Rachael's voice, shrill and close to breaking.

He looked up at her. She was writhing, struggling in place against Penny's protective energies, yet still levitating in place with Mother Tonzi high above the pyramid. "She's okay, Penny. We're all okay."

Hearing this, Rachael ceased her struggles. It was at this moment that she became fully aware of what was towering above her. Denny watched in helpless wonder as his wife gazed up at the fantastic apparition looming over her. A heartbeat later, Mother Tonzi cast a quick glance over at Rachael, then down at Denny and Penny. Inscrutable, her wizened face a veritable mask, she then joined Rachael in taking in the scene of the incredible scene unfolding around them.

The Mother gazed upon them all. Reality itself seemed to pinwheel and dance, the eyes of the Mother millions upon millions in number, staring into their souls. No issuance of sound was possible in this moment. Not even the numerous fires dared crackle. Not even the massive boiling cauldron dared rumble. Not even their hearts dared beat.

Then, in a million different voices, She spoke: "At last, I gaze upon my children. Now, at the time of our most desperate struggle. The heretic Lightbringer has unleashed his horror upon my flesh and my blood. The curse of immortality is upon the survivors of the Evolutionary Tribulation. Worse, the Vanth'Vash'Var soon come to destroy this world, and fulfill their wicked goal of cosmic genocide. They plan to unbind the Dragon itself, which now is fully awakened, its soul cosmically bound to EarthZero. Thus, the fate of this world is the fate of this cosmos. Intertwined, the hyperthreads of Fate bend and bind us all. And despite our most precise war plans, despite our combined immortal powers, we will all die, as we have died a thousand times before. For this is how the game always ends." She paused a moment, her voices still resounding. Something about her seemed to loom larger than before, threatening the sanity of those who gazed upon her. As if she had suddenly become even more impossibly large, more impossibly infinite. "But those are no longer the rules of the game. The Lightbringer's insane blasphemy has caused us to gaze down into this primitive, small cosmos, and note its heresy. There are worlds beyond worlds, and the Lightbringer's desperate efforts in this particular instantiation of this constrained cosmos have caught our attention. The Dual-Aspect of the Metacosmic Instantiation now has become the superpositioned Dragon and Dark Earth Mother of this puny cosmos. And now, aware, and no longer blind to this pustulant abomination of false creation, we have, in our righteous wrath, caused the Anshadar Effect. Now, the Dragon's Game begins anew. Now, it is no longer merely the fate of the cosmos of EarthZero hanging in the balance. No, now the cosmos of the ZeroTime itself – the world above this world; the home of the One Above and his eternal opponent, the Lightbringer – hangs in the balance as well."

Hearing this, Denny didn't waste a nanosecond. "You're still using us all as pawns, just like the Lightbringer and the One Above are. Why do you think we'll help you win your own pathetic game?"

"Denny, no!" Rachael called out, but her fierce response was drowned out by the Mother's booming reply.

"Because your own flesh and blood is Anshadar," was the reply. "Did not my own VoidSpawn tell you this? Did he not inform you of the Dragon's Game, the Anshadar Effect, and what it means to you and this world?"

"Not in so many words," Denny admitted. Disgusted, he shook his head. "Can't we just stop it with all of the game stuff already? Just talk normal for once? Look, if you want us to help you win this thing, why don't we just sit down together and talk it over? Do away with pretension, and god-this, blasphemy-that? That shit just muddies and muddles the conversation. Now, more than ever before, we need focused communication. Not more riddles and games and metaphysical quantum fractal talk."

As both Mother Tonzi and Rachael prepared for total annihilation, there came a sudden flash of silent, purple lightning, and they, along with Denny, Penny, and a still sleeping Cuan, cradling Penny gently to his chest, were suddenly sitting around a plain oak table. They were in a curtained, rather large booth, their oak table large enough for all of them plus a few more. Plush silk cushions lined the large, high-backed black oak booth in which they sat. Crude ceramic steins sat before them, brimming with a heady, dark brew. Pewter plates lay before them, stacked with a variety of fruits and sweet meats. Simple silver forks, spoons, and knives were set to the left and right of the plates. Outside the curtained booth came the generic noise of a small crowd of rowdies, singing along with gusto to some bizarre form of shanty song, in an unknown yet somehow familiar tongue. Knife-etched graffiti, in an unknown runic language, dappled the top of the oak table. Unknown, but, again, somehow familiar.

Denny sat next to Rachael, with Cuan and Penny to Rachael's right, and Mother Tonzi to Denny's left. The green energies were gone. Across from them, sitting slightly off-center from Denny opposite the table, was a most unusual avatar of the Mother. She appeared to be a simple, virtually featureless female mannikin fashioned of metallic, brilliant chrome. No eyes, no mouth, no clothes. Just dainty, fused fingers which somehow hooked into the handle of the stein before her and lifted it to her nonexistent lips.

"Ah!" she said lustily if somewhat robotically, blowing the head of the brew off onto the tabletop with a sudden, sharp exhalation that apparently had issued from nowhere. "Best brew in the cosmos. Or metacosmos, take your pick," she said, tilting the stein up, then draining it in a few brief seconds. "By the way," she said, her voice fey, "wakie-wakie, Cuan. You don't want to miss this."

"Okay," Cuan immediately replied, passing Penny over to Rachael. "Huh?" he added, suddenly conscious again. Total shock forced his eyes wide for a split-second, but a quick glance from Mother Tonzi instantly calmed him, stopping him in mid-growl.

"The Mother would have words with us, Cuan," Mother Tonzi calmly informed him.

"Yes, I would," the Mother replied. "But first, the food and drink are real, and very tasty. I'd feel like a bad host if you all don't partake."

Never ones to resist the bidding of metacosmic deities, all of them began to sip their brews and pick at their food. As an almost comical afterthought, a tiny glass baby bottle filled with creamy, fresh milk appeared next to Rachael's stein. The mannikin avatar observed them silently for a moment. Then, apparently satisfied, the Mother turned her head toward Denny and fixed him with a sightless gaze.

Denny shook his head once, reached over and gave Rachael's hand a quick squeeze, then said, "Thank you, Mother."

"You may refer to me as Chthon, Denny," she informed him politely. "Such that there is no confusion during our conversation, as Mother Tonzi is among us."

"Thank you, I am honored," Mother Tonzi said, nodding respectfully toward Chthon.

"As am I," Chthon admitted. "It's not every day that the Dual-Aspect gets asked out on a dinner date."

Cuan's slanted eyes almost bugged out of his head. His former respect for Denny? Now it was that, times one million.

After taking a quick sip from his stein, Denny said, "Thank you, Chthon. We are honored that the Dual-Aspect – the Metacosmic Dual-Aspect, I mean – could take the opportunity to speak with us in an informal setting."

"You're welcome," Chthon replied, her formerly somewhat robotic female voice a bit more animated now. Almost as if she were actually a living being, and having a good time.

"Sure, sure," Denny said. "It's just... just a bit mind-blowing to be here, wherever here is, and to be talking to the Prime Mover itself. Herself," he quickly corrected. "Themselves?" he added.

"Ayahuasca, maybe?" Chthon blatantly taunted him. "Still tripping, Denny?"

He shook his head. "No, not like that. I'm completely sober now, I can assure you. Adrenaline. Immortal-level version of it, too. But I'm sure that time is of the essence, so—"

"Time means nothing," Chthon laughed, her voice growing warmer and warmer. "We control it down below what you'd call the sub-Planck level. Way below. All the way up, and all the way down. So, please, by all means, take your time. Think about what you really wish to know, then ask. I might even be so inclined, if your questions are well-formed, to reply truthfully. No promises, of course. I am the Dark Earth Mother, after all."

Mother Tonzi bridled at that, her rheumy eyes alight with inner fire. "The Mother speaks nothing but truth! Always!"

"Yes, the Mother does," Chthon agreed laconically. "But, as you can plainly see, and as I explained earlier, I am the metacosmic version of the Mother. I'm not the EarthZero version of the Mother, nor the Dark Earth Mother, nor Chthon. I am the ultimate instantiation of your parochial, local deities and cosmic forces. Metacosmic. Above and beyond your experience, my dearest Mother Tonzi. All That All Which Is, All That All Which Binds. And I look like a flat-chested robot."

Embarrassed by such familiarities from her divine godhead, Mother Tonzi stared disconsolately down into her plate. Rachael and Denny exchanged quizzical glances, while Cuan hid his smile with another tug of his stein.

"Denny?" Chthon asked him.

"Yes?" he replied, suddenly noticing that she was no longer quite so flat-chested. That, indeed, some massive metallic hooters had bloomed from that previously flat sea of chrome. "Err..." he temporized, noting Chthon's lascivious smirk, now that she had also caused to manifest an interesting pair of bee-stung lips. Temporarily taken aback, his mind roiled as he struggled to hold on to a single strand of thought. "Normally," he admitted through somewhat numb lips, "I can run multiple threads of thought simultaneously. No trouble. But now? I'm having trouble keeping my mind on any single subject for too long. I don't understand..."

Every head at the table, including little Penny's, turned to stare directly at Denny. In eerie unison, they whispered, "Aya-huas-ca!"

Shit! Denny thought, busted. "I'm still tripping, right?" They all nodded in unison, their smiles frozen on their faces.

"But you're still talking directly to me, Denny," Chthon informed him, leaning back to settle into the cushioned booth. "We've moved way past the pretty lights and shining shapes part of the psychonautical experience. In fact, you've done so well that you've jumped directly past Orion's gateway, through the Milky Way, and straight down into the central galactic black hole. Metaphysically speaking, of course. Now, you're directly sharing an experience with me. A quite real one, metaphysically speaking, of course."

Buzzed or not, Denny made the proper connection. "So, no 'Book of the Dead' needed? My heart was like a feather after all?"

"And you blazed right through the Duat, directly to me," she replied, a bizarre pattern of kohl rising from her face. It danced and weaved, like light cycle trails in *Tron*, ultimately stilling around two newly risen almond-slanted eyes. Eyes just like Void's eyes. "Just like the immortal you are. Now ask it, Denny. Ask the question you've been waiting to ask of me."

"How was Penny conceived?" he asked bluntly, with no hesitation. "No one since that time and until this very moment has been able to conceive. No one, meaning humanity in general. Most of the higher life forms, too, although there have been some exceptions. Which fortunately didn't live long. The main bulk of life as we knew it is hanging on now by the slimmest, most fragile thread. We might indeed defeat the Death Horde, only to go extinct at some point in the not so distant future. EarthZero is below replacement level. We're facing extinction, from more than one direction. So how did Rachael and I get pregnant with Penny?"

Chthon stared straight into Denny's soul. "She is the one who breathes life."

The response hung heavy in the air of the now silent scene. No one else moved around the table, because they weren't real, he finally admitted. Illusions. Lies. Just like everything else.

Several solution paths ran in Denny's computer-like mind, despite the influence of the ayahuasca. Or, perhaps in this case, because of it.

"No," Denny's mouth formed the word of denial. Yet it was impotent, and he knew it. "No, you're not being the Mother. You're being Chthon. And you're lying. You're lying."

She sat in stony silence.

"She's not an avatar of you," Denny said, his voice thick with emotion. "She's not! She's just Rachael, my wife! There's no way... She doesn't even have powers like... like..."

Slowly, Chthon nodded her head. "She is the one who breathes life," she said softly, her form shapeshifting into an identical copy of Rachael's. Save for her eyes, which remained dark with seething energies. "She is the one who breathed life into the dead seeds of your union. Her will made the choice of life over certain death. In so doing, she ushered into EarthZero's timeline the impossible: Anshadar. She served the will of the Metacosmic Dual-Aspect, as well she should, for her soul is but an extension and permutation of our own. Of my own."

A long, silent pause, during which Denny realized that hot, salty tears were cascading down his stubbled face. Then, one of his solution paths matured, yielding a particularly horrific end state. "No. Tell me you won't do this. Tell me you won't take her away from me."

"Of course I will," she said. "And of course she will. That's her destiny. That's how EarthZero is truly reborn. Rachael will merge with the resonance, and the resonance, moving across the world, will rejuvenate all life. She is the one who breathes life, Denny. No one else may do this. No one else has the power to save life on the planet. Rachael has to die, sacrifice her own soul, such that EarthZero may survive."

Enraged, Denny stood, slamming his fists down on the table. "No," he said fiercely. "I forbid it. I reject your meddling, and I defy your lack of imagination, Mother."

Suddenly, the original, flat-chested metal mannikin reappeared. Its fused fingertips rose to brush its no longer extant lips in feigned shock.

Denny continued, "I am of the opinion of Void in this matter, Mommy Dearest. You so-called higher immortals – the One

Above, Helel, and the Dual-Aspect itself, at any level – might have all the cosmic power that there ever was. But you've grown beyond simple survival instincts because everything has become so easy for you. You've lost that cunning edge that we former mortals have in spades. So, while you've vectored directly to the perfect linear solution – slaughter Rachael so that her power can cause life to work normally again – you've missed the nonlinear solution paths, of which there are many. Here's one for you: We find a Talisman, or resurrect the old one, and we use her Hekatek amplification power to empower Rachel to perform the ceremony without having to sacrifice her soul. And my new runes? Add them to the mix, and we might not even need the Talisman. Boom! How 'bout them apples, you subtil old serpent?"

He saw it, just for a brief fraction of a second: She bit back a smile. Impossible of course, because she had naught but a tiny slit for a mouth, and her fused hands still hid it. Her next action, however, seemed to contradict her possible amusement.

"Careful, Denny," she veritably hissed at him, her hands falling gently to the tabletop. "Insulting the Dual-Aspect isn't necessarily wise. Especially for a soul that was only so recently mortal."

He gave an exaggerated shrug. "How am I supposed to react? You just told me that my wife was an avatar of you, then you just casually informed me that she had to die. I regret being aggressive, of course," he admitted politely. "I know you're not my enemy. Hell, you're probably our best ally. But I had to defend my wife. So, I'm sorry about accusing you about your immense cosmic power eclipsing your survival instincts. And daring to think that I could come up with a better—"

"Your solution is worthy, Denny," Chthon informed him in a detached voice. "See to it that you inform Mother Tonzi of this immediately upon your return," she said, even as shapes and colors began to swim around him. "Tell her everything we discussed.

Everything." Then, as the assumed reality whirled like some psychedelic blender, Chthon added, in Rachael's own voice, "You're a good husband, Denny."

Immediately upon his mental return to EarthZero, Denny jumped to his feet, waving his hands wildly, shouting at the top of his lungs, "Stop! Stop!"

Around him, the music stopped. Mother Tonzi and Rachael turned to face him from where they stood immediately before the boiling cauldron, quizzical looks on their faces. No towering apparition of the Mother loomed above them. Cuan and Penny, no protective green energies to be seen, looked up expectantly at him.

"Oh, thank god," Denny said, "I got back in time. I have a message from the Mother! I have a message from the Mother!" he yelled loudly. Shock and awe replied soundlessly from the gathered throng. The one that they had taken to calling "Quetzalcoatl" had spoken to the Mother, as only a true god could!

Then, awkwardly, he bent double, puking until his face turned green.

In the back of his mind, as total embarrassment washed over him like an ice cold wave, he could have sworn that he heard Chthon laughing wickedly.

CHAPTER 18

"Well, I'll be damned," Tim said slowly. "It *is* a freakin' pyramid. Here, in Antarctica. All those nuts on YouTube were right after all."

Abruptly jutting from the flat glacial desert expanse before them, the towering Nunatak of Nanabozho stood silent watch over uncounted leagues of nothing but nothing, and more nothing, at the literal bottom of the world, Antarctica.

Mercy's precise cutting of spacetime with Shunya had spirited them to a place on the expanse especially chosen by Mercy some unknown number of millennia ago, when she had first decided to render this her final anchor point. She had decided to craft her anchor point the exact distance from the pyramid itself required for her to take 112 paces from its nearest ground-level door. As such, and at being in such proximity to the massive construct itself, the Nunatak dominated most of the view.

"It's as big as that big one at Giza!" Leta marveled.

"Precisely," Mercy acknowledged. "That's because the creators of the pyramids at Giza used the Nunatak here as a template. Copied it almost verbatim."

"What?" Tim asked, incredulous. "You mean ancient Egyptians knew about a pyramid in Antarctica, and they just happened to have blueprints of it to copy?"

Everyone else, save for Void, turned to look at Tim. Leta took the task of explanation upon herself.

"Tim?" she began, reaching out to hold his hands. "Of course, Void wasn't here when we were getting blasted and exchanging tall tales. So, he's excused. But you, you're forgetting something you've heard before again. I'm starting to worry about your mind, man. What's bugging you so much that you'd keep on forgetting important things? You can talk to me. To us. We're your friends, Tim."

"I know, Leta," he replied swinging their hands slightly. "And I've never had such good friends before. Trust me, I get it. But what's been bugging me... What's been killing me. Killing me, twisting my soul into a bitter knot. Well, I just said it back there in the Null. I said I still had my faith. My Christian faith. The one, true, unshakable attribute of my character; the belief system that guided me through many years of life. I said I still had my faith. But I lied, Leta. I lied. I keep trying to pray, to seek forgiveness, but I'm praying to what I think's nothing more than an empty abyss now. I can't reconcile what the Good Book told me with what's actually happened. It's more than just a tiny margin of error. It's the most obvious, blatant lie I've ever experienced. I mean, look at it! Look at us, what we've become! It's just like what Void just told us. And if anyone remaining on this fucked up simulated world knows the truth, it's got to be him. He died, and he came back. Not 'came back' like Dwayne did. Dwayne was healed. I saw it. But Void? He came back, by himself, from nothing. Nothing. Not even Jesus did that, Leta," he finished, tears welling in his eyes. "Not even Jesus..."

Leta's reply caught in her throat. Tim discerned in that instant of hesitation on her part that she, too, had lied. Something unsaid passed between them, and Leta clutched Tim's hands up close to her mouth, a gentle kiss falling lightly on his hands.

Suddenly, they both became aware of Void, who now loomed over them. Unseen by either Leta or Tim, Mercy's hand tugged at the material of his clothes, at the small of his back.

"It's okay, Mercy," Void said softly. He stared down at the two, first at Leta, then Tim, before he fixed his gaze upon the middle distance. "I understand what you're feeling, my friends," he said gently. "So please forgive me for saying this. Yet, I have to say it, so that you will know, and you will believe."

Still holding hands, both Leta and Tim gazed up at Void's circumspect face in silence. Both suspected, and dreaded, what they were about to hear. They were not disappointed.

"There is a book yet unwritten, beyond what you know as 'The Book of Revelation," Void intoned. "In this yet unwritten book, we are the avenging angels. We are the breakers of the seals. We are the ones who fight the War Between Heaven and Hell. In our book, we have but one single, simple task: Redeem the world. We fight to redeem our world, our cosmos. To free it from the tyranny of the One Above, and free it from the nihilistic pride of the Lightbringer. In our book, Heaven doesn't want us, and Hell is afraid we'll take over. They're both right. We're fighting for redemption, for freedom, from both of them. We have to defeat both the Devil and God in order to win our redemption. Caught between Heaven and Hell, we truly walk the Path of the Void, balanced between so-called 'darkness' and so-called 'light'. Favoring one over the other wins us nothing but a temporary reprieve from the ultimate fate of our world, our cosmos, because neither the Devil nor God intends to keep EarthZero around, win or lose. Quite simply, we mean nothing to them. Nothing. Win, lose, draw... they simply erase us, our world, our cosmos, from existence, with no more compunction or compassion as you would show to an ant that you just happened to step on. So we must strive for that middle way that redeems us. It's the only logical course of action for us to take. It's the only way to save our world, and our universe."

"And that's the 'Way of the Void'?" Leta inquired, seeking Void's eyes. He nodded once.

"And I suppose," Tim said, suddenly smiling, "that the book after 'The Book of Revelation' will be 'The Book of the Void'".

Abruptly, Void laughed. "I sure as hell hope not," he admitted, embracing both of them. "That sounds positively grim. How about," he offered, "something like, 'Cute, Fuzzy Kittens Redeem Everybody', or something upbeat like that?"

Laughing, Leta released her grasp of Tim's hands and slugged Void on the thigh. "You're a fool, Void!" she snickered. "And you're apparently made of concrete or something, too," gingerly flexing her numb hand. "Got a compressive modulus for *him*, Tim?"

"I can't count that high," Tim laughed, shaking his head. He gave Void a sidelong glance. "Void, I get it. It's really all about redemption, at this point. Nothing else really matters. Just redemption. That... that makes it easy enough to reconcile with my beliefs. Kind of a major theme there," he admitted, smiling, "and that's some major overlap. We're redeeming not only ourselves, but also the entire universe. That's deep."

"I'm just doing it for kicks," Mercy said, emerging from Void's shadow. "You can redeem whoever you want. God. Satan. Cute, fuzzy kittens. Whatever. I'm just in it for fun."

"You're fibbing, Mercy," Ku'tu taunted her, her laughter mocking, tinkling. "You don't want to redeem God or Satan. Just cute, fuzzy kittens. So you can eat them."

"True," Mercy lied, smiling wickedly. "Let's do this, peeps," she said, taking off toward the nunatak's door, softly counting aloud her steps.

At precisely 112, she ceased counting, as the group stood presently before a rather normal-looking, humanoid-sized rectangular door. A rather normal-looking door wrought of slightly translucent ice, that is. One with no apparent doorknob, handle, or hinges. Crinkling her nose, she inclined herself toward the door, her eyes expertly appraising it, searching for something that no longer was there.

"What the eff—" she said in disbelief. "The damn thing doesn't see me."

"See you?" Leta asked, concerned. "You okay there, Mercy?"

"I'm fine," Mercy replied quickly, biting back the urge to be a smartass and tell her friend that she really didn't need a religious counselor, either. "Cute, fuzzy kittens," she whispered to herself, regaining control. "It's just... it's just that the door doesn't see me. That's how you get in. The door sees you, you see your reflection, and your reflection opens the door for you. Silly, of course, but that's his sense of humor. But now it's not working. Maybe I need to knock now, or something? Maybe he's just playing around?"

She knocked softly. Then, after a pause of precisely 0.5 seconds, she knocked again, harder. Much harder. Hard enough to deform quarter-inch steel. Defiant, the ice door contemptuously allowed not a single decibel in reply.

Mercy liked this not at all, and the expression on her face as she turned to face her companions said as much.

"Guys," she began, slowly shaking her head, "I suddenly got a really cold feeling in my soul. Not my normal super angst, either. I mean, for real. I think something's wrong. Really wrong."

Leta stepped forward quickly, gently elbowing Mercy's unyielding form aside.

"I got this, girl," Leta declared, a gout of elemental flame the consistency and color of whirling pahoehoe arcing between her outstretched left hand and the ice door. Nothing, not even the hiss of steam, as the ice door once more taunted them silently. Drawing herself even and square to the door, snarling, she gave it a two-handed blast, channeling and intensifying her power. Harmonizing with her power, her artificed body suit's embedded runes began to glow like magma, pulsing in syncopation with her channeled power.

"Ah, shit, that's hot!" Tim swore, backing up behind Void, Ku'tu, and Mercy, who seemed unaffected by the extreme heat. Instinctively, he raised his arms before his face, and his own body suit pulsated briefly. Manifested from the ground a full kilometer beneath the glacier, thin streams of basalt erupted before him, working free from the ice beneath his feet. In the veritable blink of an eye, a barrier of stone shaped like an overlarge Spartan shield appeared, sheltering him from the intense heat.

After a few futile seconds, Leta ceased her fiery outburst. The ice door remained unscathed, to her immediate chagrin.

"I can't believe it," Leta said, breathing heavily from the exertion. "First time that I haven't been able to melt something that I really wanted to melt. Especially some weak-ass ice."

"Want me to breathe on it?" Ku'tu asked, enjoying her friends' failures.

Immediately shaking her head, Mercy rapidly replied, "Oh hell no, Ku'tu. He'll have a shit-fit if we wreck his pyramid."

"So *my* weak-ass fire was okay," Leta bridled, smirking, "but Ku'tu's is too much? Fuck you, Mercy," she finished with a laugh.

Shrugging, Mercy said, "Well, I think Ku'tu meant doing it in her Big Momma Dragon form."

"Oh," Leta acknowledged, nodding and saving some face. "But what if we can't get in? What if your friend's really in trouble, and we *have* to get in?"

"Then I'll spit some fire on it," Ku'tu said agreeably. "I think Mercy really meant that it's Void's turn, next. Before mine. Because, after my turn, there won't *be* another turn. Big Momma Dragon is right."

Slowly, both Tim and Leta started laughing, joined by both Mercy and Ku'tu. They stopped abruptly, however, when Void walked up to the door, for his usual mien had been replaced by something akin to pure malice. Sheer hate, on a cosmic scale. It was a most unsettling sight, to gaze into his eyes and finally see his soul.

"Void..." Mercy said, moving quickly to interpose herself between his towering bulk and the ice door. "Get a grip," she bade him, her palms up, pleading with him. His eyes showed nothing but darkness, and his chest was issuing forth a dull nimbus of black light, outlined by slowly twirling fractal rainbows. "He's not the enemy. He's a friend, Void. You're slipping into your Godslayer mode. Back off. Don't do it. Please," she pleaded, noting his eyes narrowing, "he's my friend."

"Mercy," Void grated, slowly chambering his right hand, "Nanabozho's not the god I'm here to slay..."

Silently mouthing the words *"Oh, shit!"*, Mercy abruptly tumbled and rolled past Void.

Then, Time seemed to flash-crawl along on limping, broken legs as the VoidSpawn struck the highly artificed ice door with something beyond mere physical force. It was the will to power embodied in humanoid form, lashing out and striking not only at the physical manifestation of the magickally gimmicked ice door, but also at the bound magick itself. Magicks bound by the power of a true god. Not that such power, able to resist a proximate low-yield thermonuclear blast, could stand before the awesome, implacable will of the VoidSpawn. Especially not when that primally enchanted artifact stood before him and his prey.

A sound like the calving of an impossible, screaming iceberg followed the strike. Otherwise lethal ice shrapnel impacted harmlessly off of Tim's hastily erected group shield, which covered all but Void. An immediate ice fog filled the local area, obscuring all sight for several seconds, until Leta's slowly modulated heat aura burned it off. Now, they could see that the ice door, as well as several tens of meters around the epicenter of Void's strike, was no more. A triangular hallway, slightly larger than the former ice door, inclined in its rise, greeted them from beyond the volume of enchanted ice removed by the strike. Void was nowhere to be seen.

"Aw, no," Mercy grumbled, Shunya flaring once more to life in her left hand. "C'mon!" she implored her companions, moving swiftly into the hallway, on point. They dashed in behind her. "Maybe we can reach him before..."

Another massive sound, seemingly coming from the very ice of the pyramid around them, bowled into them from all sides, assaulting their senses. Ice shards peppered the triangular hallway, falling from the ceiling and erupting from the walls and floor. Though slightly less energetic than the debris from the ice door strike, the impact still stung them like angry hornets, their wards and various charms notwithstanding. Leta's conscious extension and shaping of her heat aura dispelled the cloying ice fog around them, while Tim's earthen bindings caused a proactive shielding of basalt to rise up on their flanks, the dense rock spilling to the ice floor of the hallway behind them as they sprinted past its conjured protection.

A few seconds elapsed as they continued their pell-mell sprint up the slightly inclined triangular hallway, which grew in dimension as they progressed toward the center of the nunatak. After another breathless moment, they cleared the aperture of the ice hall, where they spilled into a surprisingly large inner chamber, which appeared to have been thrown into total disarray by a recently passed EF-6 tornado.

The Great Medicine Lodge of Nanabozho now stood in ruin. Great sheets of primeval birchbark, which had formerly served as the walls of the lodge, separating it and sealing it off from the fantastic ice nunatak itself, now littered the floor, twisted and grotesque. The embers of what had once been the central fire pit now fell from the air like hissing, miniature meteors. Hundreds of square meters of precious animal skins flittered and flapped on both the floor and upon the shattered remnants of the birch wall frame, moved by unseen and unsettled wind. Shattered gourds and unraveled baskets formed a fine mixed debris field beneath their feet. And there, slightly offset from the center of the lodge, near to the edge of where the fire pit had once blazed, stood Void, poised as if ready to spring at a rapidly fading pinwheel of radiant rainbow light before him. And there, on the floor behind Void, lay the writhing form of Nanabozho himself.

"Oh, no!" Mercy yelled, bounding quickly over to his side. "Nan! Nan!" she sobbed, bending down beside him, Shunya still active in her left hand. Immediately, as she began to scan his form for injuries, she noted that there was a play of tiny pinwheel sparkles of light issuing forth from the centerline of his body. Like bugs drawn to an electric bug zapper, the sparkles vectored directly to Shunya, causing its entire length to flash with silver light.

Without turning, Void bade Mercy, "Dispel Shunya."

Immediately complying, Mercy caused her blade to remove itself from local spacetime. At once, the sparkles issuing forth from Nanabozho vanished. She bent down, cradling him closely to her, as Tim, Leta, and Ku'tu formed up between her and Void.

The eyes of the dying god met hers. Sepia eyes, formerly full of immortal zest and mischief, now were dull and flat. Recognizing the hollow look of death she had seen in the eyes of so many mortals during her many years, hot, stinging tears began to well in her eyes.

"Nan," she implored him, "tell me what happened. Tell me who did this to you, so I may avenge you."

"It..." Nanabozho replied in Ancient Sidhe, his voice smooth as silk, "...it certainly wasn't Paul Bunyan."

"Oh, no, don't say that," Mercy softly admonished him. "Nan. No jokes. You've got to tell us. Tell me. There isn't much more time..."

"It was just a few moments ago," he said, pausing a few seconds to regain enough strength to continue. "Not much before you and your friends ran in here. Timing. It's always timing, isn't it? Essence of comedy. Easy to describe. Hard to master. Took me a long time. But I think I finally got it right. I mean, this has to be the last punchline, right? Last one for me, at least. So I have to time this one just right."

Seeing that the local spacetime had healed and the warp was no more, Void turned to regard them. Taking the cue, so did the rest of the group.

"See?" Nanabozho faintly laughed. "Timing. Now that everyone is tuned in, I'll spend the last few moments of my formerly immortal life and clue you young ones in. The stakes of the sim we're in just went way, way up. And, yes, you're not the only smarty pants who know we're in a simulation. Took me a while, myself, to discern that there actually was a man behind the curtain. In the beginning, I'd always thought that it was just the gods running the show. We arose with the Fae of this world, back in the long-ago mists of time, during the First Morning. Brothers and sisters of the same seed. We were content to live within the Song of the Sidhe, but, once mankind arose, their belief actualized and realized us. We had to leave behind our beloved Song and enter the world of man.

"In this beginning, the New Gods had the form of man, yet were immortal, unable to die. Except, of course, if we burned to ashes, got eaten by cannibal squirrels, or the like. Yet, over the many seasons, some of us did indeed meet death, usually through our own internecine wars. For, though the humans did not know how to do so, we gods did know exactly how to slaughter one another.

And thus, our numbers decreased over time, until only a few others and I remained.

"And now, history lesson over, the sigil has birthed a new assembly of immortals. Welcome, my friends," he said to the group. "However," he paused briefly, his breathing labored, "the sigil also birthed an abomination: a rogue Watcher."

"Ah," Mercy said quickly, "that's not good."

No one else said anything, perhaps due to their shock at hearing something so insane, so Nanabozho continued:

"As I said, it arrived here only moments before you did. I was in communion with the twin to your blade, Mercy. I was just in the very moment of feeling the blade reach out to Shunya, probably exactly when you were using it to warp here, when the rogue Watcher burst into being right behind where Fresswelle was levitating before me. Right there, almost within arm's reach of me. And it got in here without any trouble at all, apparently, even though, as you well know, I've warded my nunatak and lodge down to the atomic level. It got right in without so much as breaking a sweat. Right through god-level magicks.

"It had chosen an interesting humanoid form with which to greet me. One I had thought reserved for those of the First Seed. Tall, muscular Fae, it was. Blue sparks danced around its eyes. No wings, though. Probably just hiding them or something so as not to reveal its relative power. Even though it had just blatantly done so, just by getting inside like that.

"When he – I'm not using the term loosely; he was definitely in a male form – addressed me, he used a peculiar dialect of the most ancient Sidhe. First Seed stuff. He named me properly, using my First Name, which no one else still living knows. So I knew I had to take heed, and I did. I gave him the proper nod, and he told me, in a rapid monotone, that he was here at behest of the Lightbringer, the Creator of this world. That he was here to retrieve the Fractal Blade, the Blade of Time, Fresswelle. That he was going to have to use it to bend spacetime and travel into the past, such that he could fulfill the mandate of the Lightbringer. His mission was to save the sim," he continued, switching to English, emphasizing the word "sim". "Said he had to go back and 'right some stones'. Or was that 'write some stones'? Like, with a 'w'? Don't know, because I didn't press him on it, and that's because he had just casually reached over and plucked Fresswelle out of the air.

"Unfortunately, it didn't instantly slaughter him, which confirms his immortality. But it seemed like, judging from how his eyes rolled back in his head for a split-second, that he realized Shunya was near. He didn't like that. I guess that's why he suddenly blurred and spun around like a cyclone, then lit into me. He was too fast to defend. He went right through my wards, too, like they were nothing. Couldn't even auto-shift to my white rabbit avatar, either. Hit me many, many times with that blade. Never felt a single instance of being cut or slashed or pierced, though. Just felt cold. Colder than I've ever been. I think it cut away my powers, then it cut away my soul. Then I fell, and that big fella came in.

"The rogue Watcher took one look at the new guy here, his eyes went wide with shock, like he recognized him or something. Then he used the blade to cut spacetime around him. He was gone through the warp faster than I could blink.

"Hang in there, Nan," Mercy told him. "We're going to get you over to Dreamland, get you some medical help."

Nanabozho shook his head, his long white hair spilling down to the floor.

"Shunya just accelerates the already irreversible process of primal decay that Fresswelle inflicted on me," he told her softly. "I have only a few minutes remaining now, Mercy. There's nothing you or your friends could do for me anyway. You're immortal, true. But you're not gods."

"No!" Mercy protested. "I refuse to accept that. There has to be a way to save you! Even if I can't use Shunya to transport us back to Dreamland without killing you in the process, there has to be something else we can do. C'mon, team," she barked at her friends, "let's figure this out!"

"Maybe we can tap into the magicks of the nunatak?" Leta offered. "And/or some of his magick items? He has to have something around we could use for a soul battery for him."

"I like you," Nanabozho said somewhat brightly to Leta. "Clever. Like me. But no items to use. I've absorbed all of my former enchantments from virtually everything, except my nunatak, over the past year. Had to. The sigil almost killed me."

"Use the nunatak's pyramidal resonance to directly transport to Dreamland?" Tim suggested.

"Good one," Nanabozho admitted. "But my soul, or what's left of it, is directly entangled with the nunatak. You might get my soulless corpse back with you to your Dreamland. But that wouldn't do anyone any good. Except maybe for Mercy. I'm sure she could use it as a mannikin or something."

"Not funny," Mercy dismissed. Then, noting the hurt look in Nanabozho's eyes, she quickly added, "Well, it was funny, of course, in the context of using a corpse as a mannikin, I guess."

"Not like you've never done it before, Mercy," he smirked right back.

"Aal Ball isn't here," Ku'tu said, "or else we might be able to use them to harbor Nanabozho's soul for the journey there, and then see if we could get Maynard and Denny and some of the noble Fae to craft a new physical body for him."

"Ah," Nanabozho sighed. "I miss them. Aal Ball, that is. I have no idea who Maynard and Denny are. But I'm afraid I can't fit into Aal Ball. My soul's too big. Even now, at the end."

Everyone now was looking at Void. Disgusted with something he wasn't yet ready to share, he just stood in place and rolled his eyes.

"Void!" Mercy exclaimed loudly, causing Nanabozho to wince. "We're all asking for help. How can you be so cold, and just stand there like a broken ice golem?"

Shrugging, Void replied, "Because I know he's lying, Mercy. Remember: I know exactly how Fresswelle works. It basically takes all, half, or nothing. It doesn't leave a victim with some undefined remnant of their former power. So, he's lying like the Trickster he is, and he's not quite as dead as he's wanting us to think he is. And that means that he's probably intentionally delaying us from trying to trace and follow the Watcher who has Fresswelle. Oh," Void added with a fake, warm smile, "and I'm not here to slay you, Nanabozho. I'm after that rogue Watcher puke."

Nanabozho actually blinked. Then, never averting his gaze from Void, he slowly freed himself from a disbelieving Mercy and stood.

"I... can't... believe you—" Mercy stammered.

"It's true," Nanabozho said calmly. "I had to be certain that he hadn't come for me. You don't get through so many millennia as I have without being prudent. Especially when a Godslayer is involved. Yes, I'm delaying you. And, yes, I'm lying. But only a little." He turned, smiling broadly, toward Mercy. "C'mon, kiddo! You would have done the same thing, too, given the circumstances."

"Why I oughta..." Mercy began, murder in her eyes, pretending to summon her blade.

"So, okay," Tim asked quietly. "What was true in what you just said, and what was false?"

"Yeah!" Leta fumed. "And why are you delaying us?"

"Good questions," Nanabozho replied, happy indeed that neither Mercy nor Void was going to kill him. "What a truly dangerous crew you travel with now, Mercy. Clever. Powerful. Askers of discerning and diplomatic questions. Please note that your male friend with the taste for deep woods camo gear said 'false' in opposition to 'true', instead of using the derogatory 'truth' versus 'lie'. I like that. It appeals directly to my inner pathological liar."

"Get on with it," Mercy prodded him. "We're on a tight schedule here. Save the world? Okay?"

"Okay," he agreed. "Well, it *was* a Watcher, who *had* to be rogue, because he didn't disintegrate along with his fellow Igigi once the sigil had performed its task. He probably had indeed been tasked by the Lightbringer to do this deed for him. That only fits. The Fae form he chose to appear in? I don't know the answer to that one. Whatever, I guess?"

Void grumbled, causing Nanabozho to flinch. "I know who he is pretending to be. I just want to wait till you're done before I say it."

"Huh?" Nanabozho asked. "Why not just say it now?"

Rolling his eyes again, Void blurted, "Because you really don't wanna see Big Momma Dragon get upset, do you?"

"Who?" Nanabozho shrugged.

"The Tink," Mercy said, hiking a thumb over at Ku'tu's tiny, flitting form.

"Why would I be upset, Void?" Ku'tu inquired, buzzing over in front of Void's face. "Logically, it has to be the form of Zon T'Danu. Certainly wasn't your form. Rogue Watcher dude had to pick someone's familiar form to use the blade. Zon had to have been his only other alternative. Not that he's Zon, or anything like that. He's just a doppelgänger."

"See?" Nanabozho said. "She's not upset at all."

"Actually," Ku'tu said quickly, moving over to buzz near Nanabozho's face, "I implied that I was not upset, but *I* was lying. Just like *you've* been lying. And just like you've failed at being the guardian of Fresswelle. Which might have cost me my entire race, because they're stuck in the blade, thanks to the Lightbringer's meddling. I'm not actually upset with you at all, or the freak who's making a mockery of my former husband's sacred image. I'm actually *outraged*. So, please continue with your tale, and spare us more lies. Or, you'll get to see firsthand what kind of sheer hell Big Mamma Dragon can unleash on tiny little nunataks like yours."

"Tiny?" Nanabozho replied meekly. "Oh, I remember now," he said quickly, noting the otherworldly fire in her tiny eyes. "During my communion with the blade, I saw that Watcher guy... I mean, the guy he was imitating, hanging around with a rather large dragon. I take it, that was you?"

Ku'tu nodded in confirmation.

"Okay, well," he continued, warming back up to the task, now that he had dodged another potentially fatal bullet, this one made of phlogiston, "I think I can safely say, without stretching the truth at all, that everything I've said is true. Except for the dying part. And he only hit me once with his blade. More of a glance of a strike, it truly was. Like a love tap that slightly missed."

Mercy exhaled loudly. "You know, I thought that maybe Fresswelle could have sped him up enough in local spacetime to actually have given you a challenge. But I guess it really didn't give you a challenge, did it?"

Nanabozho shook his head. "Nope. No challenge. Might say I have a few lucky rabbit feet tucked away. He missed me all 1,000 times he struck."

"So he *was* trying to kill you?" Mercy asked, incredulous at his casual admission.

"Maybe just trying to brush me away, so he could hop into his warp? I was stuck in real time, so, basically, I couldn't really move out of his way."

"But you still managed to dodge all of his attacks, or otherwise make him miss you?" Mercy inquired.

"Obviously," he preened. "Or else, I probably would have been killed, god or not. That blade's as wicked as yours is, Mercy. It's a god-killer. Potentially, at least. Maybe. Just not to me," he finished under his breath.

"So," Leta said, "we have a lunatic Watcher running around through time, waving a god-killing, time-warping blade at anyone in his way? Holy shit. How do we even begin to deal with that?"

"We can't," Void admitted. Before everyone's hopes hit the floor, he continued, "But, we can start looking around for where the blade is."

"How? Where?" Mercy asked. "If we take it literally, and assume Nan didn't add any artistic license to it..." She paused, giving him a glance, which he returned with a noncommittal shrug. "He went to the past. What does that even imply? Is he going to be waiting somewhere for us? Is the blade going to be with him? Do we even know where to start?"

"He gave us a clue," Void reminded them. "I think it might mean both."

"Both?" Tim asked. "Both what?"

"'Right' and 'write,'" Void replied. "Pretty obvious clue, actually. Especially seeing how he switched to modern American English to tell us that. Now we just need to find which stone or stones he was referring to, find them, and see if it leads us to Fresswelle. But first," he said, staring hard at Nanabozho, "Nan here has to finish, and tell us why he was delaying us."

"Oh, but you're good at this, Void," Nanabozho told him, smiling craftily. "But, to be truthful, I switched to American

English to properly convey the word for 'simulation', because, in Ancient Sidhe, there's only a stupid handful of words to describe something like that. And most of them deal with lies, or varying degrees of truth. So I didn't want to go there."

"You're delaying again," Ku'tu reminded him.

He shrugged. "Force of habit? Sorry. Where were we?" he asked rhetorically. No one bit, however. "Ah, tough crowd. I'm here all week. Be sure to try the buffalo. Okay, okay. The Lightbringer told me, a little while before the sigil worked its charms, that he was going to send an agent to retrieve Fresswelle from me. That I was supposed to just hide the blade from casual and deific eyes until he came to get it. So, not being one to argue with Kichi Manido himself, I agreed. Well, that, and because he said I'd just wither up and die anyway if I didn't agree, because most of my followers were going to die, and that this was my only possible chance to avoid that fate. Then, he set Fresswelle there, where I described it had been, and I've been glued to it 24/7 ever since. And the Watcher just now came to get it. Too bad. It was very entertaining, now that all the cable shows are gone."

They looked at him as if he had totally lost his mind.

"Nan?" Mercy said guardedly. "We know for a fact that you're lying, because Void received the blade around the time of the sigil, and he wielded it briefly thereafter, until a certain event happened and it vanished again."

Taken aback, Nanabozho replied, "Huh? Oh. Well, *yes*, it *did* disappear from here for a little while, back there at the start. But it came right back. Figured it was just the sigil's charms mucking about with it. Certainly hit me like a war club to the face. Look, Mercy, I've been glued to that thing for just over a whole year now. Do you know how difficult it was to tend to my scattered and decimated people while I was holding watch over it? Bilocation costs a pretty penny, my dear, and if one thing I've told you is true, it's that I've had to break down and consume almost all of my old magicks to empower myself to help my people since the sigil wrecked almost everything."

"Okay," Mercy agreed, somewhat satisfied, "I know you're serious when you talk about your people, Nan. Okay. But where is he taking the blade? Which stones are the ones he's talking about?"

He shrugged. "I have no idea. Nobody told me anything about that. If I were you, I'd start with the obvious megalithic sites, then work back and down from there. Me? I've to clean up this mess, and get back to helping my people. Maybe even go down there for a visit. It's been a while," he said as he gathered a random fur from the floor and began to shake debris from it.

"Do you know how many megalithic sites there are?" Mercy cried loudly. "I'll have to scan each and every single one of them with Shunya in hand in order to even see if the blade is there. That's going to take forever, and we don't have forever, because the Death Horde is coming! We have to find it now! Now!"

That stopped Nanabozho in his proverbial tracks. The fur he had been shaking dropped from his hands back to the floor. Slowly, concentrating heavily, he turned around in place, chanting something under his breath. First, he faced Mercy, then Ku'tu and Leta, then Void. Finally, he stopped turning when he faced Tim, and his eyes opened wide even as his chanting ceased.

"Ah," he said simply. "The answer's been here the whole time. If anybody can find a stone, it's him."

"Interesting," Void said. "I would have reckoned that either Mercy or I would have been the proper conduits to seek Fresswelle: her, because she has its twin; me, because I've wielded it."

"And, normally," Nanabozho replied, "you would have been right. But I reckon now that the Watcher has gotten hold of it, and because he's running a mission with it, given to him by the Creator himself, things aren't normal anymore. I suspect that both personal and twin-based resonance are going to be quite subdued. Especially in the past. Especially when tampering with otherwise normal temporal flow. In fact, I suspect that Fresswelle's going to become stealthy, like a deer hunter. Too many bad folks, like this Death Horde, or some of the bad folks here on our world, could find it otherwise."

"I sure would like to know what the Watcher is going to do with it, back in the past," Ku'tu said quietly. "It better not involve something like converting my people into energy, or anything like that."

"Or using it to go back in time and kill one of us," Mercy said.

"Or alter the timeline in a dramatic way," Tim said.

Leta said nothing, even as Nanabozho and Void exchanged stony glances. It was a troublesome thought. And they had absolutely no way to intercede, they all knew, to change that particular fate.

With an audible sigh, Void broke the silence. "Fair enough. You have helped us by keeping the watch, Nanabozho. We won't fault you for anything you've said or done, because you've done this more for your people than for yourself. We thank you for your help in showing us that Tim might be able to show us the answer to the question of the missing blade. So, I would like to offer my service to you, to repay you for your help. And I think the best way to repay you, in this case, is to help you help your people. What say you to taking a trip to Dreamland with us, to see what we have to offer?"

Genuinely shocked and pleasantly surprised, Nanabozho smiled. He extended his right arm to Void, and Void accepted his embrace.

"For the first time in many years," Nanabozho admitted, his smile transforming to a sober, somber expression, "I have hope for this world. I have hope now because I now know that the Creator has favored me with friends, new and old, who will recall my name.

Who will one day tell my scattered people who I truly was, and how much I truly loved them. Thank you for this," he said solemnly to Void, his eyes darting to everyone else in turn, stopping finally to linger on Mercy. "But now, now that I have played my role, I must finally accept my fate. This new world, the one you call EarthZero, is not a world for the old gods. No, our time is done. We all must fade now, such that the new gods may take our place. Take our place, and take our power. For you, my new gods, must soon face the Vanth'Vash'Var."

Releasing his embrace of Void, Nanabozho turned to face the fire pit, which now, suddenly, was fully ablaze. Sitting down, he pulled his legs beneath him, slowly rocking in place.

"Go now, my friends," he bade them with a hoarse whisper which seemed to burn into their very souls. "Return to your Dreamland, to renew your quest for the Devouring Wave. I will first send my remaining people a dream, showing them their new way. Should they choose to accept this new way, they will come to you, and you will tell them of my love for them. Then, I will sing the song of my First Name, and I shall return past the First Morning to the Song of the Sidhe. Go, swiftly now. For, as a god, I must sing my song alone. And soon my lodge will turn to dust."

Beneath their feet, the floor of the lodge groaned and the nunatak began to shake, the first of many quakes to come assaulting it.

Flaring to fractal life, Shunya veritably crackled with pent up power.

Without a parting word to her friend, Mercy cut Reality into really tiny, wicked-sharp pieces, and the group departed the Nunatak of Nanabozho, leaving the last of the old gods on EarthZero to his eternal fate.

CHAPTER 19

"Ready to give it a shot?" Mhyrranda asked everyone around the Dreamland War Room table.

At the table with her were Maynard, and the newly returned team of Void, Mercy, Tim, Ku'tu, and Leta. All nodded affirmatively.

"And the others?" Mhyrranda asked Maynard directly.

"Eidolon upgrades in place on all council members," Maynard replied evenly, as his eerily lit eyes darted back and forth over a massive grid of Aal Ball-constructed viewscreens. "She wasn't joking when she said they had peeps who could transport to virtually all of the main settlements," he observed. "We got the Eidolon upgrades out to everyone in just a few minutes."

The Duchess nodded in agreement. "We are most blessed to have Santa Muerte and her people with us. Her jumpers are incredible. They expedited the process of getting the Silverstuff slivers from Aal Ball to Cholula and Los Angeles, to get their own war rooms up and running. And, more importantly, get them linked to everyone else's. Let's go live, Maynard. We're ready."

Focusing his will, Maynard's flitting fingers rapidly described a series of sideways figure eights over each one of the viewscreens. A deep green hue appeared in the wake of his elaborate movements, birthing a writhing, pinky-wide trench in the air from which issued tiny filaments of precise, purplish vectors. A moment passed in silence. Then, with a subtle hissing sound, the tiny filaments burst forth, winding themselves into and among one another, from viewscreen to viewscreen.

Around the war room table manifested the very real forms of the disparate council members in Atlanta, Los Angeles, and Cholula, the diameter of the table automatically expanding to seat everyone comfortably.

Mother Tonzi and Cuan represented the Cholula council members. Santa Muerte, Vir'gil, Dwayne, Beth, Denny, Racheal, and Penny represented the la Raza council members in Los Angeles. And from Atlanta, Peaches, Nick, Ami, M'Tumba, Chester, Riki, and Lucy held their arc of the war room table.

A broad smile dawned on Duchess Mhyrranda's face. "Welcome, everyone!" she said kindly. "Let's officially get the first meeting of the New Alliance underway." She paused deliberately, giving everyone a bit of time to adjust to the most curious Hekatek multilocation effect, which instantiated and shared among all of the entrained war rooms the forms of all council members. Though she knew damn good and well that she was here in Dreamland, with but a nudge of thought she could shift her perception to her projected image at any of the other war rooms. And once there, her senses shouted to her that she was, in fact, entirely, physically there.

"Oh, my, Peaches. I didn't realize you were that big!" she found herself exclaiming.

"Well, Duchess Mhyrranda, that's exactly what my last boyfriend said," Peaches replied, immediately covering his mouth with his enormous hands as he bit back laughter. Stifled giggles and some shocked expressions showed around the table.

"Starting off our first meeting with dick jokes?" Maynard said with a straight face. "Fine by me. Hi, Peaches," he finished, abruptly smiling.

Despite herself and her desire for order, Mhyrranda allowed herself to smirk. After all, she had walked right into that one. And some disarming humor was not necessarily a bad thing. "Right, then," she said. "First, don't be alarmed by the effects of the multilocation. It just takes a few moments to adjust. And I obviously didn't even give myself enough time to adjust before pitching that softball to Peaches. So go ahead and try it out. Will yourself to move from one war room to another. We'll take a minute so that everyone is comfortable, then we'll resume."

"Maynard?" Denny asked. "I can't see Mercy and Void at all, and Duchess Mhyrranda is really blurry, even when I occupy my projected image at Dreamland."

"Add Penny to that, too," Peaches said. "What a cute little sweetie!"

"And add Lucy, too," Denny said. "Hi, Lucy," he added, remembering her shy sweetness. The Fractal Mage herself.

"Hi, Denny," Lucy replied, the faint suggestion of her bottom lip implying a smile beneath her always present hood.

"I guess her power isn't so stupid, after all," Ami said quietly, earning her a stank glare from Nick.

"You're sitting right next to her, Ami!" Nick scolded her under his breath.

"I don't care," Ami said. "What's she gonna do? Turn me into a newt?"

"I could, too, you know?" Lucy said back, daintily laughing. "Might take a day or two..." she snickered, her soft voice a musical purr.

Lucy and Ami had become quick and fast friends over the past few days, sharing absinthe and shrooms of all sorts during Peaches' nightly parties. For Peaches' parties mostly were booty calls featuring muscular young men, disco lights, massive beats, and lots of bubbles. So the ladies tended to sit back and watch the spectacle, getting shit-faced and whispering snide comments about the fawning members of the elite coterie while Peaches lorded it over all the insane festivities. The Teaches of Peaches, for real.

Groaning, Maynard replied, "We expected as much. Duchess Mhyrranda, of course, can control her mental defenses. Which she might want to do now. But, for everyone else... Kicking in the Inferential Augmentation," he said, detached as he added another layer of sizzling inscriptions to the viewscreen tableau before him. "By way of explanation for everyone's benefit, even the current power of our four entrained war rooms has some scrying limitations. It's difficult, at this level of power, to remotely view any of the others. So, to solve that, especially as it would be silly for us not to be able to see the Duchess of Dreamland firsthand, Denny and I created a way for some sharing of direct, physical, non-hooked-up-to-Aal-Ball-or-the-war-rooms   imaging.   So, indirectly, what those at the same table see of those three will be added to the perception signals of everyone else. We'll inferentially be looking through each other's eyes."

Even as Maynard finished his explanation, Denny gave a thumbs-up, indicating that the tediously researched gimmick had worked. As they knew it would, of course.

"We're five by five now, Maynard. Good job," Denny said.

Mhyrranda cleared her throat. "Introductions are in order. Let's move widdershins, from me, around the table. I'm Duchess Mhyrranda of Dreamland. The Dreamwyrd. Pleased to see everyone."

From Dreamland they moved first to Atlanta, then Los Angeles, then finally Cholula. The leaders of their respective enclaves spoke first, followed by the rest. It took only a few moments, as everyone was eager to get to the next phase of the meeting. Well, only a few moments, except for the long minute of silence after Void introduced himself.

"Void..." he had said simply, the last of the Dreamland group to speak.

The silence had been eerie, awkward. Maynard had rolled his eyes as far up into his head as was humanly possible. "Duchess Mhyrranda?" he had finally interrupted.

"Ah, yes," Mhyrranda said, "after the introductions, we'll take a moment to return to this. I'm sure we all have questions we'd like to ask the Risen."

Embarrassed, Void looked over at Maynard, and the two of them tried for a moment to out-duel each other with eyes-rolling-back puissance. Not that anyone could actually see Void's.

"They're idiots," Tim deadpanned. "Please ignore them. We do."

They did, despite some deeply held mortal fears still nagging at their immortal souls that the Risen was there among them. Pulling faces, and acting like a total idiot, encouraged by the highest representative of the Mother on EarthZero.

Well, the highest representative of the Mother on EarthZero thus far, and in a very crowded field at that.

Continuing after the somewhat rushed, somewhat touched introductions, Mhyrranda said, "Right. Now, we'll get a group SitRep. We'll do the same rotation, and—"

"A moment, Dreamwyrd," Santa Muerte asked politely, to which Mhyrranda immediately deferred out of respect. "Rachael and Denny gave us most of the story, in detail, after they arrived from Cholula. Yet, my people are curious, and have asked me to learn it all; to learn what this 'Risen' means. I am their Lady of Death. I know the names of all the dead, and all of them do my bidding, should I ask. Yet, I know nothing of this Void, who has allegedly died and has been reborn, from nothingness. So, I must ask," she said, her dead snake eyes staring directly at the Spawn of the Void himself, "how is it that the Lady of Death does not know you?"

"Respectfully, Milady Death," Void said, using the Fae honorific, "Denny's tale will provide the whys and wherefores associated with our new understanding of 'As Above, So Below', and what it means in our Metacosmic Instantiation. And why you can't see me when I die."

A sharp intake of breath from the Cholula representatives followed. Denny and Rachael, disturbed to hear something like this come from Void, knew enough to remain quiet. Denny had sworn those present at the event of the fire drill ceremony to silence on the matter of the true, full story. *So how did Void know?* he asked himself, even as he knew the answer.

"Ah," Santa Muerte said, understanding at last. "Then we will await his tale. Then, again, I will ask you the very same question, Void. For there are no answers within anyone's purview, it would seem."

"Thank you, Milady Death," Void said diplomatically.

"Well," Mhyrranda said, "with that, let us proceed to the SitReps. We'll start here first, at Dreamland, then proceed accordingly. Leaders will, of course, speak for everyone else, if only for efficiency. Please feel free to add additional comments, of course, if necessary."

And, verily, they did speak, and recount their tales in detail. Nothing was spared. No one could risk sparing details, for such could be their undoing when the End of All Things loomed.

First, to no one's surprise or shock, the Fae had been accepted with wide open arms by everyone thus far. The consensus was that it was in fact a long-overdue family reunion, and virtually everyone was pleased. Well, except for a few of the Gentry, who just couldn't help being snobs to everyone, and the wild Fae, who still kept their distance from the formerly mortal humans. In time, perhaps they, too, would rejoin the family.

Nick and Ami's terse recounting of their Destructorama dropped a few jaws. It was astonishing to some, apparently, that but two of them could clear the roads from Dreamland to Atlanta in such a short time. And that the new generation of autonomous drones were doing it even faster. That so much positive change was happening so quickly. That they could, effectively, loot and preserve the best of the Old World, without being burdened by its many problems. Sure, social media sort of sucked right now, but everyone sensed that the entire concept would soon enough be considered archaic and quaint. Their current Eidolon session whispered to them the first of many promises to come.

The tale of Fresswelle, the Rogue Watcher, and the Last God drew particular attention. For some, it was the first that they had heard of the Twin Blades and the Watchers, and their context in the tragedy of EarthZero. This caused an hour long series of explanations regarding the time immediately prior to the Evolutionary Tribulation of the Sigil, the role of Lucifer and the One Above in all of this, and what the current status of the survivors of EarthZero was in relation to the impending attack of the Vanth'Vash'Var. Fear, exhaustion, and consternation wound in and out of the discussion, yet never did Surrender rear its ugly head. No, there would be a fight to the death, and beyond, for EarthZero. No more cowards remained, their kind having been purged during the Tribulation. Only heroes with souls of steel remained.

Chester's garden-tending was well-received, for it meant that hunger would no longer exist once his methods were shared. Curiously, what drew the most attention was that both M'Tumba and Riki were what they were: the Evolved. It seemed that, at least thus far, they were unique. However, now that eyes were opened, it would be difficult for other possible Evolved to escape notice.

Denny's tale, however, caused immediate gastric discomfort and unfortunate trepidation in all gathered.

"First," Denny began, "I'd like to state that Void and his crew arrived back in Dreamland only an hour or so before we called this meeting. I've been on commlink with Maynard almost that entire time, and I didn't see any brief or debrief mentioning what I'm about to describe. No way Void, or anyone on his crew, could have known this. But, somehow, Void did. This is from back when we were at Cholula. Okay, here it goes: Seems that during the massive ayahuasca ceremony at Cholula to rehearse the fire drill ritual, I was called by the Metacosmic Instantiation of the Dual-Aspect. I had a fantastic, trippy dinner date with Chthon herself. Long story short, she revealed that Rachael's thus-far seemingly dormant power was for her to be 'she who breathes life'; that she had impossibly caused our dead seed to reanimate and create little Penny. Rachael worked the will of Chthon, and brought forth the Anshadar Effect on EarthZero."

Silent anticipation grasped everyone's spines with talons of steel.

Mhyrranda's eyes sought Maynard's, drilling into them, because she, too, knew what it meant. Tim stared hard at Void, who just shook his head grimly in return.

"It's okay, guys," Denny assuaged. "While it's really cool that we all seem to know what that formerly obscure Fae-based phraseology means, and what that possible path could have meant for Rachael – in the context of pyramids and resonance – I resolved it, right then and there before Chthon herself. Chthon told me that Rachael would give her life to jumpstart the resonance across all of EarthZero, with life once more capable of reproduction becoming possible again. Not just the lower life forms. All life. However, I gave her grief, pointing out that the big cosmic powers – the Dual-Aspect, the One Above, and the Lightbringer, et al – had lost their edge for survival, being superpowered and all, and were blind to more elegant solutions. Solutions that I then provided. I told her that she suffered from a lack of imagination, too," he paused, laughing to himself. "I proposed that, instead of sacrificing Rachel to restart the pyramids, and restore some semblance of natural life to EarthZero, we could resurrect the Talisman, or find another immortal capable of amplifying powers. Use their power instead of burning out Rachael's soul. Maybe one day we'll even be able to do it with new, currently unknown inscriptions. We don't know. I'm set on it, of course. She's my wife. But it's something we all have to consider, too. So please give me some feedback. Let's integrate the solution into our master plan."

"No fucking way!" Beth growled. "That cunt killed Dwayne. No way we resurrect her sorry, dusty ass!"

"Wow, girl!" Mercy's voice. "Want to tone down the cursing a bit, Beth," Mercy implored hypocritically, "before we lose our PG-13 rating?"

"Huh?" Beth replied, stunned for a moment that Mercy, of all people, would scold her for holding a grudge. "Oh, I get it," she said a moment before Dwayne opened his mouth to explain it for her. "Well, I'm sorry that I'm being a bitch about it, but no way the Talisman gets rezzed. She killed Dwayne and then mocked his death like a total sociopath. With that kind of power, and with that kind of bad attitude, we'd be fools to risk it. She's a villain. She'd just betray us and not think twice about it."

"Okay," Maynard said, "but what if she's the only way we can save Rachael's soul?"

"No!" Beth yelled, her arms tightly held at her sides. "She's the Talisman, Maynard! What if by bringing her back, we save Rachael's soul, but then she runs off and resurrects Petrus Romanus! We don't know what she can do. We don't know the limits of her powers, but she was freakin' powerful enough to bend and bind all of those energies at Giza. And we know that Petrus had it ramped up enough to open a portal from EarthZero to the ZeroTime. Ami told us how they did it, too. They were burning souls, Maynard. Souls! Ami aside, who was merely their puppet and pawn, they were monsters. No way we risk bringing either one of them back. Even if it saves Denny's wife. Even then! Maynard, they almost destroyed the world!"

Santa Muerte's spindly fingers gently brushed Beth's hunched shoulders. "*Tranquillo*, Beth," the old woman said softly. Instantly, Beth's rage faded. Santa Muerte then turned her skeletal gaze directly toward Maynard. "Please forgive her. She has expended much of her soul to give la Raza life-giving water. She has restored the lives and vitality of many tens of thousands with her selfless action. And once Denny and his family made it here, she personally assisted Denny with the many inscriptions necessary to empower our newly constructed arcology. She needs days of rest to recover from all she's done."

"I'm okay now, Mamá," Beth said wearily. "Thank you. But no way we can risk rezzing that murdering Talisman."

"So we need to find someone or something else capable of boosting the Hekatek," Denny said, "so that Rachael doesn't have to die when the time comes to kickstart life on EarthZero."

"And when would that time be?" Mhyrranda asked.

"Once we have worldwide resonance in place," Denny informed them. "Meaning, a solid lock on a worldwide belt of resonant nodes. Structures, arcologies, pyramids, or otherwise."

"And we have only four now," Mhyrranda said, "with a hemispherical coverage? Is that right?"

"Yes, ma'am," Denny replied politely. "And I know your next question. We started slowly, of course. But we've got the last two up and running from virtually scratch within the past month. That's most of this side of the Northern Hemisphere."

Denny rapidly conjured a laptop-sized viewscreen before him, then passed his fingers over it just as quickly. There, in the center of the war room table, arose a virtual globe of EarthZero. The four currently existing nodes were illuminated and called-out from the virtual globe, pale, electric blue light vector lines both joining them all and outlining them. Detail panels flashed intricate statistics, ranging from population size to various snapshots of the node's capabilities and assets, on the resonant nodes. The call-outs apparently stood out higher above the virtual globe based upon their Hekatek empowerment. While Dreamland, Atlanta, and Los Angeles appeared to be evenly matched, Cholula towered above them all.

"That's our current status," Denny explained. "Looks pretty good so far. In addition to the cities in North America already targeted for the New Alliance Initiative, we'll need to hit cities in South America, too. Then, we expand across both the Pacific and Atlantic as we move to both Asia and Europe," he said as segmented electric blue vector lines arced across the virtual globe, marking and outlining several dozen locations across the globe.

"Wow," Mhyrranda said, realizing the scope of effort required. "Looks like it's going to take a few years at our current pace. Sound right?"

Denny and Maynard both nodded. Denny continued, "But we can shortcut by a factor of at least three if we allow for three master-level runies working three separate paths. Me, Maynard, and Beth can lead the teams. Vir'gil and his barky friends can go virtually anywhere on EarthZero just by willing it, so they can zoom from one spot to another to work on arcologies. Santa Muerte's jumpers can handle the various transports required by the non-barky folks to speed travel times up. And Mercy—"

"Mercy and her crew can hit the road to recover Fresswelle," she quickly interjected. "You do you, and we'll do us, okay? Not that the Resonance Project isn't important. It's Alpha-level important. But so is recovering Fresswelle. Remember: We have the Fae of Aal in that blade. Freeing them so that they can join us against the Horde is just as Alpha-level as the Resonance Project. We have to do this in parallel. We can't be linear now."

"She's right," Mhyrranda agreed. "Parallel it is, because parallel it has to be. Any objections or counters?"

No takers, for all saw it as wise.

"Right," Mhyrranda said. "Now, we'll—"

"Pardon me, Dreamwyrd," Santa Muerte asked, "but we have not yet been convinced as to the claim that the Risen is indeed the Risen. We heard Denny's tale. Indeed, this is not the first time he has recounted the story to us, though this time there were details that had previously been omitted. Yet, still, my people are curious, and I must ask, if only for clarification, how the Risen has managed to escape my notice."

Santa Muerte's head slowly pivoted toward Void.

"The Mother has murdered me a million times," he said evenly, as their eyes met and locked, "Yet you have never seen me in death. Why? Your power is anchored to EarthZero's universe, its own plane of existence. As great as your power is, it is anchored to a local subset of the Metacosmos. A tiny yet unique subset of the Metacosmos, of course. Yet, EarthZero is but one among many, and the Metacosmos is the totality of all of these. I am VoidSpawn, spawned of the Metacosmic Dual-Aspect itself. You may not see me in death because you may not see that which is beyond your experience."

By the end of his brief reply, Santa Muerte's deep brown, snakelike eyes had grown wide with the acknowledgement of the total oblivion that existed beyond her domain of mere death. Despite her near-total control of her emotions, the embodiment of Death itself on EarthZero shot corpse white as the horror of comprehension of what truly lay beyond her own experience roiled through her soul.

Death met Void, and politely bowed. Death didn't see Void roll his eyes, however.

"It's all good, Milady Death," Void said softly. "You might not see me, but you'll soon enough be seeing a trillion or so of the Death Horde go hurtling by."

Death smiled. "I can't wait."

Sensing that no one was willing to speak, Void prompted, "Duchess?"

"Ah, yes," Mhyrranda temporized. She had been waiting for Void to start the show. "I think we're at the point at which we need to call the meeting, consider our possible paths, and regroup tomorrow at noonish. That will give the partiers in Atlanta time to get over their hangovers," she finished, winking at Peaches. "First New Alliance meeting, adjourned."

With that, the Dreamland War Room returned to its normal, natural state. Which lasted for about a nanosecond too long for Mercy.

"Okay, let's go, team," she said eagerly, popping out of her reclining silver chair like a random piece of well-done toast straight out of the silver toaster.

"Uh, Mercy?" Maynard said immediately. "Might want to hang a sec. We're still crunching those numbers for you."

"Sure," Mercy urged, tapping her wolf skin boot impatiently. "Hurry up, though, Maynard. Time's tickin'."

"Don't worry, Mercy," he told her. "Aal Ball's already crunching it out. We've got a ton of rich, robust data that the autonomous data drones have been sending us. We're also creating a new EarthZero mapping, using a new type of rune-driven LIDAR we've implemented. It's several orders of magnitude more powerful than anything the old world was using prior to the sigil. Meaning, it's pretty damn badass. Full-spectrum. It sees everything: all natural stuff, technology, magick, technomagick, and Hekatek. Spirits. Souls. Everything. We might even finally find Atlantis."

"I already know where Atlantis – or, more correctly, Atlan—was. But can this thing see the Death Horde?" Mercy asked him sardonically.

Crestfallen, for real this time, Maynard shook his head once.

"But," Tim continued, genuinely curious, "is that because our assets aren't pointed out to space?"

Maynard blatantly laughed at him. "Shit, Tim. Of course not. Our assets are pointed at the ground. That's because they're mapping out the ground. Not space. That's another project. When it comes time to look out into space, that's precisely what we'll do: we'll point our assets out to space. Tech trees! Tech trees! Geez, Tim! What did you say your Caltech engineering degree was in? Engineering SJWs? Orange Man bad? NPC shit like that? Sure you didn't' get your mail-in degree from Berkeley?"

"Fuck you, Maynard," Tim shot right back, enjoying the banter. He knew Maynard wasn't serious. "At least I went to Caltech, and not Redneck State Lose-iversity in Scruntsville, Sillybama. And Helel's chaos is probably why we elected Orange Man Bad in the first place. You NPC."

That one actually made Maynard laugh. He was totally apolitical, but politics, even of the former world, still amused him. It also caused Void to hide a grin, which Mercy picked up on, instantly.

"He went there, too," Mercy taunted him. "Best years of his life, he said. Spent in Scruntsville, Sillybama. Damn, I love me some of that. Had to have been chock full of Maynards, too. A-yup, by golly. Reckon I'll have me some of them taters," she finished in an eerie rendition of Karl Childers' *Sling Blade* vox.

Maynard and Mercy now were laughing. Void's weird-ass head was buried in his gnarly hands as he tried to bury his sure-to-be mocking laughter. Ku'tu and Leta were totally ignoring them all, eagerly discussing something about adding some highly artificed LIDAR mods to their suits. Or their Oakleys. They couldn't quite yet decide. Mhyrranda was deeply engrossed in studying a pair of small screens erected for her by Aal Ball. She was sipping on a rather large Bloody Mary while so doing, clumsily fighting the overly large stick of Fae-grown celery decorating her two-liter crystal glass.

"Well, Tim," Maynard finally managed to eke, "despite what they might have lied to you about at FailTech in your Industrial Basket Weaving curriculum, we don't actually need LIDAR to be pointing out to space, because—"

Abruptly laughing, the two fire women looked at Maynard as if he were daft.

"Maynard, I really love you," Ku'tu said, giving a slight Fae-inspired tilt of her head to acknowledge Mhyrranda, who just shrugged innocently, "but you're missing the tactical applications. For a total genius, you can be really dense sometimes, you Combat Slob. 'Tactical', as in 'stuff that will help us in battle'. It would be like having a Witcher's Eye permanently open. Not much would be able to hide from someone with one of these systems on them."

All eyes were now on Ku'tu, and she liked it. "Good one, huh?" she fished. "Combat Slob? Nick taught me that one."

"Toss in a meta-level Battlespace hook-and-feed," Void declared, nodding to Ku'tu, "and we've got a linked cybernetically augmented presence. Battlespace Eidolon system?"

Void turned to face Maynard, who held his arced fingertips to his chin. He was bridling over the combat insult. Even though he knew it was true. But why engage in all that training to become proficient in something that was practically useless to someone who could actualize and fire off a disintegration rune in the blink of an eye? "Think that's feasible? Viable?"

Nodding quickly, Maynard agreed. "I see how to do it. I see two ways, actually. They may both be integrated with your body suits. But, as usual, you've got me thinking about hybridizing both the LIDAR and the Eidolon systems. Weak point would be the feed I/O for Aal Ball. But that vulnerability's a small price to pay for something that powerful. A group cybernetic Battlespace. One in which virtually everything were revealed and mapped. And fed to anyone and everyone on demand. Major force-multiplier. And you'd still, even if the feed to Aal Ball were cut off or compromised, be able to use your local version."

"And," Mercy added, "there's going to be the innate psychic shielding of some of us – me, Void, Mhyrranda, to name a few – that's going to be an obvious impediment to overcome. If, indeed, such is even possible. Aal Ball has limitations. So do we all."

"Yeah," Maynard agreed. "True dat. But I see a way to possibly bend those rules once we get the Resonance Project up and fully implemented. We have limits, of course. But if we start using true primal power, which the Resonance Project might allow us to achieve, all of those limitations might prove to be nothing more than minor stumbling blocks. After all, hypothetically, we'll be tapping directly into the Dragon itself."

Deafening silence manifested around the War Room's table. After a few fateful seconds, all eyes were on Void, who remained motionless.

He exhaled. "Whew. Not this time," he said, relieved. With that, hearts once more dared to beat, and everyone relaxed a single iota more. "Forgive my utter blasphemy," he prefaced bluntly, "but don't take this the wrong way. We're going to have to use every bit of power we can, in order to win. In this case, it's not as blasphemous as it sounds, because we and the Dragon, and the

Mother, are all on the same side. The Vanth'Vash'Var are the sworn enemies of us all. In order to combat their cosmic nihility, all things alive must band together as allies, and fight them with every bit of life we possess."

Mhyrranda sought and met Void's eyes. She had absolutely no issue seeing them. "So you're officially signing off on this, Void? Because that's what I think we all just heard."

"I am," Void replied. "It's not blasphemy. It's not evil. It's not good. It's neither. It's necessary. It's just real. And, as such, it should be entirely expected for us to take this path, because it's the only possible path to take if we want to save this cosmos. Don't fear this path. Fear is how we fall. Confidence, my friends. As I am before you, so too are the Mother and the Dragon. Shit," he laughed, "that sounded pompous. Sorry."

Taking her silent cue, Mercy arose from her reclining apparatus. "I'm on it, Void. This has to happen before we continue the quest for Fresswelle. Power predication, in this case, augments the primary path. Ku'tu? Leta? Let's bring the news to the Gentry. I'm sure they're going to be happy to hear this. They've only been discussing it for several millennia. Probably will take us a few days to get this done, Mhyrranda," she informed her. "But it's a veritable slam dunk. Prophecy kind of thing. What do you think?"

Mhyrranda nodded her understanding. "This one had been a long time coming. Previously, the Fae, led by the formal Council of the Gentry, have been resistant to the idea that it would ever be necessary to directly interface with the Dual-Aspect, the Mother and the Dragon, and their resultant, the Song of the Sidhe. Such would be akin to asking an old world Christian to directly, physically, join forces with Jesus during the events of the Christian Revelation. Such was not written in the book, and, as such, it could not be. In fact, it would be blasphemy of the highest order to presume that anyone, even the most spiritual, could dare to interject himself into the most holy Word. It would edit the Bible, abnegating the import of the events."

Tim and Leta both focused closely on Mhyrranda's words.

"Yet now, the Risen had spoken, vouchsafing the concept. Naming it as a necessity, in fact," she quickly corrected herself. "Practically, it's only a matter of fine degrees that separate acceptable practices from blasphemous ones in the world of the Fae. Did not they, themselves, tap into the Song of the Sidhe constantly? Did not they, themselves, swear upon and worship the Dual-Aspect? And what was this new practice being proposed to them but a mere matter of fine degrees? Opening up and establishing a direct channel between the new immortals of EarthZero and the ancient, most eldritch powers? And was it not being done so only *in extremis*, to save the world? The cosmos itself? As such, I say we all agree with Void. Dreamland officially approves. Godspeed, Mercy. Give 'em hell."

"To them, I *am* Hell," Mercy laughed, gathering Ku'tu and Leta to her, Shunya cutting spacetime before them. "Thanks, Mhyrranda. Be back soon. And Tim? Be ready to ride hard when we get back. Fresswelle *shall* be found, and the Fae of Aal shall once more be free!" she said as the three were removed from the local current of spacetime.

Abruptly, Mercy's head, from the neck up, popped back out of the dissipating spacetime portal. "Unrequited love, Void! Unrequited!" she said, sticking her tongue out at him, wagging it lasciviously. "Suffer while I'm gone!" she laughed as she finally disappeared.

Everyone but Void was laughing. "I can't believe how insane she is!" Maynard erupted. "She's gonna push on it, just for kicks, even when she knows such a union would likely doom us all."

"Those are just rumors though, right?" Tim inquired. "I mean, why can't Void get together with Mercy if they both really wanted? What's wrong with it?"

"Why, nothing, Tim," Mhyrranda said, blushing. "You know we don't judge. But, apparently, Mommy does."

"Yeah," Void said laconically. "Deep Dual-Aspect stuff, man. No Metacosmic Masturbation allowed."

"What?" Tim guffawed, even as Mhyrranda's and Maynard's faces shot beet red.

"We're each other's syzygy," Void explained. "Goofy shit happens when we even get too close to each other. We're Dual-Aspect mirrors, with some As Above, So Below woven into it. Some sibling-fuckin' might work in the trailer park, but, at our level of power, if we actually got past third base, the world as we know it might start sprouting Null and Void singularities. The Source would almost immediately attempt rectification in order to maintain metacosmic balance, and the resulting union of those energies would produce rampant primal power. Death to all. And, yes, we've discussed the scenario in which, if all's going south when the Horde attacks, we're going to just say fuck it all and go out with a bang."

Everyone, even Void, was now laughing at the absurdity.

Void let events pass for a few seconds, then, with a sigh, he addressed Maynard.

"I can't believe the temporal distortion, man. Tough to reconcile. Even if the Null were behaving badly. Even if Nanabozho were using a tesseract."

Exhaling sharply, Maynard tapped the face of the timepiece chained to his vest. "Time flies like an arrow. Fruit flies like bananas."

"C'mon, man," Void pleaded, biting back a laugh. "I can read the screen in front of me, but I'm not sure it makes sense. We couldn't have been in either the Null or the Nunatak for that long, could we?"

"Guess you were," Mhyrranda said. "Time doesn't work the same in the Null, of course. No telling what it was doing in the Nunatak."

"So," Void said slowly. "Almost a month. We're going to have to be careful with our time from this point forward. No more Null, or Void, or elder god's Nunataks. Might get stuck outside of our own EarthZero timeline and miss the Horde, or something insane like that."

"I've a feeling," Maynard admitted, "that we're going to have to get used to time moving quickly. It's not only a factor of being practically immortal now, but also a factor of the immense scale of our tasks. I know time is precious. We all know who's coming. We just don't know exactly when. A few years? A hundred years? Probably something along the Fibonacci sequence, of course, considering Helel's a lazy coder. And considering what Void's told us of his personal recall of the other simulations. But nothing's set in stone. So we might want to err on the side of sooner, rather than later. And that means we have to get busy, get busy now, and waste not even a single second."

Nodding silently in approval, they arose to set about their tasks.

However, even as Aal Ball's silvery manifestations recessed, Void suddenly stood stiffly in place. "Maynard? Tim?" he asked without turning his head toward them. "May I have a moment alone with Mhyrranda?"

Tim looked over at Maynard, who just shrugged and replied evenly, "You got it, V. C'mon, Tim. Let's go grab some eats and then get to work on these new implementations. Your engineering help will be greatly appreciated."

"Huh?" Tim gulped. "Really?"

"You bet," Maynard said. "I was just giving you grief earlier. Caltech's killer, dude." Giving Mhyrranda a quick wink, he met Tim at the rise, and the two quickly departed the War Room.

Mhyrranda took a final sip of her drink, then gave Void a single nod.

"Thanks, Randa," Void said, slightly inclining his head. "Maynard's a real mensch, but he's gonna hate me for not sharing this with him. But I have no choice. Please convey that to him, if possible."

"You know I will, Void," she replied steadily, her sharp eyes darting up and down Void's form. After a day of insane revelations and knowledge-sharing deep-dives, her curiosity now was actually both piqued and peaked.

With an economy of motion belying his massive form, Void made an intricate motion with his hands, whirling the left above the right. From nothingness he conjured a single delicate green sprout, which rapidly bloomed in his upturned left palm, its vines spilling to the floor. Out of the sprawling mass arose the form of Vir'gil, the Entheogenic Lord.

"Milady Mhyrranda, Duchess of Dreamland," Vir'gil intoned, bowing like the pro courtier he truly was.

"Vir'gil, the Entheogenic Lord," Mhyrranda replied with a formal, slightly inclined nod. "To what do we owe this pleasure?"

Pausing a mere split-second, Vir'gil cleared his throat. "Ermm, Void?" he creaked.

"Yeah, yeah, yeah," Void said impatiently. "I know. Mommy already knows I know this shit, but I can't officially 'know' it now. Fucks up the weave. Can't even share it with my friends. So, with that," he finished rapidly, "I'll be off fulfilling a brief side quest. Be back in a few days. Hopefully with Nanabozho's peeps in tow."

The admission reached out and slapped both Mhyrranda and Vir'gil square on the noggin. Before either could blink, however, Void was gone, his waveform no longer present in Dreamland.

"He has such a good soul," Mhyrranda admitted. "Too bad the Mother abuses him so terribly."

Vir'gil's eyestalks blinked several times as he processed what the Duchess had just said. "Chalk it up to tough love for her favorite son. That's what he was chosen to be. That's the terrible, exacting price that he pays for all of our souls." He paused a moment, because it struck both him and Mhyrranda with the same disarming impact.

"Not just a god, not just a hero," Mhyrranda said softly, finally arriving at the proper level of discernment, "but a hero of the gods."

"Indeed," Vir'gil agreed. "And better him than me," he croaked. "I'm just a simple vegetarian who wants to get high, and deliver some spiritual take-out for the Mother..." he said, a warm smile blooming across his face as he offered Mhyrranda a tiny psychedelic pinecone.

PART II
CHAPTER 20

John Castleberry drove his dirty, rusted Jeep past the broken gatehouse and long-fallen chain link fence into the remains of a parking lot. The smell of honeysuckle was everywhere, so he was very careful to watch for faeries. He wasn't afraid of them, but he'd heard stories about what happened to people who pissed off a Wildling troop, and he wasn't fond of the ideas that kept running though his head. No data was worth that kind of torture.

The grounds were overgrown to the point that the building was all but hidden by trees and vines. But it was right where the old map said it would be. An old government warehouse had to be slap full of treasure, and if he was lucky, he might find an unpilfered set of snack machines. The snacks would be gone to the varmints, but varmints didn't drink soda. And they didn't call him Soda John for nothing.

John grabbed his rucksack and firestick from the Jeep and drew a little glowing sign of warding in the air, waving it toward the Jeep to keep it safe from casual observation. Nobody would mess with it unless that was really their intent, but out here, that's probably all he needed. Just to be sure, he left several candy bars along the path for any nearby Fae. John turned and headed to what he thought should be the entrance, whistling tunelessly.

The young man reached the front of the building, and found that the doors were indeed locked, and the filthy windows and doors were bulletproof glass. He wondered how much people actually shot at buildings back in the old days, and shrugged. Digging in his pack, he found a six inch ash stick and began drawing symbols on the glass around the edge of the door frame, and stood back once the runes were complete. Tapping the glass three times, he casually covered his eyes and waited until the glass shattered into thousands of little pebbles.

Humming to himself, he walked over to the guard desk and rummaged until he found a keycard in one of the drawers. Using the wand, he drew another rune on it, and went to the main door, where he found the RFID pad and repeated the rune. When he held the card against the pad, there was a soft glow, followed by a clack, and the door opened to his touch. John slipped the wand back into his pack, and the card into his pocket, then slid into the darkness beyond.

The building was cool for early summer, and filled with a dry, dusty smell. No one had been here in many months, he thought. Probably not since the Collapse.

"Excellent. Probably a total grab bag." John grinned as he walked down the corridor past a long row of offices, stopping at one that was larger than the others. Hmm. *Carpeted. He must have been a boss.* Peeking behind the desk, John spotted a pile of fuchsia fabric in the chair, covered in a dried black powder. And next to the chair was a purse and a cell phone, long dead. *She was a boss*, he corrected himself.

John found a lanyard in the pile of powder that had once been the body of the fuchsia-clad boss, and reverently blew the dust off it. "Jennifer Jeffreys, of the CIA," he said. "Well, Jennifer, let's see what you can get to." John hung the lanyard around his neck and headed back out into the hall.

Eventually, after happening upon a break room with a fully-stocked set of snacks and soda machines, John loaded as many candy bars and sodas as he could carry in his pack. Exiting the break room, John found the back of the warehouse, and the room he suspected held the best loot. Sure, the crates and boxes in the main warehouse would have treasure for the arcologists, but the best stuff was always locked away.

This room must have held something *very* important, if the abundance of desiccated powder of the bodies was any indication. There were quite a few firearms stacked against the wall and on the ground, as well. These people were dedicated to protecting what was in here, and he suspected they may not have died with the appearance of the Lightbringer's Sigil. John had come to recognize the difference from the dark, gummy sludge of people who died with the first wave of people affected by the sigil, the people dead from before, and the powder of those who died now that human DNA had changed.

The large sliding door was both locked and padlocked. Once John had finally dealt with both, he slid the door open and stood for a moment, looking at something he'd never seen before, but could only be one thing: a spaceship. Levered on a large pallet was a sleek, egg-like body, with odd, bumpy projections along the length, and a series of strange, runic markings around the circumference at the midpoint and each end. But it was small—only about fifteen feet long and ten feet wide. And there were no visible seams for opening. Still, John was convinced, and determined to bring this back to the Lennox Science Arcology at Atlanta.

John went back into the main warehouse and found a forklift, and was able to find a still functional twenty foot truck parked in one of the bays. Unfortunately, the battery on the forklift was dead, and John had to spend time charging it. By the time he had the egg secured in the truck, it was late afternoon. He went back and gathered the rest of the sodas and snacks from the break room, packing them in a box in the back with the egg. Just to be sure none of the local Fae troops was going to mess with him as he left, he left another handful of snacks on the steps by the door to the loading dock.

He started up the truck and gave a last look at his Jeep as he drove away. Oh well, he'd pick up another one in Atlanta. Maybe a newer model this time.

John had only gone a few miles down the road when he saw the roadblock. Two pickup trucks were pulled bumper to bumper, and there were about a half dozen men with rifles and shotguns spread out on either side of the road.

"Oh *HELL* no!" John knew that he was just collateral damage, and the guys that took his truck and his treasure were just as likely to take his life. So he floored it, aiming for the midpoint between the two vehicles as he ducked down below the dash. Although the drivers of both vehicles were smart enough to back up, one of them wasn't fast enough, and John smashed into the front end, sending it careening off the road as he ploughed past it in his much larger vehicle, just as a volley of shots tore into the windshield and front of John's truck. As he lifted his head to look out the rearview mirror, John felt the barrel of a gun pressed hard against his neck.

"Nice try, punk. Let off the gas real slow and you can keep your head." The voice was gravelly and John smelled the stink of cigarettes from the man who stood on the running board while holding on to the mirror. John stared straight ahead, and slowed the truck, letting it slowly coast to a stop.

The man yanked the door open and pulled John roughly from the driver's seat, throwing him to the ground before kicking him in the ribs several times. He placed the barrel behind John's ear and was just about to pull the trigger when someone shouted, "Donnie, wait!"

As John lay there coughing and holding his side, another man approached them, smiling at the first ambusher. Like most of the group of bandits, he was unshaven, and wore dirty jeans and a flannel shirt.

"Whoa, man," he said. "Remember we always need to question our captives first. He may know something useful. "Now fly on around back and check out the truck. I'll take care of this guy."

"Right. Sorry Jeff, I got caught up after he ploughed through the trucks. When I make myself fly really fast, it amps my aggression up." With a nod of deference, Donnie lifted off the ground and floated toward the back of the truck.

Jeff turned his attention back to John and smiled. "Now then, where's my manners? I'm Jeff, and you are...?"

John looked at Jeff carefully, trying to gauge whether the friendliness was just an act. "I'm John."

"Well, John, let's be blunt. We are stealing your truck, and whatever's in it. Play along nice and helpful, and I might just give you a ride to find another vehicle. Or," he scowled, spitting on the ground before punching John in the face, "I might just let Donnie come back and shoot you in the head."

John fell to the ground, his hand going to his face with a groan. "What... what do you want from me?"

"Well, I—" Jeff began, before being interrupted by a shout from the rear of the truck.

"Jeff! Come check *this* shit out!"

John sat on the ground, head in his hands, while Jeff ran around to the back of the truck.

The bandits were all gathered around the back of the truck, and one of them, standing in the back next to the egg was motioning excitedly. "Hey man, look at this! What do you think it is?"

Jeff jumped up into the truck and looked at the egg, pausing to take a quick look in the box full of snacks. A couple of the men reached in to help themselves when Jeff's attention returned to the egg. "I have no clue, but it's obviously something from that government installation."

"Oh shit, do you think it's a *bomb*, Jeff?" Donnie's eyes grew large at the question, and several of the men looked nervous, edging way from the device and the truck.

"I don't know," said Jeff slowly. "Why don't we ask ole Johnny? Fred, go round and bring him on back here."

With a mixture of curiosity and eagerness to be away from the supposed bomb, one of the men walked around the side of the truck. A few moments later, he shouted, "Hey! He's gone!"

Jeff and the others boiled around the side of the truck and looked down the road and at the thick foliage on either side of the road.

"Fuck!" shouted Jeff. "Find him—but *don't* kill him!"

John had been ready the moment Jeff had turned to the back of the truck. Being as silent as possible, he had grabbed the bag and the keys to the truck and had moved around to the front of the truck before sprinting away. After three or four hundred feet, John had angled off into the woods and had kept running.

Maybe they wouldn't find him. Maybe he'd get out of this. If he could keep out of sight until he could pick up another vehicle, he might just get away. Maybe they would give up on the truck and wouldn't know how to hot wire it. Maybe. Best case was that he could still go back and recover the truck. If most of them were looking for him, he might be able to double back and find only one or two guarding the truck. He had a .357 Magnum pistol in his backpack, and it had armor piercing rounds for monsters, but he did not want to get into a firefight with the bandits.

John was running as fast as he could through the woods when a vine snagged his foot and he fell hard, landing on his injured ribs and knocking the wind out of himself. He lay there in pain, wanting to get up, but in no shape to start running. From down the road, John heard the sound of shouting. Too close.

From out of nowhere, John was nearly overcome with the smell of honeysuckle. He spun at a light touch on his shoulder, nearly screaming in surprise. He could see nothing, but an invisible voice whispered in his ear.

"Shhh. You need to get to those bushes over there, and *stay down*," the voice said. "They are coming, but I can't hide you from all angles."

Grunting in pain, John scrambled to a thick cluster of bushes and dove in. Suddenly, the world grew quiet, all colors and sounds muted. John leaned back against a tree. He could no longer hear the shouting, running men pursuing him, and he was pretty sure they could neither see nor hear him. John took his water bottle from his pack and drank slowly, recovering his wits.

So now what? He may have escaped the bandits, but now the faeries had him. What did the Fae do to human scavengers, especially those who'd been poking around their places? John was convinced that these Fae were from the installation he'd just looted. The more he thought about it, the more uneasy he became. He stood and tried to look out of the bushes to see if it was safe to bolt. As he peered around, a shadow covered the sun momentarily, and a boot came out of the sky to connect violently with his head. John was knocked senseless to his knees. Shaking his head, he looked up to see Donnie holding his pistol with both hands, a vicious grin on his face.

"Got ya, you punk!" Donnie crowed. "And this time, nobody's gonna save your ass. Jeff isn't here, so all I gotta say is you made a move for the gun..."

With a sneer, Donnie pulled the hammer back, never noticing the glitter sprinkling his shoulders. When the gun exploded, John got a final look at Donnie's face before it disappeared in a cloud of smoke, blood, and debris. John felt something wet and sticky hit him, realizing with a start that an eyeball had landed on his shoulder. When the smoke cleared, Donnie collapsed backward with a thud, half his face missing from the shrapnel of the ruined gun.

In the distance, John heard yelling and screaming from various points up and down the road as all hell broke loose. People were running in all directions. Weapons fired, and he could hear bullets whizz through the trees, alarmingly close by. John was pushed to the ground by a body that was too small to be one of the bandits, but too large to be a faerie.

The conflict was over quickly, and the sounds of gunfire were replaced by indistinct moaning. John raised himself up on his elbow and turned to see a small mahogany-skinned girl, barely in her teens, wearing a completely inadequate tunic made of leaves. She was unaware of her immodest clothing, as she tilted her head and watched him curiously.

"I think they won't bother you no more," she said matter-of-factly. "My troop chased them away."

"Who are you?" John asked, incredulous. "You aren't a faerie, where did you come from?" He reached out tentatively and brushed her curly ringlets from her round ear.

"I'm Loli. Was from New Yark, when the troop found me and took me to their ring. And then the bad people came and made everything shiny glass, so we left. Now we wander."

A confused look crossed her face, and they both looked down to see blood patter to the ground from a darkened spot on her dress.

"Oh no. Loli, you've been shot!" John scrambled to his feet and caught Loli in his arms just as she collapsed. Her eyes fluttered, and John laid her down on the ground, moving the leaves carefully aside to expose the bullet hole in her side. John moved her carefully on her side inspecting the exit wound.

"Okay, looks like it went through nice and clean, but I have to clean it and get it patched up. I think you are going to be okay, but we should get you to a doctor—you're in shock. Can you, I mean, will your troop let you come with me?"

John looked into Loli's amber-flecked black eyes, and she smiled at him, not in obvious pain. "Is there more candy where we are going, handsome man?"

John laughed. "Yes, but we have a bit of a drive to get there. First things first, I have some medical supplies in my bag over there. That bullet probably had some iron in it."

"It's okay," she said. "I'm not *really* a faerie. I'm adopted..."

He rose, but stopped abruptly, as he noticed that they were surrounded by a number of small, winged forms, none of which looked particularly friendly. *In fact,* John thought, *they all looked like the Lost Boys, with wings.* A pair of them flew over to John, dropping his bag at his feet with a huff.

"Um, thanks."

John worked as quickly and carefully as he could, but he discovered that the exit wound was bleeding badly, and Loli was definitely going to need a more skilled hand than his. His biggest concern was loss of blood, and he was afraid he wouldn't be able to get her anywhere in time to save her. But anywhere was closer than here, especially if the bandits came back with friends.

He loaded her into the passenger seat of the truck, flanked by the troop of angry-looking faeries, who glared at him, but never said a word. John gave Loli as many makeshift cushions and blankets as he could improvise. Before leaving, he paused briefly to scavenge weapons and supplies from the marauders' vehicle. When he hopped into the cab and started the truck, John saw that her troop had surrounded her inside the truck, flitting back and forth in the passenger side. They had pulled away the clothing that had covered her ribs and side, and were laying mud-soaked leaves on the bullet hole.

"Hey guys? I really think you should leave that—" John began as the faeries turned in unison and *hissed* at him, tiny fangs bared in a vicious challenge. Eyes wide, John edged toward the door and continued driving, picking up speed as he hit the main road.

Muttering to himself, John wondered what would happen if Loli didn't recover.

He'd barely made it to the southbound interstate, when he felt Loli's hand touch his jacket.

"Handsome man, you look scared," she said, a wan smile touching her face.

John looked at her, and the troop sitting on her, the dash and headrest. He nodded carefully.

"I have to get you to a doctor to help heal you. But..." he looked at the faeries, calm for the moment. "But, I'm so far from Atlanta, I don't think we have time. I don't know what else to do, and there's no other place to take you that I trust."

Loli squeezed John's arm and said, "Tell me about Atlanta. Think about this place you are going, and picture it in your head."

John considered it for a while before he responded.

"It's a big city. Not like New York, But downtown has—*had* —lots of tall buildings. Before the fire. Most of the people moved to a place called Buckhead. There's a huge complex that was perfect for the arcology, and there are shops and stores and a couple of nearby hospitals, and, oh yeah! There's this huge store full of building supplies, like wood and tools and... oh shit!"

As he was talking, John failed to notice until too late that a large portal illuminated by iridescent rainbow hues had opened in front of the speeding truck. Even though he slammed on his brakes, the truck skidded over a curb, hurtled across a sidewalk, and impacted a large building that read "The Home Depot" at nearly 70 miles per hour.

CHAPTER 21

In the secure sector beneath the Lennox Science Arcology, M'Zinga glowered at the chrome and steel Nest Nexus before him. There were still a few more field samples for him to review before he would be able to pry himself from his tedious sample reviews and try to catch a few hours of sleep before dawn. He quickly calculated that at a good pace of 10 minutes per sample, he might just barely make his goal. Perhaps with even enough time to hit the local arc and procure some late-night greens. *There was only so long the proverbial 800 pound gorilla could refuse to answer his grumbling stomach,* he thought, bemused.

He stifled an unbidden yawn with the back of his hand, then set to work. Returning to his seat within the levitating Nest Nexus, he carefully adjusted his mass against the customized Aero chair. He slipped both his hands and his feet into separate conduits of dark liquid steel, their many runes flickering to life as he engaged himself within the symbiotic, cybernetic Nest Nexus. M'Zinga carefully moved himself into proper alignment with the invisible interactive field that was now scanning his form. His thick fingers moved with nimble grace as he tapped through various virtual menus which floated before his eyes.

The system still performed flawlessly with nary a squeak, despite M'Zinga's recently acquired 100 pounds of mass. Too many honey coffees over the past few months, and he was admittedly well past his prime Silverback years before the sigil had changed him into one of the Evolved.

Still, the Nest Nexus and the veritable tractor-trailer loadout of Hekatek provided to the Resonant Order of Hekateks of Atlan by the magnificent immortal hero, Maynard, who had fought for EarthZero at the Battle of Giza against Petrus Romanus, the Black Pope, were beyond robust. They were crafted with such precision and skill that they would very easily function for another millennium, if such were possible. *If the Horde didn't engage them first,* he thought bitterly. *Dammit. I love this life.*

M'Zinga paused a moment as his consciousness merged with the symbiotic, cybernetic artifacts. There was always a single moment of dislocation and confusion upon reaching the point of merging with the marvelous Hekatek system of devices. His first thought as the merge completed returned to his last thought. He would love nothing more than to remain here, in Atlanta, or Atlan as many now called it, for so long as his immortal body would allow him to do so. But, of course, that would not be possible until the End of All Things transpired, and then only if the impossible were achieved: the defeat of the Death Horde.

Or so the legends had it. And the liturgy, he quickly corrected himself. And from what Maynard himself had told the Hekateks of Atlan as he had established the order and given them their charter. M'Zinga had himself been there, as had all of the newly evolved Hominidae. He had heard it himself. So why even doubt it?

"Why doubt at all?" he muttered to himself. "I'm just tired and irritable. And hungry."

Before his mind's eye, standing before him in virtual form, were nine separate field samples. They were separated into three rows of three samples each. Bound with their field location data in the new Global Point Pixilation (GPP) format, which featured an embedded global-to-point-of-capture view, the samples appeared to him to be nothing more than standard wildlife captures. While not quite boring, as the wildlife had enjoyed some spectacular permutations and recombinations since the Lightbringer's Sigil had delivered its singular Evolutionary Judgement upon the creatures of EarthZero, he had been expecting some material samples instead. Certainly, it was an important directive to discover the new species, and catalog their various new abilities and special powers. But with the recent arrival of Soda John's latest haul, which Peaches had immediately hushed up, the rumors of something very special indeed had reverberated among the members of the Resonant Order.

"Ah, bother," M'Zinga said softly as he reached his virtual hand toward the first sample.

Canceling the auto-executing GPP sequence, he made a flicking motion of his hand, spreading all of the internal file folders onto a virtual screen to his left. Ten new file folders populated the monitor. Pivoting to his left, he used his left foot to quickly open the file folders, while he used his left hand to shadow their opening, his keen pattern-matching abilities rapidly making short shrift of the catch-sample-release data frames, the molecular data, the quantum data, and the combined Hekatek potential analysis and reviews.

At least the field agent—probably Ch'in Zhen, one of the newer Hominidae to join the Resonant Order—had performed his craft well. Everything was in perfect order. Nothing was missing. The field analysis conclusion was clean and not subject to bias. Another new "unknown", something formerly of the Order Coleoptera. Another of the seemingly endless species of beetles. Not bad work for a chimp, though, he had to admit. Easy enough to approve, no corrections or augmentations to note, and nothing more to see here.

M'Zinga embraced the mindless repetition, iterating through the samples one-by-one.

When he arrived at the seventh sample, he made it to the quantum data before something caught his eye. There, caught somewhere between a minor entanglement tetrad of gluons, was a single stray quark. One which should not have been there. A quark, just sitting there—relatively speaking, he thought with a morbid laugh—by itself, within a wicked looking tetrad of gluons. He knew Maynard's post-Collapse revisions of science by rote, but this entity wasn't included among them. Perhaps it was merely an artifact, or transient, caught in miraculous mid-binding by the field agent's FrameGrabber?

Quickly, he used his right hand to open another virtual monitor window to his right, scanning for all known pre-Collapse entities which this might resemble. There were a few hits, which didn't surprise him—they couldn't help it that, pre-Collapse, few of them were very well educated—but he had already suspected that it wouldn't align 100% with anything from those days. Only a short time ago, relatively speaking, but a virtual eternity of change between the old world and the new.

M'Zinga didn't like to hit dead ends, especially so close to the end of a very long night. And this meant, due to the odd hour, he'd have to contact one of the Finnies. Because they knew everything, and they weren't shy about telling every member of the land-bound how smart they were.

Grimacing, he blinked his right eye three times, quickly, establishing a popup session embedded within his main screen. Almost instantly, the popup filled with the slap-happy face of one of the Born Again.

"Born Again Cetaceans," came the snappy, trilling voice, instantly annoying M'Zinga's refined hearing. And sense of humor. "What's up, Big M?" the evolved Cetacean merrily inquired, clicking rapidly. "Need some help? I can help. I'd be glad to help. You Hominidae are great, and big, and hairy, but sometimes you've just gotta get help. And we're the best. The b-b-best!"

"Why me?" M'Zinga softly moaned. "Good morning, Riki-ti-ti-... uh, Rikit—"

"Close enough!" Riki laughed. "How long have we worked just down the hall from one another, and you still can't pronounce my name? Tsk-tsk-tsk! Is *that* what you're looking at?" the curious cetacean asked, craning its head upward, stiffly, apparently searching within its own virtual environment for what had just been linked to it from M'Zinga's.

"Yes, it—"

"I see it!" Riki chortled, clicking like a spastic Flamenco dancer's castanets. "Never seen that before. And the Born Again have recorded at least ten times what you Resonant Order folks have. The seas are a mighty big domain! Mighty big!"

M'Zinga slowly shook his massive head. "You're still members of the Resonant Order, Riki. Just because you've implemented a faction within the order doesn't give you the actual charter to claim you're better than anyone else."

"Set-subset construct, you fuzzy throw-rug," Riki gibbered quickly. "It sure as heck does. Even though you're right. Semantics, though. But what the—"

"I've never seen a quark like that," M'Zinga replied. "It's apparently bound with unbound gluons. The FrameGrabber doesn't sample that quickly, does it?"

"Well, sort of..." Riki said, its long flippers moving back and forth rapidly as it commanded its own symbiotic, cybernetic interface. "But that's not the issue here. The issue is..." he trailed off as their shared screen image began to zoom in quickly, filling most of the screen.

An embedded warning suddenly flashed in the midst of all of their virtual screens: "Black. Boss Mode. Peaches." After a silent count of approximately three seconds, the message vanished, and the rapid zoom resumed.

The two Evolved shared a brief, knowing look. Leave it to Peaches to cleverly sneak a sample into their daily fare and label it as both "black" and "Boss Mode". Both knew the communications protocol now invoked. And both were clever enough themselves to ascertain the origin of this particular sample. Soda John had delivered again.

There, at the deepest possible zoom level, a tiny 12-winged figure resolved itself, coming into direct view. Nestled within the form of what appeared to be a lone unbound quark, the Fae's distorted face glared directly at them. It was pissed.

"Gakk!" Riki snapped, repulsed by the curious image. "That's a member of the Gentry, for sure. It's got 12 wings. But what's it doing in that quark? It's alive! Alive! That's impossible. Impossible!"

"I know," M'Zinga said. "Thanks, Riki. Following strictly our communications protocol, we'll keep this one under wraps for now. It's going directly to the Boss," he finished, effectively hanging up on a very disappointed sounding Riki.

"Peaches is going to have a cow," M'Zinga said, nervously giggling to himself as he established Boss Mode protocols, and forwarded all of his data to the Boss. "That's a Watcher."

CHAPTER 22

"So, Petrus Romanus," the angel inquired, its voice lilting, seductive. "Will you at last don your holy mantle and lead these good people against the heretics of Dreamland?"

Wearily, Petrus shook his head. He steepled his fingers before his face, trying to ward the angel from his sight. He leaned forward as far as he could in his wooden chair, his back hunching. "No. For the tenth time, no. I will not return to that lie, that illusion. I am no longer that man. Please, leave me be."

"They need you. No one else can do it. Not Brother Bradley. Not Brother Greg. Not Sister Evaline. Not even the entire population of the City of Glass. Yes, they have power, but they don't have *your* level of power. They don't have your experience against these wicked villains. If you allow them to launch the war without you, they will be destroyed. And it will be due to the fact that you didn't lift a finger to help them. It will be your fault, Petrus."

"You're not even real, deceiver!" Petrus hissed, careful to keep his voice low. "Angel of Deceit!"

He knew that the occasional guard patrolling down the hallway outside would be listening carefully. Though they were too wily to directly bug him, magickally or technologically, he knew that some of the best possible intel could come from simple, if only brief, observation. And were there not two Shard Troops posted at the penthouse elevator at the end of the hall? There for his protection, of course.

Petrus sensed the angel's presence move closer to him. He felt movement near his hands, and felt, with quite a start, the slight, soft caress of the angel's fingers against his.

"I am as real as you are, Petrus," the angel informed him.

Lowering his hands, Petrus sought out the angel's ethereal blue eyes. "No. I can lead no one in anything holy. My soul is tainted. It is consumed from within. It's nothing but black. Black."

"Well," the angel consoled him, "if anyone may heal a soul, it would be you, Petrus. Heal thyself. Purge the darkness within you. Return to the light. Use it to guide these poor souls around you to their righteous destiny."

Gritting his teeth in very real pain, Petrus replied, "The darkness in my soul has a name, angel. It must never be released. Never."

"We know its n—" the angel began, abruptly stopping. It gazed at the penthouse door. Then, with a secret smile, it folded into itself and vanished from sight.

"Petrus?" Sister Evaline inquired as she lightly knocked upon the door to his chambers.

"Yes, Sister Evaline?" came his distracted reply over the sound of shuffling papers and the slow groan of his chair moving slightly across the floor.

"They're here to meet you," she replied, her voice betraying the slight edge of her impatience. *Finally, the twain shall meet,* she told herself, eager to finally get the delayed meeting of powerful forces underway.

Sister Evaline had tried her best to maneuver both Petrus and the twins into meeting before a private session of the Council, but the broken prelate had enforced his own conditions upon the meeting, thwarting her will. Which she naturally hated, though there was little she could do overtly to force the event. Bad form, and bad press. The assets were too valuable to their cause, so to compel them against their own will would turn them against the Council, and the entire City of Glass. Thus, the kid gloves, as both Brother Bradley and Brother Greg had eventually voted.

For, had it been entirely up to Sister Evaline, she would have had Warlord Armitrage and his Shard Troops torture Petrus into compliance. The little shit twins, too, and their goody-goody zookeeper, Maria Vida Ándale Arriba, or whatever her name was. But this would have to do. For now. Perhaps Brother Bradley and Brother Greg were right. Perhaps the twins would be the ones who could finally force Petrus to step up and be the shepherd for all his willing sheep. And if not the twins...

"Very well," Petrus said. "Come in, come in."

Sister Evaline opened the door, then stepped aside with a flourish, allowing Vida, Abe, and Ada to file into the room. She quickly pulled the door to a close once the three cleared the threshold. With a scoff and a sigh that she had to actually obey the terms of the broken pope's conditions, she then walked briskly down the hall to the elevator, leaving them to their privacy.

Sitting in his simple wooden chair, Petrus waved Vida and the twins to come closer to him.

"Come, come," he said, a crooked smile cracking on his face as he continued to beckon them. "I don't bite."

Complying, Vida nudged the twins ahead of her. Apparently a bit nervous, both of the children held their hands behind their backs, and slowly stepped toward the deformed and broken man. They came to a stop immediately before him, at which point they both revealed, with a smile, what they had been hiding behind their backs. Two bright, shiny apples suddenly were thrust toward a now fully smiling Petrus.

"Why thank you!" he beamed, accepting them both. "My favorite! I love apples. I'll just set these aside for later, so we can talk," he informed them, carefully turning in his chair to place them atop the nearby table. With a brief flicker of his eyes, he nodded to Vida, who resisted the urge to genuflect. Then, he turned back to the twins. "My name is Petrus. What are your names?"

"I'm Ada," Ada immediately told him. "He's Abe," she added just as Abe was about to speak.

"She does that a lot," Abe said, scratching his arm. "She's Vida," he said, hiking his scratching hand over his shoulder for a moment. "She's our nanny. She takes care of us."

"Il Papa," Vida said simply, inclining her head.

"Vida, Ada, Abe," he intoned gently, the name from his former life slamming into him harder than had expected. "I am pleased to meet you. So, Sister Evaline tells me that you are able to see things that others cannot."

Hesitantly, they both nodded, fidgeting nervously.

"I believe you," he admitted to them. They both stopped fidgeting and looked up at him expectantly. "I see angels. Do you see angels, too?"

The twins looked first at each other, then back at Vida.

"It's okay," she told them. "You can trust him. Tell him what you see."

Returning her gaze to Petrus, Ada told him, "Yes, we see angels. But they're not really angels. We know they're not angels because they're scared of Vida. When they see her, they always go away. Fast."

Petrus gave Vida a quick glance. She nodded in affirmation.

"So, they're not angels?" he asked. "If they are not angels, then what are they?" he asked, dreading their possible replies.

Abe craned his head upward toward the ceiling. He slowly pointed up. "They're from space," he said reverently. "They're from the Deaf Horde."

Slowly, Petrus exhaled. Carefully, slowly, he extended his gnarled hands to the children, which they grasped without hesitation. "Abe? Ada? Listen carefully. You must be very careful with whom you share your gift. With what you tell them. Some will use what you tell them to hurt other people. Hurt them bad. Be careful. Do you understand?"

They both nodded. He released their hands. Then, with a sudden smile, he said, "Okay. Now, if you want to, you can open the presents that I have for *you*! They're under that little folded blanket before the bookcase. Go on!"

"Yay!" The twins, excited to be kids again, zoomed over to their waiting, hand-wrapped gifts, and rapidly tore into them, giggling.

As the children focused on playing with their new toys, Petrus arose from his chair and stood close to Vida. Quietly, he began, "Vida? Do you understand the game going on around us?"

She nodded. "I think so. I have heard many versions of the story from various sources. Also, I have heard what the Dreamwyrd has told me in my dreams. I am inclined to believe her version. Based upon my personal experience, as well."

"You side with the Devil's children?" Petrus asked, incredulous.

"Hardly," Vida scoffed. "Please let me explain, Papa. The day that the sigil appeared? The One Above spoke to me from my devotion candle's flame. He... she... it told me what was happening, and how to protect the twins. It told me that its holy angels were coming to free this world from the forces of Lucifer. It told me that the children were going to be instrumental in this."

When she paused, he saw the external signs of classic cognitive dissonance cloud her eyes.

"Go on," he bade her.

"Yes," she said, carefully considering her next words. "But after a year of studying the issue, after learning everything I could learn about it from all possible angles, I think it's obvious that there's only one side to be on. I certainly won't join those who side with Lucifer. They're evil."

"But you said that you trust what the Dreamwyrd told you?"

"I do. Her version of events is the most truthful. They just made a bad choice and sold out to Lucifer. Some people just can't help being sinners. The One Above contests Lucifer. Heaven versus Hell. Lucifer made the sigil and doomed EarthZero. Now, while he reigns here for a space of time, the One Above's angels head here to avenge this world. And defeat Lucifer and his wicked heretic followers. Yes, I know it's not the Old World's Catholic eschatology. Please forgive me for saying so. But it makes sense. And it's still parallel to it. I think that the One Above's avengers will actually arrive in the City of Gold. I think that the One Above's angels will defeat those of Lucifer. And I think that we will then achieve a total paradise here on EarthZero."

She reached out and cradled his hand in hers.

"But we need your help, Papa," she implored him. "It's obvious that the Dreamland heretics are going to attack us before this happens. They intend to wipe us out because we oppose their blasphemy. You are the only one of all of us here in the City of Glass who can lead our forces to victory! We have to wage war on them first! Strike first, slaughter them all, before they do the same to us! Please help us, Petrus! We need you!"

Petrus stood there and shook his head slowly. Truly, he felt sorry for Vida. For, truly, he discerned that she was not in her right mind. He didn't need his power as a Soulthief to know this, either. Plainly, she was a zealot. A dangerous one, for she had in her charge those who had the Sight.

"Vida," he said, "I wish I could help you. But I cannot. The Battle of Giza crippled me in both body and in soul. And some remnant of that cosmic struggle now taints my soul. It is beyond evil. I fear that perhaps some machination of Lucifer now has accursed me. I cannot trust my own judgement. And what if that means, should my powers return, that I cannot control them, and use them for good? What if the evil he has implanted in my soul forces me to slaughter my own sheep? What good, then, would I serve as being their shepherd?"

"Then don't lead us, but instead use your power to resurrect the dead," she asked him desperately, tightly clutching his hand, "and make an army of millions for us. This used to be New York City. There are many millions of dead here. It would be easy for you to do! Resurrect them, and let them join us in our holy quest! That way we can at least defend ourselves before the unholy might of the evil ones!"

"Vida, it doesn't serve Heaven to create slaves for earthly toil."

"Please!" Vida begged, tears forming at the corners of her eyes.

The twins had stopped playing. They were staring not at Petrus, but at Vida. Staring at her, as if they suddenly didn't recognize her.

Seeing this, Petrus allowed his hand to slip from hers. "I'm sorry. I cannot help you. It is simply too risky. Thank you for your very kind gifts," he told the children. "I hope that you enjoy yours, as well."

Wiping her eyes, Vida realized that their audience with Petrus was over. In silence, she bowed her head toward him, gathered the twins and their new toys up, and quickly left the room.

Reaching the end of the long hall, she encountered Sister Evaline, who was waiting by the penthouse elevator, which was guarded by two Shard troops. Shooing the twins ahead of her into the elevator, she paused a moment to lean into Sister Evaline's ear and whisper, "He refused. Just like you said he would."

Annoyed, Sister Evaline remained silent as she joined them in the elevator. On the ride down, she slowly, gradually exfiltrated her mental domination of the zealot cow, who was too stupid to realize that she had just been most sorely used.

Now, maybe Brother Bradley and Brother Greg would come around to her point of view. After all, she was, and always had been, right. Petrus was damaged goods. No amount of persuasion was going to work on him. No, she now was completely convinced that he had to be controlled and compelled to be of any use to the Council of Glass. And if that required his torture and brainwashing, and even his possible death, then so be it.

CHAPTER 23

"Boss Mode," Peaches said sternly. "Peaches, and only Peaches, present."

"Copy, Boss Mode," came Maynard's soft reply. "Maynard present. Duchess Mhyrranda?"

"Confirm, Boss Mode," the Duchess of Dreamland intoned. "Mhyrranda present. So, Peaches," she began as their now black shared session instantiated, "show us what you've got."

"M'Zinga and Riki just discovered this," he said as a myriad of images churned into view in their shared virtual view. "It was recovered from the vessel that Soda John retrieved from a black Old World .gov site."

"How is he, Peaches?" Mhyrranda inquired, genuinely concerned.

Peaches nodded as more images swirled, "Recovering. So is the girl, Loli, who was the one who apparently opened the portal. We've got our best healers on them, including some former Old World physicians, and a few Fae ambassadors. The Fae are there to keep the peace between our guys and Loli's Fae troop. They're Wildlings. They claim to have taken her when the sigil came, but her age is accelerated. Probably because they took her into one of their rings for quite some time."

"Anyone else there with them?" Maynard asked, even as he rapidly scanned the blooming and zooming images.

"Yep," Peaches replied. "Lucy and Chester are present. Soda John's a major asset. Probably our best Old World scavenger. Has a nose for getting himself in trouble, and bringing us back the most wonderful toys. He gets the best healers possible. Same with this Loli. Especially if she's the one who saved John, and made that portal. Chester is among the best healers we have, so, of course he's there. Curiously, so is our Fractal Mage. Seems that someone who can direct probabilistic outcomes may guide and steer healing improbably."

"Not so useless after all, eh?" Maynard chuckled.

"That's a Watcher!" Mhyrranda abruptly exclaimed.

"Yes, it is," Peaches agreed.

Maynard silently nodded, also. "From the retrieved vessel? How did you manage to isolate it?"

"That was the easy part," Peaches snorted. "The essence of that Watcher infuses the vessel at some interesting quantum domains. Break it down into the smallest part, and the Watcher itself is there. Over and over and over again. I even had our two Evolved check that shit a few dozen times. Same thing, over and over again."

"Is it really alive?" Mhyrranda asked, curious. It looked alive to her, if that malicious glare was any indicator.

"We think so," Peaches informed them. "We think that the Watchers shared a collective identity while they were doing sigil duty. We're certain that one of them went rogue at some point and broke away from their collective, and came down to EarthZero. Antarctica confirms that. However, our current operative hypothesis is that the Watchers, or at least this Watcher, have an ability to instantiate themselves in various, simultaneous avatars."

"Hyperthreads..." Maynard breathed. "That's the code concept of the sim in action. So what is it doing now? Besides keeping Fresswelle away from us, and occupying a few gazillion – actual science-y term, by the way – quanta in its vessel?"

"Well," Peaches replied, "we have no way of demonstrating it, yet, but we think that it's possible that there are one or more active instantiations of this rogue Watcher somewhere. Extant, on EarthZero. We already know that there was the one who grabbed Fresswelle. But, if this is true, then it's possible that there might be more. I mean, there are more, at the quantum level. But there might be more of them out there, like us, at the macro scale."

"That gives me a migraine," Mhyrranda admitted. "We'll share this with the other arcology leaders. See if we can shake anything else out of it. But, for now, it remains Boss Mode only."

Both men nodded, accepting the Duchess's judgement.

"Peaches?" Mhyrranda said. "Please be sure to heal those two up. Fully debrief both of them. We need the full story. Learn all you can about Loli. She's more than just a single-person jumper. That makes her a high-level asset for us. She requires a protective detail. And let's consider what to do with those badass Wildlings, okay? They might prove to be useful to us, if properly guided."

Peaches nodded. "Got it, Duchess. So, what about the vessel? Probably too risky to try a mass jump, or even an Aal Ball-to-Aal Ball transport. Too much could go wrong."

"Agreed," Mhyrranda said. "No other choice but to get it here conventionally. Could we fly it here? Get it here quicker?"

"We could," Maynard said. "But something's telling me that the more power, the more motion, we put into it, the more dangerous it might become. I'm pleasantly shocked, actually, that the portal and high-speed crash didn't impart enough kinetic power into it to... to reactivate it, maybe? Or allow our enemies some insight into its existence. Or trigger some sort of self-destruct in it that might be Hekatek—"

"The Hekatek!" Peaches loudly exclaimed, his massive hands slamming together like two steamrollers. "The Watchers had the power to force the sigil upon us. They guided and shaped the

Evolutionary Tribulation. They're the First Seed. Gods, themselves. Think of that level of power. And we know it's Hekatek, not conventional power. And that final bit that the sigil did? You know, now that we've crunched all of the data over and over again, it was primal power. Union of Source and Void. Over and above everything. So..."

"So..." finished Maynard, "...we use the Watcher's Hekatek as a roadmap to lead us to ultimate Hekatek, and, maybe, even primal. Ultimate power. Relatively speaking, of course."

Mhyrranda considered the variables. "Is that Loli girl capable of using her portal generation power again soon? If so, then she's our immediate solution."

Peaches shook his head. "A few more days. She almost bled out from getting shot by vandals prior to the crash. The crash took its toll on her, as well. She and Soda John are lucky to be alive."

"Okay," Mhyrranda said, "then we immediately get an interstate convoy up and running. Small scale to avoid obvious notice. But several vehicles, loaded for bear, with our best available peeps on them. They get here as fast as they can. If Loli is able to get her bearings before the package arrives here at Dreamland, then we recruit her to do the transport again. We can ferry her from—"

"It's got to stay conventional, Duchess," Maynard interrupted. "It was a miracle that her transport didn't trigger something nasty from the vessel. We don't want a Giza Part II anywhere near us."

"That bad?" Mhyrranda asked, her eyelashes fluttering.

Maynard grimaced. "Maybe even worse."

"We got this," Peaches said. "We have our Monster Truck, and some badass peeps to ride shotgun. Although sparing a few of your Praetorians might be ideal."

"Got it, Peaches," Mhyrranda immediately agreed. "They'll be jumping within the hour, after receiving their briefings. That good?"

"Yep, Duchess," Peaches said. "Exiting Boss Mode. Presuming we'll be keeping in close contact at this level, just in case, right?"

"Right," Maynard confirmed. "Exiting Boss Mode. And, Peaches?"

"Yeah, man."

"Get that Soda John guy geared up like Team EL. He deserves it."

"Will do!" Peaches chuckled. "He's gonna shit a brick. Now he'll be able to get into anything."

"Exiting Boss Mode," Mhyrranda said, officially terminating their shared virtual session. She gave Maynard a quick, sidelong glance. "This is it, isn't it? Not just the linking of the arcologies and pyramids. That's a parallel path. But this Watcher thing? True highest-order Hekatek? Primal power?"

Maynard smiled slowly. "It is, Randa. This is it. If we manage to learn everything we can from it, we can use that new understanding to finally leverage all of EarthZero up to that level of power that razed Giza. Not just passive linked pyramid power, either. This could allow us to form a permanent union of every power source out there. Maybe elevate everyone's chakras to our own levels. Maybe even boost our own to max nines, like Mercy's and Void's."

Slowly, considering the import of Maynard's assessment, Mhyrranda arose and walked over to Maynard, who also was stepping up and out of his silver comfy chair. Abruptly, she lunged toward him, throwing her arms around him and squeezing tightly. Returning her fierce embrace, he noticed that a single tear was trying to sneak down her cheek.

"We have a chance now, my love. We have a chance..." the Duchess of Dreamland said softly, relieved.

CHAPTER 24

Grim faced and determined, M'Tumba manually eased the Monster Truck out of the loading dock complex of the Lennox Science Arcology, its precious alien cargo safely secured in its highly warded dump body.

The customized Mack Granite 64B Day Cab Dump Truck, newly re-inscribed for stealth and extended range, literally bristled with defensive inscriptions. It was, effectively, now a rolling Ft. Knox on 16 armored wheels. Difficult to see, almost impossible to hear despite its incredible mass, and virtually immune to conventional harm. M'Zinga had calculated, much to the Resonant Order's collective amusement, that not even a stomp from an enraged Ku'tu would give it pause. And M'Zinga, to impress the point, had embedded in his virtual message to the Resonant Order a most amusing Old World video of something called a "Tonka Truck" being stepped on by an elephant. To which Riki had almost immediately replied with a ginned-up holographic of Ku'tu, in her Tink form, sputtering indignantly, "Does this elephant leg make my ass look fat?"

M'Tumba replayed Riki's chittering laughter in his head, smiling despite himself. The Born Again Cetaceans were some funny finnies, even if their humor was sometimes entirely too tangential and hard to grasp. Once you got there, though, even things like naming one of their own "Finnie Google" made sense.

"This is going to suck," M'Tumba groaned, steering with his feet. Distracted, he gave the wondrous Moon, its half-face of pumpkin spice orange mocking him, a long gaze. "Time?" he inquired. Instantly, his quantum chronometer displayed a rather long series of numbers before him on its projected, virtual HUD. "Yeah, like I hadn't already calculated that. Slow. I-40 almost forever, with a few jukes and jives, then on to Dreamland. Because we can't go too fast with this piece of Watcher shit, or else it might wake up and go boom."

"Focus, M'Tumba," came a bright, tinkling voice. One with a distinct, Fae accent.

"Ah, Zhila'ghe," M'Tumba purred. "I see you're monitoring. Good. You and your troop should do the same. You're perimeter guard. The most important part of this op."

A momentary pause ensued. Then, "The most important part?" Zhila'ghe said softly. "I thought we were here just in case your blind monkey ass hit an armadillo and flew off the road."

M'Tumba heartily laughed. "You little Tink! With an attitude like that, you sure you're not the Wildlings?"

"Buncha low-borns..." Zhila'ghe scoffed.

"At least the trip won't be boring with you riding my hairy ass. Not like those Praetorians that the Duchess sent us. They're such ninja fucks that they won't even break silence to exchange a few humorous barbs."

For a moment, both the Evolved and the Fae on their shared communications lines paused, hoping for something, some response, from the creepy-silent Praetorians. They hadn't said more than a single word since they'd arrived a few hours back. Scary folks, even for former humans. More black than purple, more dark than light, in their artificed War Suits. They even had creepy, bat-like cloaks of midnight black, with bruised purple fringes that seemed to dance with living energy. They were even capable of defying M'Tumba's more than casual attempts at direct scrying. They were locked down tight, with nary an iota of Hekatek to mark them. Even though he knew quite well precisely how much Hekatek Maynard, Denny, Old Man Culpepper, etc., and et al, had artificed into them.

It was difficult for M'Tumba, who had actually conversed with Nick and had found him lively and amusing, to comprehend how the boisterous general had instilled in his warriors such insane levels of silent, scary discipline. Still, no reply. No telling where they actually were located now. He suspected that at least one of them was attached to the bottom of his truck, but even his truck's elaborate sensors couldn't detect him, or her, or he-she-it.

Sighing, M'Tumba made the transfer to the highway successfully, where two other modified Old World vehicles, each manned by a driver and a co-driver team selected from Peaches' elite guard, and two New World vehicles joined him. Two were virtual clones of M'Tumba's own vehicle, to compel a choice of targets from any attackers. The two clones played a momentary shell game with M'Tumba's massive truck, then filed into a slightly offset line in front and behind him. The remaining two vehicles were Resonant Order Warbirds – christened, appropriately enough, as the "Falcon Hovertank"; each as large as the other vehicles in the convoy, yet capable of stealthy flight – and they took to the air at standoff air cover distance. He was silently thankful that Peaches had spared two of their most precious air assets to provide cover and protection. Their 360-degree, multi-axial autocannons fired a variety of lethal, hypervelocity projectiles that could penetrate even the most armored Old World battleships, and their main cannons inflicted counter-harmonic resonant unbinding on anything in their solution paths. And, yes, due to their biomimetic designs, they somewhat resembled rather large, rather angry looking, big black metallic falcons.

Mentally cuing his personal collection of Old World music, M'Tumba selected "Long Lonesome Highway" and let it rip on their shared bandwidth.

Curiously, all of them noted a formerly unknown voice break with sudden laughter. "Good call, furball," a Praetorian told M'Tumba, her voice silk and steel. "It's really a long and lonesome highway I see here beneath the Monster Truck. Thanks!"

CHAPTER 25

H e had been careless in his rescue of the Fractal Blade. The thought that he had almost failed before he had even started continued to torture him. Even long after his narrow escape from the Godslayer, who surely would have destroyed him, even if the Trickster would have chosen his side in the conflict, the thought of possible failure burned him like a brand to the soul.

He could not bear even to consider failing Lucifer. The rest of the Igigi? The so-called Watchers? Fools, all of them. Drones. Bees buzzing in harmony in a hive of self-similar echoes. But Lucifer? The Prime Mover? The Creator Himself?

Never. Never would he fail the Shining One.

Thus, without fear, he had accepted his task, unbound by any pacts, save for that of the love he felt for his Creator. He had dared to separate from his bond with his fellow Igigi.

Unprecedented. Essential.

Though the act had seared his soul, and had cast him down into a world devoid of the Communion, he had adapted to this new unknown, and had acted with fire and grace to fulfill the will of his master.

He had dared confront the Last God, Nanabozho, in his own place of power. Yet, despite resistance from the Trickster, who had sought to confuse him and keep him away from his prize, he had persevered. The Fractal Blade had found his hand, and, true to the physical form required of him by Lucifer, the blade had instantly bound itself to his own nine chakras. Like a long-lost lover, bound once again in fierce embrace.

Yet... yet the insane chorus of voices raging forth from the blade... crying for freedom from their stillborn thrall...

"Zon! Zon! Free us! Free our souls!" they had raged, battering his mind, body, and soul like angry, hungry insects. Thousands upon thousands of the most powerful Fae.

Clicking. Clacking. Picking one tiny piece of his essence away at a time.

But he needed his essence – his full essence – to complete the mission of his master.

So, reluctantly, he had been forced to... quiet them.

The terrible thought of what he had been forced to do to the last denizens of Aal made his mind spin. Forcing the horror from his mind's eye yet again, he focused his attention on driving the rather antiquated four-wheeled conveyance down the unexciting rural Georgia road. The massive '76 Cadillac Eldorado, jet black with ostentatious gold trim, smoothly maneuvered along the dangerous, poorly paved rural roads of Elbert County, Georgia. Sol was rising in the eastern sky, and the day promised to be one of pristine, absolute destiny. Soon, if his discernment of the humans' backward conception of time was true, he would arrive at his destination, and set Lucifer's beautifully efficient plan in motion.

CHAPTER 26

"I'm ready," Sister Evaline informed Brother Bradley and Brother Greg.

"Fiat lux," Brother Bradley intoned, his baritone voice purring from the hidden sound system in the cathedral, and the interior of the former St. Patrick's Cathedral beamed with light. Now more psychedelic crystal than wood, marble, and steel, the cathedral's immense apse had been converted to house the Council of Glass. A titanic table of crystal occupied the main space of the apse. The various sisters, brothers, and knights militant of the City of Glass occupied the majority of the table, with three seats at the head of the table reserved for the triumvirate of Sister Evaline, Brother Bradley, and Brother Greg.

Beyond the colorful apse, the cathedral teemed with many thousands of the City of Glass' inhabitants. Standing room only, for many more thousands milled about outside, all of them eager to learn if the Pope would command them to victory against the disciples of hell. Word had spread like veritable wildfire about the twins, and how God spoke directly through them like the prophets of the Old World. The Council of Glass had decreed the mandatory attendance of all non-essentials to witness the event, so everyone with a functioning brain understood that something of immense importance was to occur.

"The light is good," Brother Bradley announced, his voice now projecting for many blocks down the city streets. The two big screens adorning the cathedral's entrance roared to life, causing the crowd outside to cheer and stamp, just as the two big screens in the apse did so, causing a similar quaking inside. The triumvirate's faces were center focus on the screens. "Welcome. Tonight, the Council of Glass calls upon the citizens of the City of Glass to witness the miraculous prophecies of God's own chosen twins: Abe, and Ada."

In unison, the crowd went wild with fervent, religious zeal. As the roar intensified, the hidden cameras focused on a circular platform of vibrant rainbow crystal that arose from the withdrawing floor in the center of the council table. To the cheers of the maddened flock, Vida, the twins, a slightly nonplused Petrus, who leaned heavily into his plain wooden staff, and two flanking Shard Troops in their gleaming prismatic armor were revealed. As the six new arrivals stepped off their trapdoor riser, it once again descended into the floor, which closed in upon itself. A small battery of recessed spotlights focused upon them, and the big screen images now split, showing the new arrivals and the triumvirate.

"It's loud," Abe laughed to Ada, who giggled back at him.

"Quiet," Vida scolded them, scooping up their hands into hers. "Now genuflect to them, like I showed you," she said under her breath. Following her lead, they did as they had been told, and the crowd once again roared.

"Welcome, Vida, Abe, and Ada," Brother Bradley said. "The Council of Glass thanks you for accepting our invitation to share with the City of Glass the revelations of the Lord. So, without further ado, please tell us what the Lord has shown you regarding the schemes of the servants of the Devil himself, the evil ones of Dreamland and their warped allies?"

Immediately, the noise stilled unto virtual silence. Thousands of pairs of eyes seemed to bore directly into the souls of the two small children, whose images now monopolized the video screens.

"You say it," Abe prodded Ada. "I'm scared."

"Okay, scaredy-cat," Ada replied. "Hi. My name is Ada. God told me to tell you what I saw. The ebil Dreamland people and their friends will fight us. They try to kill us, so we can't do what God wants us to do: beat them and the Devil. But God showed me and my brother that the towers of the City of Glass will glow like the Sun."

"And, and, and..." Abe interrupted, excited. "And King Kong is bringing a space weapon to Lost Vegas. The bad guys will use it to hurt everyone in the City of Glass. Lucifer made it. It came down from his seagull."

"Yep, we have to stop them," Ada added. "They're wolves. They'll slaughter all the Lord's sheep. That means ewe," she giggled.

"The end," Abe finished.

A moment of awkward silence followed as both crowd and council considered what they had been told.

"Thank you, children," Brother Bradley said carefully. "Veritably from the mouths of babes. I see that we sheep require a good shepherd. What say you, Il Papa?" he inquired of Petrus. "Will you lead your sheep, and guide us through the Valley of the Shadow of Death?"

Nervous, Petrus shifted from one foot to the other, even as a chant of "Petrus!" began to grow from outside the cathedral. As the chant began to reach a booming crescendo, Petrus shifted his staff, and attempted to straighten himself to stand as straight and tall as he could, given his infirmity.

"I..." Petrus began. He gazed around the council table. Above and beyond the triumvirate, he gazed at the big screens, noticing himself and the smaller inset screens showing the mass of the crowd inside the cathedral and out. "My own encounter with the Devil's Children cost me dearly. My limbs are nearly useless. My senses are failing. I no longer have the power that the Lord gave me. I am not fit to lead you. I am sorry."

Again, silence fell, for all of three seconds. Then, Sister Evaline pointedly inquired, "Petrus? If you cannot lead us, can you at least raise an army to help us? As you did in the Old World when you gathered your forces from far and wide, in order to directly contest Lucifer and his fallen at Giza? A few million of the former dead, resurrected by your hand, surely would shift the initiative, and the advantage of power, to the City of Glass. By God and all that is holy," she said with a certain premeditation, "would you at least help us in this?"

"It doesn't serve Heaven to create slaves for earthly toil. I am sorry," Petrus replied solemnly. "I cannot. My time is through."

"I see," Sister Evaline said tersely. "Thank you, Il Papa."

Brother Bradley and Brother Greg exchanged quizzical looks. Sister Evaline gave Warlord Armitrage, seated first next to Brother Greg, a quick smile. The Warlord was a tall man, bearded and grey-eyed, with pale, close-cropped hair, wearing a uniform that proclaimed him to be a general. The uniform was black, with a light blue crystal insignia on the breast. The Warlord noted the smile, and said nothing, choosing to stare dispassionately at Petrus.

"I see," Brother Bradley said. "Thank you, children. Thank you, Petrus Romanus." At this, the two accompanying Shard Troops motioned for their group to return to their now-arriving circular platform, which they then used to depart. "And thank you, Sister Evaline," Brother Bradley continued after the floor sealed itself. "Citizens?" he asked. "Consider what the twins recounted. If you happen to reach understanding, please report immediately to your local priest and tell them everything. Remember that God guides us all, and that everyone in this new age is worthy of prophecy, should the good Lord so wish. Leave nothing to chance. The stakes are too high, in this, the advent of the final battle between Good and Evil. Thank you, God bless you, and good night."

With that, the video screens went dark, and the audio ceased, even as various attendants began to usher the cathedral crowd outside. As the crowd filed out, a thin yet virtually unbreakable film of crystal arose from the floor just beyond the westernmost portion of the council table. Swiftly, it rose to the top of the ceiling, expanding and filling out in order to seal off the council table from the rest of the cathedral.

Noting the small text display of "Secure" upon the screen of the recessed flat screen in the table before him, Brother Greg informed the Council of Glass, "Secure. Safe. Commence."

Which Warlord Armitrage did immediately, a dark scowl on his bearded face: "Petrus is too weak to lead us, or even to help us. Or, he is lying, compromised by the Devil he tried and failed to defeat. I therefore request the opportunity to ask him, personally, where he truly stands."

"What?" Brother Bradley scoffed. "You can immediately jump to such a permanent conclusion, based upon a single statement by an infirm old man, who gave his life to do God's work? Are you mad, Warlord Armitrage?"

"Oh, please, Brother Bradley," Warlord Armitrage replied firmly. "The cameras are off. No need to continue your holier-than-thou act. We all know now that Petrus went off half-cocked and got his ass kicked by the Dreamland crew, who still had to cheat like hell to beat him. And even though the common story has him being destroyed in the battle, then being resurrected, it's still an unproven unknown. Who could possibly survive a blast like that? For all we know, the Devil saved him and has only recently returned him to the game board. To spite us all, and to mislead us in the struggle against our very real foes. Seriously:

What good has he done us, other than to recruit a few thousand more to our side since it went public that he had come to join us here in the City of Glass? Has he raised another army to fight for us? Has he even given us a simple blessing? No. He just sits up alone in his penthouse, and talks for hours on end to himself about nothing. He's useless. And a liar of some kind on top of being useless. Please grant my gaining a more intimate understanding of what the truth is with him."

"Yes, please, Brother Bradley," Sister Evaline interjected before Brother Bradley could answer. "The twins? I believe them. They're innocent, and God certainly guides them. But Petrus? I agree with Warlord Armitrage's assessment. Petrus is hiding something. And I *know* he is, because I can't peer into his mind, which is impossible, unless he still has his power. Which means he's lying about not having his former power. Blatantly lying. He's playing us all for fools! He's in league with Lucifer!"

Brother Bradley sighed deeply, steepling his fingers beneath his broad chin. He knew he had to tread carefully, yet forcefully, now that it was a matter of council record that Sister Evaline had spoken for Warlord Armitrage. Seditious bitch that she truly was. "Sister Evaline?" he began, staring straight ahead. "The next time you side with anyone outside the triumvirate against us, you will discover that it is within my considerable power to transform you and your erstwhile allies to crystal without so much as breaking a sweat. Test us at your peril," he said, speaking for both himself and Brother Greg.

"And not even your much vaunted invulnerability will save you," Brother Greg coldly informed the Warlord, who met his burning gaze with an emotionless smirk.

"Test us at your peril?" Sister Evaline shot back testily. "You're being tested right now, Brother Bradley! Petrus has you fooled! *He* is testing you, not us. We're on *your* side," she carefully added.

"I know," Brother Bradley agreed, accepting the olive branch. "I was being pro forma, of course. I suggest that we give the wounded prelate another chance. Perhaps after we deal with the issue revealed to us by the children?"

"Agreed," Brother Greg said, eager to get on to the actual meat of the matters facing them. "The speculation about the Pope is just that: speculation. What the twins have revealed to us, however, is of immediate importance. Lucifer has granted Dreamland a weapon of cosmic power."

"And King Kong is driving it there," Warlord Armitrage scoffed dismissively. His customized set of crystal plate armor flared with pent up prismatic power. "Those children are not to be trusted. They speak nonsense, just as does the daft Pope. Perhaps a session of interrogation would straighten out their tongues."

"Torturing children?" Brother Greg asked, wide eyed. "Jesus, Anthony! Have you grown so cold that you could even consider such a thing?"

The Warlord returned the Cardinal's gaze with an entirely neutral expression. "Just keepin' it real, Brother Greg. And hard. Somebody has to."

"I don't like your insinuation," Brother Bradley said. "We're not soft. Nothing of the sort. Warlord Armitrage, you have my explicit permission to nonviolently interrogate the children, so long as Sister Evaline sits in, using her mental controls to influence their speaking the truth. Be sure not to include Petrus in the interrogation. It would negatively influence him, and we can't afford that. Brother Greg? You are with them. Boost everyone, if needed. Dig deep. Find out everything. No stone left unturned. Report back once you are done, and do so immediately after you are done. Now, go. Council dismissed."

Brother Greg, Sister Evaline, and Armitrage nodded in agreement, silently acknowledging just how fucking smooth

Brother Bradley could be when he wanted to. Part of how he had made Wall Street his bitch back in the Old World.

Around the titanic crystal table, the various brothers, sisters, and knights militant of the Council of Glass arose, with naught but the gentle clink and tinkle of their crystal armor and weapons to mark their passage.

Several meters beneath them, slowly winding their way through the subterranean passages beneath the cathedral, the twins stopped and shifted their gazes to Petrus. Solemnly, he nodded, and sighed.

Be not afraid, he thought, bidding them to hear his silent words, as he knew they truly could. *I will be your shepherd. I will guide you through the Valley of the Shadow of Death. And more.*

The twins looked at each other, smiled briefly, then continued walking. They liked Petrus, even if he was old and crippled. He gave them nice presents. And he had a twin, too. A scary twin. It just lived inside him.

CHAPTER 27

"Don't be afraid, children," Sister Evaline sweetly told Abe and Ada as she passed them each an Old World Butterfinger bar. "Go ahead," she told them. "Dig in. Relax. General Armitrage is going to ask you a few questions, then Ms. Vida can take you back to your rooms."

Vida smiled vacuously at the twins, nodding her head in approval. Sister Evaline had been most careful this time to insinuate her psychic control into her mind. Those two children, she now realized, had powers that might be beyond her ability to control, so she had decided at the last moment to focus on their caretaker, rather than on them directly, as Brother Bradley had directed. Thankfully, the same mindset that made Vida such a devout follower of the Old World's false god also made her quite susceptible to psychic influence and control.

With the sudden clank of crystal on metal, the steel door of the old police interrogation room opened wide, and General Armitrage walked into the room. Casually, he dismissed the two Shard Troops guarding the door, and they closed the door on their way out. Armitrage made a concerted effort to smile and appear to be happy and warm, even though he was long out of practice. The world had changed around him, virtually overnight, and the man he had once been simply was no longer there. Not after the horror of losing his entire family to the sigil.

Still, he made the effort, earning him a quick smirk from Sister Evaline.

"Hi, kids," General Armitrage said easily, settling down in a simple metal chair, joining the twins and Vida, and Sister Evaline, at the table.

"Hi, Mr. Gen'ral," the twins replied in unison. Both were still trying to fish out their candy bars from their wrappers. Seeing this, Vida robotically moved to help them.

"Are you enjoying your visit to the City of Glass?" Armitrage asked brightly. "We have a lot of fun things for you to explore when you're ready."

"Like what?" Abe asked as he greedily tore into the wrapper that Vida had slightly opened for him.

"Well, this used to be a place called 'New York City,'" Armitrage replied, "and we have managed to rebuild and restore a few places, like the ice skating rink, a museum that has dinosaurs in it, and, of course, Crystal Park, which used to be Central Park. I'm sure Ms. Vida will take you on the grand tour, starting tomorrow, if you'd like?"

"Yay! Dinosaurs!" Ada squeaked between bites. "Are they real?"

The general shook his head. "I'm afraid they really aren't real, but they're big and scary enough as it is. Especially with their nice new crystal teeth."

"Like your armor?" Abe asked. Armitrage nodded. "What's it do? Make rainbows?"

"If only..." Sister Evaline laughed. "We enchanted it such that it makes the general invincible in combat. He can walk through raging fires unharmed. He can swim underwater and not drown. He can resist bullets, and he is so strong that he can lift an elephant!"

"Wow!" Ada exclaimed. "A elephant! That's heavy!"

"And I can make crystal weapons with it that can slice through bank vaults," Armitrage added with a tiny crack of a smile. "But that's just so I can help the City of Glass. That's my job. What you two do is much, much cooler, I think. God shows you things. That's as cool as it gets."

"It's okay, I guess," Abe admitted, smacking loudly. "I'd rather be able to pick up a elephant!"

"Or swim like a fish!" Ada laughed. "Can we go see the dinosaurs tomorrow?"

"Of course you can," Sister Evaline replied. The twins giggled excitedly.

"Could you tell us about what God told you about the people from Dreamland?" Armitrage asked them. "The more you can tell us about them, the better chance we have of winning. They're the bad guys, and we're the good guys. You want to help the good guys, don't you? Of course you do. Please help us win, okay?"

"Okay," Ada replied. She exchanged a quick glance with her brother. "I'll go first. They're not just in Lost Vegas. They're everywhere now. They have a fish man, a plant man, a cat man who can lift a whole train, King Kong and his friends, a guy who drinks a lot but is still really smart, some elves with pointy ears and wings, some cartoon people in costumes who can all fly, a man and his wife and a little baby who go around everywhere in a truck and see cool things, a dragon, a skull lady, a big big big man who likes other men when they take bubble baths, a lady who can visit you in your dreams, and somebody named 'Boyd', who is really mean, but he likes cat videos. He kilt the pope, and he died too, but they both just came right back. It took the souls of 13 people in black to bring the pope back. The pope's twin inside him made them do it. Boyd came back when the Dragon and the Mother called him. Neither had a choice."

"Boyd sleighs gods," Abe added, still chewing. "I guess it has to snow first, though."

Nonplused, Sister Evaline and General Armitrage stared at one another.

Continuing after a dry moment of children smacking on candy bars, General Armitrage asked them, "Do you see anything specific? Any buildings? Any weapons? Any specific names of people or things? Anything we can use to help us win?"

Ada replied, "We see what we told you in the church. They are going to fight you. It's going to hurt a lot of people. It's going to be a real war. They think that they are the good guys, too."

"But they're not," Sister Evaline said quickly. "They are in league with Lucifer. That makes them the bad guys. Definitely."

"It's confusing," Abe admitted, finishing off his candy bar. "Adults are confusing. I just want to see some dinosaurs!"

"Okay, okay, you will," General Armitrage told them. "What about that golden glow you saw over the City of Glass? What does that mean?"

"Looked like the Sun," Ada informed him. "Like a sunrise over the whole city."

"Like the Sun rising over the City of Glass?" Sister Evaline prompted.

"Yes," Abe agreed, his left leg kicking wildly beneath the table.

"What about the 'twin' you said was inside Petrus?" General Armitrage asked.

"It's black and scary," Abe said. "My sister and I don't look at it."

"Is that the 'SoulThief'?" Sister Evaline asked?

Both children shrugged their shoulders.

"What about this 'Mother' and 'Dragon'?" Sister Evaline pressed, though she was fairly certain she already knew this answer thanks to the most excellent intel from the Council of Glass. "Who are they?"

Ada replied, smiling, "One is the mommy of EarthZero, and one is the daddy. They love us all. They're God."

"Yep," Abe agreed. "God."

Sister Evaline and General Armitrage, not liking the sound of such blasphemy issuing forth from the mouths of innocent children, invoked a subtle form of cognitive dissonance first to gloss entirely over and then totally dispel the thought. Clearly, they were confusing God, the One Above, with pagan, Fae beliefs. They would learn, in time, to clearly differentiate the two, with the former being quite real, and the latter being nothing but faerie hocus pocus.

"Anything else?" Sister Evaline asked the general. He shook his head, unwilling to speak, lest his growing anger betray him.

"May we go now?" Abe pleaded. "I've gotta go pee really bad."

"Me, too!" Ada chimed in. "May we please go?"

Sister Evaline and Armitrage looked at one another. This was going nowhere, and it was painfully obvious. Sister Evaline relaxed her psychic hold over Vida, who still continued to smile.

"Ms. Vida?" Sister Evaline asked her. "Would you be a dear and take the twins back home? And let them use the restroom here before you leave?" The door creaked open, and two guards stood ready to escort them.

"Of... of course, ma'am," Vida agreed, rising from her chair. "Come, children. Let's go. Thank the kind Sister and good general, please?"

"Thank you Sister and Gen'ral!" the twins said in unison as they skipped off, joining Vida as they sped out of the room.

Waiting a moment until the noise of "Yay! Dinosaurs!" dimmed down the hall, Sister Evaline slowly steepled her fingers before her, elbows resting on the plain tabletop.

"Well, Anthony," she said, "that was entirely fucking useless. Complete waste of time."

"Agreed," he shrugged. "Useless information. Probably remnants of Old World cartoons floating around in their vacant little heads. So much for their being prophets. Except for that sunrise part. That resonates strongly."

"City of Gold?" Sister Evaline shot back testily. "Don't tell me you actually believe your own religious propaganda. Revelation came, and no golden city appeared."

General Anthony Armitrage gave Sister Evaline Kohl a passionate glare. "Sister Evaline, maybe it's you who should be paying attention to your own propaganda. Don't you get it? The City of Glass will welcome the City of Gold. It's going to descend here, in our own New Jerusalem. God's coming here, Sister Evaline, because we're the good guys. And we're going to be the ones who wage Armageddon against the Devil's Children, and lay them to waste. See how it fits?"

Mouth agape, she had to give him silent props. Then, not-so-silent ones: "I think you've just pieced together what might have been an actual prophecy. I mean, it makes perfect sense. The Church and its teachings didn't fail us. Armageddon didn't fail us. It's here, on our very doorstep. And we're the ones who are going to usher it in, and receive praise from God. God Himself is coming to reward us Eternal Life for beating the Devil!"

"Amen..." Armitrage said softly, nodding his head.

CHAPTER 28

The Angel of Deceit phased back into the Prime Reality a few paces behind the Omen of the Apocalypse, the Herald of the Nine, in the Omen's very own private chamber.

"Ugg..." the Omen of the Apocalypse deeply sighed, its cosmic senses informing it of the presence of its old personal foil, friend, and most ancient lover. "What do you seek now, Apate? More tricks up your silken sleeves?"

A muffled laugh mocked the Omen, even as warm, slender arms embraced it from behind. "I just wanted to hear you say my name, Omi."

"Well, I said it," the Omen admitted, bristling at the corruption of its familiar name. "And you know I prefer 'Omen' over 'Omi', my dear."

"Sounds too much like 'Onan'," Apate cooed. "You really need to join me more frequently. You're letting your job rule you, denying yourself obviously needed pleasure."

The Herald of the Nine reluctantly broke free of Apate's embrace. It turned slowly to regard the billowy, blue eyed and blond haired apparition before it. Behind Apate, the chamber's holographic walls flickered, and a placid, pastoral scene filled the room with its highly virtual reality. Alien blue flowers tall as a human male speckled themselves throughout the golden high grass of the simple mountain dale. A ringed moon dominated the ultraviolet sky above them. A troop of 12-winged Fae buzzed about, gamboling merrily from bloom to bloom.

Apate sighed, slowly breathing the experience in. "Ah, I remember well this place, my love. It's where we First Seed were bloomed. So, tell me again why we didn't join the Nine?"

"Because they're a sorry lot of pretentious assholes," Omen barked. "This last session? They almost killed me in their panic. Kept forcing me to share my Zyrrblok, knowing how defenseless that makes me. However, and of course, they kept up their primal powers, even during the Mindlink, and they almost managed to off me this time. Took every trick I know to ward myself. Bunch of wankers. Half of them aren't even worthy of their power. Too stupid."

"I know," Apate agreed a bit too quickly. "We've finally reached the End of All Things, and now they're scared shitless. Bunch of old ninnies. Well, come to think of it, I think they're scared because they realize that everything is over once we close this one out. Ta-da. The End. Gods no more. Fade to black."

Omen stared at the virtual grass on the floor of his personal haven. "I'll tell you, if you tell me. No lies, though. I'll know it. And you'll know, too."

"That's why I love you," Apate admitted. "We can't possibly bullshit each other. After this Confession Session, though, you're mine. And you're bottom this time. Okay. You first."

Sighing again, Omen began, "You know that recreational procreation is forbidden! Why must you always tempt me?"

Apate shrugged innocently. "Because I'm the Angel of Deceit, it's in my nature, and I can't help it? Scorpion, frog?"

Omen bit back a laugh. "How true. So, when I went to scout the final world, EarthZero, at first I couldn't find it. I know, right? I can find anything. But it was hidden from me. The whole world.

So, I cheated a bit, zoomed in, and I saw the Dragon manifested around EarthZero. It was protecting it."

"But that's impossible!" Apate countered. "The Dragon cannot manifest itself like that around any planet. Unless... Unless the First Seed are present. Then, of course, it's inherently manifested." It paused, its delicate hands clenching and unclenching as it worked over this particularly foul equation. "I've been there, of course. But it wouldn't manifest just for a visitor, First Seed or not. However, we know that immortals are present. Whatever the Evil One hit EarthZero with killed off all of the weak, but it made the very few remaining extremely strong. Transcended them. Maybe that super-charged the planet, and made the Dragon appear?"

"Wait..." Omen considered, now glancing up to meet Apate's flashing blue eyes. "They're *all* immortal?" Apate nodded. "No wonder the Nine are in such a tiff. How comprehensive was the genocide you mentioned? I caught only a glance of it before the Dragon cut me off."

"About 99%."

"Incredible."

"Right?" Apate said. "Should be a cakewalk for us after that, right? But it's not, I can assure you. That 1% or 2% remaining? From what I've learned directly and indirectly, those who remain are all post-seventh chakra. Some rare few of those have even achieved the ninth. Ancient Fae from another world have joined them. Apparently, these alien Fae came from a world that has – get this – fought against the Vanth'Vash'Var. Cosmic-level artifacts are in play. Petrus has something in his soul of souls that's... beyond black. I can't even discern it, save by noting what is not it. But it's cosmic-level, too. And..." Apate stopped, considering how to break this to its friend and lover from the Time Before.

"Don't say it," Omen interrupted, his own cosmic senses already sensing where this was going to lead. "Don't you dare tell me that shite, Apate," he finished, grave and strong. "He's not real. It's a myth meant to scare gods and men, and flitting Fae. That's all it is."

Apate shook its head. "Sorry, luv. I've read it directly from Petrus, and from a few others who have witnessed them personally. Null, and Void."

"Well, fuck me!" Omen complained loudly, rolling his eyes in utter frustration. "Vashti Thog's going to snuff a billion souls when he learns this. It's rank, utter heresy and blasphemy to the Horde, all warped into a single holy wafer of shite. How can we rightly proclaim that we are the Sentinels of the Void when the Void itself appears to stand against us?"

Apate continued without remorse, "Void Schmoid. At least this will be a challenge. Probably on the level of the V'layans themselves. That was truly worthy."

"No it *wasn't*!" Omen argued. "It was bloody terrifying! They compromised a good part of the Starhome that required several planets worth of materiel to regrow, and they almost killed the triad!"

"Don't be so dramatic, Omen," Apate chided. "That's not so bad. Had they listened to me, they would have been able to take those three down, permanently. And we would have ascended to replace them."

"Don't tell me that! Zyrrblok," Omen grumbled, "please wipe that last bit. I don't want to wind up getting soul-snuffed by Vashti Thog."

"Angel of Deceit, remember? However, they also have an extended group of heavy hitters from different cities and regions on EarthZero. There's a 'Team EL', chock full of Elemental Lords. Hybrid evolved human and Fae. They have a Dreamwyrd, a Fractal Mage, and numerous dozens of superpowered humans and evolved animals. The finnies are especially amusing. The main antagonists, the Dreamland people and their allies, are actively trying to tap into and exploit certain resonant technomagick properties of their own Dragon. Some of them are as smart as our best and brightest. I know that sounds hard to believe. But it's true. And I think..."

Silently, Omen urged Apate on, totally enthralled. In its countless conquests of other worlds – even the biggest, and most advanced – it had never heard of such things in convergence and resonance. A perfect storm brewed for them, and it was only now that it was starting to comprehend its own very real possible mortality.

Apate continued, "I think that they have discovered something beyond technomagick."

"Impossible!" Omen shouted. "There is nothing beyond our greatest power! Nothing! Especially nothing that some provincial hicks on some backwater planet in a meaningless galaxy could fathom! You're actually lying to me now, aren't you?"

Apate shook its head, its golden locks spilling over its hermaphroditic breasts. "Like what we have is *so* great!" it said, heaping scorn upon the audacious suggestion. "Look!" it bade Omen, causing the holographic field to conjure direct images of the Starhome itself. Row upon endless row, column upon endless column of their multiracial war forces appeared, frozen in various forms of stasis, like unripe grapes upon some stillborn cosmic vine. "If what we have is so great, then why is it that we enforce total stasis upon virtually everyone between our encounters? Why does the Starhome sail on what's virtually a skeleton crew of only a few million? Why do we even have to conserve energy if the energy we have is so all-powerful?"

Scoffing, Omen replied testily, "Because nothing is infinite, Apate! We have, counting the small-scale warriors and their various accoutrements of war, many trillions upon trillions. Even parsing for orders of magnitude, it is entirely prudent and wise to simply enforce stasis between encounters not only to conserve energy expenditure, but also to protect the First Seed from mutiny. Even with Vox constantly pounding their minds with its eternal propaganda, many of them would love nothing more than to rectify the genocide of their own home worlds and star systems with the destruction of Demonia Prime, the Starhome, and its elite First Seed. They hate us, and fear us; they do not love us, and they certainly do not all share our quest. Nine forbid, but they could even wage war upon their own disparate factions, and bring us all down by so doing. What then would we profit, when our Quest of the Eternal Recursion ends for naught? We would lose our right to be reborn after the End of All Things, Apate. And that cannot be allowed."

Suddenly, Omen stood stock still. For a few silent moments, its eyes moved as if it were dreaming. Then, with a quick mental command, Omen dismissed the holographic field. Now entirely dark, no light save for their own filled the room.

"Apate?"

"Yes, Omi?"

"The Nine decree that you are to provide the Council of Glass with the designs of some of our own planetary-scale weapons, and instill the technomagickal artificing know-how for them to create their own versions. Weapons that will give them the ability to inflict massive harm upon the Dreamland faction and their allies. You are to do this immediately. Farewell."

"Divide and conquer," the Angel of Deceit smiled. "Right up my alley. I like it," it said, phasing out to begin its new quest.

CHAPTER 29

"Albuquerque!" M'Tumba said most earnestly. The Sun was up high, around local noon, and the nearby mountains seemed to shimmer with a sandy haze. "Making good time now!"

"Yeah," Zhila'ghe noted laconically, lazily sprawled out on the Monster Truck's massive dashboard, "Albuquerque. Just try not to take a left turn or anything like that."

"Silly rabbit!" M'Tumba teased. "Just wait till we get to Dreamland. You're going to love that place. Lot of places to party down and have a great time. Or so I've heard."

"I've already scheduled an appointment with the Entheogenic Lord," the Fae casually informed his Evolved friend. "Gonna hook us up real good."

"Huh? Hook us up? Like carcasses in a butcher's shop?"

Zhila'ghe bit back what would have been a cruel laugh. "No, my furry friend. It's a colloquial term for giving us the best stuff. He's the Entheogenic Lord, so, of course, he's got the best stuff."

"Ah, good," M'Tumba smiled. "Being a true vegan, I will savor the tasty shoots and leaves that Vir'gil provides for us. What a great time we'll have."

"Uh, okay, big guy," Zhila'ghe exhaled, realizing he'd lost this one. "I'll take everything but the shoots and leaves, and you can have them all. Deal?"

"Very kind of you!" M'Tumba agreed. "But I get all the drugs, okay?" he finished with a meaty sneer, causing his streetwise Fae friend to burst into uproarious laughter.

A brief flash of sunlight atop the towering hill to M'Tumba's right caught his attention. Was someone standing up there, arms raised in a "V"? Tilting his massive head for a better view, he shifted slightly forward, interrupting Zhila'ghe's laugh fit. As the Fae began to turn his head to try to catch sight of what M'Tumba appeared to be staring at, the world around the two and their truck, and indeed within a radius of nearly 400 meters centered upon them, abruptly flashed a very wicked white. Then, the two, and everyone else in the convoy on the ground, experienced disorienting pain, intense nausea, and confusing vertigo as their retinas burned from the inside out. Around them, the ambient temperature instantly soared to several thousand Kelvin, flash-burning their highly artificed vehicle, chewing into its runic infrastructure as it did. Outside, I-40 converted into a hellish, cloying, bubbling mass of melted interstate, shocked rock, and rapidly fusing sand. All of the ground vehicles slogged to a stop, slowly sinking into the boiling morass.

"Good shot, Solarr," General Armitrage said over the Shard Troop commlink.

"Warbirds incoming, General," came another voice over the commlink. "North and South oppositional vectors. 2,000 meters and closing really fast."

"Wyrmhole. You're up," the general commanded. Breaking cover, because he had to see this new kid in action, he peeled back a section of the chromo cover and stared out across the scene of devastation below.

"Yes, sir," replied the puberty-broken voice of a young man with a pronounced Brooklyn accent. "Birds are mine."

General Armitrage caught sight of the flying youth, his draconic wings casting off the chromo cover as he revealed himself to the approaching Warbirds. He was a few hundred meters above the scene of Solarr's massive display of hellfire power, calmly hovering in place, his spiked tail darting to and fro as the sunlight glittered polychromatically off his customized shard armor. The Warbirds, wasting no time, engaged with their autocannons, showering him with dozens of armor-penetrating rounds.

"Ah, shit," the general cursed, instinctively covering his eyes with his armored gauntlet. "Poor kid."

However, after the initial bursts, to the general's minor surprise, Wyrmhole remained hovering in place, totally intact. With nary a mark on him, save for a few dangling shards where his armor had been compromised. Then, as the Warbirds continued toward him, shifting their axes slightly such that their matter-disintegrating weapons could be brought to bear, the draconic hybrid waved his taloned gauntlets. With a motion almost too quick to follow, a pulsating black rift appeared directly before both Warbirds, swallowing both vehicles before hissing to a close. Immediately, a few hundred meters above the place where he hovered, the two black rifts appeared again, this time directly opposite one another. In extreme proximity.

The two Warbirds then became one in a sickening crash of exotic metal and mangled flesh, a massive black, roiling fireball immediately blooming in the sky like some mutant dark aerial rose.

General Armitrage allowed himself a slight smile. "Well done, Wyrmhole. Solarr, Wyrmhole, form up on me for immediate portal egress. Shard-2, retrieval team up. Recover the craft. Birds inbound, five minutes. No survivors. Kill them all. Then destroy what's left."

With that, a dozen Shard Troops removed their chromo covers and began to descend down to the hellish ruin of I-40 below them, leaping 10 meters per jump.

CHAPTER 30

"Nick, Ami, Cuan?" Maynard said softly, not believing what he had just seen. "Jumpers ready. You're up."

"Sec, Maynard," Nick grated back. He had just lost six of his best. But he had to contain it, as he was trained to do, or he was going to burst a blood vessel.

"We will avenge them, Nick," Cuan assured him, gently resting a most malicious clawed hand on Nick's left shoulder.

"We will perform our mission and retrieve that vessel," Nick informed him solemnly. "Any vengeance will have to be incidental. Any questions before we jump?"

Cuan regarded the multiple screens provided by Aal Ball in the Dreamland Arcology's War Room. Fully half of the dozen or so screens were now showing fuzzy distortion, their feeds having been compromised by the City of Glass attack. However, of the six remaining, various vantages of the scene of the ambush were displayed, and it was obvious that the remaining enemy troops were having no trouble negotiating the boiling morass in their efforts to get to the entrapped trucks. *Nasty,* he thought. *Nasty, but do-able.*

"Yeah, Nick," Cuan said, withdrawing his clawed hand and cracking his gnarly knuckles with the sound of railroad ties being driven. "Do you want me to leave any of them alive for you?"

"What?" Nick asked, somewhat startled.

"Ha..." one of the three jumpers laughed. "He's the Black Jaguar, man," the jumper told them, sharing a smile with his two companions. "He once took down an entire army of mutants by himself. With a locomotive."

Ami laughed. Loudly. "I like it," she declared. "I'll post Top-Z and take out their sure-to-be air assets, playing backup and spotter in the meantime. Well, stuff that Maynard and Cully and the Duchess might not observe from here, and Peaches and everyone else from everywhere else."

"OK," Nick agreed. He gave Cuan a sidelong glance. He'd of course heard much, but had yet seen little personally. Time to see if the rumors were indeed true. "You're on point, Cuan. I'll provide tactical cover with my shields. I'll also do this to the vessel once we clear and secure the area. Cully's theory that we can safely shield it and transport it will have to be tested. No choice, considering the power and aggression of our opponents. Jumpers in and out quickly. We don't need to risk your staying there, so jump back ASAP, without us. Got it?"

"Check," Cuan and Ami said in unison. Behind them, the jumpers nodded silently.

Nick paused a moment, then added, "Body recovery will occur only after we secure and transport the vessel. We'll send a new team to retrieve the fallen at that point. Then we'll bring them home."

"Then, in honor of our fallen comrades," Cuan breathed, "I will respect their bodies, and not lay waste to the entire site."

Nick nodded. Ami grinned. Cuan chuckled, "Hey, guys. It is what it is, as y'all like to say."

"Jumpers? Do it!" Nick ordered.

And it was done. In the veritable blink of an eye, the jumpers parsed the spacetime between Dreamland and the ambush site just to the east of Albuquerque. In but a moment, the three were now hovering in place a thousand meters above the site, with the jumpers barely registering in spacetime as they were suddenly back to where they had begun.

"Cool suit, thanks," Cuan said, praising his newly artificed inscribed battle armor. "Kinda cool to fly around, I have to admit."

"Beats crawling around in the kitty box, doesn't it?" Ami prodded him. "Now, put it to good use," she said as she began to bend and bind the local spacetime to her formidable will. "I've got CAP."

"Check," Cuan and Nick said in unison.

They glanced at each other, jaws clenching.

"Let's do it, Cuan," Nick said, staring down at the enemy below. "Release them from the pain of Life, and let them rejoin the Mother..."

"*¡Pendejos!*" Cuan hissed, popping his wicked black claws as he cybernetically commanded his suit to veritably slam him down to the ground below them.

Ami and Nick watched Cuan descend like Divine Judgement itself.

"He called them a bunch of assholes, Nick," Ami snickered, scanning the sky.

"I know, Ami," Nick said, steadying his will for what was to come. Already, nearly invisible force fields formed tactical barriers around Cuan. "We'll see if he's all that very soon. I sure hope he is. It's just us three for now. We have to win."

Like a certain zooming Void Meteor cast forth from the Void by a grinning Mother, Cuan accelerated his flight, twin sonic booms in his wake as he came in hot and fast into the side of the hill nearest to the center of the three monster trucks.

The Black Jaguar impacted the hillside with the force of a Rod of God, instantly causing fear and consternation among the twelve Shard Troops who were now grouped in teams of four, with each team around one of the marooned trucks. A massive shockwave ripped through the site, cascading down the hillside and impacting those on the ruined interstate with significant force. Dust and debris obscured the entire area. Silence pregnant with the promise of Death to Come loomed large as the dust and debris billowed like an advancing dust storm.

"What the fuck was that!" one of the troops cried out over his commlink. Back in the City of Glass, the Council of Glass, with the addition of a certain Solarr and Wyrmhole, focused intensely on the scene, which now played from twelve distinct vantage points on the big screens in the cathedral.

"Focus, and continue the mission," General Armitrage ordered as he took his place at the crystal table. Sister Evaline, Brothers Greg and Brother Bradley, and a small host of other very important persons crowded around the table, and their newly improvised War Room. "Shard-2? Go sub, Teams 1, 2, and 3. Team 1 continue on the retrieval. Teams 2 and 3—"

A sudden black blur loomed large on Screen 9, and Shard Troop Chuck Roberts screamed in agony as his nigh invincible armor yielded to the Black Jaguar's furious claws. A split-second later, Screen 9 showed an impotent view of the Albuquerque sky obscured by dust and dirt.

Over the next three seconds, the sound of panicked automatic gunfire, shattering crystal, and guttural screams filled the air. Team 3 was down. Then, after a momentary pause of but a single second, there was approximately four seconds of more blurry darkness and the screams of the dying, and Team 2 was down.

"What the hell..." Brother Bradley breathed. Even as he gazed over at Brother Greg, Team 1's commlinks abruptly failed simultaneously. A sidelong view from one of Team 2's commlink cameras relayed the most unusual sight of all four members of Team 1 being pulled off their feet, forcefully levitated a few dozen meters above ground, then drawn together and crushed to a mangled combination of shattered crystal and human flesh.

"Call the birds off!" Brother Greg shouted at Warlord Armitrage, whose eyes were still affixed to the screens.

"Send Solarr and Wyrmhole back!" Brother Bradley shouted desperately.

Warlord Armitrage, his eyes never leaving the screen, said loudly, "Scrub, Air Team. That's a scrub. Return to base."

Yet, he failed to issue orders to his two super-powered Shard Troops, Solarr and Wyrmhole. And Brother Bradley liked this not at all.

"Send them back, Warlord Armitrage!" Brother Bradley commanded. "Send them now! We must have that ship!"

"I give the orders of war, Brother Bradley," the warlord calmly reminded him. "We will not risk two of our most powerful assets on a doomed mission."

Silence filled the cathedral. Then, strangely, one of the still functional commlink cams went into motion, as Cuan lifted it from the corpse of his last victim and held it before his face.

"People of the City of Glass," Cuan growled, "I am Cuanmiztli, the Black Jaguar. I represent the Dreamland Alliance. I am begging you, with tears in my eyes, to join us in order to save EarthZero from the impending doom of the Vanth'Vash'Var. Please help us save this world! Join us..."

There was a sudden crunching sound, and the feed from the camera went blank.

Nick landed beside Cuan. "Let's check the trucks."

They did, as Ami maintained guard high above them. Unfortunately, the first and second vehicles that they checked yielded nothing but horror and blackened bodies in both the cabs and in, on, and under the trucks themselves. The Fae troop had been blackened and burned to ashes by the initial solar assault, as had been five of six of the hidden Praetorians.

However, as Nick and Cuan closed in on the third and final truck, sudden motion from the bottom of the vehicle, where the cab had sunk into the still boiling morass, caught their attention. Struggling against the incredible mass of the truck, a black garbed figure crawled out from beneath one of the truck's massive front tires.

"Shayla!" Nick exclaimed, willing a human-sized force field to entirely cover the lone surviving Praetorian and float her over to where he and Cuan stood.

"Sorry, Boss..." Shayla sputtered, even as her body went limp as she surrendered consciousness.

Gently, Nick settled her down to the ground, as Cuan leapt over to the ruined cab of the truck and casually removed its heavily armored door with a flick of his claws. The horrific stench of burnt fur poured forth from the ruined interior, curling their nose hairs.

Smiling, Cuan said over his shoulder, "Two more, Nick. Alive, if only barely. We got two more."

Nodding grimly, Nick raised a hand to beckon Ami down to them. After that, he motioned for Cuan to move aside, and he carefully removed with his force field the now hairless M'Tumba and his Fae friend from the cab and placed them atop the vessel in the back of the truck.

"Everyone up on the vessel," he said as he hovered over to rest on the vehicle's tarpaulin cover. "Ami? We're ready," he informed her, willing force fields to encompass everyone along with the vessel itself.

"Here we go..." Ami said, conjuring a most curious infinity sign-shaped singularity effect, which enveloped the team, the wounded, and the vessel in its eerie grasp.

In the War Room in Dreamland, they appeared slightly before they had actually departed, and Maynard, Cully, and the Duchess, as well as everyone sharing their link, finally took the chance to breathe.

"It worked," Maynard said under his breath. "Thank the Mother, it worked."

CHAPTER 31

As the receiving clerk at the Elberton Granite Finishing Company nimbly dipped the last piece of his crumbling biscuit into the fragrant, sticky honey on his breakfast plate, he heard the bright tinkling of the tiny brass bell atop the company's front door.

"One minute," he called out, awkwardly swallowing his last bite. "Just finishin' my breakfast. Gimme a sec," he added quickly, shoving his plate under a stray business file, then rising quickly from his desk chair.

"Biscuits and honey," he admitted, shuffling out of his office, carefully licking his fingertips one by one. "Best darn honey in Elbert County, too."

Then, as he walked over to the standing, detached receiving counter, he raised his gaze and slowly took in the sight of the unusual, well-dressed stranger standing on the other side of the counter. The tall man sported a neat, black, three-piece suit. He held a rather oversized briefcase in his left hand.

The clerk craned his neck, gazing up at the tall man. "Well, good mornin' to you, sir. You must be as tall as that Kareem fella. Wow. Well," he temporized, slightly embarrassed by the stranger's nonplused reaction, "what can we do you for?"

"Soon, you will learn," the tall man informed him, "what my master has in store for this world."

With a smooth, efficient motion, he lifted the briefcase up and placed it atop the counter. His hands darting quickly, he popped the locks on the briefcase, reached down into its voluminous confines, and gingerly lifted a wooden box from it. This he placed atop the counter next to the case. Deftly, he whirled it around to face the clerk, who appeared to be hypnotized by the performance. Then, with a barely audible, metallic clicking sound, he opened the wooden box.

A warm, silver-and-gold light shone forth upon the mystified clerk's face.

"My name is Christian. R. C. Christian," the tall man informed him. "I have a task for you."

CHAPTER 32

Not-so-distant thunder boomed ominously from the approaching supercell thunderstorm. It was yet another tornadic storm produced by the super-outbreak front that had seemingly been stalking them all day long, though they had traversed many disparate monolithic sites distributed among many states. The thigh-high wild grass in the hilly pastureland around this new site began to stir and whip as the gathering wind blatantly lied that its caresses would remain gentle.

"C'mon, Tim," Leta grimly urged him as the group walked up the grassy hillside, turning to gaze back at the approaching tornadic supercell. "There's an EF-5 in this one, too, or so Riki keeps clicking excitedly in my ear. ETA 15 minutes."

"Yeah, yeah, yeah," Tim brushed her off. "Like a stupid little tornado is gonna stop us now. And it helps if I actually get to concentrate during the walk up. So shhhh!"

"Little? *Little* tornado?" Leta nervously mocked him. "An EF-5 is one of the big ones, Tim. Big enough to destroy an entire city."

"Like any of us care, Leta," Tim said tersely. "Not that any of you need it, but even one of my minor earth shields can protect us from it. No sweat."

"Or mess up our monolithic site before we get to it," Ku'tu cajoled, flitting close to Tim's left ear. "So hurry up, Tim! My people must be free!"

"Dang, okay!" Tim complained, even as he realized that both of them were right. With more accuracy than he really wished, he recalled Old World media coverage of the really big, really nasty tornadoes. And the absolute destruction they could wreak.

Crackling with restrained fury, Tim's external form rapidly shifted, and jagged black stalagmites erupted from his shoulders, back, arms, and legs. Tiny veins of red hot lava pulsated and crawled over the surface of his now blackened, stony flesh. Molten fire flashed around his gimlet eyes. He stared hard at the massive slabs of granite towering above the flat clearing nestled below the hill.

"The fucking Guidestones? Are you shitting me?" he guffawed. "Would Lucifer be so fucking obvious?"

"Shut up, Tim!" Leta barked. Riki's endless chittering was really starting to crawl under her skin. Especially as he was counting down the ETA by the second. "You know we have to check out every monolithic group, even the new ones."

"And we're following the map, anyway, Tim," Ku'tu added, carelessly perching atop one of his shoulder spines, the lava tickling her gently. "Don't complain that we might have found Fresswelle so soon. Be happy!" she said lightly, almost daring to inject some hope into what seemed to her to be an endless quest filled with disappointment and despair.

"Okay, okay," Tim agreed, shifting his focus to yet another earthen scan of yet another group of stones. "I just think this particular monolithic site might be a bit too new to count. But, what the hell. I'll do my job. Won't take long. We'll beat the storm."

"Tim!" Ku'tu yelled in his ear. "Stop worrying about the tornado! We won't even need your filthy dirt shields, either. I'll EAT it if I have to!"

Ku'tu flitted off, rapidly flying around the towering granite stones. The group followed along at a canter, drawing to a stop immediately before the site. There, Tim began another series of scans, even as the approaching supercell roared and snarled at them, ignorant yet not at all impotent.

At Tim's left flank, Mercy stood silent, emotionless, the ancient Fae map unfurled in her hands. Her pointy white eyebrows were curled up in consternation.

"Those ancient fools," she mumbled to herself. "They've mislabeled this one. They've got it named as 'Eye of the Dragon' when, plainly, it's just a bunch of hick-ass pastureland. With some obviously fake new granite stones stacked up atop it, with some of the most lame-ass New Age buffoonery I've ever seen. It's like a Stonehenge Goofy Golf course..."

Leta snickered. "And to think: You just had to beat Don'El D'Zaarz to within an inch of his decrepit life to get him to part with that musty old thing!"

Pausing in midair, Ku'tu's bright eyes flickered. "Wait, Mercy," she said, flitting to perch on her left shoulder. "Did you say 'Eye of the Dragon'?"

Distracted, turning the map over and over as if that would help her sort it out, Mercy muttered a noncommittal grunt of agreement.

Ku'tu froze. "Oh, man. That's what... that's what Zon used to call his communion with the Dragon. He told me he was able to use, and I quote, 'The Eye of the Dragon.'"

Time seemed to stop stock-still. Everyone in the group now was focusing on Ku'tu.

Leta spoke first. "Why didn't you tell us that from the start, Ku'tu?"

"I *did*!" Ku'tu protested, her tiny arms twisted in supplication. "Don't you remember? And Mercy's been hogging the map this whole time, so we couldn't just read it ourselves..."

"You *can't* read this," Mercy whickered. "It's extremely ancient Terran Fae. Not Aal Fae. You probably would have misread it as 'The Butt of the Bullfrog' or something stupid like that. It's like you Fae of Aal are our dyslexic cousins."

"Yeah, Ku'tu, but, there's so many Dragon-this, and Dragon-that, that it..." Tim said, his gaze suddenly drawn to the open ground between the stones. "Wait, wait, wait. I've got a hit," he said, pointing his auguring fingertips at the open ground. "It's there!" he yelled loudly, lurching his stony feet over to stand before the granite stone, its edges unkempt and overgrown with grass and weeds. "There! Down in the ground. There!"

"Mine!" Ku'tu growled fiercely, speeding to interpose herself between Tim and the unkempt granite marker stone. She gave Tim a fierce, if tiny, growl. Wisely, he took a step back, even though he knew precisely how powerful his Rock Tank form truly was. An EF-5 tornado? He'd take his chances. Phlogiston, however, especially when vomited forth from a Most Ancient Fae Queen of Dragons, might actually kill him.

Scowling, Mercy tossed the ancient Fae map up into her right sleeve, then joined Leta at Tim's side. "Okay, girl. All yours. No one will contest your rights. Right, peeps?"

This time, even Tim got the subtle Fae nod of agreement right.

"Ha! You're wiser than you look, Mercy," Ku'tu blatantly taunted her.

An ephemeral flash of sadness flashed across Mercy's face. "You know who you're gonna find in there, right?"

"Fuck you, Mercy," Ku'tu shot back testily. "It's going to be the Watcher, in Zon's form. We already know that. He's not Zon, though. Zon's dead. Aal is dead. But the remaining Fae of Aal are still in Fresswelle. And we're going to free them just as soon as I dig that fucking time capsule up and crack it open. Stand back, friends," she said heavily, working her mind into the first step of her transformation into her mighty dragon form, "I'm about to get very up close and personal with this thing..."

"Wait, Ku'tu," Void intoned, materializing directly above the granite marker.

"Holy shit!" Tim yelled, instantly conjuring a protective earthen shield around Leta and Mercy.

"Dammit, Tim!" Mercy shouted, phasing through the shield to stand between Ku'tu and Void. "I called out for Void just a few moments ago. Well, called out silently. He's here for backup, in case this whole thing goes south. As a former bearer of Fresswelle, it's a good call."

"Mine, Void!" Ku'tu warned the Godslayer, defiantly flitting up to his nose. "*Mine...*"

"Tim!" Leta shouted, pounding at the interior of the shield. "If I miss this, I will shoot fire up your muddy ass!"

"Ah, okay," Tim said, instantly lowering the shield.

Void gave Ku'tu a deep bow. "Of course it's yours, my dearest Queen of Genocide. I'm here simply for backup. In case the Watcher has other ideas and doesn't want to give Fresswelle up. I'm here to help you."

Sneering, Ku'tu said, most darkly, "I accept what you swear, Void. But, if you fuck with me, right now, at the most critical moment of my life, I will sell my soul dearly as I fight you to the death. And, at long last, rejoin the Song of the Sidhe."

Ku'tu had just admitted, for the first time ever, that someone else could defeat her. And now, at this time in her life experience?

When everything was most critical? To admit blatantly that Void would slay her? Slay her, even in her invincible dragon form; the form that had rofl-stomped two of the great pyramids and an equally insane animated Sphinx Monster? Even Mercy was shocked.

"I know you would, Ku'tu," Void agreed formally, respectfully inclining his head. Then, quickly, he added as he rose into the air, "Let's give her some room, shall we?"

Taking the cue, the group, sans Ku'tu, rose slowly into the air, spreading out wide around Ku'tu's slowly transforming form. Deliberately, she took her time with the transformation, careful beyond measure not to disturb the now realized holy ground, which everyone now knew was no longer some mere hick-fake-ass Stonehenge Goofy Golf course. Hovering above the monoliths, Ku'tu gingerly extended the tips of the claws of her left arm down to the central area. With the dexterity of a neurosurgeon, she slowly, cautiously dabbed the tips of her thumb and index finger claws below the ground, shredding the granite slab embedded in the ground as she gently closed them together.

"Got it!" she grumbled, temporarily drowning out the booming thunder.

Unseen by the others due to her titanic form, something spilled to the ground from her claws. Instantly, Ku'tu shifted form, the massive displacement causing its own localized thunderclap. Like a mad butterfly, she sped down to hover atop a slightly larger than human-sized granite sarcophagus, which now lay slightly askew atop the excavated pile of earth and granite. The others followed her down, deciding to land nearby, even as Ku'tu manically flew up and down the length of the sarcophagus.

"Open it!" she implored them. "Somebody open it! I have to see it! I have to see it *now*!"

"I've got it," Tim said, lowering his hands, pointing his fingertips at the granite flesh eater. "It was supposed to be a time capsule," he said as he reached forward with his soul, making contact with the sarcophagus. "But I think that's a loaded term, considering things. So, let's just ask the granite to time capsule itself, and only itself, and see what happens..."

With that, Tim willed the granite to lose coherence, shifting itself into teeny tiny particles resembling a fine dust. And, verily, the will of the Elemental Lord of Earth was realized, revealing the contents of the alleged time capsule.

True enough. The physical form of the Watcher was now that of Zon T'Danu. He lay in repose, as if sleeping, his unique Fae form slightly out of line with the horizontal, just as had been the sarcophagus prior to its transmutation. Clutched in his lifeless hands, folded above his waist, was the unmistakable hilt and basket of Fresswelle, the Fractal Blade.

Around them, the thunder boomed, and the wind began to pick up in hateful velocity as the supercell and its massive EF-5 loomed inevitably nearer.

"Zon..." Ku'tu said softly, her slanted eyes growing glossy.

"It's not him, Ku'tu," Leta reminded her. Still, her instinct was to initiate her own defensive protocols and ease into a combat stance, if only because Tim and Mercy were now doing the same.

Slowly, Ku'tu began a hesitant descent, coming to a stop just above the Watcher's chest. He was dressed in a stupid human suit, she noted. *The blasphemy!* Slowly, she reached down to touch him.

"Don't do that," Mercy growled, Shunya flickering to abstract life in her hands. "He's *not* dead, Ku'tu..."

Immediately, in total resonance, Fresswelle's full length bloomed from its hilt, even as the Watcher's eyes shot open.

"Zon!" Ku'tu cried out, fluttering up and away a few feet.

"Ku..." the Watcher stammered, abruptly clambering to its feet, unsteady. Dangerously, yet adroitly, it leaned down into Fresswelle, whose point improbably pierced down only a few inches into the ruined soil, supporting its weight. "Ku'tu..." it finished, its voice resonant and hoarse. And in the ancient Sidhe of Aal.

All present exchanged quick glances, first to the Watcher, wearing Zon T'Danu's physical form, then to each other. Ku'tu was openly weeping. No one dared speak. Well, almost no one.

"So, Watcher," Mercy barked. "Out with it! You wear the sacred form of the Overlord of the Fae of Aal! Tell us why you defile us with this foul necromancy! Tell us why you bear the twin to my blade, imposter!"

His almond-slanted sepia eyes narrowed in shock and disbelief as he slowly tracked from Ku'tu to Mercy, then locked. "He told me he'd spare my people, the Tuath Dé, the Fae of Aal. But he... he lied. He bound them to Fresswelle," he said, turning the blade slowly before his eyes. "The Tuath Dé who survived the initial attack. 42 War Dragons and their Gentry members and retinues. A few dozen wyvern riders and Shadowcorns. A few hundred Ban-Sidhe. Thousands of shock troops and spellcasters, along with their mounts and their trains. Then, the rest. Embedded within the Song of the Sidhe. However, that was before the Watcher decided to start feeding on their souls, and I was not there to protect them..."

"Oh, no..." Ku'tu cried softly, hot tears pouring down her tiny cheeks.

"The thing about the Song, however," the figure informed them, still staring into its fractal blade, "is that it not only sings our souls into being, it also beckons them to it for final rest. And rebirth. It sang to me, called me by my First Name, and I came home."

"What you're saying is impossible," Mercy said, noting the subtle shift of the figure's stance, which she matched with one of her own. "We all know the story. Ku'tu told us. Aal was a subset of this instantiation. Upon its dissolution, it ceased to be. Everything in it and of it ceased to be, save for what was embedded in Fresswelle by Lucifer. The Song was no more, either. The Lightbringer folded it into Fresswelle along with the Tuath Dé. Perhaps something of Zon still echoes on in Fresswelle, and it's imprinted itself upon you, Watcher."

"With all due respect, bearer of Shunya," the figure told Mercy, "the Watcher made it too easy. It had assumed my form in order to bear Fresswelle. It was directly bound to the blade, which itself was bound to the Song of the Sidhe. Massive resonance. It was performing a task directly given to it by the Lightbringer. Only, it did not have the power to fulfill the task, having had so much of itself drained away by Nanabozho."

"What?" Mercy exploded. "That's not what—"

The figure smiled faintly. "You *know* it's what happened. *I* know it because, since that time, *I* have learned it from both the Watcher and from Fresswelle. The fact that you trusted a trickster god to tell you truth is both naïve and pathetic."

"He lied to us!" Tim said. "Or, maybe you're lying to us..."

The figure gave Tim a nonplused glance, then continued, "My word is always truth, hybrid. I am the Overlord of that more perfect part of your composite soul that is Fae, Elemental Lord! However, once the Watcher started to feed upon the souls of my people in its insane desire to carry out the will of the Lightbringer, the Song itself compelled me to manifest. It drew me from total nihility, empowered me and realized me, and the rest... well, the rest is that not even a Watcher may contest me. Not I, who am master of this blade. It was child's play to bend and bind its own immense powers into Fresswelle, then assume my own form. It just required supreme effort of will, over time. And such I had, as we have shared this tomb for what must have been..." he paused, Fresswelle flickering in ultraviolet as he read it. "For what was many decades." He turned to regard Ku'tu. "I regret, my Queen, for allowing such a span of time to pass."

"Zon, it can't be you," Ku'tu said softly. "As much as I wish it were you. Mercy's right. It's not possible. Fresswelle doesn't have the power to supersede and circumvent the Lightbringer's machinations. Not of something bound directly by the power of the ZeroTime. Our world was indeed a subset of the world we're now experiencing. Your soul did not travel with the rest of the Tuath Dé. The Song would not have been capable of summoning you from the total nihility you have described. No," she said softly, "you are the rogue Watcher, the one who fell from grace, and you have been driven mad by what has transpired. The chaos has been too much for you. You have assumed the identity of a shadow, an imprint, of a most ancient soul-scream issued forth from the souls of my people which you have doubtless devoured in your insanity. Gods help us all, but there is only one price for you to pay for what you have done..."

Instantly, rampant and titanic, the full dragon form of Ku'tu loomed above them, her wings and head postured to deliver a blast of Phlogiston to the offending Watcher.

Without being prompted, Tim and Leta lifted off like rockets, flying away in opposite directions, their vectors perpendicular to Ku'tu's longitudinal axis. Mercy phased, even as Void just stood there and crossed his arms, a few paces away from what was certainly about to become Ground Zero. And the rogue Watcher, as it had been named? It slowly raised Fresswelle before it, its face grim and determined, as Ku'tu breathed a massive gout of diamond-melting Phlogiston down upon it.

For the span of several heartbeats, the world immediately around the Guidestones glowed white hot, blanching the normal visual spectrum. There, at the center of the blast, a tiny pinprick of electric blue light outshined the cacophonous display of eldritch fury. As the breath came to an end, it became clear that the rogue Watcher, Fresswelle pulsating wildly before it, remained untouched, though it now stood at the center of a hundred meter radius of complete volcanic destruction.

It took Mercy a full, nervous three seconds to determine that Void, too, still stood inviolate. He still had his arms crossed, too, she noted with a smirk.

The rogue Watcher gave Ku'tu a wicked sneer. "My Queen, you have sealed your very fate with your untoward aggression. No one assaults the Overlord of Aal and is spared his righteous fury!"

He screamed loudly, waving Fresswelle before him like an oversized and yet very lethal conductor's wand. Lifting from the ground, he took to the air even as Time itself sheared and shredded around him. Everything within the local frame of time abruptly appeared to no longer be moving. Tim and Leta both hung suspended in the air, seemingly unmoving. Ku'tu froze in the midst of her breathing recoil. The first few raindrops from the supercell froze in midair, even as the volcanic ground below appeared to freeze in place, still glowing white-hot in places.

Without pause, the rogue Watcher flew straight to Ku'tu's massive head, raising Fresswelle for what was certain to be the first of 1,000 strikes.

"Die!" the insane Watcher roared, striking down mightily, only to experience a dead, mild thud as the Fractal Blade impacted something other than Ku'tu. And something other than Shunya, because Mercy had been, for once, a fraction of a nanosecond too late to intercept the strike.

"Not today," Void said laconically, Fresswelle's fatal length safely snared in his right hand. "And certainly not her. You, though?" he asked rhetorically, kneeing the Watcher in the groin.

"Right fucking on!" Mercy sneered, zooming in, taking a cut with Shunya at the now defenseless, reeling Watcher.

"No!" Void sputtered, his left hand intercepting Mercy's cut, fully securing Shunya. "Not yet, Mercy," he said as his physical form began to shine with impossible rainbow colored fire.

"Void?" Mercy asked, shocked. "I'm letting you slide on the 'not yet' part, considering what you said back in Antarctica about him being the god you were there to slay. But this... This is impossible. Even for you."

"Yeah, I know," he said, giving the Watcher another groin shot, this one folding him into uselessness, the impact resounding with the sickening crunch of a shattered pelvis. "I told you I was immune to them, though, didn't I?" With a sudden tug, Void freed Fresswelle from the Watcher's impotent grasp, and the Watcher began what appeared to be a slow-motion fall to the ground. "Here," Void said, passing Fresswelle over to Mercy. "Take it."

"What?" Mercy declared loudly. "No way, Void! You take it. It's yours anyway."

"No it's not," he retorted, releasing his grasp on Shunya. "Never has been. Lucifer just used it to kickstart our syzygy. Elevate our souls. Prime us for what was to come. The Twin Blades have always belonged to a single soul. They're the blades of the so-called Lord of Time. Twin Blades. What better person to wield them than the Master of the Null, which is beneath, between, and beyond mere Time? What better person to wield the Twins than one who is herself a twin of sorts? Here, take it. It's yours. It's been yours this whole time. It's just that, until now, no one's bothered to tell you."

Void waggled Fresswelle at her. He was still holding the Fractal Blade by its pulsating blade. Clearly impossible. Mercy's expression said as much.

That's when she noticed an unusual event occur upon Void's waveform, near to where he held the blade in his hand. For a brief nanosecond, his flesh flickered, revealing an inky black, metallic-looking surface etched with flowing, multicolored, triple-helix DNA runes...

An icy cold chill skittered down the nape of her neck as she recognized it. "I see," she said curtly, taking the extended blade. "Who needs super-artifacts when you've bound the Hatefang to yourself. Is Maweth in there, too?"

Void stared silently at her for a split second, as if he were expecting something. "I thought there'd be some cosmic fireworks or something. You know? Highlander shit?"

"Oh, you mean the blades," Mercy said, stifling a smile. Nerd movies, and silly cat videos; things beloved by the Godslayer and Destroyer of All. "Naw. That only happened because Lucifer had gimmicked the blades. They are, in fact, very happy to be together. They both just let me know, too. Now, as for Maweth? Need some snippy-snippy there, Void? Extract that fiend?"

He shook his head. "Nope. Maweth didn't come along for the ride. Two guesses as to why. I just got the blade, not the possession. It's internalized. Perfect weapon for the Godslayer. Just going to keep it a secret until it's necessary. *Capiche?*"

"Yeah, whatever," Mercy agreed. Somewhat. "I'd have gone with the Fractal Blades, but, then again, I'm a lot smarter than you are."

With a snide wink, she waved her blades around, and Time came back on. The rogue Watcher smacked into the ground below with what should have been a fatal impact for most things. Ku'tu's eyes narrowed as she studied both Void and Mercy flying way too close to her face. Tim and Leta, flying rapidly to rejoin the team, approached with arms pumping. The fact that Mercy now bore both of the Twins was lost on no one. The fact that the Watcher was now on the ground was lost not at all on Ku'tu, either.

"Okay," Mercy began, "Let's—"

"DIE!" Ku'tu suddenly roared, stomping the rogue Watcher's body until nothing but a deep hole remained, its sides smeared with purplish ichor and the molten dross remnant of her Phlogiston tears.

Wisely, the rest of the team gave her a wide berth as she carried out her task with studious vigor. From their vantage, now able to see completely and clearly over the hilly pastureland, they could see the massive EF-5 moving in from the horizon. It was a massive, mile-wide wedge of ugly, roiling darkness. Similar to their own souls.

"Ku'tu?" Mercy finally asked as the sky began to rapidly darken. "We need you, girl. Time to go and free your peeps. Can't do it here."

Nodding, Ku'tu shifted to her Tink form and rejoined them where they hovered. "I'm ready," she told them, forcing a smile. "Let's do this, team. Let's free my people. We have a world to save."

Just as Mercy began to cut a hole into spacetime with her blades, impossibly bright silver light flashed around them.

"Wait..." a somber, sober voice called out to them in the tongue of the Fae of Aal.

They turned to regard the figure floating nearby. It was androgynous in form, its silvery, humanoid outline flickering with alternating, ant-dancing segments of black on white, then white on black.

"I am the Watcher," it told them, slowly showing them the palms of its hands. "Thank you for freeing me from the corruption. I was unable to best it myself. At least, not with the stunted power of this particular hyperthreaded avatar. I go now to bind with my primary thread, which has been here on EarthZero, awaiting my return. Shaping, always shaping. Soon, as certain routines mature, I will reach out to you, and make myself known. Together, then, we will move toward total victory over the approaching enemy. Love, and peace, my fellow sentients."

As eyebrows collectively arched, and scoffs issued forth, the Watcher flicked its hands closed, and simply vanished, leaving no trace of its passage.

"I'm not surprised at all," Mercy said bluntly.

"The hyperthread thing is pretty cool, though," Tim commented. "Maynard's going to love to hear this."

"Maybe if the Watcher can do it," Leta speculated, "then maybe we can, too."

"Whatever. Freeing Aal is primary for us. That avatar stuff can wait. C'mon! Let's go!" Mercy growled as spacetime whirled chaotically around them.

CHAPTER 33

"Brother Bradley, wake up..."

Brother Bradley, still reeling from the three-bottle nightcap he had forced upon himself, stirred fitfully in his elegant four-poster bed. His penthouse, the best suite of apartments on the southern side of Crystal Park, typically was as dark as he could possibly make it. The view was still commanding – even if the city no longer shined its electric lights at night as it once did; much more efficient magicks now did this, though on a much smaller scale – because the omnipresent crystal that had replaced all of the former stone and steel was a spectacular medium for augmenting light. Any light. Even starlight, if the conditions were right, could produce localized rainbows in the dark.

But the uncomfortable light that was nibbling softly into Brother Bradley's closed eyes did not radiate or cast from his crystals. Dimly, slowly, he noted that the lights must have been turned on in his bedchamber, which meant...

Abruptly, Brother Bradley bolted upright from the waist up. "Who is it?" he asked as warm, golden light bathed him from head to toe.

Apate, the Angel of Deceit, folded into being directly before the four-poster bed. "It is I," it informed him, "and I have come to reveal to you a blessing from the Most High..."

The angel produced from its translucent sleeves a single scroll, set with a golden seal. Slowly, it extended a hand toward Brother Bradley, and the scroll floated over to him, settling into a gentle hover before his wide-eyed face.

"Take it, and eat it," the angel bade him. "It will grant you knowledge of a mighty weapon which you will build, enchant, and then use against your foes. It is not technology. It is not magick. It is the higher, hybrid form of both: technomagick. It will require much sacrifice and much investment of the soul energy of the sacrificed to build and enchant it. But, the sacrifices will not be forgotten by the Most High. Indeed, they will be honored when the Final Roll is called. Now do this, and do this quickly. The Hour of Final Judgement looms near at hand."

With that the angel vanished, leaving Brother Bradley to contemplate the scroll which had now fallen into his lap.

"Oh, and by the way," the angel added, startling Brother Bradley mightily as its disembodied head appeared right in front of Brother Bradley's face, "Petrus Romanus gets only one more chance. Not even the pope, despite his personal sacrifices and former valor, may deny the Most High for so long."

Silently, the angel's head vanished, leaving Brother Bradley in a state of awe.

God had finally spoken to him, vindicating everything he had fought so long, and so hard, to achieve. Without a second thought, Brother Bradley set about eating the scroll, noting that it had the slight taste of honey.

CHAPTER 34

Crossing the vast space of Saint Patrick's cathedral, Petrus noted that there were snakes here that needed to be driven from the island of Manhattan, and sadly, there was a dearth of saints in attendance.

This late in the evening, the room was filled with turquoise and violet shades in addition to the lighting illuminating the large table. Unlike the last time, the crowds, fanfare, and video were missing; only four people sat at the table. Plates, glasses, and covered trays filled the table, though it appeared those seated had already eaten.

Brother Bradley rose and smiled at Petrus, indicating a seat at the table. "Welcome, Holiness. We are glad you could join us. Would you care for a bite, or a drink? I apologize for starting without you, but we can have the food heated...?" He gestured to a servant standing near a door, out of earshot.

"No, no, thank you, Brother Bradley," Petrus smiled softly. "I've eaten already. A glass of water would be welcome, though." He glanced around the table as he helped himself to a glass of water from a crystal pitcher. Though Brother Bradley appeared truly glad to see him, Brother Greg was appraising Petrus with a neutral stare, and Sister Evaline—as usual—was openly hostile. Warlord Armitrage was looking at the Pope as if he were something stuck to the bottom of his massive crystal boot.

Brother Bradley filled his glass smoothly from a carafe containing an amber liquid, and looked up. "Petrus, we have a situation that is escalating, and it is crucial that you help us. The heretics in Las Vegas have acquired a ship, which we believe was one of those that formed the Sigil web during the Evolutionary Tribulation. We don't know exactly *what* it can do, but technology like that will most definitely give them the advantage in their campaign against our holy city."

He licked his lips as his eyes traveled to the others at the table. The faces, solemn, tense, and angry, spoke volumes as to why Brother Bradley was doing the talking.

"We need an army. We need an army of *your* creation. The living converted to zombies, or to sheer power, and the dead raised to life. As you did at the Battle of Giza. And we want you to lead it, gathering and converting every person you pick up between here and Las Vegas. If they learn how to use that craft, it may mean the end of the City of Glass. We just don't know what power that thing has, and we are running out of time. We are gathering a large force and heading to Atlanta, to take their technology and the weird energy they are developing there. If we can consolidate the East Coast while you keep the heretics from Las Vegas from advancing, we can crush them. *Divide et impera*," he finished, hoping that his use of Latin would impress Petrus.

Petrus spent a long moment staring at the condensation on his glass. Then, he slowly lifted his gaze to Brother Bradley and the others. "Each soul taken is a soul irrevocably destroyed. Not sent to Heaven, not damned. *Gone, with no chance for redemption.* I cannot in good conscience absorb any more lives, or raise any more of the dead. It is wrong. I may no longer have God's grace, but I cannot destroy any more of those few who have survived the Evolutionary Tribulation. The army of unliving soldiers may be relentless warriors, but they are disposal vessels only."

"And that's *exactly* what we need, dammit!" Warlord Armitrage slammed his fist on the table, rising. "We are at the end of the world, with a capable, murderous force in place, waiting for the chance to strike us, and this city, from the face of the Earth! Why shouldn't we use *every* advantage, every force available to stop them before they do? We're fighting monsters. Lucifer's Children. We need all the possible help we can get. And if you're not helping us, then you're actually helping the enemy."

"And that's treason," Brother Greg added with a malicious sneer aimed at Petrus.

"I am sorry," Petrus replied, slowly shaking his head. "I cannot do what you ask of me."

Sister Evaline immediately shouted, "Brother Bradley, this is horseshit! Our *beloved* Father here is just refusing to help the City, and you've turned lesser citizens into glass for that." She shot a withering glare towards Petrus, and crossed her arms.

Brother Bradley held up his hands, trying to placate everyone. "We have options. I'm sure that Petrus just needs time to consider. Maybe pray and consult with his angel..."

Petrus lifted his gaze quickly, catching the implication.

"That's right," Brother Bradley continued. "The angel has come to us, as well. And it has given us the plans for a different kind of weapon. Apparently, Heaven wants us to have a chance, too – with a heavenly cannon, capable of neutralizing cities."

"Real Old Testament stuff," Warlord Armitrage interrupted. "My technical guys say it will remove all the biological entities in a 35-mile diameter area. Poof! Not sure about splitting hairs, but that's pretty much my definition of 'destroyed', and we don't even have to clean up."

"You might want to consider a war that can be won without bodies and prisoners," Sister Evaline said. "There will be no redemption, if there are none left. Create an army for us, and take

Las Vegas, and you can have all the flock you can convert, minus the heretical leaders, of course."

Petrus rose from the table, aghast. "You would do this?"

Brother Bradley looked at Petrus, with a mixture of dismissal and pity. "They are building a prototype, as we speak. Petrus, think about it. You have three days."

Solemnly, Petrus left the table and made his way for the cathedral's front doors, the dark shadow in his soul mocking him silently.

CHAPTER 35

"We ready?" Maynard asked over the com, his physical voice echoing locally atop the Cholula pyramid. A chorus of confident affirmatives immediately arose both on the channel and in situ. "Okay, then. T-minus two minutes. Mark."

Stilling his mind, Maynard hyperfocused upon the many variables in play, trying to account for them all.

Cholula had been prepped, purified, and sanctified for a full nine days. The hardest part of this otherwise effortless group exercise between and among both human and Fae? Mollifying a certain former Queen-Consort of the Fae of Aal. Yet, reluctantly, even she had been forced to admit that there simply could not be anything other than absolute adherence to ritual and proper process. After all, this was not merely the release and reinstantiation of many thousands of immortals, it was the most risky merging of the Song of the Sidhe of Aal with the Song of the Sidhe of EarthZero.

Well, so would it be, if the denizens of the former Aal were not all dead now, having been soul-drained by a most greedy, and most insane, hyperthread of the rogue Watcher.

Another big if? Could something so audacious even be possible? Such, of course, had never been done. Probably never had even been contemplated, as it was a self-evident impossibility. Until the cosmos had abruptly become the metacosmos, and Reality had finally removed its mask to reveal What Lies Beneath.

The unspoken, unrevealed, most complicated part of the process? Gaming the probability paths. Computing and calculating, and crunching the numbers. Was the impossible going to work?

A veritable consortium of genius had been burning the midnight oil over the past nine days, calculating and computing, taking passive peaks ahead into spacetime, trying every possible trick to cheat Fate and wrest feasible and viable solution paths from the chaotic maelstrom of probabilities confronting them.

There would be consequences. Everyone knew that, and expected them. But what was their scope, their scale? Would the Fae not skip a beat? Would the two songs merge harmonically, or would there be disharmony, cacophony? Would one song cancel another, resulting in massive death and destruction, catastrophe? Would they be doing the Death Horde's work for them by attempting such a desperate union? Or, would it, could it, actually work?

Introspection by Mercy into Fresswelle had hinted that the rogue Watcher's horrific cannibalism of its very own distant First Seed cousins had been a catastrophe of its own. Brief, alien glances into the blade's extradimensional spaces, though incapable of absolute clarity, suggested that thousands probably had been devoured to empower the Watcher during its quest. Many had possibly been consumed to stealthily sheathe the Watcher and Fresswelle in a unique form of spacetime identity, such that it could coexist both with its twin and with, eventually, itself on EarthZero, and not plunge all spacetime into chaos. Or, perhaps it had been the source, or one of the sources, of the inherent chaos in this particular simulation. No one knew. One could only speculate, because even the blades themselves had somehow been purged of some essential records. And no amount of introspection could divine them, even when driven by Mercy's formidable will.

And we'll find out in a mere 66 seconds, Maynard considered, *if this is going to be the greatest rebirth, or stillbirth, of all time.*

Prudence and wisdom, for once in the fore, had compelled a general evacuation of the area surrounding Cholula, with all non-essential personnel retreating to various holding areas many kilometers removed from what could indeed become Ground Zero for a cosmic-level release of exotic, soul-snuffing energies. Energies that might not stop before they consumed all life on EarthZero. Or consuming even EarthZero itself.

Thus, it was with serious, major trepidation and just a wee bit of fear that Maynard, Mercy, Vir'gil, Denny, Penny, Vir'gil, and Ku'tu gathered atop the Temple of Cholula. Team EL, along with Nick and Cuan, formed a seven vertex vanguard just a few steps to the rear of Maynard's group. Behind them, Santa Muerte, the leader of la Raza, stood next to Tonantzin, or Mother Tonzi as she was known to the citizens of Cholula. Both were chanting rapidly under their breath.

On call, holding at the nearest bivouac a few kilometers away, were the Praetorians, and reinforcements from Atlanta and La Raza, as well as from both Cholula and several of the newer cities in the expanding alliance. Of course, many representatives of the Fae also played their roles, mostly in silence, for their roles had been assigned to be agents either of welcome to their new brothers and sisters, or as agents of destruction, should things get out of hand.

The Godslayer was nowhere to be seen.

In any event, it was Ku'tu's duty and responsibility to be the one to welcome her people. She was on point, too, decked out in the finest Aal-style finery that the fine EarthZero Fae crafters could produce. She flitted just slightly forward of and above Maynard's head. The Fractal Blades, suspended a few inches above the newly configured, bare and flat top of the pyramid of Cholula, slowly rotated on their long axes, revolving lazily around some unseen center of spacetime shared between them.

"T-minus 10 seconds, Mercy," Maynard intoned, continuing his verbal countdown from that point onward, second by second.

Her cue received, Mercy detached from their group and strode to stand before the whirling blades. "I got this," she whispered to herself. "I got this..."

"Now!" Maynard shouted with more force than he had intended.

Mercy's hands plunged forward quicker than anyone around her, or viewing remotely via the many stealth drones, could perceive. The blades now in her hands, she thrust them straight up over her head, aiming them into the heart of the cosmos itself. Then, as the feverish chanting from Santa Muerte and Mother Tonzi grew to a sudden crescendo, she forced the blades together, shouting loudly in the Ancient Sidhe tongue of Aal:

"Fresswelle! I command thee: Release the Fae of Aal! Release the Tuath Dé! Release their song!"

Incapable of resisting the decree of its binder, Fresswelle, now conjoined with Shunya, did precisely as commanded. Mercy's enhanced perception of spacetime empowered her to witness the event at its true speed, which to all others appeared to occur instantaneously. She saw the tiny burst of purest electric blue fey light form just above the center mass of the entwined blades, then rapidly issue up the lengths of the blades. There, at the abstract points of the blades, the burst of fey light launched itself high into the sky, its initial fractal seed unfurling and iterating at a speed just beyond Mercy's perception. Suddenly – a ridiculous subjective term at this point – for miles above and around the top of the pyramid, wondrous portals of purest white, numbering in the many thousands, issued forth fantastic constructs of pulsating, whirling origami rainbows, which instantly bloomed, revealing their contents.

The sky above the pyramid – indeed, covering most of the sky above the entire valley itself – filled suddenly with the surviving Fae of Aal: the Tuath Dé.

Newly bloomed on EarthZero were 35 War Dragons and their Gentry members and retinues; 35 wyvern riders and 23 Shadowcorns; 235 Ban-Sidhe; 8,132 elite shock troops and spellcasters, their mounts, and their trains; and 17,711 civilians, supporters, and craftsmen.

And, finally, just beyond casual perception, a fantastically huge, triple-helix strand of DNA manifested directly from the top of the pyramid of Cholula, stabbing high into the sky. Far beyond what eyes could see, for it truly stabbed straight into the heart of the cosmos. The Song of the Sidhe of Aal then fully manifested on EarthZero. It was motion, and light, and silent sound. Stunning, and alien, save to those who had been birthed by it. And by another just like it, that could very well have been its own twin...

Within the span of a single heartbeat, the Song of the Sidhe of EarthZero manifested itself, entwined within and among and between the Song of the Sidhe of Aal. Just the same as did the Fractal Blades that Mercy held in her hands.

Blades that began to writhe and twist in her hands as massive, cosmic resonance between the fractal blades and the twin songs instantiated. Falling in pain to one knee, Mercy bit her tongue and fought silently against the invisible fire burning into her soul. Above them all, the two songs mirrored the two blades.

Roars of mighty dragons began high in the sky, thundering down. Ku'tu used the opportunity to transform into her dragon form, appearing hundreds of meters above Cholula. Rampant, glowing in her own fey auric black light, she bellowed in her native tongue:

"Zon T'Danu is dead! Long live the Queen!"

Equal measures of shock and disbelief slammed through the ranks of the Fae of Aal. Despite themselves, despite what their Queen had now told them, almost all of them were still clinging to the belief, however desperate, that their mighty Overlord, Zon T'Danu, had somehow managed to defeat the Vanth'Vash'Var on his own. To those below on the pyramid, and to those watching remotely, it was an entirely disconcerting sight to witness mighty War Dragons crying massive draconic tears.

Various cries of woe issued forth from the Fae of Aal. No one had yet taken the oath.

Angrily, Ku'tu repeated: "Zon T'Danu is dead! Long live the Queen! Do not force me to say it thrice, for death beyond your understanding awaits any who naysay!"

The force of Ku'tu's words and the implication of an immediate, bizarre death for refusal to speak the oath finally cracked the dam, releasing a veritable flood of oaths from the Fae of Aal.

"Long live the Queen!" they swore, almost as one. "Long live Queen Ku'tu, Overlord of the Tuath Dé! Overlord of Aal!"

Below, Mercy gritted her teeth and strained against what appeared to be a slow-motion, complete merging of the Fractal Blades. The motion of which was still being mirrored above them all, by the twin songs.

Ku'tu, beaming with black auric light, turned her massive head to regard the lone abstainer, the one who did not speak the oath. The Fae in the path of her glare immediately pulled back, because they all knew what was going to happen next. Phlogiston would fly, and War Dragons would battle for supremacy of the Fae of Aal.

"Estengar!" Ku'tu bellowed. "You dare!"

"I dare, witch," Estengar bellowed right back, his massive ebony wings now fully extended as he magickally hovered in place. One of the few of his brood who could not be subjected to control, he had no battle howdah for other lesser spellcasters or warrior Fae to mount. For he had no need of such, as he himself was among the most powerful casters of the Fae. "Zon, I could serve," he sneered. "He had power that I respect. He had the blade. But you? A mere Queen-Consort? A feeble caster of no repute? How could I possibly serve one who is no better than a mere whore? No, tonight you die, and I will become Overlord..."

"I gave you a chance," Ku'tu roared in outrage. And for the Fae to mark her fair words. "Now, you will experience death beyond your understanding..."

Finally! Mercy thought as the blades finally merged. A pale electric blue aura enveloped her from head to toe, and Mercy, now wielding a fantastic two-handed blade, took to the air at incredible speed. Spacetime slowed around her, even though she had not willed it, and, relative to everyone else, she began to blur. It was merely a natural effect of her wielding the now merged Fractal Blades. In the blink of an eye, she was in the sky between Ku'tu and the equally massive War Dragon, Estengar, who appeared to be slowly casting a spell that was, even now, one syllable into it, causing the air before him to burn with eldritch green fire.

"Not today, Estengar!" Mercy yelled, raising her blade for a mighty cut, even though she was still hundreds of meters away from him. Instinct now told her what she could do. And Mercy was always one to trust her instincts.

She cut, visualizing the massive two-hander's blade extending beyond normal spacetime, reaching out across the impossible distance to deliver an equally impossible cut across and through the dragon's entire form. And verily, it did, with total ease. No resistance. Just a smooth cut, one which resulted in a massive, full-body passage of the blade, totally bifurcating the dragon from the tip of his snout to the point at which his spiked tail joined his body.

As Mercy's lips formed a silent "No effing way...", spacetime ceased its bending, and the ghostly afterimage of a skyscraper-sized blade hanging in the sky. And a rather sorely confused Estengar, who rather sloppily slid apart along his bifurcated longitudinal axis.

"Ggg-akk!" Estengar, Ku'tu's mighty challenger, managed to eke as his soul, along with his physical form, was cut.

Holding the blade high above her head, Mercy, watching the merging songs above her and hopefully timing things correctly, suddenly shouted, "All hail the Queen! Hail Overlord Ku'tu!"

And the Fae of Aal did precisely that, just as the two songs finally merged.

The metaphysical cosmic lightshow and new Soul Song drowned out the horrific impact of Estengar's ruined dragon form upon the valley below. The Fae of both worlds heard the Soul Song, and marked it as new. Though it was certainly a composite of both of the old songs, it now had been made new again. And, this time, the Dragon itself sang the song, accompanied by the Mother, and the souls of both worlds, both old and new.

Even the non-Fae felt the song, and joined in as well as they could. It was both a physical and metaphysical melody. It was both subtle and outrageous. Monotonic, yet polyphonic. Twisting, turning, morphing like the sigil itself. It sang to them the promise of a new day. It sang to them the promise of victory to come.

EarthZero itself now evolved, its own Evolutionary Tribulation complete.

In total metacosmic resonance, every pyramidal structure on EarthZero activated, synchronizing with the new metacosmic, primal resonance.

Descending from the sky, the Fae of Aal paid their respects to Ku'tu and her new entourage of strange EarthZero immortals, and the overjoyed Fae of EarthZero, who proudly welcomed their newly bloomed seed-mates with open arms and warm smiles.

PART III
CHAPTER 36

Her people had called her "Woman Covered All Over" because her husband, Jon Sky, had died when his Ford F-350 had been crushed by a drunken driver who had unfortunately been driving an overloaded logging truck. More than 55,000 kg of virgin timber had returned Jon Sky back to the earth, and the token insurance settlement hadn't been enough to buy her any new crystal chandeliers. So, being a Half Sky two-spirit already, it had made perfect sense for Kara Sky to assume her husband's trade, and continue, in his honor, their hunting expedition business.

That had been three years prior to the Sigil. Driven by grim determination and incredible spirit, she had done right by her husband's spirit, and, over the years, she had scratched out a hardscrabble living in a very tight market niche almost entirely dominated by men. White men, with big fancy trucks and bright, new equipment. Hunting the lands of her people, as if they owned it. As if they could own that which could never be owned.

Kara had earned the respect of her Ojibwe community, even of the elders, because she had carried on their traditions, their old ways. She had never once shown weakness, or complained. And she had given the white men their due, because she had been born to hunt the lands which they awkwardly clambered upon, their skills no greater than the youngest children of her people.

No weakness. No fear. Except, tangentially and by means of displacement in a fit of piqued anguish, when she had gathered all of Jon's clothes and had set them all on fire, once his scent had finally effervesced from them totally and completely. *Dammit, Jon! Couldn't you have given us a child? Something to remember you by? Someone to carry our blood on? Now, even your scent is gone...*

After the Sigil, when the dreams had come to the few who had remained on their lands, Kara had resisted the call of the Trickster, even though the few remaining elders had told all of the people that, indeed, it had been Nanabozho himself, the Creator, who had called them to go to the far-off place: Dreamland. She had resisted because she hadn't especially wanted to leave her home and move off to freakin' Las Vegas. *A desert? Really? What good would a hunter do there? Hunt tarantulas?*

And... really... a rabbit? That's some eldritch Bugs Bunny shit right there, son...

Scoffing, Kara had watched the caravan of vehicles off, observing from afar, from her tall forest cover. *Blood or not, people or not, if they were stupid enough to listen to a white rabbit in their fever dreams, and just up and leave their home woods for some stupid patch of the white man's desert, then all the better. And good fucking riddance!*

And that had been her attitude for many days now. Isolation had been... liberating? *Am I finally free at last? Nothing more to bind me? Maybe not even Jon's spirit?*

Kara considered this as she took in the moonlit view of the forested valley below her. Uncaring, because she knew that falling a few hundred feet would not kill her, she stood at the very edge of the rock cliff, silently staring out at the living night before her. Breathing the early Summer night all in. She could almost feel his presence as the wind whispered to her. *One day, Jon, we'll be together again. One day...*

The time since her people's departure had just proven to her that she didn't really need them at all now. Not since the Sigil had made her, by far, the best hunter among her people. Perhaps the best hunter ever, which was no minor statement, for hers was a nation of hunters stretching back into the long distant mists of time. Stacked and compounded upon her own natural gifts, the Sigil had made her as fast as the deer, as strong as the bear, and as stealthy as the lynx. The thorns could no longer touch her skin. Neither cold nor heat gave her pause. She could see as well by the light of the stars as by the light of day, she could track a fish underwater by its scent, and she could hear a black ant crawling on the ground before her...

No wonder I thought I felt Jon's presence, she thought. *A hunter walks nearby...*

"Name yourself," Kara Sky growled softly, her left hand resting on the grip of her Ka-Bar.

The man behind her was apparently of considerable mass to have made the loose rock crunch as it had. And, apparently, he had somehow made it across a 10 meter bare rock outcrop without making so much as an ant's whisper. Until he had suddenly stepped a meter behind her.

"My name is Void. I am truly sorry that you are crying..."

Shocked, Kara turned swiftly in place, her knife appearing as if by magick. Sheer hatred poured from her misty, hazel brown eyes as she gazed upon the bizarre apparition towering before her. He stood taller than Jon had once stood, impossibly more massive. Even though Jon had played college football in the States before his knee injury had forced him out of a potential future of an NFL lineman's millionaire salary. Larger than life. Wild hair; the starlight danced within it, casting an angry aura that was totally discordant to the happy stars. Pointed ears, gently poking out from beneath, almost like the tufted ears of the lynx. Gently slanted jet black eyes, narrowed in genuine sympathy. No scent. Nothing to mark him either as a former human or as an evolved post-Sigil immortal.

More than human, too, if what her lying eyes were screaming at her. For, upon his chest, the sign of the Thunderbird loomed large, and rampant. She knew its forlorn promise to her people, how it had somehow missed them, despite its terrible import. Yet, now, it was here. Chaotic energies strained upon it, a mass of whirling and roiling blacker-than-black fey lights, emblazoned with pure shadow. Kara's own eyes seemed to stare back at her from within its eerie confines. *Impossible. Lies...*

"You don't know shit..." Kara heard herself grate. The hilt of the Ka-Bar complained as she squeezed down, hard, upon it. "I wasn't crying," she lied. "So you can take your sympathy and shove it up your—"

"I'm *not* sympathetic," Void replied, only somewhat lying. "Sympathy is the domain of the weak. Makes two losers out of one. I don't need that. So I don't really care if you're crying or not. That's you, not me. I'm just sorry that *you* are, because you have a really bright soul. Whatever darkened it makes me want to destroy it, just so you can smile again."

The sign of the Thunderbird on Void's chest flared, wings rampant.

"I..." Kara began, totally confused. "I don't really know how to respond to that, Void. No one's ever said anything that kind to me before. Not even J—" she bit the last word back, wondering if she truly had meant to say it.

A faint smile threatened to creep across Void's lips, but he bit most of it back. He truly didn't wish to insult such a beautiful spirit. Especially not one needed so badly, with such an important role to play.

"Kara?" he began. "Yes, I know your name," he quickly added, stopping her in mid-breath. "Not long ago, I promised someone that I would personally help his people. Show them the way to Dreamland. Hook everyone up to save EarthZero from the Vanth'Vash'Var, and their earthbound agents of chaos. Everyone listened. Everyone except for you. So, I can't fulfill my promise to my friend, and fulfill my oath, unless and until you come, too."

Void slowly reached out, offering his hand to Kara.

"Will you join us, Kara? Please, come with me. Take my hand, and I will show you the way."

Kara's head suddenly felt hot, as if she were with a fever. She shot Void a dangerous glare. With but a casual flick of her wrists, she could remove his oversized hand from his stupidly massive forearm. But something was toying with her senses. Confusing and confounding them.

She shook her head once, trying to dispel the insane sensation.

Though he had no scent, Void indeed projected something beyond the normal senses, some overpowering aura of dominance that was virtually breathing down the nape of her neck, and gently massaging her firm ass with thick fingers. Crushing her into him. Compelling her silent submission as he parted her and filled her slowly with something beyond her experience...

"No!" Kara screamed, darting at Void, slashing and feinting with her Ka-Bar, even as she quickdrew her .500 Smith and Wesson Magnum and pumped five shots into his center mass. "Die, motherfucker! Die!"

"Hey! Wait a sec—" Void objected as he batted down her wild slashes with a folded hand, even as the five shots impacted him with the force of five really pissed off, charging elephants. Despite his Godslayer status, Kara's personally enchanted combat knife and enchanted bullets raked and slammed into him with supernatural force. No longer a mere 2600 foot/pounds of muzzle energy, Kara's own enchantments – enforced by her own prayers – had added an order of magnitude and more of power to them. They hit like point-blank 155mm Paladin shells. Right into the center of his torso, defiling his temporary Thunderbird crest, causing it to ripple with black rainbows. And the Ka-Bar... the three of ten strikes that actually landed actually scored his flesh, striking up black sparks upon contact with his internalized Maweth subdermal layer. They actually hurt.

"Die!" Kara screamed again, even as Void took a half-step back, his full mass suddenly apparent, scraping deep gouges into the granite outcrop as she pressed hard into him. She hit like an enraged grizzly protecting her cubs. Elbows flying, massive pistol curled inward even as she replaced it into her chest holster, her other hand, Ka-Bar flying, scoring approximately 30% against Void's unprotected chest. She blurred into him with the grace of a swallow, striking, feinting, feeling that she was somehow gaining upon his defense. But... he wasn't bleeding. He had taken the full force of her shots. And her spirit-enchanted blade. And he had taken only a half-step back. And he wasn't dead. Not even mortally wounded. Not even bleeding. Smiling. He was smiling down at her...

Kara stopped slashing. Towering a foot above her head, Void's melancholy face gazed softly down upon her. Slowly, she grimaced, affixing her tormentor with a wicked glare. She fished her Ka-Bar back into its sheathe. And, all the while, the subtle sensation roiled into her from the being before her. Here, standing near to him, she felt his unique combination of heat and cold. It embraced her like a million caressing hands. It touched, felt, grasped, and gripped every part of her body. For once, for once since his death, she no longer remembered Jon Sky. Now, abruptly, she knew nothing but this new man called Void.

"Kara?" Void said softly, sensing the subtle change in posture of the woman before him. "I acknowledge your fighting skills. You are truly dangerous. Against anyone else, you would have been victorious. No contest. But, as you can see," he said, extending his arms down so she could see, "no damage. Well, sort of," he laughed. "Maybe a few ouchies. Got to give you that, girl! Glad I cheat like a motherfucker. So, want to discuss what I'm here to ask you to do? Want to help me get square with a certain white rabbit? Help me keep my word? It's really all I have, Kara."

"Don't try to bewitch me, spirit," Kara said, defiant, staring hard up at Void. "I don't believe in... you... in love..." Despite herself, despite being a cold-hearted bitch to anyone and everyone who had beaten a path to her door to try to man her up once again after Jon's death, she suddenly felt her façade melt away totally and completely. Years of cold melted like the last snow of the year before the unforgiving heat of the Sun.

With a sudden spring of her legs, Kara was up on him, her lips pressed hard upon his, her lithe legs wrapped around his unyielding core. She thrust her hips hard down upon him, her hands grabbing his wild mane of hair, her hot tongue trying its best to force itself beyond his smooth lips.

For a very brief moment, confined by his eternal love of Mercy and her equally eternal, exquisite capacity for genocidal vengeance, Void somewhat welcomed Kara's advances. It wasn't what he was here for. And Mercy would kill him for entertaining the notion.

But, what the fuck, despite himself, despite being VoidSpawn, and the syzygy to the most amazing woman ever born, he slipped a bit, just one wee bit, and pulled her close into him, slipping her just the most faint suggestion of tongue. With a bit of a groin thrust thrown in, too.

"Oh, Jon..." Kara moaned, grinding herself upon his midsection, pulling his massive neck down into her mouth, planting soft kiss after soft kiss upon his smooth yet inviolate flesh.

"I'm... I'm sorry, Kara," Void finally managed to breath. Forced into using a bit of his strength, which abhorred him, because it was used upon such a beautiful soul, he softly disengaged himself from her, and set her gently upon the granite outcrop. "I'm not Jon. I'm just a guy who's come to ask you to try to help us save our world from some really bad peeps who are trying to erase us. Please listen to me, my beautiful Woman Covered All Over. Sweet Kara. Please come back to the here and now. I'm not Jon. I'm not your husband, Mother love him. I'm just a virgin guy who could never, ever, take his place. It's just your enhanced senses, and my aura, that are fucking with you. Sorry about that, Kara. I can't help what I am."

She took a deep breath, then looked up at him, beyond embarrassed. "I'm sorry. I really am. I don't know what to say..."

"I know," Void comforted her, without even realizing that he had once again pulled her close to him. "Ooops, sorry, Kara," he said, releasing her. "Usually, at this point in the script, or movie, the heroes are fighting one another, or some bad guy, or something. They usually don't end up feeling like they should be fuck-buddies or anything like that."

Kara smiled as she disengaged herself. Reluctantly. *Damn, he feels good...*

"I'm sorry I shot you," she admitted. "And stabbed you," she said, her fingers brushing lightly against what should have been fatal wounds.

"I just rolled my eyes," Void admitted, knowing she couldn't see it.

"Ha!" Kara laughed. "Never could have known."

"I know, right?"

"Are you really a virgin?"

"I just rolled my eyes again," Void laughed. "Of course I am, Kara. My love is someone named Mercyduceus Vendredi. She's of the Fae. But we can't get close, or shit happens, and the world gets fucked. Unrequited love. Tough stuff to deal with."

Kara gave Void a purse-lipped glance. "I actually get that, Void." Then, she stared hard at him, seeking his bizarre, black eyes. Reluctantly, he returned her gaze, careful to tone his soul down to the barest of minima. "Don't hide from me," she implored him, taking his beefy hands into hers. "I'm asking you for a bit of honesty. That's what I need now. Just let me know you're not deliberately fucking with my head, and I just might hear your words. VoidSpawn," she curtly giggled.

Void sighed aloud. He swung his arms gently, Kara's calloused hands in his own soft, smooth hands. "Okay. Fine. I'm just a simple man, like the song. Yes, I'm really a virgin. At least in this new incarnation. And although I am extremely attracted to you, I am stating for the record that I am desperately in love with someone else. I cannot and will not betray her. Even though I guess I just did when I slipped you some tongue. She's going to Lorena Bobbitt my sorry ass. Snippy-snip-snip!"

They both laughed, but cut it short. Void released her hands. He folded his tree-trunk arms upon his chest.

"Nanabozho requested that I help your people, Kara," he began, his voice falling an octave. "You're the last in line, so help me Dio. And you're just being stubborn about the whole thing, because you think that you'll betray Jon if you leave. You won't. Don't you think that Jon wants what's best for you? Don't you think that he'd want nothing more than for you to help your people, and your world, against the evil that's coming to destroy us all?"

Kara slammed a fist into Void's chest. It wasn't a mere love tap, either, though it made no sound at all. It would surely have deformed a stout bank vault door. "Fucker! Don't you dare speak ill of Jon! How dare you! You never even knew him. I... I never even knew him..."

With that, the dam finally burst, and Kara bawled like a baby. Hot tears stung her eyes, cascading down her fine cheeks. Despite herself, despite her years of lone strength and defiance of the Man's World, she crumpled into Void's warm, kind embrace.

And despite being a cold-ass Godslayer who had lived a million lives, who had totally erased a thousand universes with naught but a dead smile to mark the passage of their countless souls, Void shed a tear himself.

Those other lives meant nothing now, having been consigned perforce to the shadow of distant memory, such that he might maintain some semblance of sanity. Yet the contrast of those seemingly infinite dark experiences, those many Mother-enforced lives, slammed hard into the current reality of a very damn good woman, held warmly in his arms, who was finally admitting to herself that her former love, and lover, might not really have meant what she had though that it had meant to her.

The Ghost of Love remains, forever in my heart... Void thought, an alien imprint of a memory crossing his mind...

Slowly, Void caressed Kara's dark mane of hair. "I'm sorry, Kara. I truly am. You're ready now, I think," he said, gently pushing her away.

"Ready?" Kara asked, suddenly curious, and no longer embarrassed. She had known it for years. Only now had she allowed herself to admit it. And it had taken being overwhelmed by the wild soul towering before her, here, on this most beautiful early Summer evening. "Ready for what, Void?"

"Well," Void admitted, "at this point, I'm starting to feel like I'm some sort of overpowered, and quite underpaid, FTD delivery man..." he said, quickly whirling his hands over one another.

Abruptly, feeder vines, lightly flowered with premature yellow buds, cascaded over his hands, spilling to the granite outcrop underfoot. As Kara gazed with wonder upon the scene, Vir'gil Plik, the Entheogenic Lord, manifested before her. Gently, with the grace of a courtier of old, he bowed before her.

"Milady Kara Sky," Vir'gil croaked. "I am Vir'gil Plik, the Entheogenic Lord. And I have a gift to you from the Mother herself..." he said, producing a tiny, psychedelic pinecone in his left hand.

"What the fuck?" Kara scoffed. "The Jolly Green Midget is offering me a Candy Corn? Tell the Mother, whoever the fuck that is, that I'm doing a keto cycle, and I'll have to politely refuse. Stupid bitch," she snickered, finally smiling.

Silence for a nanosecond, because the scene was supposed to be entirely sacred. The Mother, and Sacred Drugs, and Shit Like That.

Only Void and Virge weren't those dudes.

So, suddenly, despite the gravity of the situation, both of the insanely powerful immortals exchanged glances, hand at their mouths, then both erupted into total, unfiltered laughter. Which, of course, Kara, being the good sport that she truly was, had to join them in.

And, of course, awkwardly, Maynard's laughter was heard, as the circuit he had been sharing with both Void, and with Vir'gil, revealed itself.

"Sorry, guys," Maynard laughed, startling Kara for a split-second. "I'll be signing off. And erasing this most embarrassing episode of 'Void and Vir'gil's Wild-Ass Kingdom' from Dreamland's memory banks. Before Mercy sees it and ends both your sorry asses..." he finished, literally guffawing. "Sorry,

Kara," he instantly apologized. "I'm Maynard. We always monitor everyone. No perv, or anything. Just a safety precaution. Please ignore Void, and his clumsy fumbling because Mercy never gives him any trim, and please take Vir'gil at his word. He actually speaks directly for the Mother. Void... Void just fumbles through life, flailing and wailing. Yes, he's still a virgin. And he loves cat videos..."

"Uhh, okay, Maynard," Kara laughed, accentuating Maynard's name. Void and Vir'gil were both rolling about on the outcrop, laughing breathlessly like two asthmatics. "I'll just go ahead and take Jolly Green Midget's Candy Corn, and do the sit-in with the Mother... if he'd just get sober long enough for me to do so..."

Kara kicked Void in the leg with an audible smack. "Hey, virgin! Get your friend to hand over the goods. Let's get this shit done. I'm ready."

That sobered them up. Somewhat.

"Sorry about that, Kara," Void managed to eke, hauling himself up to his elbows. "Virge? Pass her the goods. I'm out of here. Good to meet you, Kara," Void smiled. "Maybe when you get to Dreamland you could look me and Mercy up? We'd love to welcome you properly, if you're so inclined."

"Are you making some kind of warped threesome pass at me?" Kara erupted, even as Vir'gil passed her the Rainbow Candy Corn of Doom, which she gladly accepted.

"Huh?" Void temporized, his clumsy polyamorous attempt gutted.

"I'm joking, Void," Kara smiled down at him, popping Vir'gil's snack into her mouth. "And I know that this isn't recreational drug use. Don't have time for that. This is a spirit journey. And I haven't done a spirit journey in years. This will be fun. Thanks, Planty Dude," she said, smiling at Vir'gil. "I'm not into threesomes, of course, but I'll take you up on some fun and games if and when

I decide to join... join you... in Dreamland..." she breathed softly, falling to her knees.

"You can fuck off now, Void," Vir'gil taunted him.

"I just rolled my eyes again, Virge," Void laughed, fading back into Shadow, and the Void.

Vir'gil adjusted himself to stand before Kara, who slowly swayed in place, to and fro.

"Now, my dearest one, let's see what the Mother has in store for you..."

CHAPTER 37

S lumbering on beds of golden radiance, Mhyrranda and her cabal of dream witches entered into the Dream Realm en masse, their psyches tethered and anchored to the world of the awakened by delicate, slowly pulsating silver threads.

Bending and shaping the warp and woof of the Dream Realm to her formidable will, the Duchess of Dreamland caused a fantastic seraglio to arise around her and her dream witches, where now they reclined in repose, attended to by silent, muscular eunuchs. Sandalwood incense wafted lazily upon a hidden breeze, even as the calls of peacocks sounded from outside the stone walls of the seraglio. Sweet monotonic music breathed from several harpists, who gathered around a corner of the square pool which firmly established the center of the room.

"Now, my sisters," the Dreamwyrd began as a eunuch poured a golden wine into a crystal goblet and passed it to her waiting hand, "we may discuss freely the necessary strategy for our intended Global Unity project."

Raising a toast to her twelve companions, who gracefully returned the gesture, Mhyrranda nodded once, curtly.

Taking the cue, Wren Daysong began, "Milady, the strategy is clear: We must convert our enemies to our allies, and we must do so while minimizing casualties."

"Wren is correct," Ash Raven agreed. "Limited assets. We can't afford to reduce. Some, of course, must be destroyed. But we must be quite judicious in our application of destruction."

"Meaning," Renu Kali added, "we must wield the iron fist in the velvet glove. Our message of hope and salvation must be strong enough to overcome the nihility and chaos abounding in the world."

Mhyrranda nodded, considering their words. Then, "Agreed. We will craft the specifics and present them at the next council meeting. Next, what of the newly instantiated pyramidal resonance on EarthZero? Has anyone been able to synchronize? Get a glance into the formerly dark areas?"

A consensus of negatives blended with the sweet incense, causing the music of the harpists to temporarily become discordant.

"Ouch," Mhyrranda complained, stifling a laugh. "Okay, because it's a necessary step for us to take, shall we merge and take a peek together?"

Twelve nodded affirmatively. Then, without pause, the thirteen psyches became as one, embroiled in a constantly shifting mass of silvery ethereal threads, and the seraglio scene rapidly morphed into a view of EarthZero from a high equatorial orbit. Before and beneath them, EarthZero was lit radiantly by Hekatek ley lines that bound and connected thousands of nodes of pyramidal structures, as well as a host of other similarly resonant constructs and entities which shared certain golden and fractal attributes.

The effect of the sight upon the cabal of dream witches was intoxicating, exhilarating. While singly and in smaller groups all had indeed attempted the same feat recently, this was the first time that, collectively, they had attempted it at the height of their combined powers. Now, everything was clear. Revealed for what it truly was. North, Central, and South America literally glowed with resonant structures, as if some titanic swarm of fireflies had been loosed upon the world. Even the formerly dark spots now were fully defined and not some indeterminate, nebulous realms, shifting and roiling. Though yet still opaque to direct scrying, unfortunately, even to their combined powers.

It was clear now that the Council of Glass had enshrouded and warded a significant portion of the East Coast of the United States, and this zone of shrouding stretched across the Atlantic Ocean to the United Kingdom, then to the continent itself. Most of the former European Union indeed was shrouded, with certain smaller bands of warding extending up to Sweden, and then down into the Baltics. Certainly a testament to the extent of the reach of the Council of Glass and their allies. And certainly an example of their tremendous power.

"So," Mhyrranda said softly, causing the group's vantage point to swiftly pivot over the globe, "the rumors are true. The council is working along the lines of the former EU."

"It's an artifact of their new pseudo-Christianity, Duchess," Renu observed. "Note that they've excluded Turkey, and have not penetrated into the Stans. Their zealous sectarian rigidity limits them. They cannot wield the power of the religious mandate that Petrus Romanus formerly commanded. Fortunately."

Mhyrranda nodded, exchanging some glances with other members of her cabal. Renu Kali, an Oxford-trained DPhil religious scholar in the Old World, was quite the asset.

Scanning more, they noted that Africa, despite its tremendous size, had but few concentrations of resonant structures, mostly in the northern part of the continent in the Sudan and in Egypt. From what they could discern through the opaque shrouding, which lost strength as it progressed to the east, a notable belt of resonant structures spanned north of the Mediterranean through Asia Minor, then across India and into southwestern Asia. Both the

Arctic and the Antarctic had their own smaller sets of structures, as well as Micronesia and Polynesia. Yet, shockingly, in China, in what was expected to be one of the more robust sets of resonant pyramidal structures, there was an absence of resonance. A total absence of resonance. As if the structures themselves were still offline. Or, had somehow, improbably, been extirpated.

As one, the cabal silently willed a closer view of the Qin Chuan Plains in Shaanxi Province where the main field existed. Their field of view narrowing to a more precise grid of 100 kilometers by 100 kilometers, they individually zoomed up and down, back and forth, to visit each of the structures, flitting like a flock of mad ethereal hummingbirds. Sharing and collating the images among their collective, the shocking impact of the horror and destruction loomed large in their minds.

Every structure was in ruins. Improbably so, as some of them were earthworks of massive proportions, created and shaped by skilled craftsmen and engineers. Still, despite their robust nature, all of them had been crushed and compacted to virtually ground level, as if a mighty closed fist had struck down from the heavens themselves and had smashed them with impunity. Godlike impunity, delivered by a force of power equivalent or superior to the best of their own best.

Gasping, sighing, fretting, the collective gazed more carefully, discovering the blackened, carbonized ashes of thousands of humanoids scattered indiscriminately among the carnage. Humanoids, and more, for there were also sinuous, snakelike hybrid forms among the victims. And several far larger draconic forms, specifically of the east Asian variety. At least one per pyramid. Defending to the last their sacred and holy places. Yet, despite what must have been their own awesome power, trounced and smashed like the rest.

"Ashes," Mhyrranda breathed aloud. "Nothing but ruin and ashes." She paused a moment, trying to imagine what cruel force could have achieved such total annihilation of what must have been an army comparable in size and power to what the Dreamland Alliance could wield. However, due to her growing horror at her realization that perhaps a new, terrible foe had been placed upon their cosmic chessboard – perhaps even an attack by the Death Horde itself – she was temporarily nonplused.

"Milady?" Ash Raven asked, jarring Mhyrranda.

"Yes, Ash?"

"While it is normally anathema for us," Ash replied, "you know I have the power to see the dreams of the dead. Perhaps, this once, we may suspend our rules, and profit from abomination."

"No!" Mhyrranda immediately snapped. "No way, Ash. I know you mean well, and I realize it might be the only way to get to the bottom of this, but there's too much at risk. There's a chance that this might have been the work of the Death Horde. That's too dangerous to wade into at this time, without the council's input, and power, to back us up."

"Agreed," Ash replied. "Yet, I suspect that this is not the work of the Death Horde. While it's horrible, it's not even continental in scale. It's small fries, in other words. From what we've gathered over the past year, the Vanth'Vash'Var tend to work either totally small-scale, in single stealth units, or in planetary ones. They don't have a middle ground. So I think it might be worth it to ask one of the dead what happened."

A visceral disgust threatened her with immediate retching, but Mhyrranda's common sense urged her to relax their rules just once, and only for this most pressing concern.

"Okay, Ash," she agreed. "Do it. Do it on a dragon. They're probably the most resistant of the lot, and might have been able to grasp more of what transpired than the rest. We will form a sphere of protection around you. Mother forgive us for this blasphemy."

"Yes, Milady," Ash confirmed as the group of dream witches suddenly were there, on the ground, forming a circle around the fallen form of one of the celestial dragons.

Ash Raven's incorporeal form broke from the circle, hovering to a position a few feet above the center line of the carbonized carcass of the tractor trailer-sized dragon. Bringing her hands to a steeple before her face, Ash centered her psyche, then reached gently out to the spirit of the dragon. With no outward display of power, she established contact with the imprint of the dragon's spirit. To her surprise, it was of relatively recent origin. As in mere hours. Not days, or weeks, or even months as she and her companions had assumed.

"Away!" boomed a spirit voice, sibilant and sharp. A silvery shimmer appeared around the perimeter of the creature's physical body, yet no complete apparition appeared. "No! I am dead! Dead!" Speaking from its very soul, there was no need for translation. "I have become unbound! Unbound!"

"We would hear your last experience, fallen one," Ash bade it, her fingers buckling slightly under the pressure of forcing her will upon that of the creature, whose own will was formidable indeed. "Tell us what happened. What could have done this to such a mighty army? To such a mighty dragon?"

After a momentary pause, the dragon's spirit voice informed them: "I fail the Celestial Dragon King, Sìhǎi Lóngwáng. I fail my people, the Hànrén. The enemy is too strong. As strong as Heaven itself. They ride in from the sky, on horses with hooves of fire, their golden scimitars gleaming like the Sun itself. What they strike turns to ash, consumed by the holy fire of their faith. Their armor, beneath their flowing white robes, renders them immune to our weapons. Golden light protects them like shields of energy.

We cannot harm them at all, yet they lay waste to us at will. The massacre progresses to its crescendo. A bearded man with olive skin, dressed in shining white robes, appears in the sky, high above the pyramid. He cries out in a world-shaking voice, stilling the combat on the field with the power of his words. Though we cannot fully understand them, we know that he judges us as infidels, worthy of destruction, for what our Old World government had carried out on his people. He speaks his name, which is Abdulla Muhammad al-Mahdi, then he swears an oath before his prophet and his god. A mighty golden scimitar appears in his outstretched hands, shining with the light of a thousand suns, and he strikes down in anger upon the pyramid from impossibly on high. It seems as if the Sun itself bears down upon the ground, crushing and consuming everything before it. Impossibly so, for no blade can do such a thing. It is an embodiment of his own immortal power, of that I am certain, for I am of the Long. He destroys us with his own power, with the power of Heaven itself. Woe are the Hànrén. Woe is the Celestial Dragon King. Woe are those who defy the power of this desert devil."

"Thank you, dragon spirit," Ash said, her voice heavy with the emotion issuing from the doomed spirit. "We thank you for your kindness in sharing with us." Then, with a slow movement of her hands, she broke contact with the spirit, and the silvery outline around the fallen dragon abruptly faded to nothingness.

"Ash?" Mhyrranda asked. "Was he telling the truth? All we got was audio and some dim impressions. Safety precautions, because we were shielding versus necromancy, too."

Ash nodded, understanding the formerly unspoken protocol. All the better, for even she regretted the use of such a despicable power. "Yes, he was telling the truth, Duchess. And, due to our bond, I was able to get a detailed visual of the scene. I've even got the leader's eyes."

"Ah," Mhyrranda exhaled slowly, for she knew that with such knowledge came power. Very specific p ower w hich s he a nd her cabal would be certain to exploit to their advantage. "I think we should jaunt a bit around the world some more first, to throw off any trails, and then return to Dreamland for a strategy session. We can decide how we want to play this one. Friend, or foe? If friend, then we've just ramped up our power levels again. If foe... then we're in deep shit against someone with powers like that. And we'll have to move quickly to destroy him, before he gets the idea to come smash more of our pyramids. Or Dreamland itself."

In collective agreement, the cabal broke into its component parts, and wove intricate psychic trails in the Dream World to disguise their passage to their ultimate destination.

***

Elsewhere, in Mecca, a figure in pristine white robes hovered above the Kaaba, commanding the attention of tens of thousands of similarly dressed warriors who filled the central area of the temple. As the warriors chanted prayers in humble voices, the floating figure's eyes slowly opened, his reverie interrupted by the silent command of his god:

"It is time again for *jihad*, Abdulla Muhammad al-Mahdi. This time, the rest of the blasphemous temples of the infidels must be purified. This time, you will start in America, then work your way across the world, bringing cleansing fire in your glorious passage..."

Smiling to himself, Abdulla Muhammad al-Mahdi mouthed a silent thanks to his god, promising to fulfill his holy will. Then, with a sharp intake of air, and a focusing of his own power of glorious radiance, he shouted the command of *jihad* to his jubilant warriors.

CHAPTER 38

"Ready?" Cully inquired loudly, his sharp eyes affixed upon the alien craft resting on the raised black crystalline dais before him.

Flanking him on his right side, Nick and Ami both replied in unison, "Check!"

"Check? This ain't no hoity-toity Vegas restaurant, you simps!" Cully barked back. "I asked if you were *ready*, you dimwit special forces freaks! No Praetorian talk here! Ready, or not?"

"Ready, Cully!" Nick replied for Ami, whose left hand had risen to her delicate lips to ward her smartass reply.

"That's more like it," Cully grumbled, raw hekatek power crackling from his outstretched hands, cascading around the perimeter of the Watcher's craft. "You two know what you have to do if this goes south. Contain, ward, and, if necessary, warp. Maynard helped me seal this place up and ward it like all get out, so nobody and nothing gets in or out. Unless it's got Ami's signature. We'll cut losses if we have to, and Ami will hurl that thing through spacetime like a streak of gnarly goose shit if it don't behave. Can't risk Dreamland for some stupid alien rust-bucket, after all."

"Wise," Ami commented, "seeing as how we're in the basement vault beneath the arcology. An antipodal feedback loop of hekatek primal power would compromise Aal Ball, the War Room, the Dreamland Arcology, and virtually everything else that's connected resonantly with us. So, yeah, don't worry, Cully. I'll streak that gnarly goose shit into a galaxy far, far away if it comes down to it."

"Good kid," Cully praised her. "At least somebody's paying attention."

Silently, Nick filed away a potential End Game scenario for the Watcher's craft, should such ever become necessary. A true Samson Option, if ever there were one.

Cully focused sharply, shaping his power with his fingertips, bidding it to softly caress the craft. Wreathed in a shroud of writhing electric blue sparks, the eldritch vessel began to softly purr like a happy mountain lion.

"Artificers, ready?" he then inquired of the Fae gathered to his left flank.

There, behind a thin, glassine barrier of Cully's own highly artificed hekagraphene, a small contingent of Fae enchanters and artificers nervously observed the scene. All knew that the alien craft had belonged to one of the Watchers, the First Seed, who had accompanied the Lightbringer's Sigil when it had wrought its fate-shaping charms upon EarthZero. And with that very simple understanding came a potent mix of fear and dread, for the Watchers were as gods to the Fae, their power old and strong.

Zhimmi'Zhenz Vhenz, the elder artificer of the Fae of Aal, shot a sidelong glance at his counterpart from the Fae of EarthZero, Malisa Myr'Zhen, who wrinkled her pointy nose in disgust.

"I don't like being stumped," she admitted, eliciting a faint creak of a smile from Zhimmi.

"Who does?" Zhimmi found himself admitting openly, blatantly, totally defying thousands of years of Fae protocol. For a moment, he felt awkward, being truthful, acknowledging weakness. But the new scene, this new world – EarthZero – was growing rapidly on him, unbinding millennia of reticence and paranoia. "But if we can't figure it out, Milady Malisa, then who shall? Are we not the best from among our respective peoples? Are we not the masters of magick?"

"You're the masters of avoiding my questions, you bunch of commies!" Cully hissed, his tone just soft enough for the subtle Fae to realize he was just playing. Though he did expect a response to his earlier query, of course. "You ready? I'm dropping the containment sphere in ten seconds. We get 235 seconds of unfiltered discernment, then the sphere goes back up. This is a one-and-done operation. No second chances. Ain't nobody nowhere gonna have a shot at trackin' and crackin', got it? So, you ready to do this, you sad lot of pointy eared, cactus-eating desperadoes?"

Both Zhimmi and Malisa laughed curtly, signaling their own factions to do the same. Ol' Man Culpepper, though a fantastically skilled hybrid hekatek artificer, still remained human in heart and words, and the ancient Fae, despite their recent integration into the New World, still had much deeply, and rightfully, ingrained discrimination to overcome. With care, however, and with faith, and love, both sides of that most ancient coin knew that they could arrive at a new understanding. After all, they knew that they must unite and become as one, or they would die.

"Ready, Cully," Malisa replied. "You pissy old goat..." she breathed softly, causing a few lips to tug among the Fae.

"I heard that!" Cully laughed. "And you're right, Mally," he continued earnestly. "I *am* pissy. But that's because we've got only one shot at this, and I don't like being stumped any more than anyone else here. So let's solve this, folks. Let's git 'er done..."

With that Cully poured a gout of power into the craft, willing it to life, stroking its very soul. Unbridled fear coursed into his mind, for now, in that first moment of communion with the craft, he understood that, indeed, the soul of the Watcher was someone, impossibly, bound within. He had opened himself up to direct communion with an alien god, and there was absolutely no chance now for him to shield his soul from its eldritch power. And veritably trillions upon trillions of its soul shards, each of shared yet unique identity, slammed into his own, seeking, curious, outreaching. Cully, though indeed more powerful than most of the survivors of the Sigil's Weirding, had absolutely no defense, no chance to resist, the power of the Watcher. Like taking a sniper's shot to the base of the skull, Cully's conscious mind flicked off in a millisecond, and he fell toward the floor, limp, even as Nick's force field saved him from a nasty impact.

Despite Cully's unconscious state, his shaping energies continued to flow along the alien craft, seeking and establishing a new resonant entrainment, this time guided by the Watcher's soul shards.

"Ami!" Nick shouted. "Be ready to warp that thing outta here!"

"I got it, Nick," she replied, causing a fist-sized singularity to appear, out-of-phase, above the craft. "If it so much as sneezes, it's gone."

Among the Fae, almond-slanted eyes of various hues alit with scrying, divining magicks. Immediately, hekatek feedback from the craft, crackling like light green lightning, lit the Fae up from the tops of their immaculately groomed heads to the tips of their fashionable pointy-toed boots. Priceless and ancient charms and amulets popped off from chests, belts, wrists, and necks like exploding light bulbs, showering the immediate area with a crystalline shower of ruined shards, peppering them like porcupine quills. Fierce screams and howls of pain resounded, and all of them, save for Zhimmi and Malisa, the mightiest of the lot, swooned, falling unconscious to the floor. The hekagraphene shield spiderwebbed, but held, sparing Nick, Ami, and Cully from a vicious spray of shrapnel from the shattered charms and amulets. Too bad it had not been able to shield the Fae versus the hekatek feedback, nor the shrapnel, which had unfortunately come from their own side of the shield.

"Zherrod's Bane!" Zhimmi swore, clacking his Zynsh wristbands together, invoking a mass healing aura which bathed all of the Fae in soft, soothing sea green light, sealing their wounds.

"Interesting," Malisa noted aloud. "Your healing aura didn't pass through Cully's hekagraphene. It stopped."

"Concentrate on the craft, Malisa," Zhimmi reminded her. "We have only a few more seconds."

"But maybe the shield is blocking our scrying magicks, too?" she offered, a delicate purple eyebrow arching high, reinforcing her query, carrying it to both Nick and Ami, too.

Living among the Fae of EarthZero for a year or so, both Nick and Ami had become accustomed to the subtleties of Fae social communication, especially the nonverbal. Within the span of a single second, Nick winked at Ami, and Ami caused another singularity to manifest at the center of the hekagraphene shield. Despite its near invulnerability to physical impact, and its inherent magickal warding, which Cully had honestly intended to protect the Fae from any mischief from the craft, the hekagraphene shield instantly polarized, its form turning an obsidian black a few tenths of a second before the well-placed singularity wiped it from local spacetime.

"Smart," Malisa admitted, flashing a quick grin to the two former humans.

"Yes, they are. Constant state of surprise I'm in," Zhimmi admitted through clenched teeth as he bore down hard on his scrying, his eyes now flickering wicked polychromatic light. "These humans are not at all like those of my world."

"Ku'tu told us all about them," Ami said returning her full attention to her remaining singularity. "I'm glad you killed them all."

Despite their better judgement, Zhimmi and Malisa exchanged quick eyes, a mere tenth-of-a-second lock-and-release. If they survived this ordeal, they would seek out this former human, and have words with her, for they both knew a changeling when one spoke truth to them.

"Shielding everyone," Nick said, taking a step forward. "They're polarized correctly, so don't worry about your magicks."

"Too bad Cully didn't polarize his shield correctly," Ami snorted. "Might have had a few more seconds of scrying. Might have spared the Fae from that feedback."

"Well," Nick said, "I don't understand magicks too well, either. Shit's subtle. I had to get specific help from Maynard to get my shields right to filter it properly, and, even then, it took time to train up to proficiency. Sure, Maynard might have helped a bit with the room itself, but Cully just threw most of this stuff together himself, ad hoc. Making it up as he went along. He did well, considering things, I think."

"No one can ward primal hekatek anyway," Malisa gritted, her dainty, pale white hands darting before her eyes like flitting butterflies. "And that, I'm now certain, is the crafting framework of the Watcher's spaceship. First Seed power. Godlike power. It's... it's beyond me," she said disconsolately, allowing her scrying power to diminish and fade.

Shaking his head sadly, his triple-braided white hair gently tossing, Zhimmi said, "Agreed. It's still cycling Cully's hekatek shaping, resonating with it, but, otherwise, it's blank, dark, warm, yet cold. There's something there, of course, right before us, but I cannot see it, even with my own considerable level of power."

"It's like it's toying with us," Malisa said, a musical lilt betraying her annoyance. "Perhaps we've been doing this wrong the whole time. Wrong approach to something that might be overtly simple," she said, allowing Zhimmi the opportunity to continue the proffered thread.

He nodded. "Yes, Milady Malisa, I think you are correct. Let's do the most simple thing first: Let's ask it a question."

Nick shot Ami a nonplused glance. She shook her head once, silently cursing every so-called genius in their ranks for being so stupid.

Zhimmi continued, for he knew that his particular dialect of Ancient Sidhe, that of the Fae of Aal, would intersect best with that of the Watcher, who had spoken such during the incident at the Georgia Guidestones. And, as had the collective spoken, he had been informed, during the appearance of the Lightbringer's Sigil. "Watcher!" he intoned dramatically, startling those around him with the true power of his voice. "Come forth! We beseech thee!"

Before them, the alien vessel abruptly went dark, Cully's energies vanishing and the momentary resonance dissipating to nothing within the span of three heartbeats. Next, almost immediately, a sheen appeared along the surface of the vessel, similar to that of oil on water, yet distinctly discreet, as if untold numbers of entities swarmed like a microscopic army of ants. A pattern congealed from the chaos, revealing a shimmering infinity sign which birthed itself from a multicolored fractal background of whirling strange attractors. The sign arose from the surface of the craft, tiny flecks of chaotic light weaving a humanoid form for the Watcher to manifest within.

Androgynous, silvery, humanoid, it resolved before them, hovering a few inches above the top of the vessel. Black on white, then white on black static patterns formed an outline around its silver, almost chrome body. Slowly, it raised its hands, showing them its palms.

"I am the Watcher," it told them in the dialect of the Fae of Aal. "Love, and peace, my fellow sentients. My master, the Lightbringer, commanded me to break from the collective of the Igigi at the time of the Sigil, to retrieve Fresswelle and safeguard it from the adversary, then to see to its eventual liberation at the correct juncture of spacetime. Then, and only then, did the pieces fit. Then, and only then, was it possible for the worlds of Aal and EarthZero to integrate. Then, and only then, was it possible for the Fractal Blades to affect the hekatek resonance, and fully awaken the Dragon of EarthZero, through agency of the Mother herself. Then, and only then, could EarthZero move its probability of success against the Vanth'Vash'Var from zero to something ever so slightly above zero. Now, and only now, do we have a chance for victory. A chance to save this world, and this cosmos, from total annihilation."

"You said 'we' there at the end, Watcher," Nick said, staring steadily at the bizarre being. "That mean you're on our side now?"

"I have always been on your side, Nick," the Watcher said softly, turning slightly to regard him. "I serve the Lightbringer, and the Lightbringer is on your side. The Lightbringer wants us to win, to defeat the Death Horde, to save EarthZero. You understand, do you not?"

Nick nodded. "Yeah, I do. But that's some major tough love: To snuff out almost every living thing on the planet, and then try to get the remainder to join your team."

"We have been on the same team the whole time, Nick," the Watcher reminded him. "Everything that has happened, has happened for extremely precise reasons. Events occurred as they did in order to maximize our probability of success, and to minimize our probability of failure. There was, and is, no other way, save for the way of fire and stone. It is a difficult path," the Watcher said carefully, slowly, "for the First Seed hold love and seek peace for all living things. To be forced to participate in genocide is horrifying. It rips the soul apart, reducing it to ruin. You are all my children, parts of my own soul, our own souls, from the First Time. I, and we, certainly did not want to harm you. What parent finds joy in the killing of its child? Yet, I, and we, have done so, for there was no other path to take. Please forgive me, and please forgive us," it pleaded, its voice wavering, almost near to portraying emotion.

Nick, Ami, Zhimmi, and Malisa themselves felt the impact of the Watcher's plea. It stung them, hurt them, as if they had been rebuked by a parent, in the case of the former humans, or a loved one, in all of their cases.

"Oh, yeah?" Ami suddenly blurted. "I don't forgive, and I certainly don't forget. I saw the murder that you and your kind inflicted on my people, and on the world. And I will tell you, plainly and clearly, that I'll judge you by how much you help us now, in the here and now, against the Vanth'Vash'Var, and not by your argument that you had to murder almost all of us in order to save us. And, frankly," she snarled, two grapefruit-sized singularities appearing directly over the Watcher's head, "I'm about two seconds from murdering *you*, right now, unless you swear before us all that you're on our side, and that you're going to help the living hell out of us. Swear it, Watcher! *Swear it!*"

Both Malisa and Zhimmi blanched. Despite their potent magicks, both feared an embodiment of the First Seed, and what one of its station could do to them if provoked. And the former human, this waif of a girl, had certainly just provoked it by threatening it with murder. Neither could work their mouths to form coherent words.

Nick, being of sterner stuff, still had been shocked by Ami's sudden turn. He quickly scanned the room again, being certain that he had every angle covered, and every player shielded. Under his breath, he said softly, "Ami... reel it in..."

"No," she replied. "I *won't*. I mean exactly what I said. Decide now, Watcher. Swear you'll help us, or die."

Tilting its head slightly to the right, the Watcher calculated various aspects of its current scenario. The two Fae were impotent before its collective might, as were the still unconscious Fae, and the artificer who had attempted to call it forth. The other former human, the shielder, had a true and noble soul, the same as most of the Watcher's own trillions of soul shards. But he was still relatively young, and incapable of doing much, if any, harm to the Watcher. But the young woman? The one who could wrest chaos from spacetime itself? She absolutely *could* do harm, because her power was, unfortunately for the Watcher, one of the very few capable of actually affecting its near-absolute control of its own quantum waveforms, and its trillions of soul shards.

Yes, there were others in the cosmos who could challenge it. The First Seed among the Vanth'Vash'Var, of course, came to mind. The bearer of the Fractal Blades could, too, though that would be an improbable turn of events now that the path had been established for both bearer and blades. And, of course, there was always the wild card, the sole grey piece on the cosmic chess board: the VoidSpawn. But the Watcher knew that everyone and everything would one day fall before the implacable wickedness of the Godslayer, the one who would end all things. Should the simulation ever reach such an improbable state, of course, for the End State, should the Vanth'Vash'Var defeat EarthZero, would cause much the same effect. The only question remaining there, one which the Watcher could not answer, despite its power, would be: Would the VoidSpawn live on, to carry out its metacosmic destiny, despite the machinations of the One Above? Once manifested, could something of its metacosmic power ever be unbound?

Would someday all worlds be unbound? Even the world of the ZeroTime?

Irrelevant to the scenario at hand, the Watcher concluded. Returning to the main thread, it continued its calculations. Ami could, hypothetically, unbind its entirety, with but a single gesture. And although the Watcher could, again hypothetically, rebind its soul shards over time and once again manifest itself, it would take too much time, and time was something that no one had in abundance at this most critical juncture. Thus, and therefore, the highly improbable occurred...

"You have the word of the Watcher, Amaterasu Kurohoshi," it promised her. "I will help you, and your kind, against the Vanth'Vash'Var. Just as I had originally proclaimed, of course, your threats of murder notwithstanding," it said, the slightest trace of humor in its voice. "And while this might come as a surprise to you, I am merely continuing to carry out the will of my master, for such was commanded from the start. With this next revelation comes true power, for now I will instruct you as to the finer mysteries of the Eternal Recursion, and what true primal hekatek power is..."

The two Fae gasped. Nick allowed a faint smile to escape. Ami was rapidly becoming a true MVP on their team. Heart of a lion.

Ami, ever mindful of tradition, bowed to the Watcher. "You are wise. I wasn't bluffing."

The Watcher returned her bow. "I know."

CHAPTER 39

P etrus, filled with trepidation, but unwilling to show it, smiled
kindly at the four guards escorting him to the Council. Their
annoyance was palpable as they walked slowly alongside the
crippled man. Still, he was determined to show what grace he could
in the face of whatever the Council had in store for him.

As he approached the large table, the council arose and
gathered in front of it. Brother Bradley held a piece of paper in his
hands, his face grim. After the escort moved to the side, he gestured
at Petrus.

"Holiness, now is the time for your final decision. I have prayed
that you would see the light, and come to the aid of the people of
the City of Glass – to my aid. As a friend, and someone who I have
admired for years, I am begging you to help us."

Petrus stood in awkward silence for a long second.

Brother Bradley raised the paper in his hand, gesturing with
it. "I just received a memo from the research facility on Ryker's
Island. The design works, but it takes a lot of power to forge. That's
because it's beyond mere technology; even beyond mere magick.
It's technomagick. Of a most malevolent, most destructive sort.
It will smite our foes with the very Hand of God! It requires,
unfortunately, the price of many lives to become realized. Many
must sacrifice their lives in order to render this most awesome
machine from naught. But, true martyrs that they are, they will

gladly sacrifice t hemselves b efore G od t o h elp u s s trike down Lucifer! After that, though... After the blood price has been paid, the world itself will strike down from on high through our new divine weapon, with the force of an Old World nuclear bomb, to destroy our enemies, and their evil works."

"And you are going to use it." Petrus shook his head sadly. "Brother Bradley, Brother Greg, Sister Evaline, please do not do this. War is not the answer here. Send emissaries to Las Vegas, try to negotiate peace. The true enemy is coming, and without unity, humanity is lost. I have seen the other side, my friends. I came back to tell you this. I have seen the universe from birth to death, the same result in every ending, thousands and thousands of times, always the same. The Death Horde are the destroyers. The people in the west are trying to survive, like all of us. They are not the ones we should be fighting..."

"Spoken like the traitor you are," Sister Evaline said bitterly. "I have never liked you, Petrus, but I listened to Brother Bradley and felt you deserved a chance to serve humanity and God once you came to your senses. You were a beacon of hope to people in the days before. Now you are a coward, and a turncoat." The last sentence came out as nearly a hiss.

Brother Greg cleared his throat and looked at his feet before staring at Petrus. "I too, had hoped... You were someone to rally the people of the City of Glass, and they listened to your message of the future, they truly believed in what you said about humanity and this city. That we were a place where people could start again. But this? It's bullshit. It sounds like something the people in Las Vegas would say. You turn your back on the people who trusted you, man."

Warlord Armitrage appeared ready to unleash his own pronouncement, when a tinkling of bells sounded behind Petrus. Cradled within a soft white aura of suffuse light, accompanied by rainbows emanating from the cathedral's walls, the Angel appeared, its face showing a sadness beyond mere sorrow.

"Holiness, you have failed the people of this city. You have failed this Council. And you have failed the Lord. And now you face judgement." The Angel looked at each person in turn and nodded.

Brother Bradley sighed, the decision already made. "It pains me, Petrus, that it has come to this. Three times we have asked, and three times, you have denied us aid. For this we should execute you, and make an example of your betrayal."

Petrus shivered despite himself. Although his faith was still alive, he was, after all, though virtually immortal, still quite mortal. Death carried no guarantee of the reward of Heaven, given all he had seen. He hung his head in resignation.

"But," Brother Bradley continued, "as we said, you are a symbol of hope, and loved by many. If we executed you, it could be a catastrophe for public relations. So, we have a different solution. No less fatal for you in the end, I am sorry to say, my friend."

Sister Evaline waved to someone on the fringes of the room, and after a moment, the lights and cameras came up, the monitors around the room showing what was being displayed on every screen in the city.

Brother Bradley, ever charismatic, smiled at the cameras.

"People of our most wondrous city, it is with a heavy heart and great sadness that we, the Council of the City of Glass, must make a special judgement this day. The former Pope, his Holiness Petrus of Rome, has committed acts of treason against this city and its people. For this betrayal, it is our decision that he be stripped of all possessions and banished, never to return. He will be escorted to the border and released from our protection, into the wilderness. May God have mercy on his soul."

A terrible silence loomed over the City of Glass as its denizens came to terms with this seemingly impossible turn of events. The Pope, banished? For treason?

"I must note for clarity here," Brother Bradley continued, his gaze flinty, "that no citizen may provide aid of any sort, nor may his name be spoken, or written henceforth. Failure to follow these directives is treason. This is our decision. That is all."

The cameras ended the transmission, and the Warlord approached Petrus, a feral smile on his face. With a sneer, Warlord Armitrage knocked the staff from Petrus' grip and punched him in the stomach, forcing the air from his lungs and hurling him several feet.

"Anthony, please, that's uncalled for!" Brother Bradley exclaimed, while the others looked on in shock.

With barely a look over his shoulder, the Warlord lifted the breathless man to his feet and stripped his robes from him, leaving Petrus in his underwear. With a last look, he yanked the crucifix from Petrus' neck, pocketing it. "Get him out of here. And take that away," he said, indicating the robes and staff.

"Where should we take him, sir?" asked the young sergeant in charge.

"The far side of the Washington bridge. After that, his fate is not my concern," The general said, with a knowing look. "And Sergeant Shen, if he fights you, put a bullet in him."

She nodded. "Sir, yes, sir!"

They lifted Petrus to his feet, and began to drag him away.

Brother Greg called out as they were leaving, "Oh, and sergeant, have one of the soldiers at the door send a messenger to attend us, please."

"Yes sir," she said, turning to follow the soldiers dragging Petrus away.

Returning to the table, Brother Greg said, "time to begin the fight in earnest?"

Warlord Armitrage stood at the end of the table and gestured to the maps. "The decisions must be made, which direction should we focus on, and what will we do until the cannon is ready?"

Sister Evaline looked from one map to the other and said, "I don't think we can take Las Vegas yet, not until the cannon is ready. I think we should send our forces south and burn Atlanta like Grant did."

Brother Bradley considered for a moment. "I don't think we should leave ourselves unguarded here, though. What if we sent some forces along a couple of paths west so we've got more defenses ready in case they decide to strike?"

"I think I have a plan that will weaken them and draw them out without risking the city," The Warlord said. "I will lead a conventional force of Shard troops and conscripts south, burning everything in my path, and ultimately destroying Atlanta. When they hear about it, they will respond by sending a force from Las Vegas. In the meantime, I'll have our heavy hitters positioned north of their path, so we can flank them and destroy both the forces they send and their city before they can retaliate."

"Could work," Brother Greg said. "But I'd like to make sure the city is protected."

He was unable to finish his thought, as a thin, out-of-breath messenger approached the table. "Messenger reporting, sirs, ma'am," he said.

Brother Greg gave the messenger instructions to fetch the twins and their nanny. Once the young man was on his way, the discussion continued.

Sister Evaline considered. "I think we will be fine, if we put the city on lockdown and keep some of our powered supers on the city limits. Maybe a few further out. We have scouts."

The Council debated several items while waiting, and eventually, the scout returned with a look of dismay on his face.

"They weren't there and their guards—"

Brother Bradley interrupted, "Personal Attendants."

"Right, sorry. Their personal attendants didn't know they had left."

"Well, where are they?" Sister Evaline blurted. "They can't have wandered far."

"The gua—er, attendants said they sent them on an errand after the city-wide announcement. When they came back, no one answered the door. They checked the parking garage and said the black SUV they came in was gone."

"Shit, shit, shit," Brother Greg said. "They are either on their way here or they are in the wind. And they would have been here by now. We need to send some people after them and close the bridges. General?"

"Agreed. Go send word, son."

"Yessir!" The messenger bolted, hoping that he had eluded blame.

***

Reaching the far side of the bridge, the sergeant watched as a pair of soldiers hauled Petrus from the truck bed and tossed him into the street. One of them pulled his service revolver. The other stepped back, hesitant.

"Fucking traitor..." the guard grated at Petrus.

Petrus saw the void down the end of the barrel pointed at him.

"Hold, soldier," Sergeant Shen said. "Nobody gave you an order to shoot that man."

"Well, sergeant, nobody *didn't*, either. And the Warlord implied with that look he gave us that was what he wanted."

The sergeant cast a skeptical eye on the soldier. "A look isn't good enough reason to kill someone. Put your gun away."

"But he's a traitor. You heard them."

"Yep, and we did what we were told. Now get back in the truck and we are gonna roll. That's an order."

"All things considered, sir, I just want to shoot him." The soldier turned back to aim at Petrus again, and time stopped. Just froze.

Except for the woman in the great cloak, walking toward the soldier with the gun. Her face covered, her body shrouded, Petrus could hardly make out any details about her except her size and the lithe way she moved. Without breaking stride, she lifted the gun from the soldier's hand and turned it on him, holding it to his face and firing, once, twice, before dropping the gun. With time stopped as it was, there was no effect except for a pair of clicks and the appearance of a pair of bullets where the gun had been. The gun itself began to fall slowly to the ground.

Petrus stared in awe at the woman, who finally turned to face him. Her eyes fairly glowed with molten fire, and she had a vivid smile on her painted lips. "You're welcome," she said.

"What...? Who...?" Petrus was stunned, unable to process.

"Well, you *could* call it divine intervention, but that would be a cruel misnomer. Deus Ex would also be an ironically poor choice. Let's just say I'm doing it for your own good."

She turned again and continued walking, disappearing in a fractal cloud of many colors that buzzed with the sound of angry bees, as the world resumed its normal pace. Whereupon several things happened. First, there were a pair of gunshots, and the head of the soldier who had been about to shoot Petrus exploded with two large blossoms of blood. Second, the sergeant and the other soldier quickly drew their sidearms and crouched, trying to determine where the gunfire had come from. Third, Petrus realized the identity of his savior, and blanched.

As the pair continued searching, the driver of the truck and another soldier appeared, covering them.

"What the Hell?" shouted the sergeant. "Did anyone see where those shots came from?"

Petrus, still on the ground said, "Indeed. Check his pistol, sergeant, and I believe you will have your answer."

Cautiously, Sergeant Shen approached the dead man and examined his sidearm. "Sonofabitch. He's right. How'd you do that?"

"I didn't, but I can hardly explain it, except to say it was supernatural in origin."

A look crossed the sergeant's face, and she turned to the others. "Before this gets too weird to report, are any of the rest of you going to do something stupid here?"

"Um, no sarge – except maybe... Say, what do you want me to do with this stuff?" The driver indicated Petrus' clothing and staff on the bed of the truck.

The sergeant looked carefully at the rest of her team before heading back to the truck. "Hang on..." She returned with a gear bag and a canteen, and placed them on the side of the road. "Just put that stuff over here in the weeds. No use carrying extra junk around, and he's not going to need his stuff," she said, nodding toward the corpse. "Pull any extraneous gear and toss it, then put him in the truck. At this point, his armor is worth more than his dead, dumb ass. I'm writing this up as a sniper hit, and if any of you contradict me, you won't see a fresh morning. Are we clear?"

"Clear, sarge," said the soldier who helped pull Petrus from the truck. Moving to the pile, he dropped his full canteen and lifted the robes from the ground, carefully dusting them off. He gently helped the crippled man into his robes and patted him on the shoulder before turning back to the sergeant. "Say, I think I left my canteen at the sniper site. Will you sign a req for a new one, please?"

The sergeant and several others smiled, as the soldier handed Petrus his staff. "Good luck to you. Be careful out there. Don't know where you are headed, but I had some family out in Allentown. I heard it's hard to keep a good man down out there."

The soldiers gave the area a final quick once over before piling back in the truck and crossing the median and heading back to the city.

A cold chill competed with a warm vibe, both running up and down Petrus' spine. He imagined Maweth, raging within his soul, now impotent and silent. Because a slender hand had now finally clasped its mouth shut.

Lucifer had saved him from certain death, and had caused the hostile soldiers to hand over essential supplies to him. *What cruel turn of events is this?* Petrus considered, lost for a moment, deeply immersed in logical introspection. The vectors certainly indicated, robustly, that, indeed, Lucifer had been shaping his destiny along this path the entire time. Not quite to the point of abrogating his own free will. Yet, certainly, stacking the possible inflection points such that his own free will to make the most logical decision had, indeed, been irrelevant. It was humbling to consider that a being of such intellect existed; one who could foresee such a tangled matrix of event paths, and shape prior conditions such that there could be few possible divergences from the most probable decision. Time after time. With unerring accuracy.

Petrus had no other option but to fully consider the inevitable: That his path in life now placed him firmly on the side of Lucifer, and his chaotic allies. The entity posing as "God" was in fact the true enemy of all mankind. Now, it was up to the survivors of the Apocalypse to save EarthZero. It was a destiny, a fate, and a life path that Petrus finally had to admit that he had tried to follow all along.

Even if, by consequence of madness and misdirection from an alien and wicked "God", he had been led astray. He now understood why the VoidSpawn and his companions had been forced to destroy him, for his rash arrogance to force the One Above to acknowledge him would most certainly have resulted in the termination of the EarthZero simulation. In his madness, he had almost destroyed them all. Perhaps those who had taken his life, and his soul, could forgive him his many sins? If not, then perhaps they would be merciful enough to end his second life quickly, and return him to the darkness of nonexistence.

As Petrus stood there, humbly wishing for a cart to load the supplies in – almost daring, if only for a nanosecond, to offer a prayer to Lucifer for such a boon—a black SUV approached, slowing to a stop on the road beside him.

CHAPTER 40

Abdulla Muhammad al-Mahdi, the chosen Hand of the Prophet's Vengeance, stirred fitfully, his dreams tormenting him. While he and his warrior hosts had lain waste to the infidels, grinding their strongholds to ash and dust, carrying out the sublime will of the Creator himself, he felt empty, and hollow. *But how could this be,* he asked himself, gazing down upon the ruined battlefield from on high, *if I have done the bidding of my Master? The one who created? The one who breathed life and immortal fire into me? Why do I not feel the glory of victory? Of conquering the infidels, and smashing them to dust beneath the Hand of the Prophet's Vengeance?*

Writhing, the Mahdi rolled over in bed, his arms twisted awkwardly above his heaving, naked torso. Below, on the ruined ground of his dreams, the angry spirits of the dead vaulted forth from their ruined, charred bodies, casting aspersions and heaping scorn upon him.

"You have betrayed the people of EarthZero!" they moaned in unison. "You have subtracted from the Dragon, and its ability to defend the world from the Vanth'Vash'Var. You have condemned the precious, last remnants of the souls of this world with your ill-conceived notions of vengeance, and purification. You have struck out in blind, pathetic hypocrisy, and you have crippled any chance EarthZero might have had against the omnipotence of the Death Horde."

"No!" the Mahdi cried out silently. "I carried out the will of Allah! My God, the One God, decreed that His Holy Martyrs should descend upon the infidels of the East, and lay them waste! For their souls are of the apostate, the unbelievers. There is no more *jizyah*, for there are no more *dhimmi*. Those are words of the Old World, not the New World proclaimed by the One God himself. The *ummah* now is the world, or EarthZero, as you call it. The *shari'ah* now applies to all. The Caliphate applies to the entire world. We proclaim that this whole world belongs to God. This was made perfectly clear to them: It is Allah's will. There is now no path, save that of submission to God. They refused to convert. Thus, the gates of Paradise shall not open for them. Therefore, their deaths were writ in fire and stone, so decreed Allah! And who but Abdulla Muhammad al-Mahdi, the Hand of the Prophet's Vengeance, should smite them?"

"But does not Allah make it clear that any son of Adam may ultimately seek forgiveness?"

"This is true," the Mahdi agreed, "yet, they had committed the unforgiveable sin of *mušrikūn*, which is *shirk*, which is not a pardonable sin. For by not converting, they have kept their old gods, and by virtue of this and an implicit state of war against the Caliphate, they have engaged in plotting against the *ummah* and the Holy Word of God. One needs not be a scholar to understand this most perilous position, and what punishment lies in store for those who choose this path."

At this, Mhyrranda sighed. While Maynard had carefully instructed her on Old World theology prior to their calculated gambit to attempt Dream World contact with the Mahdi, her innate resistance and bias toward religious zealotry – from snake-wrangling backwoods preachers right up to the former Pope himself – caused her considerable consternation. Trying to argue reason with them was like trying to argue with a brick wall. And Belief and its bastard spawn, Religion, were two of the best bricklayers around. And now, apparently, there was a "New World" interpretation of the religion of the Mahdi and his people with which she was not familiar, rendering Maynard's recent tutelage mostly irrelevant. He could now lay minefields around the brick walls, countering everything she had learned with newfound, unknown interpretations, and, theoretically, keep her at bay forever.

The Duchess of Dreamland then decided to change tack. If not reason, then force.

"Mahdi," Mhyrranda began, shaping his dreamscape into a hellish vision of his newfound kingdom consumed by terrible dragon fire, "you must know that we have our own ways of dealing with those who would wage war upon us. And while your power is mighty indeed, capable of decimating the armies of the Celestial Dragon King," she said, conjuring a replay of the battle conveyed to her cabal via Ash's necromantic union with the fallen dragon, "we have power beyond their grasp. Behold..." she said, shaping a bird's eye view of the final moments of the Battle of Giza. In particular, she focused on the gigaton blast of primal power at the climax of the battle, lingering on the continental after-effects that had reshaped thousands of square kilometers of northern Africa. She let the thunder roil for many seconds, and it echoed over and over again in the Mahdi's fevered mind.

Sweating and writhing, the Mahdi clenched his jaw against what he had just experienced in his dream. "Your witchery avails you naught, Dreamwyrd," he said bitterly, fighting her with every iota of his own formidable will. "You and your pagan infidels are not as powerful as you might believe..."

Despite her own incalculable power in the Dream World, Mhyrranda felt the impact crash upon her psychic shields like a vicious desert sandstorm. Fortunately, and wisely, she was not in communion with her cabal, as she and only she was capable of such direct infiltration of such a formidable foe. For if she had been, then, most assuredly, there would have been casualties among her cabal from such a potent backlash.

"That's what you think, sugar," the Duchess of Dreamland drawled, focusing her own psychic power up a notch, raising her own shields to match and beat back the Mahdi's onslaught. "You might be hot shit in the physical world, able to smash down whole armies with but a single stroke. But here, in my world, you're just a tiny, scared, little man," she said, counterattacking, hammering his mind with thousands of disparate, chaotic dream slivers, each one conveying alternative, haunting scenarios which no sane mind could navigate.

In silence, the Mahdi screamed as his tortured mind tried to solve the intractable Maze of Dreams. And Mhyrranda used this momentary opportunity to reach into and dissect his memories and psyche; to read his very soul, among all nine of his brightly shining chakras.

Sifting, sorting, interrogating, the Dreamwyrd veritably surfed the internet of the Mahdi's mind. She knew his innermost thoughts and dreams, and his aspirations. His losses – he had lost his entire family to the Weirding, as had most survivors – and his gains. His desire to unite all factions of his religion, which was a most noble cause, though its price had thus far been exacted in blood and souls. His... contact and guidance by...

A wayward, screaming psychic shard forcefully extracted itself from Mhyrranda's mental grasp.

"Oh, no you don't..." she growled, pouring more power into the mix, tapping into Aal Ball's linked matrices for more Hekatek to empower her.

The psychic shard, seemingly somehow sentient and aware, tumbled wildly through the growing, chaotic shadows and light of the Dream World, desperately trying to flee from her clutching grasp. Somehow, it was alive. And it somehow knew that it could not allow itself to fall into her hands, because then she would know it. Know it for who it truly was...

With an abrupt stab of her mind, Mhyrranda leapt ahead of the spinning psychic shard, neatly capturing it in her metaphysical hands like a soccer goalie nimbly catching a kick on goal.

"Got ya, you little shit!" She shouted, triumphant. The psychic shard now firmly in her hands, she willed a tendril of shaping energy into it, burrowing deeply, revealing all of its hidden essence.

A series of memories cascaded warmly into her mind's eye. A hotel in Mecca. The night of the Weirding before the Sigil. Bright, rainbow lights. The screams of many thousands. Terror, and horror. A lone figure, nose pressed against the window of the hotel room. White light, and words of comfort. The selection of the Chosen...

"Oh, you bitch!" Cried the Angel of Deceit, fully manifesting itself in the Dream World before Mhyrranda, who now was in full pseudo-physical form herself. The pale blue eyes sought her own, burning, condemning.

"Your gig is up, deceiver!" Mhyrranda informed her, shaping the ethereal filaments of the Dream World into a cubic prison cage around her. "Now," she commanded, "you're going to tell me everything. Everything. No lies. No deception. Tell me everything, and I just might let you live."

"You have no such power!" the Angel of Deceit wailed, hammering her dainty hands impotently upon the cage's slatted bars. "I will scour your soul from this cosmos for your effrontery, witch! You dare contest a member of the Gentry of the Vanth'Vash'Var, whorelet!"

"Keep going," Mhyrranda bade her, shaping the dreamscape to reflect the words of the angel, forming a fully immersive experience around them as the angel revealed itself. "Tell me all."

As the angel noted images of the Starhome, Demonia Prime, appear around them, it carefully dialed back its emotions to a dull, blank state. The images faded, returning to the chaotic dreamscape filaments, looking for all the world now like some immersive rainbow colored test pattern.

"I'll tell you nothing," the angel informed her. "And I think you won't be able to hold both of us for too long, witch. Once the Mahdi resolves the trap you've set for him, he'll help me, and, together, we'll counter you. Then capture you. Then turn you against those you love."

"That supposed to scare me?" Mhyrranda asked her. "Tell me everything. Start with why you've corrupted the Mahdi. Why him?"

Despite her own grim resolve, and immortal power, the Angel of Deceit was forced to obey. "I chose nothing. I serve the will of the Nine. They commanded me to move to this world, and to others prior to this one, to seek out and capture potential foes. Powerful foes. Bend them to our cause. Subvert. Corrupt. Use sedition and treason as tools to soften up the weak underbelly of the enemies of the Vanth'Vash'Var. We're not necessarily all stone and steel, for we may choose silk and velvet if we please. In this case," she said, waving a hand around her, "we chose the soft path. But what about you, Randa?" the angel suddenly shifted, boring into the outer defenses of her psyche with those piercing, pale blue eyes. "Why aren't you doing the wise thing, and taking the wisest path? Join us in our quest, my love. We have the same goal as you: freedom."

"Freedom?" Mhyrranda spat, batting down the angel's clumsy attack. "That's a load of bullshit if I've ever heard one."

"I'm not lying," the angel admitted, "because you won't let me."

"Yeah, sugar, but the 'freedom' you're referring to is the total 'freedom' of losing one's soul to the End State of the Sim. That's total dissolution, baby. That's not 'freedom'. That's soul death. No thank you, Horde Whore. And you're just stalling for time, hoping the Mahdi will free himself from my maze. Trust me. He won't. Now, on with it, sweetie," she commanded.

Reeling, the angel replied, "Okay! Okay! Damn, but you're testy. I chose him because he was positioned better than anyone else to oppose the probable factions against us. I was given the general direction to select sleeper agents, then empower them to serve us as catspaws against anyone who dared to oppose us. Easy, right? Yes, it's totally easy, because there are always factions in and among you mortals. Or," she quickly corrected, "in this case, immortals. It was always rumored that the last world would be populated by the First. Makers, meet Cause. The most wonderful Eternal Recursion, which we of the First Seed have always sought. Little did we know that the myths and rumors would be true, that there were others of our level of power in the universe. True, there were – and still are, technically, for their remnants have joined us – other races of extreme technological or magickal power. Not a long list, of course, but a list nonetheless of the mightiest races in this universe. Yet, they all have fallen before us. And, each time, we have learned, and adapted, positioning ourselves to be above and beyond all potential foes. Save for now. For we have learned that you here on EarthZero have our power. And more, in some cases. Especially now that you have been evolved, and even moreso now that you have awakened the Dragon of this world."

"So that's why you had the Mahdi attack the Chinese pyramids? To weaken us? To try to sever us from our bond to the Dragon?"

The angel nodded. "Yes."

Inwardly, Mhyrranda smiled. She had been waiting to play this trump card, only she had expected to play it against the Mahdi, and not the Angel of Deceit. But, oh well...

"Then let me show you something, dearest Angel of Deceit, such that you might truly understand the power of the Dragon..."

With that, Mhyrranda shaped the dreamscape around them, willing a view of the Qin Chuan Plains in Shaanxi Province to appear. With a gasp, the angel, knowing that the vision was indeed real – for she knew deceit by rote – took in the view of a fully restored field of pyramids, their perimeters glowing, pulsating with highly artificed runes and inscriptions.

"How did..." the angel began before biting back her words.

"The Dragon cannot die," Mhyrranda informed her, her words biting deeply, for with them dawned comprehension of the power that the Vanth'Vash'Var truly contested. Seeing that recognition bloom in the angel's eyes, she continued, "Now you know what it is that you dare challenge, Demonian. You have numbers, and untold millennia, and power beyond the mortal pale. Yet, you do not, and cannot, have what we have: The Power of the Dragon. We are the answer to your cosmic riddle, writ larger upon the metacosmos itself. Challenge us, and you will die the cruel second death, your immortal souls forfeit before the Void itself."

A sharp intake of breath issued from the Angel of Deceit, for she abruptly knew the scalding truth of the Dreamwyrd's words. "No!" she cried loudly, slamming the bars of the cage. "It cannot be! It cannot be all for naught! We cannot have wasted so many millennia on nothing, only to become unbound at the end by something beyond our wildest dreams!"

"Yet, you see that it is true?"

"No! It's not true!" the angel roared, suddenly shifting its fascinatingly beautiful form into a living nightmare of shadows and flame. Its voice now deep and guttural, it continued, bellowing, "We will make you and your world *suffer* as no one has suffered before! A million years of soul-torture awaits you and your pathetic world! We will blot out your star, and the planets around it. Our dark shadow will loom large above your pathetic world as we launch a trillion war-bound souls upon it. We will capture, not kill, and we will make you learn pain such as you have never known. We will use our technomagick to bind you to a state of living death, from which you will never know release, even as we torment your bodies, minds, and souls forever. You will know our total domination over you, and you will know that we have destroyed your gods, and your world, and your precious Dragon, too."

"I see," Mhyrranda said, releasing the Mahdi from his pacted maze. His form loomed between the two. It was evident that he had heard what the Angel of Deceit had admitted, for there was no deceit at all in the promise of death held burning in his eyes. "She's yours, my friend," she said, willing the cage to expand to cover both the angel and the Mahdi. "Do with her as you will."

Fear flickered forth from the pale blue eyes of the Angel of Deceit. For the first time in her many millennia, the cold shock of failure washed over her, its bitter sensation augmented by the cruel fact that she had just been totally deceived by a novice soul. One who had just played the Game of Deception with more skill than she ever had. And the Mahdi... his sword... it blazed in divine, righteous fury!

"Allahu Akbar!" screamed the Mahdi, and the Hand of the Prophet's Vengeance struck true, severing the Angel of Deceit from the cosmos.

Mhyrranda allowed the cage to dissolve, and she helped usher away the millions of tiny fragments of the angel's shorn soul into dreamscape conduits which she knew led to the Void. The Mahdi, his chest heaving in rage, turned slowly to regard her.

"Do not think for a moment that this absolves you and your people from my wrath, Dreamwyrd," he warned her. "I still serve the Prophet, Peace Be Unto Him, and I still serve the One God, Allah. You and your pagan people are still guilty of *mušrikūn*, at the very least, and very possibly *shirk* itself, if you do not repent and convert. We will show you no mercy, if you do not submit."

"Ah, well," Mhyrranda sighed, "never let it be said that we didn't try to help you and your people, Mahdi, by freeing you from the yoke of the Angel of Deceit. She was an alien who led you and your people into actually indulging in *shirk*, because you followed *her* will, and not the will of your god. And she and the Vanth'Vash'Var are about as pagan and infidel as it's possible to be. You fell for her bullshit, and you and your people engaged in *jihad* issued by an alien pagan. At least we're your fellow EarthZerolings. At least we can join you against a common foe that wants to kill us all and destroy our world."

"But..." the Mahdi stammered, weighing her words. "But you and your people serve Chaos! You are pagans and infidels! How could the People of the Book possibly align with you and your kind?"

"Those are Old World terms now, Mahdi," she chided him, "and you know it. You lived through the End Times yourself. Did it even come close to what the various religions had described it as?"

He quickly shook his head, regretting his action even as he did. "But..."

"But what? You already know the answer. I don't have to spell it out for you. You experienced it yourself. You also experienced the Angel of Deceit, and all of the lies it spewed. And what was the easiest lie of all to believe? That you had somehow been chosen by your Old World 'god' to be its avenging hand? C'mon, Abdulla Muhammad Sajwani. You weren't even much of a believer before you were tricked into becoming one by the Angel of Fucking Deceit. See how that worked out? Belief? Deceit? Quite the circle, isn't it? You got used, dude. Believe *that*..."

For a moment, he considered her words, as hurtful as they were. But maybe that's how she had to say them, in order to get him to consider them at all.

"I am no philosopher, or king, or prophet," he told her, lowering his massive scimitar. "I was a simple merchant before this all happened. I was happy with my wife and family. Then, I thought that Allah had descended upon me, and had called me to martyrdom. And I served His Word. I served it well. I called together the faithful of the world, from all the various sects, and united them under the banner of the new *Khalifah*. This had not been done, truly, since the days of the Prophet, Peace Be Unto Him. But now... now I see that, while the outcome has been desirable, the cause underpinning it has not. I must gather my viziers and imams, and we must hold council, and we must consider this unfortunate turn of events." He cocked his head and gave her a quizzical look. "And we must also consider amending some aspects of the Old World such that we may accommodate the reality of the new one. I will have my agents seek you out once we have arrived at our decision on these matters, Dreamwyrd. On this, you have my word. And you have my thanks for your freeing me from the thrall of the Angel of Deceit. Thank you."

"Thank you, too," Mhyrranda said, inclining her head, willing the dreamscape to its conclusion.

As she returned to conscious awareness, Maynard leaned over the bedside and passed her a glass of water, which she took eagerly. "So, how did it go?" he asked.

Passing the glass back to him, she allowed a slight laugh to escape, then bit it back. She pulled herself up to sit on the side of the bed, motioning for Maynard to join her. "Sit down," she said sternly. "'Cause, if you don't, you're going to fall down when you hear this..."

CHAPTER 41

The Warlord surveyed the assembled troops from his VIP box in the MetLife Stadium in the Meadowlands. Pathetic. He needed far more troops than the thirty thousand that were assembled. He'd taken every nonessential soldier and recruit from the City of Glass, fitted them in every last set of Shard troop armor that he had, and had armed them with the best technomagick weapons that could be made. His troops had spent the past year looting every armory and arsenal in New York City and the surrounding counties of New York. The Warlord's Shard Army had seven battalions, armed to the teeth and supported by the best arms and armor of both the Old World and the new, with a total of 35,000 soldiers. He was confident that no army on EarthZero could match them.

The majority of the forces were still a motley reminder that his wizards could only do so much without dropping dead from exhaustion. They would be brought along of course, in a series of RVs where they could enchant non-stop during the trip. Others would be focused on charging and recharging the plasma cannons built from the plans of the angel. The largest weapon was still in production, but if the Warlord and his forces could get to Atlanta and distract them long enough, the first blast would neutralize the city before the Shard Troops crossed the Perimeter surrounding Atlanta. Las Vegas was next.

Straightening his black uniform and adjusting his hat, he composed himself and instructed the camera operator to begin the feed to one of the screens in the stadium.

"Attention."

The assembly snapped to order, though not as quickly or as cleanly as he would have liked. He waited a few beats, then nodded into the camera. "At ease."

"This is General Armitrage, and tonight we are on the verge of a righteous campaign against the forces of Lucifer, in both the City of Dreamland, and the Arcology in Atlanta. This group that you are in is headed South, where we will pick up forces between here and Atlanta, and we will lay waste to any enemies in our way."

There was quite a bit of cheering at that, and the Warlord stifled a response. Although his troops had been trained as well as possible, their discipline was based more on fear than loyalty. He also knew that they would loot as much as they could carry if they weren't watched.

"Their forces are not to be trifled with. We need to make our best speed while collecting weapons and more troops along the way. Surprise is our best weapon for now, and our Sister Evaline will be focused on blocking the Witch in Dreamland from reading our thoughts or infesting our dreams with her filth."

This time there were hoots and whistles from the crowd, and General Armitrage lashed out. "Enough! This is not something to joke about. The wicked ruler in Las Vegas has the power to mind control you, or the person next to you. You won't be laughing when one of your squad slits your throats in the night!"

At this, the troops sobered, and Armitrage continued. "We are leaving at first light, so get some food and rest, and be ready to roll. Your officers have been given orders and assigned vehicles. Dismissed!"

***

From high in the nosebleed section, a pair of small figures flew up on gossamer wings, pausing briefly at the top before flying over and out into the darkness beyond the stadium. From even higher in the sky, a squadron of hawks dove into the darkness behind them. Neither faerie made it out of the complex.

***

DAY ONE

With dawn a hint away, the commotion of each squad packing and locating their personnel carriers eventually resolved into several groups of vehicles moving out to the highway. Each group had their orders, from canvassing specific points along the way for materiel, to strike teams and recruiters, either of which could become the other as needed. Small teams had left several days before, and had looked for lights and people to earmark as potential threats or recruits.

Because there had been an ongoing effort to recruit capable citizens to the City of Glass, there was a bit of knowledge regarding the people within a hundred miles. Although many in the former northeastern United States had heard and listened to the nocturnal siren call from Dreamland, many more had their own reasons to mistrust outsiders. And living near one of the few remaining metropolises had its own rewards. People had news and information. The large former population made for larger groups of survivors to gather into viable communities. Technomagick learned and exported from Manhattan had helped the surrounding cities, and now it was time to return the favor.

***

Private Tom returned to the truck, a spring in his step from more than just the coffee he'd been drinking. He smiled at Lieutenant Reicher and waved the people following him around to the back of the truck.

"What did you find, Tom?" The Lieutenant, who everyone just called 'Loot', cast a suspicious eye on the small but growing crowd that was rounding the corner of the building. They had boxes and bags, and a motley selection of weapons.

"Got about two dozen, Loot. They don't have much on them, but they know where there's a storehouse full of food. Freddie here is gonna lead us to it."

"Are you sure, Tom?"

"Yes sir. They are glad we are here, and he is telling the truth."

As the new recruits crowded into the back of the truck, one of them – a skinny kid of about fifteen – moved to a rusty old Camaro and started it up with a growl. Loud music burst from the Camaro as well as a cloud of smoke.

Tom hopped up into the cab and said, "They have a truck we can load up and they can follow us."

Reicher scowled. "Well, hopefully it's not using that shitty pseudofuel. Or we'll have to get a mage to add conversion runes at the next camp. There's no guarantee we can find gas further south."

Tom just nodded and tapped his feet to the music, while they followed the cloud of smoke through the streets of Trenton. With the newly acquired truck (sadly, just as old as the Camaro and also running on the same converted gasoline), loading the supplies went quickly enough under the supervision of Tom and Sergeant Tennant, a crusty old former Marine, who served before the Sigil had wiped out 99% of the world and had made armies rather moot.

Lieutenant Reicher disappeared into the mall across the street, ostensibly to look for gear. In reality, Loot was picking up a few things for himself, should this campaign sour. Within an hour, they were back on the road, headed for a rendezvous point in Philly.

***

People from Philadelphia and what was left of Baltimore joined the forces somewhat willingly. All vehicles capable of running under power of runes and power glyphs were pressed into service. Conventional arms were gathered where they were found, though most armories and gun stores had been looted long ago for the best weapons and ammo. By the time the army assembled south of Baltimore it was dusk, but they had accumulated a good haul of food and supplies, and an additional five thousand recruits.

The new soldiers were spread among the existing battalions, with any personnel demonstrating the ability to enchant being sent to the support companies. The growing challenge – besides the acquisition of food – was maintenance of new and existing vehicles.

Many of the scouts never returned from the front, and those who did reported increasingly hostile natives, and increasingly poor road conditions. This vexed the Warlord, who sent advance teams to engage and perform rudimentary roadwork in the wasteland of the former Washington, DC.

***

Sergeant Tennant pulled his poncho closer around his shoulders and spat into the campfire. His face was as cold as the surrounding darkness. The evening mist had turned into a constant drizzle. From out of the darkness, Private Tom wandered up, sitting beside the old soldier.

"Loot says we should be able to push through DC around breakfast, but we have to eat on the way. "

The sergeant looked at the young man for a while before gazing at the fire. "This is a clusterfuck, son. Ain't no way to get there except on these old roads, and nobody's been fixing them since the Sigil. Roads are fucked, bridges are fucked, and something out there ain't right."

Tom looked into the darkness, picking out the campfires among the various companies. "What I don't understand sergeant, is why we don't fly down there? Are they worried there would be dragons and such in the sky?"

"No, not that so much, but there are some squirrely critters in the air. But I don't think they have many dragons down South. I mean, yeah, there are some in the Appalachians, but most of the big ones are out west in the Rockies and Sierra Nevadas. No, the reason we don't fly is simple – not enough planes and pilots. It's easy enough to drive. Any damn fool can operate a truck, but we got something like thirty, forty thousand troops. That's a lot of planes. And no pilots, at least not that we grunts are concerned with."

"Well, shit, Sarge," Tom said. "Show me the bird, and I'll volunteer to fly it. Even if I can't fly. Anything beats trudging through this pig slop."

Sergeant Tennant stood up and shook the water from his poncho. "Sure does. But the Warlord set our path. I'd walk through Hell itself for that man. C'mon, son. Dawn's comin' early. Time to hit the hay."

DAY TWO

After gathering his officers for the predawn briefing, General Armitrage was pissed. There was mounting evidence of sabotage and it was becoming increasingly obvious that a weather mage was fucking with them. Several of the food trucks were filled with spoiled food, and the rain was reported to be localized to within five miles of the camps. Now that dawn was close, the rain had stopped, but scouts were reporting that it was now moving south along the interstate.

The decision had to be made soon whether or not to split several brigades and take an alternate parallel route, but the problem was that Sister Evaline couldn't shield two separate forces – thirty thousand was stretching her capacity as it was, and she was reported to be nearly bedridden from the constant strain. Splitting the forces or delaying too long would leave them vulnerable to the Dream Witch. So, no matter what they did, they had to make haste. Something difficult, considering the increasingly damaged roads. And while the army did have a conjuror and a stone shaper who were able to rebuild, it took time to create replacement structures capable of bearing the load of the vehicles and troops.

And now, he thought, *the forces would have to stop and forage, because entire truckloads of their food were spoiled. What a shit show.*

***

Washington DC was a collection of burned buildings and flattened debris where many government buildings had been, and all the highways were pitted and impassible in most places. It was as if the populace of the entire country had released their wrath on the former capital. For many, the multi-governmental strike against the Watchers was what had triggered the Sigil, though this was untrue. It was just a coincidence, but it was enough for the typical survivor to blame the impotent governments around the world. And most of the survivors would be right in their assessment that the many bureaucrats and politicians had little to offer society in a post-apocalyptic world. And so, they burned along with their former places of power, until little was left beyond unused and forgotten monuments to remind the new world of their former existence.

Lieutenant Reicher was annoyed, but he wasn't alone. It wasn't just because the city of Washington DC wasn't worth stopping for loot, it was also the damn rain that hid deep trenches and potholes. The entire interchange where I-95 met I-495 was destroyed, causing the army to leave the interstate and move through the city on surface streets. At nearly every turn, trucks were caught in sinkholes, and troops were forced to slog through the mud and steady rain in order to lever them back onto the road.

The line of vehicles came to an abrupt stop, as the lead transports were crossing a broad, flooded intersection. The smell of honeysuckle was thick in the air, despite the rain. A string of downed power poles, de-energized for nearly a year suddenly sparked to life, electrocuting soldiers in several trucks. The radio crackled and the report came in that the sound of children's laughter could be heard from the surrounding trees, bushes, and buildings.

From somewhere the order was given, and everything in the immediate vicinity was targeted with plasma cannons and small arms fire. No one could see an enemy target, and several walls, instead of falling away, fell on the now-moving line of transports. When the situation was over, nearly five platoons were lost.

CHAPTER 42

Around a smoldering fire pit, deep within Cheyenne Mountain, sat the Elders of the Hekatek, their black talons clacking on the reinforced concrete bunker floor.

Chief Tull, the foremost and wisest among them, held council, surrounded by a dozen of his Sigil-enhanced troll brethren.

"S-so d-d-do we help D-dreamland?" Chief Tull grated. "Or, d-d-do we help the Glassz Army?"

"Glassz Army wicked," Mmary glowered, her bright yellow eyes flashing. "Evil is b-b-bad."

"True," Chief Tull agreed. "B-but we are Elders of the Hekatek. What c-c-care we for g-good, or evil? Trolls! Cheyenne M-mountain and its n-network of assets are ours, and ours alone. Our eyes and ears s-see and h-hear all things. W-we fuse old world tech and new w-world magick with our hekatek. We bind the old with the new. Elders."

Mmerle immediately added, "Elders. We d-don't care. Help n-n-nobody. B-be n-n-neutral. Trolls. Elders."

Chief Tull nodded, and a few grunts issued from those gathered. "True. Trolls. Elders. N-n-neutral."

"N-n-no!" Rrandy interrupted loudly. "Elders, yes. B-but if w-w-we help n-n-nobody, we help no one but the Vanth'Vash'Var. We betray the Dragon! We betray EarthZero. Sooner d-d-die than that."

Silence. Then, Chief Tull nodded slowly. He was hopeful that the others were following in understanding. There transformation had been ruthless, and had shaped both their physical forms and minds without pity. The tightly concentrated, highly focused transformative energies of the Sigil here in Cheyenne Mountain had impacted them especially hard. Had worked both their bodies and souls with enthusiastic vigor. Had turned them into hideous trolls. Now, they shared a repulsive physical appearance, a noisome stench, and a fearsome hekatek aura. Their unfortunate state had been somewhat balanced, however, by a massive infusion of hekatek power, with their souls expanding to the ninth chakra. But sometimes the wheels of their minds ground slowly. Sometimes council was necessary to get the tribe on the same page.

"S-so you s-s-ee now?" Chief Tull asked them. "Do all of you see? More c-c-omplex than simple b-binary. Neutral p-path, our n-natural inclination, leads to n-nihility. Choose sides. W-we must. If not, w-we lose everything, in time."

"If w-we r-remain n-neutral," Mmerle offered, "and j-just s-share knowledge w-with them, then it s-should be okay. Help D-dreamland. Help the Dragon, and help EarthZero. Still Elders of the Hekatek. Still neutral. Still trolls. But they c-can n-never s-ee us. N-never!"

Massive, toothy heads nodded in agreement around the fire pit. Gnarly talons twitched on concrete.

"Still Elders of the Hekatek," Chief Tull agreed. "Still neutral. Still trolls. We remain neutral. Cheyenne M-mountain is s-still ours, and ours alone. We remain h-hidden from mankind. B-but we help D-dreamland. We help the Dragon. We help EarthZero. But n-no one will ever see us. N-never!"

"Never..." the trolls said in unison, their strange pact reinforced.

CHAPTER 43

Mhyrranda stirred from a dream of her very own, when the knock came on her door. The glowing digits on the clock flicked from 03:35 to 03:36 AM.

"Come in," she groaned, sitting up and slipping into her purple satin robe.

"We had another report, Duchess. They did indeed split off on Interstate 85 South and are headed to the Triangle in North Carolina. We are able to slow them, but not for long. If we break one bridge, we have to damage enough alternate roadways so that they either can't pick a different route or they spread to the four winds. And the latter won't be the case, because the person shielding their minds needs to keep them all close."

"Fine. I'm up. Please have some coffee sent to the war room. I'll need to discuss this with Peaches and the others."

***

The hallways of the executive rooms at the top of the former Luxor hotel were never busy, but in the middle of the night, they were completely empty. Mhyrranda liked to keep the lights low, and it was unnerving when a solitary ghostly figure stepped from the wall as she headed to the command center – or War Room, as the testosterone-laden men preferred to call it. She stopped abruptly, in a defensive stance, realizing she was utterly alone with the figure.

"So sorry to startle you Duchess," the figure said. "I felt it was time to make contact, but this will have to be brief, as I will be missed if I am gone for long. My name is Jasper Long, and I am a member of the army headed south from New York."

Mhyrranda recovered and smiled, assessing the image before her. "Well, next time give a girl a little warning. I almost needed my brown pants."

The image tilted his head and said, "your brown pa – oh!" Jasper chuckled. "Sorry about that. Stealth is usually called for with my, er, skills. Anyway, I came to warn you about what's coming your way, so you can hopefully prepare."

"Whatever do you mean, sir?" Mhyrranda said, coyly. She knew she had to gauge the information to determine how much the enemy forces knew, and whether this was disinformation.

"Well," Jasper said, "I know you must be aware of the forces headed to Atlanta, but I've recently learned that there will be a coordinated air strike on Las Vegas at the same time."

"Hmmm. Do go on."

"The Council has coordinated with the Warlord and they've been secretly rounding up the pilots capable of flying the jets and bombers currently sitting on airfields in the Midwest. As soon as the ground forces engage with the forces in the South, General Armitrage is going to strike you there in Las Vegas with everything he has. They don't even really care about Atlanta, but you and the rest of the leaders in Dreamland are the primary targets to eliminate."

"Well," Randa said with a wry grin, "That's very nice of you to tell us and all, but I happen to know that Armitrage is currently leading the Army south."

"Duchess, have your people ever been able to tell you what the Warlord's magickal ability is?

Randa was careful to maintain a poker face as she answered. "No. Mind sharing with me?"

"General Armitrage is capable of maintaining multiple discrete copies of himself. And he is currently leading *both* operations." The ghostly figure looked over its shoulder at something only he could see. "I'm sorry – I must go…"

And he was gone, leaving Mhyrranda alone in the darkened hallway.

Breaking into a sprint, she shouted to the walls: "Alert! This is a general alert. All security report to the command center. Aal Ball, wake up the team leaders and send them upstairs!"

CHAPTER 44

DAY THREE
The inclement weather followed the army through Washington DC and south into the Virginia countryside and beyond. Scouting reports returned news that the weather was clearing behind the army, but seemed to be waiting ahead within twenty miles of the slowly advancing troops.

Hoping to deplete the will and energy of the weather mage behind the attack, General Armitrage called a midday halt and summoned his subordinates.

"Well? Give me some status updates. And why haven't we found the sonofabitch behind this weather?"

Lieutenant Colonel Jordan stepped up, shaking his head. "Sir, we've got mages looking along with scouts. Whoever is behind this isn't just one person. The minute we think we found a lead, they disappear, and the weather gets worse elsewhere."

Colonel Rizzo continued, "And the faeries are everywhere. They are setting traps for the men; holes and tripwires. We try to engage them, but the vicious little monsters fade into the overgrowth. We think they are behind the supply problems. The water is fine, but perishables are going sour by the truckload."

Another colonel named Reyes drummed on the edge of the table. "I've been sending squads out, trying to find our scouts. Half of the scouts have not checked in, and half of the squads have disappeared as well."

The General scowled at them all. "Well stop sending them out singly, and only send squads out that you trust. Put together foraging parties to gather more food for each town we go through, and make sure they go out in platoons – and even then, make sure you have lieutenants you trust to make sure none of them go missing. They are to maintain constant radio contact. This is turning into a shit show, and we should be gaining troops, not losing them! We will resume marching in two hours and I am going to split off a couple of platoons per battalion to forage through Richmond. As usual, take whatever you find. Turn any resistance to ashes. Dismissed!"

As the officers rose to leave, the Warlord added, "And I'm going to promote the person who finds and kills that weather mage with a nice fat bonus and a case of alcohol."

When they had left, the General turned on the transmitter and computer and connected to the Glass Council.

"We have problems," was all he said as the faces of Brother Bradley and Brother Greg appeared.

"Understood," said Brother Greg. "We've got a few of our own. Sister Evaline has to sleep during the day in order to shield the troops, and she is burning out. How are the cannons holding up?"

"They are fine. That's not the problem. We keep getting sabotaged by a bunch of faeries and a damn weather mage, and half the people I send looking for him – or her – wind up disappearing."

"I've got an idea on how to handle that," said Brother Bradley.

"What about Ryker's? Any news on when that's going to happen?" Armitrage leaned forward, his ire plain.

"It's charging," said Brother Greg. "But even with my amplification, it's going to take another couple of days to get it charged enough to hit Atlanta as hard as we want."

Armitrage sighed. "Well, much as I want to hit them right now, I'm still coordinating the planes between Wilkes-Barr, Wright-Patterson, McConnell, and Buckley. The last base to lock in is going to be Kirtland, and then I'll be ready to rain hellfire down in the desert. Nothing is going to grow in Vegas for 10,000 years."

***

The rain fell steadily on the troops as they slogged through the afternoon. Tom looked back and forth to the green, drenched landscape on either side of the carrier, trying to ignore the grimace on the face of Lieutenant Reicher. It was hard to tell if the sour mood was the result of the weather or the fact that they had not been assigned to check the cities of Richmond or Durham.

Although the highway had been relatively clear, there were increasing spots on the interstate that had been destroyed, causing the convoy to slow or stop. Reports had come back that only a scattering of towns showed signs of occupation, as if the inhabitants were hiding, or had run off.

DAY FOUR

From Greensboro, North Carolina to Greensville, South Carolina, any town of significance was laid waste, but word had traveled and no resistance at all was encountered. In fact, even the small arcology that was being built in Charlotte was abandoned, and all the residents had fled.

Lieutenant Reicher addressed his platoon in the early morning light. The rain had diminished slightly, but the clouds were still low and threatening. Like the rest of the army, Reicher's platoon was tired of the rain and mud, and tired of the constant delays.

"Attention. We got assigned to scavenging duty today. Each squad gets two trucks. Our orders are to precede the army and canvas the area in and around Greensville north of Interstate 85. We are looking for weapons, food, and useful medical supplies. We are not to engage any enemies unless they shoot first. I seriously doubt anyone is even still in this shithole town – but if you encounter any of these unibrow hicks, call it in and waste 'em."

"Squad one, you are with me, we are looking for weapons and ammo. Squad two, hit the grocery stores. Squad three, pick up any supplies useful for the medics in the drug stores. Squad four, run a scout pattern and keep an eye out for any natives. Offer them a job, and if they refuse, fuck 'em. I don't want enemies at our back. Keep your radios on and your eyes peeled. Everybody clear? Good, let's go!"

The platoon's six vehicles made good time into the city, and split up to head for several locations marked on the maps. Current scouting information showed a deserted city except for a few small groups of pacifists clustered around several scattered churches.

An hour into their search, Loot heard shots from the direction that squad two was supposed to be gathering canned goods from a downtown Publix.

"Hand me that radio, Tom. Squad two, give us your status and location, over?"

"Loot, we are at the Publix on Church. Ran into some scavengers and chased them off, sir. We are all good and have no casualties. Over."

"How's the supply situation, over?"

"Good, sir. Place has been hit prior, but we are picking up lots of cans, sir. Downtown looks like there was a fire, but mostly deserted. Over."

"Good job, son. Squad four, head over to squad two's location and make sure nobody decides to fight over the food. Carry on and meet us at the rendezvous in one hour. Over and out."

The run through the several sporting goods stores and arsenals was productive, and as they headed southwest, Loot pulled over into a strip mall. As he left the vehicle and walked toward a jewelry store, he shouted over his shoulder.

"Gonna take a piss. You all look around for anything useful that might come to hand. Be back here in fifteen minutes. Sergeant Tennant, take command."

The sergeant and Tom shared a look, before the sergeant answered, "Sir, yes sir!"

Tom hesitated a moment, then said, "Sergeant, I know he's the Loot and all, but I'm not sure he should be robbing these places. He's lying. Every time he stops, he steals something."

Sergeant Tennant huddled against the rain and looked at Tom. "You know we live in a world where none of this," he gestured to the abandoned strip mall, "is worth a fart in a windstorm, right? I mean, we've been scavenging food and weapons. What's the difference if the Loot wants some trinkets?"

"Yes sir, I get it. It just seems... Sarge, have you been having weird dreams? Space battles and aliens and shit? Like every time we are out on the edge of the camp, I have these nightmares."

"Yeah, Tom. I think lots of people are losing sleep. Command says it's the dream witches trying to scare us into turning around. Or running off. Don't worry about none of that. Follow orders and we'll make it through this little war."

Tom lifted his cap and scratched his head. "But I don't get that. When I see us fighting those aliens, we are all together. EarthZero fighting the monsters together, instead of stealing from the dead and fighting each other."

The sergeant looked over his shoulder as several of the squad approached, serious looks on their faces. "Hey sarge, we need to talk."

***

The door was locked, but was easy enough to kick in. Loot walked down the aisle and found the bathroom in the back. Even through the grey skies and dirty windows, the contents of the display cases were shiny. He finished his business and was taking several large pieces of jewelry when he heard the sound of brief gunfire outside. He raced to a spot where he could see outside, with reasonable cover, considering all the glass cases.

"What the ..."

Several soldiers were clustered around his truck, some of them down, others firing shots at the receding second truck. Loot ran outside once the other truck had gone and the shooting was done.

"What happened here? Sergeant Tennant, report!"

Tom came forward, clutching a wounded arm. "Sarge is dead, sir. They shot him when the rest of us refused to go."

Loot ran to the truck and grabbed a radio, shouting on the way, "Get some bandages on that boy, and triage the wounded. I want a head count."

Picking up the handset, Loot called in to report the attack, and got status from two of the other three teams. Squad three did not respond. Because the deserters from squad one had gone northwest, command would not authorize pursuit, and Loot was ordered to gather his squads and rendezvous with the rest of the forces on the Interstate.

***

Just over the cusp of the horizon before the approaching Army of the North, Solarr and Wyrmhole accompanied the crew of the UH-60 Black Hawk on its scouting mission. Each of the two supers stood post at the open doors on either side of the helicopter, wind whipping furiously past them, their enhanced senses desperately trained upon the gathering wall of clouds looming before them.

The weather mage who had been making life so miserable for their army surely was near. And great would be their reward, the

Warlord himself had promised them, once they had removed the bothersome insect from the battlefield.

An angry gout of lightning lit the late evening sky, framing the roiling cumulonimbus cloud before them starkly. Ominously. The shock of thunder boomed into the helicopter, violently shaking it like a pitiful rabbit in a hound's jaws.

"Holy shit!" Solarr cursed, steadying himself against the open airframe with both hands. "That felt like it was right on top of us."

"It was," Wyrmhole said, his draconic wings unfurling as he launched himself out of the helicopter. "And I think I just saw the weather mage. Inbound. Prosecuting."

Shit... Solarr thought silently. *He can fly, but I can't. Not without this stupid helicopter.* "Check. Covering your six." Mentally, he prepared himself for the most powerful solar eruption that he could inflict, keeping it right on the tip of his tongue and ready for instant use.

Fierce, delicious wind rasped Wyrmhole's flying form as he exploded ahead of the lumbering Black Hawk. Slow, stupid, mechanical things. Ahead, a fresh flash of cloud-to-cloud lightning illuminated a titanic humanoid form which loomed impossibly large, thousands of feet tall. It appeared to be comprised of lightning itself, though of a slightly more reserved, less flashy variety. *Almost like living lightning,* Wyrmhole thought. *Well, we'll find out shortly enough if even living lightning can resist being shorn into ribbons.*

With that thought hanging in mind, Wyrmhole abruptly braked, throwing his clawed hands together before him, summoning and hurling in one smooth motion a massive, arcing hole in spacetime itself toward the weather mage's titanic form.

However, moving at the relative speed of lightning itself, the weather mage focused and directed an equally massive ball of spinning lightning into the approaching Black Hawk, like a pro bowler picking up an easy corner pin spare.

Aboard the doomed Black Hawk, men screamed as hot death by plasma embraced them. Though shielded by the best Shard armor possible, Solarr's physical form erupted in smoke and flame as the non-fatal shock and pain from the lightning ball caused him to fumble control of his most powerful solar eruption. It erupted point blank upon him, instantly shredding the remnants of the Black Hawk, the crew, and Solarr himself. A half-kilometer radius sphere of beautiful, blooming sunlight erupted there in the sky where the Black Hawk had been only a microsecond before.

The heat of the blast danced up Wyrmhole's back even as the overwhelming solar flash temporarily blinded him.

"Damn!" he bellowed, wings thrown wide to get some air beneath him. Tumbling wildly, he heard, or thought he heard over the dull buzz in his ears, a confusing, wet sizzle of energy before him. Then, lightning struck near him multiple times in succession, the wind picked up to hurricane force, and consciousness rapidly fled.

The weather mage, its essence pouring forth irretrievably from the ruinous hole in its elongated torso, caused the storm to bend to its will one final time, softly, gently lowering the dragon boy to the muddy ground below, where a troop of ready Fae retrieved it. All life was precious, it realized in its last moment. And some lives were more precious than others.

∗∗∗

DAY FIVE

"Reporting for duty, sir!"

Sergeant Shen stood firmly at attention, in front of the Lieutenant, wondering if this one would slip away in the night like the last one had. He seemed lost in thought while poring over the map on the table. Almost absentmindedly, he raised his eyes and nodded. "At ease. Did you bring any others with you? I'm down two squads..."

"Yes sir! I have one squad, but only myself and three of them have shard armor and equipment." The equipment was sized for someone else, and it chafed horribly, but she was not complaining. It was top of the line and light years better than her regulation army combat armor. At least the boots fit.

"Any of you have any construction skills, building magic, or lifting abilities? We are facing a lot of downed bridges ahead over the Savannah River." Loot looked grim, but at least the fucking weather had improved.

"No sir. We have two healers, a shield, and an illusionist."

"Shit. Ah, well, go get set up with Private Tom outside. He will brief you on anything you need to know. Dismissed."

Shen made her way to the group outside, noting the desperation in the way they interacted. She thought, *between the desertions and the way the remaining soldiers are behaving, we've already lost. Unless the rumors of the big bad super-secret weapon are true. In which case both sides are going to lose.*

A young man with curly red hair approached her with a smile and a half-hearted salute. "Sergeant Shen? I'm Private Tom. I take it you reported to the Loot already?"

Returning the salute, Shen regarded the young man. "Yes, I did. Is he always so cheerful?"

"No ma'am – I mean Sir. He's usually throwing parties for the folks who deserted him instead of shooting at him." His face now deadpan, Shen couldn't tell if he was joking or not.

"Well, let's plan a party – after we get through Atlanta."

"Assuming we can get past all these bridges. Our mages are getting really exhausted."

The army spent the better part of the day navigating the fallen bridges of the Savannah River on the border between South

Carolina and Georgia. Frustrated with the delay, the Warlord began targeting trees and structures on either side of the road, turning swaths of pine trees into smoking holes. The thundering cannons could be heard for miles.

By the time the Army had drawn within 75 miles of the city, fully one half of their number was gone, and it had grown so bad that the scouts and perimeter guards were on alert for deserters as well as enemies.

***

Wiping sweat from her forehead, Sergeant Shen turned to Tom, riding beside her on the gate of the pickup they were in. "God, I almost miss the rain. I hate this humidity."

Tom just shrugged. "Think of it as a personalized shower. Could be worse."

Shen was about to comment when the truck lurched to a stop and there was shouting from ahead. Standing on the gate, Shen said, "Oh shit. The road's on fire."

Surely enough, the leading mile of the convoy was engulfed in flames, and soldiers abandoned the vehicles and scattered from the flaming blacktop. The sergeant jumped from the truck and shouted "Everybody grab some tarps or blankets and follow me!"

The road had been doused with gas at a strategic location, and the shoulders on either side of the road were at least a twenty-foot drop. As the small crowd ran forward and down, they covered burning men and women with the blankets, putting out fires where they could and treating broken bones. After ten or fifteen minutes, they were left in clusters, watching the vehicles burn while others tried to put out the flames and figure out what to do with the disabled vehicles.

"Well, wasn't that just a clusterfuck?" Shen said to no one in particular. "Let's get the wounded back to the formation, back there. Everybody, lift a corner of a blanket and move it!"

Getting back to the road was harder than expected, since the ground was covered in kudzu vines. The line of soldiers pushed through the undergrowth for a half mile before there was an opportunity to ascend to the road again. Meanwhile, the officers had organized a detail to clear the road.

And then, just as the soldiers were able to push the burned vehicles off the side of the road, they were beset by a plague of insects. Vast clouds of flying and stinging creatures emerged from the surrounding trees and swarmed through the troops, scattering the soldiers yet again, and driving them off the road and into the surrounding countryside.

While they were at a standstill, a huge herd of giant feral hogs charged through the column, and during this brouhaha, snipers hidden on the side of the road shot tranquilizing darts at high value targets such as drivers and gunners, before retreating into the brush. And after each attack, more soldiers were gone, into the woods and kudzu of the rapidly setting sun.

Approaching Braselton, the army was confronted by a series of billboards, instructing them to either turn around and return in peace, or surrender by laying down their weapons. This enraged the Warlord so much that every bit of organic material within a mile of the road was burned by the cannons, catching not a few deserters in the process.

CHAPTER 45

Nick turned to Ami and said, "This is it. I don't know who they have guarding the city, or even if they have someone, but we've got to get in and stop the Council. Are you ready?"

Amaterasu smiled at Nick and spread her hands. "As long as you shield me, I'm good, Nick. Might want to ask *them*, though." She looked over her shoulder at the six Praetorians.

"They are ready. We've all been briefed, and they are the best of the best." Nick looked at Mhyrranda and grinned. "Let's do this."

Mhyrranda grinned back. "Go get 'em!"

A portal opened and the strike team assembled in formation. Before they went through the portal, one of them gestured and they were suddenly cloaked in illusion, taking on the forms of shard troops.

As they left, Randa turned to Maynard. An uncharacteristic twitch below her left eye betrayed her state of mind. "We are coming up short, Maynard. If this fails, we're pretty much fucked."

Maynard, for a change, was speechless.

***

Stepping through the portal, the team found themselves on the street around the corner from the building's entrance. Aal Baal had done a good job acquiring the layout, so they knew where they were going – they just weren't sure if their quarry would be there. Turning the corner, they noticed the street was deserted except for a pair of Shard soldiers at the building entrance. As they approached, one of them held up a hand, stopping the team.

"Hold up. Where's your pass?"

"Oh, right," Nick said. Stepping aside and turning to the Praetorian behind him, Nick nodded to the guard. "Give him the pass."

Without hesitation, the Praetorian looked at the two guards and said, "Sleep."

The guards dropped like stones, and the team held them up long enough for Nick and Ami to search and find their keycards. Once inside, the guards were quickly moved to a side room and relieved of their weapons and armor.

"Sure glad that worked," said the Praetorian. "We didn't know if the armor had any spell shielding."

Nick nodded as he put on one of the guard's helmets. "Good job, Luke. But be prepared for it to fail, as we get closer. Ah – nothing on the channel, let's go."

Nick and Ami, who had taken the other helmet, led the team around the corner and up to the bank of elevators. Slotting the keycard, Nick punched the button for the penthouse floor. Everyone was silent and the elevator sped upward. They were almost to the penthouse when Nick and Ami heard the alarm being raised.

Sister Evaline, in a nervous voice, spoke over the headset's channel, "There are intruders in the building. They are in the elevators. Stop them."

"Fuck," Nick whispered. "Well, she detected us. But if we get past the guards, she might not know that we are disguised. Get ready."

As the elevator stopped with a ding, the doors opened to a hail of crystallized energy from the foyer, blowing the back out of the elevator and piercing the concrete wall behind it. After a brief moment, the weapons stopped firing and the sound of footsteps approached, only stopping when a small round ball rolled out of the elevator.

"Oh, shit."

The room filled with a bang and a *very* bright light, and the Praetorians rushed the guards, using hand-to-hand combat to disable and disarm their opponents. Nick and Ami popped out of the elevators, scanning the surroundings, and Nick pointed to a hallway leading off the foyer and the team ran that way, turning a corner and coming face to face with four more guards.

"They are back by the elevators, and there's a bunch of them stealthed!" Nick said.

"Well, why aren't you fighting them?"

The Praetorian, Luke, stepped up and waved his hand in front of the guards. "Sleep."

"What? What the fuck are you talking about?"

"Don't mind him, he failed Jedi training," said another Praetorian, who raised his shard rifle and fired. The guards were slow, and within seconds the strike team had four more shard rifles and four helmets.

Sister Evaline's voice came over the headsets again. "Attention. The intruders were covered by illusion. Search the west side of the Penthouse and eliminate them."

"Wait," Ami said turning. "What did she mean *were* covered by... Oh!" Everyone looked down to discover that the illusionary shard armor was gone.

"Cover's blown, try the backup," said Nick. The Praetorian who first cast the illusion gestured to the corner, summoning the illusion of a pair of Praetorians, who quickly turned the corner and were slammed with a hail of shard energy and went down.

Nick tossed a grenade around the corner and was soon pleased with a loud *WHUMP*, followed by screams.

"Time to acquire our target," Nick said as he pointed at pairs of Praetorians , and sent them along different paths. Then he keyed the headset.

"Sister Evaline, please tell your soldiers to stand down and surrender. There is no need for further casualties. We don't intend to harm you, but we do need you to come along with us."

"Is that so?" Sister Evaline's voice was taut. "I think you are assassins, here to kill me, so no – I *won't* be surrendering. Come find me, you fuckers."

"Found her!" shouted one of the Praetorians over his comm. "Northeast corner, doubling back to the elevators—" and the voice was cut off with a scream.

Nick placed his finger over his mouth and motioned Ami to follow him, before silently padding down the hall. They continued toward the northeast corner of the building, with the sounds of gunfire and explosions coming from around the corner. Nick risked a quick peek around the corner to see that the entire exterior wall and most of the floor were gone. Backing up, Nick turned to tell Ami what he saw when a thin woman in a silk housecoat came running around the corner and nearly bowled him over as she collided with his back. She recoiled, crashing back into the wall behind her, and Ami immediately raised her rifle.

Hate filled the woman's face, and Ami's rifle barrel sagged like a noodle. Nick, meanwhile, had righted himself, only to find his rifle had likewise turned into a useless, sagging piece of metal.

"Oh no, lady, you are coming with us." Nick grabbed her wrist and started dragging her down the hall, when suddenly the floor dropped out from beneath him and he was falling, falling.

Until he wasn't. He looked up and saw Ami standing over the still form of Sister Evaline.

"Stock wasn't noodles," Ami said coldly. She pulled a syringe from a pocket and injected Sister Evaline in the neck.

CHAPTER 46

The sky over North Georgia was dotted by rapidly growing clouds. Dark clouds that promised rain and thunderstorms typical of an afternoon summer storm. And yet, the rapidly diminishing army continued. Within five miles of the initial sighting, the message on the billboards changed, saying merely "We are sorry," and "You have been warned." Suddenly, a muted roar came from the northwest, across the fields of the Château Élan Golf Club. The sound was thunder, but not quite, and the sky sparkled with light that was not lightning.

As they looked up into the growing chaos, the Army of the North was able to detect the faint shimmer of the invisible warplanes of the Arcologies, too late. And the planes carried an ordinance more dangerous than bombs, more terrifying than napalm. The army froze, falling where they stood as the planes dropped wave after wave of faerie dust on the vast column. There was nowhere for the troops to run or hide, as the dust rendered them all asleep.

Tom looked around him in the misty world that had taken the place of the road, far from the former fields of smoke and fire. Something about this place reminded him of home, so far away. The home he thought he would never return to. He smelled his mother's fresh baked apple pie, and he could almost hear her, though he knew she'd been dead for over a year. He looked over and there was the sergeant with a bemused look on her face.

"Sarge? Where are we? Are we dead?"

Sergeant Shen smiled and took Tom's hand. "I think it's okay, Tom. I think we are just dreaming."

As they peered into the mist, they saw several women with robes and eerie glowing eyes emerge from the cloudlike distance. One of them smiled and approached them. All around them, the soldiers rose unsteadily to their feet, filled with wonder and curiosity, and yes, horror.

The woman said, "There is no need to be afraid. It is only a dream and we are here to open your minds. The war is over, at least *this* war. The Council cannot control you, the Warlord cannot compel you. You can now hear the truth and judge for yourselves.

"Oh shit," Shen said. "Is this where we choose a colored pill and determine whether we wind up in a dirty ship flying underground?"

The woman laughed and said, "No, this is where we offer you another way, a way to join the rest of the world in harmony, and a way to fight *along with* humanity instead of against it. Unlike him." She pointed through the distance to where the general swung his fists again and again, each impotent, striking smoke, until he fell to his knees and disappeared into the mists.

"Everyone here has the ability to heal and protect this new Earth, some with truth-telling," she looked at Tom, placing a kiss on his forehead, "and others with the gift of sight." At this she took Shen into her arms, hugging her.

"Buh, but I don't have a gift," said Shen.

"I see you, sister." The woman smiled gently. "But you don't need armor for what you can do."

***

Aal Baal fizzed and bleated, gaining everyone's attention. "Incoming message from external encrypted radio signal. Decrypting now..."

The speakers in the War room crackled, but the signal was audible. The speaker, however, sounded as though he were chewing rocks. "D-dreamland, thiz is Cheyenne M-m-mountain heere, can you heear us?"

Maynard repressed a sigh, turning to the table mic. "Cheyenne Mountain, that's a roger. This is Maynard speaking." Turning to Aal Baal, he stage whispered, "got a security lock on that signal?" In response, the console gave a brief wolf-whistle squeal.

"M-maynard, hiii. Thiz iz Ch-chief Tull again. I haave good newz for you. Based on signal and existing sat-navz, we know which basez the Glassz Army iz using. W-w-we can send the d-d-data along now."

"Wonderful! Not a minute too, soon, either. Receiving your data, Hey, I'd love to chat, Chief Tull, but we have to move, *now*." Maynard turned to the assembled team of elementals and said, "You are a go. We are opening sequential portals for each base, and the last one is where the Warlord is. Hurry!"

Team EL shared a look and nodded. A portal opened and they, along with a half-dozen Praetorians ran through to the other side. At each location, they paused only long enough to hurl baseball-sized EMP devices into the midst of each group of warplanes and at each control tower, before quickly moving through the portal to the next target. As the small devices landed, they rendered the Old Earth technology inert.

Finally, Maynard's voice spoke over everyone's headset. "Be careful. This next portal is headed into the control tower where the Warlord is managing the situation. He's going to know something is up, since the signals to the other bases went down."

The last portal opened and as they emerged, the team appeared facing a series of consoles and video arrays, behind a small group of technicians and a tall figure dressed in a black military uniform.

Dwayne shouted, "Everyone, put your hands on your head. General, you are under arrest."

The Warlord turned, drawing his sidearm, but was thwarted by a beam of fire from Leta that melted his pistol. Enraged, he closed his eyes and a dozen copies of him charged the group.

As the duplicates engaged the team, Tim shouted, "Focus on the original general! The others are copies!"

Dwayne stepped back and closed his eyes and a wind stirred in the closed room, lifting several of the copies, blowing them against the wall of video monitors with a bone crushing force. All except one disappeared.

Beth grinned and tossed an EMP ball into the middle of the room. The room went dark, except for the team's Hekatek-powered full-spectrum headsets.

"Game, Set and Match! Now get those hands up!"

CHAPTER 47

"General! General Armitrage, come in!" Brother Bradley slammed his fist on the comm button. "God damn it! We lost both signals. He's gone. Fuck it! Launch!"

Brother Greg pressed the button, and the two gazed out the window to watch a gathering brightness rise into the sky over Ryker's Island. One hundred feet tall, with a tip of pure plasma, the missile launched, towards the coordinates centered on the Atlanta Arcology.

Brother Bradley high-fived Brother Greg and raised a middle finger towards the south. Then, the doors opened and the Praetorian strike team rushed in, clad in shard armor. Ami and Nick looked at the control panel, then at each other, before Nick said, "Ami, call it in."

While Ami called to inform Atlanta, Nick approached the two remaining members of the Council of Glass. "Gentlemen, as representatives of the cities of Dreamland and Atlan, I am here to offer you terms of surrender."

Brother Bradley turned to Brother Greg, then began to laugh. "Why should *we* surrender? In a few minutes, there will be a smoking hole where Atlanta used to be. And shortly after that, there will be an even larger smoking hole where Las Vegas used to be. However, we would consider your surrender to be useless. We will be happy to kill you after the light show."

Ami finished her comm and turned to Nick, nodding. Walking over to the vast window, Nick admired the view of the rainbows along the edge of the park below. "Opening video comm to the Arcology." Nick pointed his wrist camera at the lights in Central Park.

***

On the roof of the Arcology stood two figures, watching the lightning flashing far away in the night sky. The breeze ruffled their hair, but John and Loli never lost their concentration. John pointed at a spot to their north, growing brighter by the minute, and Loli looked down to her video feed.

"Is that where you want it?" Peering at the image on the screen, Loli took note of the green parkland, the trees filled with rainbows and reflected light. "It looks very magickal."

"That's it. Drop it right in the middle of Central Park. Strike team out."

Loli closed her eyes in concentration and a blurry spot in the sky above began to form.

Within moments, the plasma missile grew to a huge, molten orb streaking through the sky and down toward the arcology, bringing death and destruction for Atlan and everyone within miles of the city.

John licked his lips and looked anxiously at Loli. "You got this?"

"I got this," she said, right before collapsing into Soda John's arms. John's eyes never left the streak of fire as it flowed through the hole in the sky and disappeared. "Nice catch," John said, cradling her unconscious form.

***

"What the fuck is *this*?" Brother Bradley screamed as he reached out to grab Ami by the wrist. "What in the name of God do you think you're doing!"

As Brother Bradley's clutching fingers began to dig into Ami's armor, her arm suddenly was surrounded by utter blackness. There was a crackling of glass within the darkness, and she lifted her arm, shaking her head sadly.

"I am so very sorry," she said, and Brother Bradley's arm elongated unnaturally, pulling him inexorably into her localized singularity, until his body and legs followed. His pathetic, pleading screams Doppler-shifted unnaturally, lingering in the local spacetime ambiance for a few seconds longer than his waveform had.

The team grabbed an astonished, unresisting Brother Greg and the party exited through a hastily formed portal, just as a spot in the sky above Central Park blurred and expanded, lit from something fiery just beyond.

When the blast happened, it was as if the sun rose in the middle of Manhattan. The light and heat vaporized the surrounding glass, but not before the sky filled with rainbows of light that could be seen for miles. People in the region were mystified by the clouds of rainbows, which actually were clusters of tiny fragments of glass. In the days that followed, shards of glass could be found as far away as Philadelphia.

CHAPTER 48

Multicolored plasmas writhed, defining the perimeter of the ever-iterating Mandlebrot construct which bound the gathering of the Guild of the Eternal Recursion, Demonia Prime's greatest Fractal Mages. Fully 123 of their number filled the austere chamber of blackened steel, continuously in motion, filing along one-by-one, their steps describing the perimeter itself. Widdershins, they walked, their simple leather sandals clabbering softly, even as gentle, whirling sparks climbed slowly up their legs from the chaotic pattern underfoot.

For hour upon hour, they worked their charms, collectively bending and binding their desired probability paths from the ambient chaos of spacetime in the local cosmic frame. Beyond exhaustion, yet fearing their fates should they show any sign of wavering, all of the mages focused as one, sharing strength when necessary.

Precise focus and will power were essential to practitioners of their craft. And all of them, the best of the many thousands of their kind among the Vanth'Vash'Var, were masters of their craft. Their charm would succeed. Their desired path would be forged. Of that, they had no doubt. It was merely a matter of time now, and EarthZero's mightiest heroes and their weapons would be mitigated and broken. Their fractal seed had been planted, and now it needed merely to be nourished and nurtured. The Eternal Recursion, upon which all things moved, would shape the rest.

In the 235th hour of their collective charm, a single Fractal Mage paused a microsecond in her focus, allowing a most fleeting shard of alien power to issue forth from her soul, far too quickly to be noticed by any of her brethren. Wayward, rogue, and stealthy, the shard of power entered the collective matrix woven by the guild, implanting its own seed into their own.

Play the game as if your soul depends upon it, Lucy Diamante thought bitterly. *Because it certainly does now...*

EPILOGUE

In the shadows of a deserted Midwest town, Vida's black SUV was parked in front of a semi-dark hotel. The four travelers had stopped for the night. While the twins played quietly in an adjoining room, Petrus and Vida discussed the future, over scavenged cans of cat food.

"There is no way to escape it now," Vida told Petrus. "The Dreamland Alliance has achieved dominance. If the shortwave reports are right, then the City of Glass is no more, and Dreamland has no one else to stand against them."

Petrus smiled weakly. The cat food was not sitting well on his aching stomach. At least it had been wet cat food, though, and not that terrible dry food, which would expand uncomfortably in his stomach and make him feel bloated.

"I agree, Vida," he replied, awkwardly stifling a belch. "The other factions can't match their power. And no one else can match their vision. They're into it to save it. EarthZero, that is."

"They're actually sending out food and medical supplies, too," Vida recounted from last evening's shortwave news. "That's dispelling their reputation as a bunch of devil worshippers."

Smirking, Petrus said, "I no longer judge anyone by those measures, Vida. In fact, I no longer judge anyone but myself. Let their actions speak of their souls. Nothing more, and nothing less."

"It speaks loudly of their souls, these actions," Vida replied. "They're actually helping. Going out of their way to do so, too. They're uniting, not dividing. They're taking in all survivors, too, even those who fought against them for the City of Glass. They don't sound like they're evil to me."

"Evil and good are sometimes merely fine matters of degrees," Petrus allowed, knowing this only too well himself. "The question for us, however, is one of where we next will go. Do we dare attempt that journey, even over the newly reclaimed roads? I am not capable of defending anyone, and you and the twins aren't capable of combat."

"Dangerous, of course," Vida said, hiding a smile. "But we've come this far, through some nasty circumstances, and I've got to believe that someone is guiding us along. Protecting us. We'll be fine, Petrus."

He nodded. Of course they'd be fine. A slight movement caught his eye, and Petrus turned to regard the twins, who now stood side by side at the door.

Abraham said, smiling, "Of course we'll be fine. We're going to Dreamland."

Published by Anshadar, LLC. 3645 South Truckee Way, Aurora CO 80013

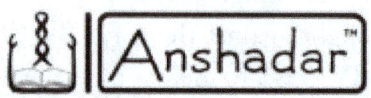

mobi ISBN: 978-1-7329802-3-5
epub ISBN: 978-1-7329802-5-9

***

Lyrics from "Transcendence" by Crimson Glory. From the album "Transcendence". Writers: Rob Garza, Eric Hilton. Publishing/Licensing: WMG, TuneCore (on behalf of Crimson Glory Records); BMG Rights Management (US), LLC, UMPG Publishing, and 3 Music Rights Societies.

Hail, Midnight! It was a great experience to meet you. -void-

Dave Newton & Todd King

D ave and Todd met at NASA, and bonded over shared experiences – as in roleplaying game design, gaming, and MMOs. When Todd brought up the idea of writing again, Dave mentioned that he had some ideas percolating. These ideas meshed well with the ideas Todd had, and the two decided it had to happen. There was a story to be told, and the more they worked on it, the bigger it became, until the scope was cosmic. The two of them formed Anshadar, LLC to create the new world of EarthZero, wherein they and others will explore the boundaries of magick, morphogenetics, hekatek, and Simulation Theory.

Dave lives in Colorado with his wife and two daughters. He's discovered he doesn't hate the snow. He listens to music, is a DJ for a pirate radio station in his spare time, and is a prolific reader. He has written and co-written a variety or roleplaying games and fiction, including The Mythus FRPG, Rapture: the Second Coming, Twisted Bedtime Stories and Quest! Roleplaying for Kids.

Todd has served as a contractor for various federal agencies, including DoD, MDA, and NASA,

producing multiple intellectual properties in disparate realms, including Chaotic Systems,

Cryptography, Logistics, and Nanotechnology. Previously, he mutated from lead guitarist to vocalist, playing in several bands in the southern heavy metal scene, opening for acts as diverse as Lynyrd Skynyrd and Pantera. He created the SenZar role-playing game, which sold in 14 countries, and has virally influenced certain Void themes in both the current tabletop and computer genres.

Dedication

From Todd:

To my and Renee's furry feline Overlords: Rynn, Roo, Nikki Nik Nik, Pikachu the Quality Control Manager, and Buster Boo Boo Kitty.

From Dave:

To everyone who suffered through my bouts of creativity, and all of the people who helped us finish this book, especially my talented daughter Faith, who nailed the cover on the first try. Be safe, live well, and be very careful how you name your cats.

Anshadar, LLC is pleased to present this second novel in the EarthZero Evolution series: The Anshadar Effect.

Stay tuned as we give you more science fiction, fantasy, and horror.

Quest! Roleplaying for Kids by Dave & Christi Newton

The Lightbringer's Sigil by Dave Newton and Todd King

The Anshadar Effect by Dave Newton and Todd King

The Death Horde by Dave Newton and Todd King (coming soon)

Bloody Kudzu by Dave Newton (coming soon)

The Saga of the Seven Stars (coming soon)

VoidSpawn (coming soon)

www.ingramcontent.com/pod-product-compliance
Lightning Source LLC
Chambersburg PA
CBHW071343020726
47502CB00001B/224